GOD
MODE

GOD MODE

PURIFIER ■ BOOK 2

Curator Omega

Podium

ISBN: 978-1-0394-1797-7

Published in 2022 by Podium Publishing, ULC
www.podiumaudio.com

Welcome back, wanderer. Now that you've heard the first act of Dak Korasa's struggle, do you wish to turn away? If so, who could blame you? By the standards of human minds, this tale is one of bloodshed, abominations, and exceedingly confusing details.

Perhaps you, like me, delight in such a story for the very same reasons. There is a certain forbidden pleasure in learning the details of another's misfortune. This pleasure is only heightened by the fact that you were never meant to hear them.

Should you choose to proceed, wading deeper into the oceans of death and madness, I will gladly share the next volume of Dak Korasa's account with you.

Ah? Is that a nod?

Very well. But before you carry on, let us refresh the most pertinent details of our unwilling hero's saga. There are so very many names, faces, plots, twists, and turns to recall . . . I would not expect your mortal memory to comprehend all of it.

Our protagonist is, of course, Dak Korasa, a man who believed himself to be a peaceful archaeologist. When his tale began, he was scavenging on long-lost planets for Chanzig, a vile crime lord, trying to afford the life-saving surgery included in his contract.

There were a great deal of things Dak didn't know at that time, including the most obvious: He hadn't been hired by Chanzig, but rather created. Grown in a time-accelerating laboratory to serve as Chanzig's personal tracking dog.

And what was he tracking? Why, the chok'tal, naturally. An alien parasite that was rumored to turn ordinary men into godlike conquerors. Through divine revelation or simply error, Chanzig had encountered the maker of these creatures: the enigmatic cross-dimensional entity known as the Unmade. Sadly for Chanzig, his body hadn't been prepared for such an experience. Only the chok'tal could ensure safe passage for one wandering in the land of the Unmade.

Thus, Chanzig set out on his grand quest, turning over every stone and searching every dark corner of the universe for a chok'tal to complete himself. The search was a failure . . . until Dak Korasa.

As you may recall, Chanzig had engineered this poor fellow by merging two halves. The first was the nervous system of Jekra Modri, a former soldier who'd served as a host to Chanzig's precious chok'tal. The second was the body (and to some extent, recycled memories) of the real Dak Korasa. Through fusing these elements, Chanzig created a man with no past, no present, and no future, born only to find what he desired.

Things didn't go so smoothly, however. Instead of merely finding the chok'tal, Dak Korasa accidentally absorbed it into his body. He became a fabled Purifier, killing to keep himself alive. But Dak didn't stop there. Desperate to pull at every loose thread, he followed the trail of breadcrumbs back to Chanzig's home planet, where he met up with a curious alien seer devoted to wiping out the chok'tal . . . and their creator.

With this unlikely bond in place, Dak Korasa and his new companion set their sights on Chanzig and his gateway back to the Unmade's dimension. They succeeded in killing the visionary, but not in solving this cosmic quandary. In fact, they departed from Chanzig's world in more peril than ever before. With their presence revealed to both the Unmade as well as the tyrannical Halcius Hegemony, there was nowhere to run but deeper into the storm.

My, that was a mouthful. But I believe we're caught up. So, pour yourself another drink, sit, and indulge in Dak Korasa's second volume. If memory serves, this installment opens with our strange pair about to arrive on a world of monks. I shall say no more to avoid spoiling your experience.

If any questions bubble up, do not hesitate to ask. I am here, as I always shall be.

Such is the work of Curator Omega.

GOD
MODE

1

Throughout my archaeology career, I'd always viewed myself as an optimist. If it started raining on an important dig, I was the first one to camp out under the tarps and wait for the clouds to thin. If a colleague dropped a priceless artifact, I comforted them by mentioning that there were countless other treasures to unearth across the cosmos. Such an uplifting and frankly naïve approach hadn't made me popular with many employers, but at least it had gotten me through the storms of life with my chin held high.

Only it hadn't. That cheerful perception of myself—and indeed, all the memories connected to it—was just a looping echo in my mind. The positive, lighthearted demeanor of Dak Korasa was as impersonal to me as the birthing fluids I'd seen in Chanzig's tanks.

I'd come to the triage module's bathroom to pace a bit, to shake off the dust and keep on trucking, but I'd ended up with an existential crisis. As I gazed into the mirror, focusing on my own eyes, I kept returning to one question:

What are you?

Until a few hours ago, I had defined myself as a lovable, capable nerd. A bookworm. A *bon vivant*, in the right situation. But now . . . what could I call myself? What memories could I lean on as proof that I could handle this hellish quest?

The hard truth was: Chanzig had both given and taken away everything I associated with the name "Dak Korasa." All I could grasp at were the qualities of my original genetic templates: the original Dak and Jekra Modri, the former owner of the voice in my head. Both of those men had gone on adventures. They'd learned and loved and sampled every delicious flavor in the universe. They'd made a name and reputation for themselves over decades of living.

And me? I hadn't done shit. All this time, I'd believed I was the rightful owner of Mr. Korasa's life. But in reality, I was just a hollow imitation of the man. Worse still, I was *literally* an infant. I hadn't pieced together Chanzig's exact schedule, but it was clear I'd been "alive" for less than a year. Even in that short span of time, all I'd experienced were the sights, sounds, tastes, and sensations Chanzig permitted. I hadn't lived in any real sense of the word.

"Come on, Dak," I whispered, slapping a bit of cold water on my cheeks. "You've got this. You know who you are."

Despite trying to reassure myself with those words, they seemed to have the opposite effect. Because as I spoke, I heard only the voice of a stranger: Dak Korasa, Hegemony citizen and archaeologist. If I adopted a harsher tone, I'd only hear Modri's words. More than anything, my attempts at self-hypnosis only reminded me of two unpleasant truths.

First, I did *not* know who I was . . . mainly because I didn't exist, in the conventional sense.

And second, I did *not* have this. Not at all.

The task ahead of Akasha and I was already impossible, and the latest message from the Hegemony hadn't made it any easier. How the hell were we supposed to track down and kill a bunch of highly ranked Purifiers, *then* take on an interdimensional horror, all while evading the gaze of this galaxy's most powerful military?

Maybe Jekra Modri could've done it. But I wasn't him. I was just some speed-cloned infant having an identity crisis in a stolen ship's bathroom.

"You know," Modri said through our telepathic link, *"not to heap any more burdens on you, but uh, this whole 'talkin' to the mirror' thing is giving off some serial-killer vibes."*

I stepped back and sighed, regrettably admitting he was right. Introspective brooding wasn't going to fix anything about this situation. I needed a voice of reason—and that voice, for better or worse, was the blue-skinned alien priestess on the bridge.

Akasha.

After toweling off my bruised, gash-covered face, I palmed the door lock and prepared to find my confidante. But in a twist that nearly ruined my new pants, I found I didn't have to look for her—she was standing in the doorway.

"Yes?" she said evenly.

I blinked back at her. "Yes?"

"You summoned me."

"Absolutely not."

Akasha tilted her head. "I heard it, Dak. You called out with your mind."

"Maybe you're just hearing things." Thinking on it, though, I leaned against the frame and narrowed my eyes. "Is that something Purifiers can do?"

"Of course," she said easily, stepping aside and motioning for me to follow. She led me down the corridor at a relaxed pace. "It's the same skill that allows you to commune with your chok'tal."

"How would you know about it?"

"Every text I found along my journey spoke of the 'silent tongue.' A way for Purifiers to contact one another using their mental faculties."

"Or to contact Purifier hunters, I guess."

She nodded. "I am not one to speculate, but I do believe my unique connection to the Unmade has made me sensitive to this ability. Which is why I'm confident you summoned me."

"Well, it wasn't intentional," I said, as we passed into the recreation module, "but I did want to talk with you."

"That is fortunate, because I wished for the same opportunity."

"Oh?"

She gestured for me to sit down in one of the module's satin-lined booths, where she'd already arranged a variety of juices, teas, stim-drinks, and water carafes. I gladly accepted her invitation, on account of my broken body.

"Look at this," I said, as I started pouring a citrus-smelling liquid. "A full buffet spread, and all for me?"

Akasha sat down across from me and folded her hands on her lap. "In a matter of minutes, we'll be dropping out of subspace and landing on the target world. It is important that your body is nourished before training."

"Hitting the ground running, huh?"

"We have little time to spare. In fact, we are indebted to time. This scourge should've been erased the moment we discovered it."

Nodding in solidarity, I sampled my juice. Sweet, but undoubtedly produced in some sort of genetic-modification wonderland.

"While we're on the topic of precious time . . ." I hedged.

Akasha lifted her chin. "You already know."

"Eh?"

"You forget that your mind is somewhat translucent to me, Dak. You viewed the transmissions. That much is clear."

I nervously swallowed my juice. "What transmissions?"

"There's no need to fear alarming me," she said. "The Hegemony's transmissions also arrived on the bridge terminal. We have a mutual understanding of our delicate situation."

"Oh, thank Halcius. I didn't want to overload you."

"On the contrary, Dak—it is you I am concerned about."

I poured another cup of chemical juice. "Why? Because I'm a Purifier?"

"That is another conversation," Akasha said in a flat tone. "Here, I am referring to your discovery of the Hegemony's messages."

"That . . . makes you concerned about *me*?"

"The training you are about to undertake will require complete control over the body, will, and mind. I had hoped you would be able to progress without distractions."

"I'd say a galaxy-wide Hegemony dragnet is a little more than a distraction."

Again, she nodded. "Speaking with honesty, I had already predicted Chanzig relying on this sort of desperate act in his final hour. Many years ago, I overheard him recording just such a transmission. The Hegemony was not fond of him, but they respected his power. They kept a close eye on his doings." She took in a long, deep breath. "They will locate the ship, but with luck, the trail will end there."

"So, we're just going to ditch the ship in orbit or something?"

"Not quite."

"Oh, right. Surveillance." I gestured to the embedded cameras all around us. "Do you know how to scrub the systems, or is that a question for the chok'tal?"

"Neither."

I gave her a puzzled look.

"When the time arrives, I will take care of all this," Akasha explained. "Your training will not be altered by this development."

"Even if we abandon the ship, there's a chance they'll land ground forces on anything in the area. How many planets are in this system?"

"A successful hunter must know the shape of their prey."

"In plain speech, please? I'm too banged up to catch your poetry."

She hummed. "Due to the nature of your existence, I doubt Chanzig would want the Hegemony to identify you. As such, your appearance has likely been removed from all of his archives. Your genetic makeup—" Upon seeing my face, she stopped. "Yes, Dak. I know what you uncovered on Kagu-9. I know your origin."

"How?"

"When you were lying in the triage module, your mind was in a suppressed state. Not quite a coma, and yet . . . defenseless. I saw everything."

"Oh." Well, that was one long and awkward conversation out of the way. "So, it doesn't bother you that I'm . . . not a real person?"

"You are exactly as real as any other being: a body, mental intentions, and consciousness. All else is a concept."

Her words were simultaneously the most and least inspiring things I'd ever heard. Maybe she was right. Maybe there was no secret sauce involved in creating a genuine "person." On a purely factual level, I *was* equivalent to any other living creature. But still . . . the doubt was hard to shake. Deep down in my core, I still felt like a science experiment playing dress-up. And taking on a grand quest to stop an ancient evil.

"Alright, so in simple terms . . . you think they won't be able to find me because they don't know what they're after," I said. "Maybe it's good not to have a personal history on file. Makes things a lot cleaner."

She gave a dim smile, but only briefly. "This returns us to the original matter I wished to discuss with you. A matter that seems most important to discuss before we arrive."

"Which is?"

"You asked me why I viewed you as a candidate for the monastic order's mission," she said quietly. "In other words, why I believed you were worth training instead of slaying. I promised that the relevant qualities of such a candidate would be described soon, and so they shall. But in my eyes, Dak, there was one specific factor within you that changed my mind . . . yet also haunted me."

"Is that good or bad?"

"Most chok'tals change their host every few days or weeks, depending on the Purifier's progress. Yet some Purifiers have lived a long time with their chok'tal. A very long time. These Purifiers are exceedingly powerful, but also tainted by all the evil in their minds."

"Okay? But what does that have to do with me?"

"The order has always sought a Purifier with the power to contain their teachings and serve as a champion. A Purified One. But in the pursuit of this power, every Purifier has been corrupted."

I set down my glass. "But that's just it, Akasha. I *don't* have any special power."

"No, but you are fertile for its cultivation."

"Can we not say *fertile*, please?"

She grunted. "Your power is not as important as the mind that wields it. Because of your birth, your mind is largely empty."

"Thanks."

"It is simply the truth, Dak. You have not been sullied by decades or even centuries of immoral conduct. You have not tainted your natural compassion and wisdom."

"How do you know it's there at all?"

"Because it is *natural.* Inborn. It is your birthright. All beings possess such wisdom, but few are able to develop it instead of being dragged down by their evil."

I nodded slowly, trying to grok her meaning. "I'm a *pure* Purifier, then."

"If you wish to verbalize it this way, then yes." Akasha's brows tensed. "But with this inherent purity comes weakness."

"Yeah, you're telling me."

"It is the vulnerability of the naïve. Such a young mind is flexible, open to possibility, but it has also not been immunized against the cruelties of this world."

"I think I've battled enough cruelty for a lifetime."

"Perhaps," she said, "but to accomplish your task, you will need to directly understand the roots of evil. You will need to guard your mind against its influence. The chok'tal may be part of you, Dak, but it is equally part of the Unmade. It *will* exploit any cracks in the walls of your awareness."

"I understand . . . probably."

Akasha nodded sharply and stood. "Good. Now go and collect whatever belongings you wish to take off the ship."

Finishing the dregs of my juice, I tossed her a grin. "Why? So it doesn't get destroyed when the ship crashes?"

"Yes," she said, as she headed back toward the bridge. "Precisely for this reason."

2

Akasha, you were kidding, right? Right?"

I'd asked the same question twelve or thirteen times in the last few minutes, and with each attempt, I'd received only a noncommittal shake of the head. From the looks of it, she really *did* intend to crash us. My confidence in this conclusion was only cemented when she led me to the row of evacuation capsules on the ship's underbelly.

"This is insane," I said. "You really think I'm gonna get inside that thing?"

Akasha stepped into a capsule's bright, red-cushioned interior and held the triple-plated door open for me. "Our window of opportunity is shrinking, Dak. We don't have time to discuss this right now."

"If this is a joke, I really need to know."

"It is not."

"Listen, I don't think this plan is going to work out how you're thinking. You really think the Hegemony is just going to throw up their hands and walk away when they see that an empty ship nosedived onto a very specific planet?"

"Of course not," she said, still waiting for me to board.

"So, what the hell are you thinking?"

Akasha sighed. "The ship has been programmed to make slow, circling passes over a planet on the other side of this system. But the planet *we* wish to inhabit will soon be within orbital range. We cannot delay our departure."

"How is putting the ship on a looping course going to help us? Once they find it and see an evac capsule is gone—"

"They will not."

"How do you know that?"

Without warning, Akasha reached out, grabbed my wrist, and tugged me inside the capsule's claustrophobic shell. She was strong—painfully strong. I'd forgotten that lesson since the last time she picked me up by the throat.

Before I knew it, I was slumped down on one of the velvety seating benches and pouting.

Akasha dialed in a few commands. The thick door locked in place, followed by a mechanical screech as the capsule's exterior locks disengaged. When the ship's ever-present hum faded, I knew we'd dropped, regardless of what the underfoot grav-panels suggested. We were currently plummeting through the void, steering limply in whatever direction Akasha had specified.

"Now I shall explain," Akasha said, as she sat primly beside me. "The ship is en route to a world populated by mechanized armies."

"A permawar world?"

"I do not understand this term."

I scratched the back of my head. "It's, uh, a bit of a legend among archaeologists. They used to always talk about worlds where two or more factions had developed automated 'smart' defenses." Akasha looked at me like I'd peeled off my own skin. "Basically, the machines fighting these global wars got so developed that they were able to repair and reproduce themselves, but they're not intelligent. It's all sensors and metal."

"Ah, I see. This creates an eternal and unwinnable conflict."

"Yeah, hence 'permawar,'" I explained. "I just didn't think they really existed. Imagine finding one near a planet of monks . . ."

"This connection is not mysterious. The monks *are* machines, Dak. They fled from their prior world's devastation."

"Wait . . . I'm gonna learn how to master my mind . . . from machines?"

"Minds are not limited to organic beings," Akasha said, her voice surprisingly defensive.

"It's just a lot to take in," I said, fully aware of the irony that this was the *least* "lot to take in" thing I'd had to process in recent days. "Okay, fine, machine monks and a permawar world. So, what's the idea? The automated defenses will target the ship, destroy it?"

Akasha hummed. "Even if it is not destroyed, the Hegemony will need to expend valuable time and resources attempting to recover it."

"Got it. So, this is basically a way to waste their time."

"A way to ensure you are able to train."

I leaned back. "You really think this world is still here? I mean, maybe we should've sent a hail before we left the ship and all that."

"I have contacted them," Akasha said. "As I said before, Dak, there is no other goal for you other than the refinement of mind and body. Allow me to handle the mundane tasks."

"A personal secretary. I could get used to that."

Akasha's grimace let me know I'd taken a step too far. Waving my hands in surrender, I took a long breath and decided to review my Status Display for peace of mind. I knew I had a handful of hours to spare and a rank-up in the chamber, but seeing as I had nothing else to do except brood during this eternal plummet to orbit, checking data felt like a comforting distraction.

STATUS DISPLAY
PURIFIER RANK: 10
RANK-UP AVAILABLE: RANK 11 (204,800 KP required)

Kill Points: 213,250
Genofacturing Points: 9,890

Rank Points: 0

Rank Time: 5 Hours, 17 Minutes, 8 Seconds
Storehouse Time: 6 Hours, 0 Minutes, 0 Seconds

Anima: 300%
Dominion: 0/4

The fact that I had only five hours until I started eating into my Storehouse Time shouldn't have frightened me, but it did. Not because of the time, really, but because of the rank-up requirements. Up until this point, I'd been playing in the shallow end of the pool. At one time, 5,000 KP had seemed like a daunting amount to rack up, now it was little more than an afternoon snack. A drop in the bucket in my current situation. Once I triggered the rank-up to 11, I'd need to gather a heart-stopping 400,000 KP. After that, 800,000. After *that*, I'd step well into the millions and beyond.

So, in reality, my fear had nothing to do with the actual amount of time left in my current rank-up. Instead, it was linked to the realization of what was coming. With every minute, every hour, my Kill Point needs ballooned to new and extreme heights. If I didn't become an uber-Purifier and take down the Unmade post-haste, I'd be a goner.

But even that was a distant concern. More pressing was the planet below us. Akasha had said it was full of beasts, but was that *still* true? She'd last seen it thousands of years ago, after all. And even if they did exist, how many Kill Points did they grant? Would I have to kill an entire den of murderous spider-dragons just to buy a new rifle with the Geno-facturing Spore?

I didn't know the answers to any of it, and that chilled me. Almost as much as the realization that I'd placed my life in the hands of a near-total stranger sworn to kill "my kind."

Feeling more perturbed than before my review, I shut the Status Display down and looked over at Akasha. She was studying her golden cube with extreme fascination, prodding at various panels and tugging at others to release tufts of blue light.

"Still have the magic touch?" I asked.

The moment I spoke, the light shrank back into the cube's crevices.

Akasha cautiously moved her hands away. "I do not wish to cause offense, Dak, but I believe it's best if you do not inquire overmuch about this device. Not until the monks have deemed your mind sufficiently trained, that is."

"I get it. You're afraid I might use its knowledge against you if I go all evil-Purifier mode."

"A simplification, but it shall suffice. Thank you for your understanding."

Honestly, I didn't *really* understand her reservations—she'd already shared a fair amount with me back on Kagu-9—but I also didn't feel like pushing her buttons. Mainly because my survival depended on it. Even though I was now heading to "safe" territory, a part of me knew that this was no different from scurrying around in Chanzig's city. I was still in the hands of a powerful faction that knew far, far more than me. Asking too many questions about sacred artifacts was a surefire way to guarantee my own execution.

Worse still, I was back to square one, relatively speaking. My Genofacturing Spore, nano-carbon sword, and Plague Burst shotgun had all been abandoned during our escape from Chanzig's fortress. All that remained was my semi-trusty Plopper pistol, which had miraculously stayed put in its leather holster during the chaos.

Sure, after a few good fights I'd earn enough Kill Points to restore my arsenal, but I wasn't jazzed about needing to spend so much just to get back to where I'd been. Especially not with the exponentially rising cost of rank-ups. Oh, and then there was the whole matter of needing to vomit up another spore . . .

Suddenly, the entire capsule shuddered. Sounds of pinging and rattling leaked through the ultra-dense outer shell.

"We have entered the stratosphere," Akasha said calmly.

"How long until we touch down?" I asked, feeling ridiculous the moment the words came out. She was a mystic seer, not an astrophysicist. How the hell would she know the time it took for a capsule to make landfall on a planet she hadn't seen in thousands of years?

To my surprise, however, Akasha had an answer ready. "Approximately twelve minutes."

"You're a woman of many secrets, Akasha."

There's no reason to describe the following ten minutes, mainly because nothing of note happened. Right about now, however, you might be wondering why I've written ten minutes instead of twelve. Well, buckle up, because the remarkable part of our descent happened in those fateful last minutes.

In one instant, just as I'd leaned forward to grab the strap of a stolen rucksack, the capsule was rocked by what felt like a class-five explosion. A tremendous force kicked up through the floor and nearly snapped my ankles. Emergency lights winked on and off. This was significant, mainly because I knew that high-end evacuation capsules featured gyroscopes designed to prevent injury from hard landings.

But here, now, that machinery wasn't firing—because we hadn't landed. We'd hit something. Hit it hard enough to mess with the grav-panels, no less.

Suddenly the capsule spun. Down became up, left became right. My feet were peeled off the floor, and the entire interior became a dark, whirling expanse of flying equipment and wires. Alarms shrieked as my back collided with the ceiling cap. Then the world shifted again, and the floor came rushing up to crack my cheekbone. Akasha's knee pounded into my kidney.

Second by second, twist by twist, all remnants of logical thought disappeared. All I knew was motion, nausea, pain, shadows. At a certain point I ceased to grab at anything, already knowing I'd be thrown loose an instant later.

Then, like sunshine poking through a blizzard, the tumbling slowed to a stop. The ringing in my ears faded, replaced by groans and desperate breaths. When I opened my eyes, the formerly tidy capsule interior was nothing but a jumble of strewn-about supplies and busted electronics. The capsule was tilted at a slight angle, meaning we hadn't landed on flat ground.

"Akasha?" I managed.

"Yes?"

She sounded rattled, though not exactly banged-up—not like me, that is. Glancing over with my aching neck, I found her sitting comfortably on the bench. She was strapped in with a series of reinforced buckles.

"Did you . . . secure yourself?" I said, wincing.

"Of course," she said. "That is what such features are there for, Dak."

I just flopped back to the floor panels. "We need to stop crashing."

Akasha undid her buckles, stood, and moved to help me up. Given how badly the Unmade and Chanzig had shattered my body, I couldn't tell if my handful of broken bones were old or new. Not that it mattered much. Either way, everything *hurt.* Just standing and limping over to the capsule's side door proved a Herculean task.

But before we could even touch the release valve, let alone start the pressure-equalization process, a larger problem appeared. Or rather, it spoke.

A series of deep, creaking groans moved through the capsule. Then I noticed that the craft's angle had moved. Not by much, granted, but still . . . movement was not good. Even as I stood there, staring at the flat lines of the wall for reference, I noted the capsule's mild seesaw motion.

"Akasha," I said, my chest tight, "I don't think we're on the ground."

Her hand shrank back from the release valve. "No, we are not."

Confirmation of that fact petrified me. But the fear didn't come from her agreement, per se. Instead, it came from the way in which she'd spoken. There was a frank and unyielding certainty to her voice. Considering all I knew about Akasha, it wasn't impossible that she'd sensed something even worse than our altitude.

It didn't take long to figure out what had put the chill in her. After a few moments of tense stillness, which the two of us spent silently tiptoeing about to balance the capsule's weight, there was a fresh sound. A growl, to be precise.

"Is that what I think it is?" I whispered.

Akasha nodded, but kept her face angled toward the door. "We are not on the ground, nor are we alone."

"How many are there?"

"Three." She paused, frowning as though in reconsideration. "Five. Seven."

"I get the idea," I muttered, unholstering the Plopper. "It's going to turn messy, isn't it?"

Akasha swiveled her head as though tasting the air. She must've sensed some flow of data that my juvenile human mind didn't even know existed. After a short bout of investigation, she pursed her lips. "Their minds are . . . unsettled. Chaotic."

"You think?" I asked, scoffing. "That growl told me all I need to know. Our capsule sure isn't surrounded by a horde of monks right now."

"Perhaps we should remain here. The order has received our transponder signal, so in time—"

Akasha was interrupted by a massive, rage-filled impact on the door side of the capsule. Our temporary home shifted backward, its exterior scraping with the sound of a thousand dying critters. If we took one or two more hits like that, we wouldn't need to worry about being up in the air. Gravity would handle that issue—and our bones.

"Don't do it, Dak," she told me.

I glanced her way. "What do you think I'm about to do?"

"Open the door and begin firing at them."

"Well, alright, you've got me pegged there."

"This capsule is designed for high-impact landings," Akasha said. "If we open it, we may compromise the—"

Again, the creatures pounded against the walls. Our capsule slid even farther back, this time accompanied by the supersonic *kr-krik* of a massive tree branch straining under an excessive load.

"I've got to do this," I said, as I checked the Plopper's ammo count. A full mag. "We can't just sit around and wait to be rescued. If they slap us down to ground level and we don't end up in a peaceful meadow, we're screwed."

"Combat at such elevations is a grave risk."

"So is landing in ten meters of mud . . . or opening the door to find twice the number of whatever the hell is out there now."

Akasha seemed to weigh our options for a time, her eyelids shifting under the cover of the blindfold. Eventually, she stepped back and nodded at the release panel.

"Thank you," I said, as I got to work. "When it opens, just . . . stay back. Let me handle it."

Keenly aware of the gibbering sounds outside, not to mention the capsule's general swaying pattern, I cautiously triggered the release mechanism and let the pressure equalize. Cold air came misting through the ceiling vents. For a moment I stared at those glistening puffs, wondering if Akasha had—through some seriously bad calculations—led me to a world that couldn't support a human respiratory system. But sure enough, when I tested the air with a brave inhale, it was workable . . . albeit a bit thin.

The panel's light flashed green, indicating the pressure was equalized, and I shifted my free hand to the door lever. *This* was the part I dreaded even more than the air exchange. Still, it wasn't like there were any significant decisions I could make inside. The only way to back off the growing crowd of savages, and thus avoid falling to our deaths, was putting on a show of force.

Summoning the dregs of my courage, I wrenched the lever down. The door popped a hair's width open, bringing with it a rush of dry, chilled wind and the stench of decaying plant matter. Next was daylight—muddy, close to sunrise or sunset. Gradually, inch by inch, the door swung farther . . .

"Remember," I whispered to Akasha, my Plopper raised and aimed, "no matter what, I want you to keep at a safe distance. If the—"

Once again, I was rudely interrupted—this time by a huge, mangy hand grabbing my entire head like a grape.

Mammalian Variant (BEAST)
CALCULATING . . .
Estimated Kill Points: 9,000

I hollered into the leathery, mud-splotched pads of the palm, which felt like sheets of sandpaper against my cheeks. Either that, or a vise. The sheer force of the grip was astounding. By the time I actually realized what was happening, though, it was too late. In one vicious yank, whatever controlled the monstrous hand tugged me straight out of the capsule. My legs flailed through empty air.

Even though I couldn't see anything, I knew this was *bad*. It only worsened when the beast let out a guttural roar and began waving me about like a ragdoll, raking my legs over thorny tree branches or outright slamming me into diamond-hard bark. I had to do something before this thing turned me into jelly—or went after Akasha.

Struggling for air, I assessed my options. My right hand was occupied by the Plopper, but the left was free, occasionally bumping against the creature's coarse fur. Not that I could use it for much. The beast's twitchy strength was more than sufficient to crush my skull on a whim. Stabbing this brute—or worse, firing blindly at it—would only succeed in triggering a panic reaction. One that would most likely end in my brains being squeezed through log-like fingers.

As the creature continued swinging me about, I shifted to the idea of triggering an upgrade. It was hard to think, given the growing nausea and overall fucked-upness of the situation, but I did my best to take Modri's advice and ground myself with my heartbeat. It was easy enough to sense, on account of the beast's thigh-like fingers squeezing my neck.

Upgrades, Dak. Think. What upgrades do you have?

I ran through the list as quickly as possible.

Indomitable? Good for surviving a long, nasty fall—not getting out of this thing's grip. Still, I'd take any boost to bodily durability I could. I flicked it on, biting past the pain of the transition. What else?

Overclock? Well, it'd help to wrench my way out at the very least. Without hesitation, I triggered the upgrade and felt its stimulant-like strength suffuse my limbs.

Still, Overclock and Indomitable wouldn't be enough. Trying to pry the beast's fingers apart would likely lead to the same result as shooting them: my head being *splooshed.* There had to be something genius I'd overlooked.

Infiltrator? Useless.

Silence? Even more useless.

Telekinesis? Not while being blindly tossed around in a forest canopy.

There was just one thing left, and it wasn't an upgrade—in fact, I didn't even know what it was. A Morphic Imprint. I'd gained it just after Akasha killed Chanzig, but thus far, I hadn't learned a single thing about it. For all I knew, it could've been symbolic, some victory trophy that rewarded me for taking down the bastard. But I doubted that. For starters, I hadn't been the one to get the kill. The fact that Chanzig's essence had crawled into me instead of Akasha meant there had to be *some* resonance with the chok'tal. And besides, there was a certain power behind the imprint . . . an uneasy aura that both tempted and jarred me.

None of this went through my mind at that moment, of course. I was too busy being flung about by some oversized forest critter. Rather than analyzing the merits of Mind Cascade, I frantically poured my focus into it and tried to activate it like any other upgrade.

In that instant, my body went partially numb. It was similar to the pins and needles of sleeping on your arm for too long, only it encompassed *everything.* All the physical sensations I'd felt a moment prior were muted, hazy, as though popping up behind an opaque screen. Hearing dwindled, then smoothed out into a long, rolling hum. The panic and urgency in my chest drifted off.

By contrast, my mental sensations had been dialed up to eleven. Every thought, every fear, every intention was loud and blinding. It felt like I'd aimed an amplifier directly at my own mind, creating some twisted version of a feedback loop. Second by second, my mind further drowned out the body, expanding and evolving until it seemed to occupy physical space.

Soon enough, I didn't even have vision. Hearing, touch, and taste vanished shortly after. Was I dying? It sure felt like it. My whole reality had been condensed down to a stream of flickering thoughts and perceptions. Then, like the finale of some grand magic trick, my vision returned . . . sort of. It wasn't my usual, eye-driven vision, but rather a grainy landscape made out of the mind itself.

Far in the distance, I sensed a presence other than my own. A hungry, diseased presence that manifested as a churning tornado in the void.

Instantly, though without understanding why, I identified the presence: My furry foe.

The recognition didn't come by way of thought, however. It was simply an act of knowing, much in the same way you intuitively know two plus two is four. In fact, everything about this encounter was neutral. The creature's presence, or aura, or whatever it was didn't inspire any fear. Almost on autopilot, my consciousness swam toward the formation.

The nearer I got to the beast's mind, the more turbulent my world became. Streaks of dark, cold energy whipped about in a maelstrom. Incomprehensible whispers brushed up against my mind. Faintly, I sensed the essence pulsing deep within the beast. The core that was animating this violent display. Words will never do any justice when it comes to describing its nature, but here are a few off the top of my head: pain, fear, rage, depravity.

Everything in my rational mind pleaded to move back, to disengage from this ravenous presence. But I still found myself on a collision course. There was some sliver of consciousness that found this place familiar, and furthermore, knew what to do.

When I came within mere inches of the beast's whirling heart, my mind opened like a flower. Brilliant light shone forth from what would've been the center of my physical chest. The light condensed into tendrils, which then proceeded to slither straight into the enemy's darkness.

A barrage of sights and sounds exploded through my awareness: Gnashing teeth, strings of fatty meat, blood on the snow, howling, screeching, rotten carcasses, burning trees . . .

With each momentary sense impression, I felt the separation between myself and the beast shrinking. Panic set in. My mind was drowning, completely overwhelmed by the flood of screams and itches and dark desires. It felt as though I'd opened some floodgate. Torn a hole in whatever was holding back the depths of the beast's consciousness.

Then there was *nothing* between us. No light to push back the shadows, no spaciousness to hold the oceans of misery. I felt myself slipping under its waves. Being eaten alive.

In my final moments, I summoned everything I had left and willed myself to return to the safety of my body. It was desperate, and yet—

I opened my eyes—my real, physical eyes—to the sounds of wild gibbering. It was coming from the beast, which still had me gripped firmly in its fist. Mind Cascade had been a dud, then. A terrifying, borderline psychedelic dud, but a dud nevertheless. Yet as I fought to draw breaths, sucking down as much air as possible between the folds of the giant palms, I sensed that something was . . . different.

The creature's noises were no longer those of a macho predator. They were frantic and clipped, reminding me of an animal trapped in a nightmare. That wasn't the only change, though. The beast had stopped jumping about, and its entire body was wracked with anxious spasms. Willingly or not, I had done *something* to the creature.

Before I could figure out what that *something* was, however, the hand abruptly let go of my head.

Then I was falling. Again.

3

One of my biggest pet peeves about action vids is how easily the protagonist manages to avoid certain death from falls. It might sound hypocritical, given how many times I've plummeted and lived, but at least there were valid reasons for my survival. Plus, I'm a real guy.

The worst offender for the "get out of death free" card has to be the miraculous handhold, which every protagonist somehow manages to grab while falling at terminal velocity—without ripping their arm off, naturally. But even setting aside the dubious physics, do you know how often architects install convenient ledges, grips, or protrusions for the benefit of falling civilians? Almost never. And even if they did, the odds that anybody could even locate such a helpful grabbing point while mid-air are slim to none.

How do I know all this? Because I've fallen a *lot*, in case you haven't been paying attention. Furthermore, it's taught me a very important truth that action vids never capture: When you're falling from great heights, you can't see much of anything. Between the screeching winds and your body's general survival instincts, you'll find yourself instinctively curling into the fetal position and shutting your eyes.

All of this is a long-winded way of explaining why I didn't see much on the way down. And what I do remember seeing isn't pleasant.

Cold air lashed at every bit of exposed skin, numbing my face and hands in mere seconds. The world streamed past in a collage of glinting ice and silver and monstrous trees. On an intuitive, gut-based level, I knew I was falling. Probably to my death. Due to the abruptness of shifting from Mind Cascade to total skydive, my mind took far longer to put the pieces together. So much longer, in fact, that by the time I had the thought "I am falling," it was too late.

Suddenly, I caught a branch to the thigh. Then the face. Then the groin. A veritable phalanx of branches battered and flipped me until I was locked in a nauseating perma-tumble. At some point, a question occurred to me. *Where will I land in this fu—*

The center of my back slammed against hardwood, folding my body in half over whatever had arrested my drop. Glancing sidelong despite the excruciating pain, I found my savior: a thick, snow-laden tree branch. At least, I presumed it was a tree branch. The damn thing was several meters wide and at least a hundred long, and even my tremendous impact had hardly stirred it.

I just lay there for a moment, breathless and dazed, staring up at the alien canopy that blotted out most of the sky. Our evacuation capsule was about eighty meters above me, perched on the edge of yet another titanic tree branch. It was surrounded by a horde of large, furry mammals—the same species that had grabbed me by the skull.

Gazing from this angle, it seemed insane that we'd even managed to penetrate the forest's uppermost layers. The canopy was so dense and gigantic in scale that it resembled a city. An icy, fog-laden city reserved only for those with the claws to navigate it.

But before long, the majesty of the view faded and reality returned. I was lying on an overgrown branch, probably paralyzed, and staring up at a gang of head-snatching beasts about to kill my only help in the universe. Broken or not, was I going to allow that?

Hell no.

I struggled up to my knees, unwilling to risk a jack-in-the-box-style pop up to a standing position on such an icy surface. Not that I would've been able to do that even if the conditions were right. My entire body hummed a familiar tune: pain. A few fractures, a handful of gashes, a bad break here or there. I didn't have time to baby myself about any of that. My one-two combo of Overclock and Indomitable would have to hold me together long enough to get some proper medical aid.

"Alright, Dak," I whispered to myself, absently patting the Plopper on my side to ensure it hadn't fallen loose, "it's time to work."

Unfortunately, this was the same moment I happened to look down. I wasn't and have never been afraid of most heights, but this wasn't *most* heights. This was a thousand-meter drop into a dark, foggy nothingness.

Somewhat cowed by the sight, I glanced back up to gauge how treacherous the climb would be. The capsule was teetering on a branch of a different tree, but there was an overlap point about three-quarters up where I'd be able to shimmy across. Well, not quite shimmy—*jump*. See, the two branches didn't quite touch. It wasn't a massive divide, but at these heights, and with this accursed ice, any amount of acrobatics was a gamble.

I worked my way up to a wobbling crouch, then began moving down the length of the branch and toward the main trunk. The damn thing was as thick as a Hegemony frigate. Probably tougher than one. And jutting out of the mega-trunk, in a fashion similar to its tree kin, were growths of massive blue crystals. Not the greatest climbing course. Thankfully, when I got right up to my target, I found that the bark was grooved enough to offer handholds. Shallow, irregular handholds full of ice, but handholds nonetheless.

After a silent prayer to whatever gods managed this sorcery planet, the climb began. It was slow at first, but Overclock did wonders with hoisting and shoving off footholds. The only thing it couldn't improve was the burning in my fingers. The sting of thorny wood and frozen rivulets on squishy pink flesh. But I didn't give a damn. I couldn't. Each time my foot slid and I heard a chip of bark plink-plonk all the way down to oblivion, fear gave me another kick in the ass.

Soon, I heard something else to keep me in line: the wild screeches and grunts of the beasts above me. They were still crowding around the capsule, slapping at it or raking their claws over the panels.

Damn, were they some *claws.* I got my first look at them—indeed, at the entirety of the creatures—about halfway up my tree. There were still forty or so meters separating me from the action zone, but the mist had thinned enough for me to see the beasts in detail.

Strangely enough, the furry bastards most closely resembled . . . sloths. Big, brutal sloths with a penchant for scrambling around on crystal-covered trees.

Only one of them wasn't actively trying to shake the Akasha prize out of the box. It was the same one that had grabbed me. The same one I'd hit with the Mind Cascade imprint. It was still framed in the HUD's blue box, marked as being in combat with me. It clung to a tree far from its comrades, spasming, gibbering . . . and slamming its beady-eyed face into a patch of crystals.

I hung there in total shock, unsure what I was seeing. But there was no mistaking the beast's action, especially when I saw the bright streaks of blood running down the trunk's crevices. It was beating its own head to a pulp.

What the hell are you, Mind Cascade?

I didn't get an answer to that question, but I did get a chilling sight. The beast delivered one final face-slam to the tree and went completely limp.

Its claws retracted in what seemed to be a type of rigor mortis, and then it was falling, vanishing into the endless haze of the forest floor. All that remained of it was the splotchy, semi-frozen patch of blood on the tree's crystals.

My stomach lurched, though I didn't quite know why. That thing had been trying to kill me. Trying to kill Akasha, no less. And yet . . . it hadn't deserved that end. Nothing had. There was something horrible about that imprint. Powerful or not, it had come from Chanzig and his corrupted mind. Now it was inside of me.

"Not now, Dak," I told myself. "Akasha first. Then rumination."

Redoubling my efforts, I surged up to the overlap zone between my tree and Akasha's. All I had to do now was crawl out on a thin branch, make a jump onto *yet another* thin branch, and then climb the remaining way to the capsule—all without becoming a sloth snack. No sweat.

The only problem was that the branch, much like the tree from which it grew, was covered in a thick gloss of ice. I rested a tentative hand on it and tested the surface. Slippery as hell. The only traction came from my palms' moisture flash-freezing.

But there was no way out—or down, for that matter. Each time I looked up, another sloth was battering the capsule and bringing it ever closer to a full drop.

I saddled the branch and wrapped my legs around it, only to wince at the sudden sagging. A dull, hollow crack moved along the wood as I scooted out over the void. All I could do was pretend that I *wasn't* about to drop to my death. Inch by inch, I moved farther toward the junction point, my sweat instantly turning to ice on my cheeks. Just another scoot, and I'd be there . . .

Then I heard a roar. Not the kind of roars the beasts had been making since our arrival, but something lower, throatier.

I peered up to find that I was no longer approaching undetected. One of the beasts was hanging on a branch directly above me, studying me with small, scar-lashed eyes and a twitching snout. It bent its head low and gingerly reached down with a vicious claw. Each of its nails reminded me of a chipped scythe.

Without even a shred of conscious thought, my right hand went to my holster. I snatched the Plopper free and aimed up at the approaching hand.

"Don't do it," I murmured. "Don't you friggin' do it . . ."

But the beast, predictably, didn't heed my command. The nails came closer, wriggling back and forth as though tasting the air for my presence. When one of their tips grazed my scalp, all control went out the window.

I sent two Plopper rounds straight into the beast's palm. Both exploded in a wash of steaming sludge, chewing through fur and flesh in mere seconds.

The beast reared back and shrieked, and suddenly *all* of its comrades were on full alert, turning away from their former prize and toward the new threat. My HUD exploded with fresh targets.

Mammalian Variant (BEAST) (5)
CALCULATING . . .
Estimated Kill Points: 45,000

For the first time in a while, I was completely *stuck* in a firefight. There was no way to scoot back without sliding straight off, and no way to advance without risking a snapped branch—not to mention a face-to-face encounter with my new friends.

Still, I had to do something. The beast above me was cradling its wounded hand and letting out a frantic hooting sound, undoubtedly drawing the attention of its kin in distant woods. The sloths on Akasha's side were certainly riled up by it. They began scaling the trees and branches toward me, their unwelcome curiosity souring into rage.

I couldn't even blame them for what was happening. From their point of view, we were just tiny, hairless chimps that had come crashing down in their backyard. Even while grabbed, the first sloth hadn't shown any sign of wanting to murder me. The aggression with *this* critter had only come out when I loosed that damn shot. But justified or not, I couldn't let them go to town on us. I'd take the guilt of being an ecological nightmare over becoming a corpse any day.

With a deep breath and no shortage of regret, I took aim at the closest sloth and let loose a volley of three flesh-eating shots.

Those rounds were all it took to cause pandemonium.

The moment the Plopper bullets burst across the sloth's face and chest, it leapt back and began howling in agony. In response, its comrades accelerated to a suicide rush. A flurry of overpowered fur, muscles, and teeth came bearing down on me from all sides. All I could do was turn the Plopper's barrel on each of the onrushing brutes, striking their necks and limbs with one potshot each. I didn't know how many rounds were left in the magazine, but I was certain it wasn't enough.

The moment I heard the pistol *click* with an empty chamber, it would be game over.

But just as the horde came within spitting range, so dense and overbearing I could feel its heat on my face, it stopped. There seemed to be a seismic shift in their momentum. Even the most aggressive of the bunch, a battle-scarred specimen missing its left eye, shrank back and clawed at itself as the Plopper's caustic rounds ate its fur.

One by one, the sloths retreated around the cover of tree trunks or descended into the haze, their claws stripping away fat slabs of crystal on the way down. The few stragglers seemed content to hang back and glare at me across the divide.

Well, all except one. The sloth was medium-sized, compared to its kin, but it had eaten my Plopper volley like a champ. Even as the flesh-eating ammo did its work, dissolving entire patches of facial skin by the second, the sloth lumbered closer to the evacuation capsule.

"Hey!" I shouted, waving the Plopper in hopes it would grasp my threat. "Get away from that!"

But the sloth either didn't give a damn or didn't understand. Rather than following the others, it proceeded to slam its shoulder into the capsule. I stared in horror as Akasha's tin can rocked on the precipice, each teeter accompanied by an ear-splitting groan of metal on hardwood.

Panicking, I lifted the Plopper and fired at the bastard—only to hear the dreaded *click*. Great. The time I needed it most, and I was dry.

Again, the sloth reared back and pummeled the capsule. That was the fatal shove. The capsule lurched forward and skidded over the crystalline wood, dropping into freefall like a bobsled.

"*Akasha!*" I screamed.

But it was too late. The capsule rocketed straight down, severing branches and plunging into the—

Abruptly, there was a deafening *kreck* sound. The capsule halted halfway down in the churning mists and bobbed slightly, almost as though floating on a super-dense ocean. Had it hit something and gotten stuck? Was it trapped in some sort of anti-grav field in the middle of the forest?

I had no answer to those questions, and I understood even less when the capsule began moving *back up* and out of the fog. With my jaw dropped and eyes wide, I tracked the craft's miraculous ascent. It looked like the capsule had suddenly triggered its own landing mechanisms, but the movement was too slow, too controlled. No, on second thought, it looked like something was . . . pushing it.

As the capsule fully emerged from the fog, I noticed something strange and murky locked around its base: a series of long, moss-covered struts, seemingly multi-jointed and full of power. Then I saw what appeared to be a thumb, and a wrist, and soon an entire arm. At first, I thought I was hallucinating, but the next few seconds—which revealed more and more of the mechanical body—proved my head was on straight.

Against all odds, the capsule had been saved by a giant, robotic hand.

But my amazement rapidly turned to fear. Whatever creature had just saved the capsule was easily three times as large as any of the sloths. The thick patina of lichen and rust all over its hydraulic bulk spoke of an impossibly long lifespan—not to mention unimaginable power. No matter how incredible this feat was, it had still been performed by a strange, ancient machine on a world of strange and ancient threats. A machine that probably viewed the world far differently than Akasha or I, no less.

In light of that, all that separated the capsule from an effortless crushing were the calculations inside the newcomer's artificial brain. One snap judgment, one shift in decision making, and Akasha would be turned to an alien pancake inside a metal tomb.

Heart jackhammering against my ribs, I scooched forward on the branch and tried to form a battle plan. If push came to shove and I had to square off with this mechanical titan, how would I even do it? The Plopper was useless against metal—a moot point, seeing as it was out of ammo—and no amount of Indomitable's boosting would allow my fists to punch through tempered steel.

I could try to jump on it, maybe shimmy down and knock out its optical sensors, but where the hell would that leave us? Perched on a blind, out-of-control machine with no qualms about dropping its new toys.

Suddenly, there was a flash of movement on the capsule itself. The main door peeled back to reveal Akasha, who stood with one hand on her hip and the other waving up at me.

"What are you doing?" I hissed, hoping the machine wouldn't hear me. "Do you realize where you are?"

She sat down on the lip of the capsule's doorway, allowing her feet to dangle down by the enormous metal fingers. "This is our welcoming party, Dak."

I blinked at her. "Huh?"

Before she could answer, a *colossal* head rose out of the fog directly beneath me. The entire skull was covered in a living ecosystem—thick, spongy moss, colonies of twisting mushrooms, even a few warrens that housed small, chittering animals. It was more a grove than a head. As the strange forest tilted back, I was greeted by an even less expected sight: a pair of glowing cobalt eyes set in a weathered, yet humanoid, face.

"Greetings, human who is known to Akasha," the titan said with a warbling and bass-heavy voice. "I am Brother Tekshim. Allow me to welcome you to the Order of the Radiant Throne."

All at once, dozens of similarly large eyes began glowing throughout the fog.

I didn't know whether to laugh in relief or piss myself. "Uh, hello . . . Brother. You can call me Dak. Just Dak."

"Very well, Dak Just Dak. Let us begin your training."

4

Down on the forest floor, things seemed calm. And by calm, I mean less predisposed to murdering squishy humanoids. Then again, I couldn't say whether this was because of our new elevation or the presence of roughly twenty skyscraper-sized mecha-monks.

Akasha and I sat atop the verdant grove of Brother Tekshim's skull, soaking up a rather impressive view of this new world. Our convoy followed a well-trodden path that had clearly been carved out by the monks, judging by its massive footprints and impressive width. The trail was made even more obvious by the lack of overgrowth, which hemmed us in on all sides.

At that moment, all I could say about the planet was that it had a haunting beauty. Here, at ground level, the air was thin yet humid. Chockful of rare nutrients, if the curious smell was any indication. It lent itself to large, violet-hued bits of foliage and pulsing crystal outcroppings. I was glad for the crystals, in a strange way. If not for their light (and the glow of the monks' eyes), we'd have been moving through total darkness beneath the thousand-layered canopy above. Every so often, I caught sight of large, slinking shapes moving within the shadows. As I said before, there was something to be said about the intimidation factors of our new monk pals.

Just then, I noticed Akasha eyeing me from her makeshift seat of mushroom spores. We hadn't spoken at all since our rescue—mainly because the sound of descending through the crystal trees was deafening—but she seemed eager to converse now.

I turned toward her. "Yes?"

She gave me a soft smile. "It seems we would have been better served by following my advice."

"Is this where you say, 'I told you so'?"

"No. Simply an observation."

"How was I supposed to know the monks were as big as these damn trees?"

"You weren't," she said, shrugging. "Consider it a lesson for the future, Dak. Rash decisions may breed harsh consequences."

In truth, I *did* feel remorseful about what had happened up there. Things were hunky-dory now, but if the monks hadn't shown up at that precise moment, it would've been a much different story. Much as I hated to face it, Akasha's point was valid and worth considering. I *had* leapt into action without regard for the consequences. I'd put her life in danger because of my recklessness. I'd also slaughtered a bunch of wild animals relaxing in their native territory.

But all that guilt was mine to bear—privately.

"Maybe next time, you can let me know how large your friends are," I said, trying to lighten the mood. "That would help in forming a decision."

She glanced out at the forest streaming past us. "Not much has changed since the last time I saw this world. And yet . . . there is a difference in the qualities of the creatures' minds."

"Huh?"

"There's a darkness in them," she said quietly.

"You mean, those sloth things weren't so aggressive a few thousand years ago? Seems like a short time, in evolutionary terms."

"I cannot explain what provoked such a change in them. But it is there, Dak."

I reflected on her words, calling to mind the swirling darkness I'd encountered upon using the Mind Cascade imprint. Granted, I didn't have a frame of reference for what a "normal" mind looked like through the ability's vision, but it seemed I didn't need one. In that short encounter, I'd sensed the creature's mind—its pain, its corruption. Part of me still ached with the aftereffects of its presence.

Still, now wasn't the time to spill my guts to Akasha, no matter what I had or hadn't experienced. I had a feeling she'd tear me a new one for relying on a power as volatile and unexamined as Mind Cascade. Hell, she'd probably lecture me about the dangers of playing with abilities I'd gained directly from Chanzig. And she'd have been right.

So, with that in mind, I just shut up and nodded along. If these monks were half the geniuses Akasha had described, they'd be able to tell me what had gone wrong with Mind Cascade.

"How far are we?" I asked Akasha.

"Not far at all," she said, nodding toward the front of our procession. "The main monastic grounds, provided they have not been altered, are rather close."

"You still remember where they are?"

"Almost half my life was spent here. Such memories do not easily fade."

"About that . . ." I scratched the back of my head. "I know it's bad manners to ask for a lady's age, but, uh . . . how old are you, exactly?"

She gave a soft smile. "Years are a poor measurement of time, Dak. Far too imprecise and rooted to the relative world."

"You don't have to be an astrophysicist to know your birthday."

"Perhaps not, but you asked for my exact age. I can't calculate such a figure. What I do know, however, is that entire worlds have vanished in my lifetime. I've seen empires rise . . . and inevitably fall."

"What about the Hegemony?"

She cocked her head to the side. "What of it?"

"You must've been alive before it existed," I said. "Do you remember what the universe was like without them?"

"Glimpses still remain, yes, but as I've said . . . time is so unwieldy. It isn't as though the Hegemony appeared out of a void and changed everything in one day. In fact, I can still recall the expansion of the humans. The rippling chaos of the Microbe Tide."

I nodded soberly. "Good thing you survived it, then. Otherwise, I'd have been all the way up shit creek without a paddle."

"Come again?"

"Never mind," I said, smirking. "Just an expression."

"You humans seem to have a fascination with defecation."

I opened my mouth, ready to defend my native species, only to realize that she had a damn good point. Thankfully, I had neither the time nor the need to get too deep into that discussion. At that very moment, the trees ahead of us thinned and gave way to fields of tall, swaying red grass. Although it was difficult to see in any detail, on account of the massive heads bobbing all around us, there was an impressive mountain range that spanned the entire horizon.

I whistled through my teeth. "No wonder you stayed here so long. It's goddamn beautiful."

Rather than reply verbally, Akasha stood and went to the right-hand side of Brother Tekshim's skull. There, she ascended a small ridge and waved me over.

"What is it?" I asked as I drew closer.

She stepped to the side and gestured out across the field, which now appeared to span hundreds of kilometers. It was an impressive sight—one that took my breath away—but I soon realized she wasn't referring to the fields. Instead, she was pointing at a section of the mountains that extended straight toward us like the head of a spear. My best guesstimate placed it a kilometer away.

Nestled at the base of that mountainous spur, encircled by a ring of waterfalls and twisting stone pillars, was some sort of compound. Even at this distance, the sheer scale of the masonry told me everything I needed to know. That was the monastery.

Something shy and unexpected moved in my chest as I studied the structures. It was a feeling I recognized, though I hadn't experienced it in so long that it felt like a fluke, a fake. Against all common sense, this place felt like *home*. Granted, I hadn't even seen the monastery up close, but it didn't matter. I'd been on the run for so long that I'd neglected that critical desire deep inside of every human: the desire to belong somewhere.

The more I looked out at the monastery, the stranger I felt. When I really thought about it, I'd never actually had a home. All I had were memories of places that the "real" Dak Korasa had called home. Sad as it was to say, Chanzig's planet was the closest thing to a home I'd ever gotten . . . and we all know how *that* turned out.

So, the prospect of being welcomed somewhere, not to mention receiving some form of security from these enormous monks, felt like a godsend in that moment. Hell, I knew I would've been more than satisfied with a bed to call my own.

Midway through my navel-gazing, a low, thunderous clap rolled across the fields. Several monks turned toward the origin of the noise, as did Akasha.

"This place get a lot of storms?" I asked her.

She shook her head. "That is not a storm, Dak."

I scrunched my face at her lack of explanation, but the meaning behind her words was made clear a few seconds later, when another volley of supersonic claps split the silence.

"Explosions?" I guessed.

"Yes," Akasha said. "This planet is remarkable, but it is not without conflict."

"Between?"

"The monks themselves are surely a better source of information." She set her lips in a thin line, but continued a moment later. "This world is uniquely situated. It has drawn the monks and their order, yes, but it has also attracted attention that one may find . . . undesirable."

I kept looking her way, expecting her to elaborate, but she stopped there. Maybe that was for the best. After days of nonstop conflict, the last thing I wanted was to wade neck-deep into another war. Merely *thinking* about a fresh fight was enough to turn my stomach.

"Don't trouble yourself," Akasha said, almost as though she'd sensed my concerns. "We've come to this world for a noble purpose, Dak. The first stage of training is allowing the mind to rest."

"Easier said than done."

She rested a warm hand on my forearm, surprising me. "As of this moment, you are among allies. There will be foes to encounter, of course, but you will seek them out of your own accord. It's time to let go of the vicious mind."

"The what?"

"The vicious mind." She spoke as though it were the most obvious thing in the universe. "All beings come into this world with innocence. Over time, though, they are drawn to viciousness. They wish to protect themselves and their beloveds. In doing so, they lose sight of the pure, unsullied mind . . . and wander through the realms of hell."

"Is that why you brought me here? To make me soft?"

Akasha grimaced. "Softness is strength, Dak. Given enough time, a gentle stream will slice through stone."

"Yeah, well, we don't have time."

Again, she touched my arm. "Softness is what the chok'tal fears. It is what the Unmade fears. Such beings are fueled by domination, pain, and scorn. If you pursue their desires, you will fall into the same abyss as those who came before you. I don't wish this for you . . . or the many worlds you would bleed."

The sincerity in her words disarmed me. I just looked back at her, nodding slowly. If I wanted to get far in this brutal "game," I needed to keep doing what I'd already done: relying on the guidance of those who'd walked the same road and learned its pitfalls. Modri was a miracle for combat advice, but Akasha clearly knew more about the long-term mechanics of the Unmade and its schemes.

Speaking of Modri, you might be wondering why I hadn't spoken with him since being on the ship. Don't worry—the surly bastard wasn't forgotten. Far from it, in fact. The simple truth of the matter was that Modri had a time and place. He was a fantastic companion for in-the-field chats, general chok'tal musing, and talking trash about the various dickheads we encountered . . . but he was a poor choice when it came to meeting "good" people. The last thing I wanted was to mentally juggle his snark with whatever introduction the monks were about to offer me.

I didn't have to wait long for that introduction. When we'd crossed about half the field to the monastery grounds, a long, ear-splitting horn blast filled the air. I winced and peered around the head of the monk in front of me to get a better look.

To my surprise, if not slight embarrassment, both sides of the path leading to the monastery's gates were crowded with rows of kneeling monks. There had to be nearly a hundred of the titans, all as rigid as stone and prostrating themselves before . . . me.

I didn't know what to do as we passed the mechanized greeting party, so I settled for the sort of sloppy wave one might expect of a hungover politician touring a good-for-nothing district. After several minutes of parading past the monks, the entire thing seemed more than a little ridiculous. I'd imagine it would be similar to a bunch of humans kneeling down before a mouse. And yes, I *did* have some remarkable powers, but it didn't change the comedy of the situation. In cases like this, let me just say . . . size *does* matter.

Given how awkward the procession felt, I was more than relieved when we came within sight of the monastery's main entrance.

It appeared that the monks had carved a gateway directly into the stone of the mountain. The two weathered metal slabs, which had been flung wide open for our arrival, were easily two hundred meters tall. Probably more, but good luck measuring them. To put it in perspective, the gate was several times the height of a monk.

"Did they, uh, chisel all of this out . . . by hand?" I asked Akasha.

Despite her lack of vision, she wore an easy smile. It was as though she could sense the aura of this place—its majesty, perhaps, or its nostalgia.

"The gates, yes," she said, "but not the inner sanctum. It used to be a lake."

My jaw nearly dropped when we passed through the gate and I understood what she meant. The entire inner area—the sanctum, as she'd called it—resembled the site of an apocalyptic meteorite crater. The sides were mottled and bowl-shaped, curving up and around us to form walls that felt more like a roof. By carving out the gateway, these crazy monks had drained the entire lake and turned it into their living area.

Suddenly the monks ahead of Tekshim veered to the sides, offering me an unobstructed view of the entire complex. It was radiant.

The main grounds consisted of six or seven gold-hued buildings, all plainly constructed from the remnants of ancient colony ships. Just like the gate, the buildings were beyond massive. Their bases were covered in interweaving tangles of large, crystal-studded roots, all of which rose up through the mossy stonework that formed a sort of courtyard.

Farther back, situated just in front of the waterfalls and their curtains of mist, was a central "temple" that rose to unthinkable heights. Like the other structures, it had a faded gold coating that spoke of its impressive age. What set this temple apart, aside from its sheer size, was the design. It didn't have the sleek, industrial look of a repurposed ship segment. Instead, it resembled a permanent habitation module intended for planetary colonization. The proportions alone made me wonder . . . was this how the monks had come to this planet? If so, where was their true home?

I'd have time to ask that later. Right now, there were more pressing matters. Such as meeting the gaze of what seemed to be the monastery's leader.

The white-robed titan stood on the steps of the central temple, both hands resting on a gnarled walking stick that had probably been a full-sized tree in its former life. Sprouting from their head was an enormous fungal colony that resembled a crown. They were flanked by four guards in silver robes, all of whom bore ceremonial swords. I hoped they were ceremonial, at least.

As Tekshim came closer to the leader and their entourage, the monks who had guided us here—as well as all those who'd knelt along the path—filed out around us to form a semicircle. They bowed their heads and waited as Tekshim crossed the final distance, then sank down to both knees at the foot of the enormous staircase.

It was like looking up at a god.

"Come closer, Purifier," the leader boomed, his voice echoing like an atomic shockwave in the basin. "I wish to look at you."

Who the hell was I to refuse? After giving Akasha a quick glance for reassurance, I wandered up to the edge of Tekshim's brow and lifted my chin.

The leader's pupils narrowed, seemingly zeroing in on my face using the optical sensors embedded in their skull. "Yes . . . I see," he said. "You've come here to learn about your mind."

I cleared my throat, worried that anything short of a scream would be lost due to the vast distance between us. But when I spoke, I found that the cavernous space did wonders for the acoustics.

"I've come here to deal with the chok'tal," I replied. "I was told you know about that sort of thing."

The leader's laugh nearly knocked me off my perch. "The Order of the Radiant Throne treats the root of all evils, Purifier. Your *symptoms* will be addressed in due time."

Much as I wanted to bark something back about reducing my issue to a "symptom," I held my tongue. I wasn't in the mood for getting turned to pulp this early in the day.

"But you can teach me to take down the thing that made the chok'tal," I said hopefully.

"We can do more than that," the leader said. "We can teach you to shape reality."

5

Fifteen minutes later, I was sitting alone in the middle of a meditation hall so vast I couldn't see its edges. Braziers the size of satellite dishes burned along the walls and at the base of the room's columns, but even their towering flames weren't enough to shed light on the darkness above and around me. Between these braziers were rows upon rows of exotic flowers and fungi, all growing in long brass planters.

Brother Tekshim had carefully deposited me on the threadbare crimson rug that covered most of the hall, then left without saying a word—with Akasha still on his head, no less. The unlikely duo had also deemed it necessary to take the Plopper off my hands. It crossed my mind that I was some sort of ritual sacrifice, a victim of whatever occult game Akasha and her monks had been playing for centuries, but I quickly shut that thought down. Not because it was unrealistic, but because there was nothing I could do to prevent such an unfortunate fate. I mean, come on, I couldn't even chase down Tekshim to ask questions once he started to lumber off. And yes, I tried.

Thankfully, I didn't have to wait long with my stewing paranoia. A series of thuds rippled through the floor, heralding the arrival of another mega-monk.

Still in my cross-legged position, I turned back toward the new arrival. At such a distance, and given the chamber's murkiness, all I saw were swishing white robes. The head honcho, then.

Suddenly, this whole affair felt like the 'verse's most intimidating job interview.

I remained totally rigid as the head monk stomped around the room, attending to his plants, and finally came to stand directly in front of me. Then, without preamble, he sank down on heavy legs to mirror my own sitting stance. Unlike me and my fleshy tendons, however, he was able to take it a step further. He lifted one leg atop the other and tucked it deep into their pelvis area, forming the classic "lotus" posture seen in so many religious texts.

Once the gears stopped creaking and pistons stopped pumping, silence fell between us.

I took the initiative. "Nice to meet you."

The monk bowed their head. "Well met, Purifier. I am known as Scryer Narbu."

"Come again?"

"Scryer," Narbu repeated. "One who divines the future. But between us, since you are not a formal member of the order, 'Brother' will suffice."

"Got it . . . Brother."

That sounded weird, even to me. I made a note to think of him as simply Narbu from then on.

"It is quite rare that Sister Akasha deems any outsider worthy of instruction," Narbu said, resting their gigantic hands in the folds of their lap. "I presume that, true to her nature, she has not explained much about our order."

I squinted up at Narbu. "Sorry, did you just say *Sister* Akasha?"

"I did. She was an honorary member of our order for many, many centuries. An emissary, if you will."

"Does that mean there's a, uh . . . female . . . robot chapter?"

"Sex is a concern of biology," Narbu said. "We have transcended our organic shells, so such concerns are purely linguistic. Brother is merely the term that we adopted from our progenitors. If history had been different, we might all be sisters. That being said, various species, sexes, and forms of life have sought us out over the eons. In this way, there are sisters of the order . . . but all of them are converts, bound to flesh."

"I see. I think."

"Let us return to the matter at hand, Purifier."

I raised a hand to halt him. "Dak will do just fine. Purifier's not exactly my proudest descriptor."

Narbu nodded. "Very well, Dak." He seemed to offer a wry smile, though the gesture was less than comforting, on account of the chipped, interlocking gears that formed his teeth. "Before we begin discussing matters of training, perhaps I should explain the history of this order. It may illuminate what Sister Akasha has brought you here to achieve."

"Listen, I mean no offense . . . but if you know about Purifiers, you also know I'm on a timer. A death timer."

"This is known," Narbu said. "How many hours remain for you?"

I blinked up at the monk, wondering if his mention of "hours" was an omen about how long he planned to keep me here and explain the long, convoluted backstory of the order. Don't get me wrong—I truly didn't want to spit in my host's face, and I *did* want to know what this order was all about, but death is death. Every minute I spent here was another minute that could've been spent pursuing a rank-up or learning to hone my skills.

To answer Narbu's question, I took a split-second peek at my info.

STATUS DISPLAY
PURIFIER RANK: 10
RANK-UP AVAILABLE: RANK 11 (204,800 KP required)

Kill Points: 222,250
Genofacturing Points: 9,890

Rank Points: 0

Rank Time: 3 Hours, 4 Minutes, 29 Seconds
Storehouse Time: 6 Hours, 0 Minutes, 0 Seconds

Anima: 300%
Dominion: 0/4

"Alright," I said, comforted by the fact that I still had a rank-up waiting in the wings and several hours left before crunch time, "I think I've got enough time to hear you out."

Narbu didn't seem particularly fazed by the answer. Something told me he'd have rambled about the order whether I had ten hours or ten seconds left.

"Long, long ago, our progenitors existed as organic beings at the apex of their evolution. With vast power and unsurpassable wisdom, they aspired to banish suffering and bring about an age of infinite satisfaction. Yet our creators found that no matter how much they improved in the fields of engineering or art, it would not solve the fundamental problems of birth and death."

"Problems?"

"It is suffering to be born, suffering to age, suffering to grow sick, and suffering to die."

"That's life, though."

"We have been led to believe it is," Narbu said coldly. "Our progenitors realized this was the root of all maladies. The solution, however, was not obvious. There was no visible engine driving the process of birth and death. To this end, my brothers and I abandoned our physical forms to seek nothing but a final answer. Our sole task was to explore the stars and discover the equations that govern reality. To establish a path to the permanent end of suffering for all living beings."

"Noble. But what does this—"

"With our new forms, we ventured across the stars," Narbu steamrolled on. "Knowing that memories of our homeworld would only hamper us, our progenitors elected to erase our memories. Then, after settling us into the long sleep of cryostasis, we were sent across the stars."

"To *this* planet?"

"Just so."

"Why?"

Narbu looked at me strangely. "One could say it was destiny. Prophecy. Whatever you wish to say, the truth remains: It was known that this world would play a crucial role in the eons to come."

"Right . . . but how do you know that's true? Not to be facetious or start a fight, but you all had your memories wiped. I mean, what if you landed on the wrong world?"

Rather than reply, Narbu extended a hand to the column on his right and pressed an embedded panel. After a moment, the entire hall was flooded with the sound of clanking cogs.

I glanced about in a blind panic, trying to locate the cause of the noise. It seemed to be coming from everywhere and nowhere. When a thin streak of light sliced its way down the middle of the hall and began to widen, however, I understood.

Directly overhead, the ceiling flaps had peeled back to reveal a wide-open expanse of sky. Only it wasn't just sky. The nearby mountains loomed like a vengeful god, their crags dark and . . . magnified? The glossy shimmer over the scene suggested there was, in fact, some kind of advanced tech at work.

"Look at the highest peak with care," Narbu said.

I did as he asked, squinting to discern any important details among the sprawl of rock and snow. There was plenty to see, but none of it seemed to be noteworthy enough for a live demonstration. Except . . .

"What the hell is that?" I whispered, homing in on an overgrown fungal mass that rested atop the mountain like a crown.

Narbu gave a deep, bass-laden hum. "That, Dak, is the force that explained our purpose on this world. It is our link to universal wisdom. The Throne of Radiance."

"Alright, now I'm lost."

"Sister Akasha tells us that you had a direct encounter with the Unmade," Narbu said. "To engage with this being, you had to travel through a sort of gateway. A portal that linked its world with ours."

"And you're saying that"—I pointed up at the Throne—"is another gateway to the Unmade?"

"No, not exactly. It is a gateway, yes, but its creator shares little with the Unmade."

"Where does it lead, then?"

"Not all gateways are made for physical forms to change locations," Narbu explained. "Sometimes, a gateway is merely that which allows minds on different levels of reality to exchange information." Perhaps seeing my poorly hidden befuddlement, the monk pressed on. "Through its gateways, the Unmade brought misery and death. But through *this* gateway, the Throne of Radiance, we are given access to wisdom beyond measure."

"Maybe I've just bumped my head too much lately," I said, massaging my temples, "but I don't understand how any of this adds up. Machine bodies, gateways, mountain fungus?"

Narbu let out a curt laugh. "After we arrived on this world, we were aimless. Despite containing every byte of data our progenitors had gathered to counteract suffering, there were no organic beings to learn from, nor was there any obvious task to be done. But the elders and I soon discovered that cosmic wisdom had not vanished—it had merely changed forms. Through meditation and rituals, we were able to converse with the Throne of Radiance you now see. It taught us of reality and its laws. It understood the urgency of our prophecy. It taught us everything we know about the Unmade . . . about the true nature of the mind . . . and about how to preserve order in a dying universe."

"This, uh, Order of the Radiant Throne, then . . . was your way to pass down this wisdom."

"Yes, very good," Narbu said, for once seeming pleased with my answer. "To our order, the voice that spoke through both the Throne and our progenitors was the same. It is the voice of original radiance. The voice of that which resists darkness by its very nature."

"I'd be able to hear it?"

Narbu's eyes narrowed. "The Throne of Radiance spoke to our kind in a language organics could not understand. That is why it is our duty to translate it to a more digestible format."

"What does that mean? Did it speak to you through eating the fungus and tripping?"

I was joking, but Narbu nodded emphatically.

"Not to be rude," I said softly, "but how are you even able to trip without a stomach?"

Narbu gave me a wide smile, then activated something on his torso. All of a sudden, the two panels that formed his chest peeled outward, exposing a central cavity. Within that cavity was a wide, transparent vat that resembled the tanks Chanzig had grown me in. Thankfully, there was no body in the vat. Instead, there was a thick, bulbous brain suspended in clear fluid and wreathed in bundles of. . . something organic. Neural fibers, nerves, blood vessels? Too hard to say. At least I'd gotten my answer as to how robots could "trip balls" without a body.

"The sacrament is injected into the core of consciousness," Narbu explained, pointing to a tiny valve I assumed was meant for a drug-filled syringe. "Such things are not yet relevant to you, of course. The wisdom of the Throne is reserved for those who have proven their capabilities."

"Okay, back up, though. You told me that the Throne knew about the Unmade, and that it taught you all about it."

"That is correct."

"How did *it* know about the Unmade?"

Narbu raised a brass eyebrow and sealed his chest panels. "You said you did not have much time, Dak. I don't wish to burden you with excessive knowledge."

"This seems important."

"And so it is," Narbu replied quietly. "You are asking about the foundation of existence. Not just the existence of this universe, but of all universes."

I took a deep breath. "Alright, yeah, maybe I don't have enough time for this."

Narbu rested a palm on the ground between us. "Stay, Dak. I will make this brief." He looked down at the Throne of Radiance again, then made a slight hand gesture that caused streams of glimmering particles to form overhead. When they solidified, however, they formed a vaguely disc-shaped cloud that reminded me of galactic simulations. "Beneath and within our physical universe, there is a void. A space between worlds. But this void is not completely empty. It contains pure potential, suffused with knowledge of its own existence and all of reality. Wise. Compassionate. Perfect. Not quite alive, but far from dead."

"Okay . . ."

"The void's true nature is beyond description, but we know it as the Absolute," Narbu continued, moving his fingers and causing the swirling disc to brighten. "It is the wisdom that incarnated as the Throne, as our universe, as every sage and messiah in history. It is the basic intelligence that allows you to know you exist, or to know hot from cold. It is the radiance burning in the heart of all minds, in fact."

"Sounds like God."

"Such concepts do not apply to the Absolute." Narbu made another gesture, and the formerly bright disc became clouded with a dark haze. "The Absolute is not one being, nor is it many. It has no body, no mind. It is simply itself: perfect wisdom."

"If it's inside everyone, it seems your average Joe should be a little sharper."

"It is our original state, and our potential future state," Narbu explained. "Countless cycles of bloodshed, deceit, and apathy have dimmed the true nature of one's mind. Without the guidance of the Absolute, we are bound to life, death, and rebirth in the Endless Wheel."

"The *what*?"

"The Endless Wheel. The veil of delusion that keeps us trapped in the dimensions of matter, forever incarnating us in accordance with our own defilements. It is the reason for your low birth as a human animal." I cocked a brow, but Narbu moved on anyway. "The darkness of the Wheel is crushing, but *some* manage to escape it by discovering their own nature and illuminating the path to freedom. These beings have shed their bodies and attained mastery of reality."

"Now *those* sound like gods."

"They are beyond gods," Narbu said. "Each culture and dimension has a different name for awakened beings that have made contact with their inner nature, with the Absolute. They are known variously as Voidseers, Deathless Ones, prophets, and much more. But among our kind, they are called *Wayfarers*."

"But . . . what exactly are they? Aliens? Extradimensional creatures?"

"In their former lives, they were born as many things: humanoids, specters, animals, demons. What unites them is their shared state of being. They have all renounced their universes and gone beyond the bounds of logic. They have attained the ability to shape reality itself. To liberate . . . or vanquish."

"That's what you're all after? Becoming a Wayfarer?"

"Not merely a Wayfarer," Narbu said. "To experience one's potential as the Absolute, it is only necessary to acquire power and insight into the laws of reality. Some seek this state of being out of a wicked mind."

"Yeah, I can imagine," I said, thinking very firmly about Chanzig.

Narbu smiled again. "Some of these Wayfarers understood that their path was not yet complete. Although they had freed themselves from the physical universe and tapped into the void, their minds were still dominated by lust, clinging, aversion. They had not achieved full *expression* of the Absolute. Thus, they probed every layer of reality, continually seeking the final knowledge that would lead them to freedom and ultimate compassion."

"And?"

"Their answer rested in the one place beings forget to look: their own minds. There, they studied the nature of the Absolute until no ignorance remained." Narbu dispelled the hazy layer of his projection, bringing out the original golden glow. "Those who contemplated it long enough freed themselves from rebirth and attained supreme perfection. They became known as Radiant Wayfarers."

"You're sure they aren't gods?"

Narbu chuckled at that. "They seek to spread knowledge of the Absolute to all beings, in all times, in all universes. They will not rest until they have freed the last prisoner of reality."

"Tall order."

"One would assume so. Yet all Radiant Wayfarers, from all universes and realms of existence, have their own paths of teaching. Some remain in solitude, traveling from world to world to seek out students. Others lend their mind to their universe's Wellspring."

"Wellspring? What's that? Some kind of hive-mind?"

With a slow nod that indicated I was *almost* correct, the monk said, "Wellsprings do not exist on the physical planes. They are realms beyond time and space, each shepherding over a different universe or continuum. Infinite sources of knowledge, wisdom, and strength, free to those who know how to access their power. Even as we speak, the Wayfarers comprising this universe's Wellspring continue to work tirelessly for the benefit of all beings."

"Well, that's pretty kind of them." I thought further on it. "Wait—was the Unmade one of those Wayfarers?"

"Your mind is active," Narbu said. "As I said, only *some* of these Wayfarers understood their own nature. In their former lives, they had been monks, sages, martyrs, emperors, scholars. Their motives had been pure. Others, however, did not awaken for the good of their fellow creatures. They performed dark rituals or overloaded their minds to the point of madness. Some simply wandered too far into the riddles of the cosmos." The monk closed his eyes for a time. "Upon awakening, they found themselves overwhelmed by the intensity of the void. They sank deeper into the emptiness. They grew lost, confused, agitated . . . and they began to seek pleasure through acts of darkness. Thus, they gained the title of Defiled Wayfarers."

"Yeah, that seems about right for the Unmade. Is it in some kind of war with our universe's Wellspring? You know, radiant versus defiled? Light and dark?"

"Precisely." Narbu gestured back to the Throne of Radiance. "What you see before you is a conduit. A rift, of sorts. Its fungus allows us to commune directly with the Wellspring."

"What does it say?"

"You will find out soon enough, Dak. Just know that I am the interpreter of its will. I shall *never* lead you astray. Your path is assured."

It was a lot to take in, but I did my best. In some ways, perhaps it was easier for me to accept all this than the average person. After all, I'd only been alive for a few real-world years. I hadn't yet adopted all the beliefs, dogmas, and theories of an adult. My mind was an empty vessel waiting to be filled . . . hopefully with useful knowledge.

"I have a question," I said, raising a limp finger. "How exactly is learning about the Unmade going to help anybody? Akasha said your order's been looking for a champion, or something like that. I'm paraphrasing."

Narbu gave a sagely nod. "Such wisdom will come later, Dak. For now, all you must know is that your mind is more valuable than you'll ever grasp. It has been touched by a Wayfarer."

"Not one of the good ones, though."

"Even if a Wayfarer has not mastered the perfections to become radiant, it is still drawing its power from the Absolute," Narbu said. "By extension, so are those affected by their deeds."

"So, I shouldn't be worried about getting defiled?"

"On the contrary," he said darkly. "You must safeguard your mind against it in every moment, waking or dreaming. That is why you are here, Dak. To learn to walk the sacred path instead of wandering into the darkness."

"About that . . . have you actually met any Purifiers who've gone off the deep end?"

For the first time since we began speaking, Narbu's face displayed a hint of unease.

"It's best if we return to such matters at a later time," he said, reaching over and activating the same column's panel to close the ceiling aperture. "The question for now, Dak, is whether you are willing to undergo training with our order. If you wish to proceed, the trials will not be easy. The answers you receive may not be pleasant. If, conversely, you wish to walk away, we will do our best to ensure you and Akasha receive safe passage to your next destination."

It seemed like a weighty decision, but in all honesty, it wasn't. Akasha would snap my neck herself if I so much as thought about leaving this place. After all, a refusal to train my mind was tantamount to saying, "Screw you—I'm off to become the number-one Purifier!"

"I'll stay," I told Narbu, bowing my head slightly. "So, what's first on the list? Breaking boards with my hands? Meditating on a mountaintop?"

Narbu just blinked at me. "No, Dak. The first matter of business is finding out if your body is strong enough to endure our training. To that end, walk with me. We will see if your skills in battle are as sharp as your wit."

6

Considering how often Akasha and Narbu had emphasized nonviolence, compassion, and restraint, I'd begun to wonder how I was going to earn any Kill Points on this world. Sure, there had been brief mentions of "foes" and "battle," but for all I knew, those were just metaphorical terms related to overcoming hatred—or some other form of double-speak nonsense. With that in mind, you might better understand my surprise upon being led to the monastery's armory.

The long, candlelit area had been carved into the mountain itself, leaving rough-hewn walls threaded with veins of glimmering minerals. An impressive sight, but not nearly as impressive as what lined those walls.

The monks had covered every square centimeter with a lattice of thick, wooden beams. This lattice provided the anchor points for hundreds—or maybe thousands—of weapons. Everything from gold-encrusted glaives to composite bows hung before me like goods at the 'verse's largest martial emporium.

Of course, most of the hardware on display had been forged for the monks, not a puny human like me. Even the smallest daggers were nearly three times my height. Some of the polearms and spears resembled thin towers.

"What do you think?" Brother Tekshim asked, squatting down beside me like an attentive parent as I wandered the chamber.

"It's . . . glorious," I said honestly. "Did the monastery make all of these?"

"Yes. What you now see is the result of thousands of years of work."

"You'll have to show me the forge you used. I bet that thing has enough power to let a ship pinch to the end of the galaxy and back."

Tekshim let out a rumbling laugh. "So it could, Dak. In fact, our forge is none other than the fission core that powered our progenitors' vessel."

"Makes sense." I paused before a serrated axe, running my hands along its haft. The thing was massive, but to the monks, it was probably small enough to be used as a hatchet. "If you don't mind me asking, what'd you make all of this for? Wild animals?"

Tekshim exhaled gently, but the force of the air was still enough to stagger me. "You will learn such things in time, Dak. Scryer Narbu has maintained the order's integrity over the eons by restricting the knowledge available to outsiders. Once you've completed the requisite trials, you will understand everything."

A tad annoying, but I also understood the monks' commitment to hushed-lips policies. Countless organizations had been destroyed by letting in the wrong crowds and failing to stomp out corruption. Whether or not I was the "champion" the order sought, I needed to be vetted and allowed access to the good stuff. And I'd earn that right.

"Fine, we'll set it aside for now," I said with a sigh. While scanning the racks further, I noted glimmering, golden flakes set into one blade's steel. They had the same consistency as the particles Narbu had used for his presentation of the void. "What's that?"

"A miracle."

"Huh?"

"It's what the older brothers say." Tekshim stooped down and smiled. "They claim that the Throne of Radiance fills the waters with condensed power. It produces these small, glowing flakes. Our order considers them supremely valuable. Many say this substance is the living expression of the Wellspring, and thus the Absolute itself."

"Confusing."

"For an outsider, perhaps. Scryer Narbu does not always explain things so directly. If it helps, you may conceive of our reality in the following manner: The Absolute is perfect reality, the Wellspring is the teacher that shares knowledge of the Absolute, and the Throne of Radiance is the vessel through which the Wellspring makes contact with our physical plane."

"So . . . an interdimensional fungus turned wisdom into glowing flakes in the water? Sounds radioactive."

"That was what several outsiders with scientific knowledge told us," Tekshim said, shrugging. "I would not suggest skin contact before you have thoroughly examined the relationship between the flakes and human tissue."

"These, uh, miracle flakes wouldn't be connected to the explosions I heard on the way here, would they? Akasha said this world's got a conflict problem."

"The nature of a deluded mind is greed," Tekshim explained, by way of an answer. "When sentient beings heard about the treasures our Wellspring had sent through the Throne, they swarmed this world. They began excavating the gullies, the rivers, the mountains, eagerly hoping they might recover even a fragment of the Wellspring's artifacts and sell them for a fortune."

"Good old human looting."

Tekshim gave a solemn nod. "Our order has secured a large percentage of the Wayfarers' miracles, but this has not stopped outsiders from waging war over what remains. If they knew how many treasures we held within these walls, they would surely turn their guns on us. That is why we remain quiet and detached from their affairs."

"From the sound of it, that hasn't been enough. You mentioned that you'd been suffered attacks on the monastery."

"That is true. Every few decades, a band of outsiders grows brash enough to challenge us with force. The problem has worsened somewhat in recent years."

"Word gets around," I said, shaking my head. "Not to scare you too much, but I think you might be getting full-on planetary invasions within a decade. Us humans will go to extreme lengths for shiny trinkets."

Tekshim hummed, though the sound resembled a sputtering motor. "To circle back to your original query, Dak, these weapons are reserved for maintaining the existence of the order. Such threats may arise from anywhere."

There was a guarded, borderline coy note in Tekshim's words. Something he either wouldn't or couldn't tell me.

"What's next?" I asked. "Do I pick a weapon so we can spar or something?"

"We will not be sparring. Scryer Narbu has requested that you begin the first phase of your training immediately."

"What does that mean?"

"It means that death is a distinct possibility." Tekshim gestured across the armory with a moss-coated hand. "Fortunately, our order has made many items to accommodate outsiders over the years. Walk with me, Dak, and examine your options carefully."

With no shortage of suspicion about Tekshim's mention of death, I followed the monk to the rear of the armory and looked around. Sure enough, the weapons mounted here were far more suitable to a humanoid-sized creature. Most of them were just as archaic as the swords and shields reserved for the monks, but the furthest shelves held a few relatively modern weapons. And by "modern," I mean designs that would've been cutting-edge tech about a thousand years ago.

Primitive shotguns, dart-spitting tubes, and flamethrowers lined the walls, all coated in a thick layer of dust. It was clear that these devices hadn't been put to use in a significant amount of time.

"So, I can just . . . pick something?" I asked Tekshim.

He nodded. "Arm yourself as you see fit. Once we are in the wilderness, of course, you will be unable to rearm yourself." His glowing eyes shifted about with unease. "I should also mention, Dak, that I am forbidden from directing you in your task. Should you face a mortal threat, you must be self-reliant."

I pulled my hand away from a thin, humming sword and blinked at Tekshim. "You mind telling me what we're about to do? It sure as hell would make it easier to pick my gear."

"I would be delighted to explain the situation, but I'm certain you already know my answer."

"Rules, rules, rules," I grumbled.

"Precisely, Dak. Select your arms and meet me at the door. Be mindful with your choices."

Tekshim lumbered off, leaving me with the seemingly infinite smorgasbord of lethal instruments. You might think that having heaps of choices leads to better outcomes, but I'd disagree with that. You see, too much choice is crippling. It's a lot easier to feel confident in your decision when you only have two or three options. At least in those cases, you can narrow things down in short order.

Here, though, I had an overdose of choice. What in Halcius' name were they going to have me fighting? If it was some sort of flying beast, I'd be an idiot to rely on a melee weapon. On the other hand, how much use would a ranged weapon be if the fight took place in a narrow cave? Sighing, I resolved to take two weapons along with me—one for smacking things up close, and another for nailing things at a distance. It seemed like the surest way to cover my bases.

Now, I could spend an hour listing all the weapons and the pros and cons I assigned to each one, but I won't. I'm a man who's learned the value of time the hard way. This being the case, I'll make it easy by describing what I picked and why.

First up was my ranged choice: a snub-nosed shotgun that fired what appeared to be shards of pulverized crystal. It wouldn't be great over large distances, but I figured it didn't need to be. The monks were setting me up for a fight, not a sharpshooting competition.

The second weapon, my melee pick, was the stranger of the two. I opted to take a heavy, skull-smashing hammer off the third row of shelving. It had a wide, blunt head and a short grip. Perfect for crushing things in close quarters. The fantasy fetishists out there might be fuming that I didn't pick a symbolic weapon like a sword, but too bad. Hammers deserve more love in the world of weapon enthusiasts.

With my killing tools picked out, I trudged back across the armory and met up with Tekshim. I hefted both items up for his approval. To my surprise, he didn't give me any of the muted robotic expressions I'd come to expect. No nod, no silent, stony look. Instead, there was a deep, all too human unease in his eyes. Small hydraulics cycled in a weird display of anxiety.

Then, before I could probe further or even ask for a sling to better carry my weapons, Tekshim scooped me up and placed me back atop his skull. He headed back the way we'd come, taking me past the various meditation halls and storerooms with long strides.

I rode atop him with suspicion for a while, eyes squinted as I tried to work out what had spooked him. Nothing immediately came to mind, though, and I had to admit that trying to parse a robot's mental state using facial expressions was a losing game. It wasn't worth chewing over. Or so I thought at the time.

While Tekshim chauffeured me around, I pulled up my Status Display and had a peek. I still had a few hours before I started eating away at my Storehouse Time, but it seemed prudent to rank-up now, before we got into any new fights. For starters, I didn't know how long it would take us to reach our hunting grounds. And second, all this talk of meditation and mind training made me antsy about Kill Points. If I spent three-quarters of my day cooped up inside the monastery, I wouldn't be able to accrue the points I needed for another rank-up. It was better to bite the bullet now and start progressing toward my next rank. Otherwise, this upcoming kill would just be relegated to more Genofacturing Points—which I needed, but not as badly as, well, living.

With the decision made, I hit the rank-up button. My new Status Display was daunting, to say the least.

STATUS DISPLAY
PURIFIER RANK: 11
RANK-UP NOT AVAILABLE (409,600 KP required)

Kill Points: 0
Genofacturing Points: 27,340

Rank Points: 1

Rank Time: 21 Hours, 59 Minutes, 57 Seconds
Storehouse Time: 6 Hours, 0 Minutes, 0 Seconds

Anima: 320%
Dominion: 0/4

Four hundred thousand goddamn points. Assuming I made it to the next rank-up, I had a nearly million-point quota to look forward to. Briefly, I considered churning out another Genofacturing Spore and making one of those Kill Point-boosting tonics—then discarded the idea. After the brutal beatdown the Unmade and his goons (including Chanzig) had given me, I was in no condition to birth another spore. Not right before a battle, anyway.

No, the Genofacturing Spore and its tonics would have to wait until I'd passed this test. If I was going to spend 20,000 GP to crank out the special sauce, I wanted to do it at the right moment. Before a Slaughter Event, for example. The six-hour window for the tonic was excellent, but six hours wasn't a lot of time when half of it might be spent sitting around in the monastery.

After tabbing back to reality to ensure Tekshim was still walking (he was), I pulled up my information again and headed to the upgrades tab. The selection was just as I remembered it: two more Rank Points to unlock the next tier of Annihilation, and just one to unlock Mutation's.

A natural choice, then. Mutation was already my most invested category, and besides, I was on the edge of my proverbial seat to find out what Tier IV held. Eager to invest my fresh point, I pulled up the Mutation display.

MUTATION [Tier III] (*1 Rank Point required for Tier IV access*)

Telekinesis (REQ Rank 8): Forms a moderate quantum link between your mind and any inanimate object within 10 meters. (1/3)

Blindsight (REQ Rank 6): Projects a sonar signal up to 20 meters from your nervous system, rendering a three-dimensional readout of any environment. (0/5)

Polyps II (REQ Rank 3): Enables bonding with a second Polyp. *Does not require a Dominion slot.*

Omniphile (REQ Rank 3): Increases homeostatic efficiency in harsh environments. (0/3)

Nocturnal (REQ Rank 1): Further enhances night vision when active. (2/5)

Honestly, it was hardly even worth considering. Telekinesis had saved my ass several times already, and I'd already caught myself fantasizing about what the next ranks would offer in terms of power. Not wanting to linger too long, I added my Rank Point to hit the second stage.

That was only half the fun, though. With that investment, I'd just unlocked Tier IV access. I hastily scrolled back to see the new selections.

MUTATION [Tier IV] (*3 Rank Points required for Tier V access*)

Genofacturing III (REQ Rank 15): Enables creation of all Stage-III products. *Does not require a Dominion slot.*

Soaring Death (REQ Rank 13): Sprouts a pair of wings made from cartilage and stem cells, suitable for low-altitude travel. (0/3)

Photosynthesis (REQ Rank 11): Converts starlight into energy, enabling accelerated healing and decreased nutritional requirements. (0/3)

Telekinesis (REQ Rank 8): Forms a strong quantum link between your mind and any inanimate object within 10 meters. (2/3)

Blindsight (REQ Rank 6): Projects a sonar signal up to 20 meters from your nervous system, rendering a three-dimensional readout of any environment. (0/5)

Polyps II (REQ Rank 3): Enables bonding with a second Polyp. *Does not require a Dominion slot.*

Omniphile (REQ Rank 3): Increases homeostatic efficiency in harsh environments. (0/3)

Nocturnal (REQ Rank 1): Further enhances night vision when active. (2/5)

For a few seconds I just hovered on the menu, certain my physical body's jaw had dropped through the floor. There it was—*wings*! In some ways, flight had been my ultimate pipe dream at the beginning of the Mutation journey. It was hard to envision what sort of oddities might surpass it if I reached Tier V. Mentally marking that upgrade as a must-have addition, I moved onto the second (and weirdest) option I'd unlocked.

Photosynthesis didn't seem like a *bad* upgrade, per se, but it did give me an uneasy feeling. It was just a hair too close to becoming a plant for my liking. Granted, I could see the potential uses—it would be nice to receive patching up and a free food source just from sunbathing—but I also felt that I'd need to drop three whole points into it to see any real benefits. And considering the exponential rise in rank-up costs, not to mention my obsession with flying and telekinetic powers, I had a feeling I'd never wander down that path.

Last but not least, of course, was Genofacturing III. It would be useful, if not mandatory somewhere down the line, but at the moment, it was just a string of text. I didn't have enough points to make anything decent, and even if I did, I'd still be waiting until Rank 15 to even see what it offered.

Satisfied with my decision to make a beeline for Soaring Death and Telekinesis boosts, I shut the Status Display and returned to the world of form.

To my surprise, Tekshim had covered quite a bit of ground during my navel-gazing. We were outside on some sort of elevated terrace, supplying me with a mind-boggling view of the surrounding fields and valleys. Below, just barely visible over the ridges of Tekshim's brows, was Akasha.

She stood with a cup of tea in hand, her meditation cushion perched just a few meters from the terrace's edge.

"I suspected you'd take this path out," she said calmly, more to Tekshim than me. "Allow me to bestow upon you both my sincere wish for victory."

I rolled my eyes and leaned back. Clearly Akasha had known I'd be taking part in these combat rituals. Nice of her to mention it in advance, right?

"Thank you, Sister Akasha," Tekshim said. "May your mind merge with the unshakable, the unspeakable, the undying."

Akasha bowed deeply to the monk, then returned to her cushion and sat down.

Before I could shout any jeers down at her, Tekshim stepped over the edge of the terrace and landed hard on the grass below. We were officially outside of monastery grounds. Officially in the wilderness that would decide my fate.

"Take this time to settle your mind," Tekshim said, as he strode through the swaying grass. "Your ability to kill is not nearly as vital as the *way* in which you kill."

7

Per Tekshim's not-so-subtle advice, I did my best to "settle my mind" during our trek through the marshes and forests. This consisted of me imitating the various vids I'd seen of meditation junkies—sitting down cross-legged, shutting my eyes, and breathing slowly. It was relaxing, but nowhere near as transcendent or otherwise effective as what Tekshim intended.

Besides, I was only able to put myself through the calmness charade for about five minutes. After that, I became deeply, unreasonably annoyed with the whole affair. Thoughts ran roughshod through my mind, and every breath felt more and more like sandpaper scraping up and down my windpipe. By the eight-minute mark, I was lifting my eyelids and glancing around, desperate for any distraction from this exercise in futility.

At that point, I came to the same conclusion as most of the universe: I wasn't cut out for meditation. Maybe I was just wired wrong, or maybe my mind had soaked up too much high-fidelity entertainment to be content with sitting around and breathing. Either way, I firmly marked myself down as a "non-meditator."

Thankfully, Tekshim didn't seem to notice I'd failed in my task. By sitting in the same position and taking care to avoid fidgeting, I was able to continue pretending that I was a masterful guru. This isn't to say I was just twiddling my thumbs, of course. As Tekshim moved through the wilderness, I kept my eyes peeled for anything that might tell me where we were heading or what I was expected to do.

More than any useful details, however, I soaked up the world's natural beauty. This was a pristine world, untouched by the hands of industrialization or ecological collapse. Everywhere I looked, I found some new and gorgeous sight: waterfalls, glens, groves, ridges, caves.

This might not seem like much to you, particularly if you come from a leisure world that's chock full of pleasant sights, but this was my first taste of such a planet. Given my pitiful age and lack of real-world experience, my only reference point for nature were the destinations Chanzig had selected as part of his artifact-hunting bonanza. And even then, most of those worlds had been bombed-out, irradiated wastelands that had already been picked clean by thousands of scavs.

This world, by contrast, was a miracle in itself. Never before had I seen an ecosystem that seemed so profoundly at peace with itself. Even when Tekshim lumbered past herds of canine-looking creatures, there was a sense of rightness to it all. Predators and prey existed in an easy, straightforward relationship, sharing in the strange dance of life and death. Fish leapt up through the surface of streams, birds sang their songs, and insects chirped away amid the gargantuan trees. In every corner of this world, there was vibrance.

Yet as the journey moved into its second hour, things changed. It was a gradual shift, so subtle I hardly noticed it, but before long it was unmistakable. The sounds of a forest at play faded into silence. Rather than clusters of flowers, the ground was littered with half-decayed carcasses and deep scratches.

"Tekshim?" I ventured, hoping he'd agree I had been "meditating" long enough.

He grunted. "Yes?"

"We've been walking for a while, and I'm no psychic, but it feels like we're getting close to the destination. Think you can tell me what this is all about now?"

"According to the monastic code, I am not permitted to explain," he said, his voice carrying a wary edge. "But thus far, you have not given me cause for concern."

"So, you'll lay it out for me?"

"If you are capable of keeping this disclosure secret, then yes."

"Say no more, Tek," I said, standing and stretching. "Your secret's safe with me."

"Very well." The monk adopted a slower, quieter pace before continuing. "Within the order, there is a specific and traditional set of rites required to learn the radiant teachings. In your tongue, these rites are known as the Perfections. Several of our brothers—myself included—have mastered the Third Perfection, but only Narbu has gone beyond it."

"Doesn't that seem a little . . . off?"

"Elaborate, Dak."

"Well, I guess I'd just expect there to be others on Narbu's level. If he's the only one who's made it to the end, isn't it possible he's just making up bullsh—uh, stuff—to keep others from accessing the same material?"

Tekshim hummed with acknowledgment. "I understand your concern, but it is unfounded. There were several before Scryer Narbu who also achieved command of the Higher Perfections—those beyond the Third, that is. He is the last *living* teacher in the lineage. In any event, you needn't worry. Mastery of the three Lower Perfections is your goal."

"That makes more sense," I said, nodding. "Now, forgive me if this sounds a bit blunt, Tek, but you monks have a habit of talking around my questions. So, I'll get right to the root. How exactly do these Three Perfections apply to me and what I'm doing here?"

"All things are interconnected," Tekshim said, much to my frustration. "You cannot learn the entirety of our teachings without understanding—"

"Alright, alright, I get it. Now *please* circle back to the question."

Tekshim chuckled. "The Three Perfections are tests, of sorts. If you wish to receive the teachings of the Primordial Wisdom, you must complete the Perfections that guard the associated knowledge."

"Uh-huh. So, in order to get to the juicy stuff, I need to pass these tests. Which is what I'm about to do."

"You are about to encounter the first of three, yes. Should you succeed here, Scryer Narbu will allow you to access the restricted wisdom. The First Perfection's mastery grants access to the novice texts. The advanced materials, however, require mastery of the Third Perfection. Of course, if you manage to master all three of the Lower Perfections in your short stay here, it will also be a clear sign that you are the warrior we seek."

Mention of the prophecy re-piqued my interest. Akasha had spoken about the monks' search for a sufficient "Purified One" at length, but ever since arriving, there'd been barely a word about any of that. Tekshim's remarks, however, convinced me that Scryer Narbu and the others were simply being coy. For what purpose, I couldn't say. But I also didn't feel it was right to prod Tekshim beyond his limits. I'd just have to come back to it later.

"Okay, so I'm about to tackle the First Perfection," I said. "Sounds great. But, uh, what is it?"

"The Perfection of Power," Tekshim replied. "When our order first landed on this world, it was embroiled in constant conflict. The beasts that roamed the wilds were swift and merciless. In order to survive and practice the path, we needed to defend ourselves with force."

"Makes sense. Does that mean the Perfections follow your order's footsteps? You know, like, learning skills based on when you monks acquired them?"

This time, Tekshim's hum bordered on approving. "Very wise, Dak. Yes, one might frame the Three Perfections in such a way. But in actuality, the path of the Perfections mirrors a universal experience. It is based on the development of all organic beings."

"What's that mean?"

"When an organism takes its birth, it is without logic or language. Therefore, it must use its teeth, claws, and cries to endure. Only after surviving through strength and tenacity does a being learn to employ its mind."

"Right. So, in the eyes of the order, I'm an infant."

"Perhaps, but this perception is neutral," Tekshim explained. "An infant is also a symbol of innocence among biological civilizations. This Perfection, much like the raising of an infant, is designed to ensure that power is utilized in a responsible way."

"You do know that you could've just asked Akasha to vouch for my killing skills, right?"

"As I alluded to, not all killing is equal. Killing born from wrath will send you to the lowest hells. Killing born from compassion will liberate you."

I scratched the back of my head, awkwardly reflecting on the many, *many* lives I'd taken out of sheer rage. Thirmen, in particular, had been a clear case of wrathful killing. If Tekshim was right about this metaphysical business, I was due for a lengthy stay in the bowels of hell.

"It's just not adding up for me," I said at last. "Your entire order is against killing, unless it's for self-defense, but the first Perfection to master is based on . . . killing that isn't in self-defense?"

"It is killing based on mercy."

"How so?"

Tekshim ducked under a rotten, fallen log before answering, taking us deep into the forest's gloom. "Do you recall the miraculous material I mentioned?"

"Yeah. The radioactive flakes."

"Precisely. What I did not tell you, Dak, is the reason they are so highly regarded. They are capable of bridging the divide between mind and matter."

"Alright, you lost me."

"Through the use of one's mind, they can easily bend this material to their will," Tekshim explained.

"Sort of like telekinesis."

"Yes, but to a far more refined degree. For beings who have perceived direct reality, it is a catalyst for growth. A catalyst for incredible power. But for those who are deluded, poisoned by the defilements of lust and wrath, it is a catalyst for destruction."

"I . . . see. I think. It's sort of like fuel. If you channel it the right way, it's great. If you dump it on a raging inferno . . ."

"Just so," Tekshim said, nodding (and nearly knocking me off his head). "The power of this material makes it desirable to all beings, and most are not strong enough to resist its allure. Thus, it is not only sought by human-oids. Flora and fauna, ensnared by their primitive instincts, are also drawn to it. If they acquire enough, the consequences are dire."

"Oh, shit," I hissed, suddenly putting *all* the puzzle pieces together. "You're taking me out here to cull some sort of mega-beast, right? An animal that's gobbled up a little too much Wellspring confetti?"

"A crude summary, but not inaccurate."

"Is this, uh, standard procedure for all the monks?"

Tekshim considered it for a moment. "Not all who have undertaken the Perfection of Power have slain beasts. It is rare, but every few centuries, a monk will become overpowered by the allure of the miracles."

"You mean, monks have had to hunt down other monks that went rogue?"

"I myself had to vanquish a fellow brother." To my surprise, there was a genuinely solemn note to Tekshim's otherwise digital voice. "We do not speak of such tragedies often, but perhaps it is a useful reminder to you. None are immune from the sway of delusion."

I reflected silently on Tekshim's words for a while. It seemed incredible that one of these mecha-monks, after literal eons of training and devotion, would go off the deep end. If such dedicated students of the mind (uncon-strained by biology, no less) fell victim to temptation, what did that say about my own chances? I tried to comfort myself with the knowledge that I'd already been forewarned about corruption, and thus could sidestep the obvious pitfalls, but it still felt hollow. What if Akasha was right, and the power granted by the Unmade would be my undoing? What if I became just as soulless and depraved as Chanzig?

The possibilities unsettled me so badly that I abandoned that train of thought. All I could do was settle down, stay focused, and overcome the challenges presented by the monks. If I followed the order's magic formula down to the letter, I'd have the greatest chance of staying on the straight and narrow. That was the entire purpose behind their regimented training, after all.

Eventually, Tekshim reached a cliff overlooking a vast, mist-shrouded swamp. It wasn't a sheer drop, but rather lined with layers of scree and fallen boulders. Below, the withered and gnarled remains of trees poked up through black sludge.

"This is where we part ways," Tekshim said, kneeling so I could begin my long and tedious descent to ground level. "I will be waiting upon this rise. Should you succeed in your task, return to me so I may take you back to the monastery."

Clambering down the last of Tekshim's back, I let out a dramatic sigh. "Guess I don't have to ask what happens if I fail."

"Do not fear," he said. "Even in the case of bodily death, you will be reborn according to your karmic disposition."

"Comforting."

"Yes, very much so. Just be certain that your mind is free of aversion at the time of annihilation. It will help to guide you through the transition."

"Alright, enough death talk," I said, awkwardly adjusting my two weapons so I could carry them without tumbling down the slope. "*When* I survive this, I'm going to have quite an appetite. I hope your pantries have something more than motor oil."

Tekshim gave a thin smile. "I am sure we'll find some edible items for you. We restocked our supply of human-digestible compounds last century."

I scrunched up my face.

"That was a joke, Dak. I have learned many from outsiders."

"Yeah, real knee-slapper, that one," I grumbled.

Without waiting for another pretentious bit of advice from Tekshim, I turned and began navigating my way down the slope. It wasn't easy, given how loosely packed the pebbles were. Every step sent a mini-landslide cascading down into the dark soup below . . . where said landslides were promptly swallowed with nothing more than a fizzle of gas bubbles.

That wasn't the only ominous thing, though. The more I descended, the hazier it became. Soon, the formerly bright sky was nothing but a diffuse, silvery gloss above me. Tekshim and the cliff were reduced to blobs of shadow.

On top of *that*, the air itself began to feel like the inside of a witch's cauldron. Within minutes, the atmosphere was a bizarre mixture of humidity and biting winds. By the time I'd reached the swamp itself, I was shivering yet sweat-soaked.

"Alright, miracle beast," I whispered, squinting into the fog, "where the hell are you?"

In hindsight, it would've been helpful for Tekshim to tell me what kind of beast I was hunting. For all I knew, it could've been anything. Was it an overgrown, vulture-like monstrosity circling above me, or a bloated leech lurking under the surface? Impossible to say. What was clear, though, was that I'd need to be excessively cautious here. This was a foreign planet inundated with extradimensional energy—a far cry from the combat arenas and ordinary soldiers I'd faced on Kagu-9.

After doing a piss-poor job of tucking my hammer into my belt, I hefted the shotgun in my arms and crept up to the edge of the sludge. There was no way to tell how deep it went, but given the ease with which it had devoured the rubble, I didn't want to take any chances. Rather than simply hopping in and praying, I skirted the water's edge until I found a wide length of desiccated wood.

Good enough for a bridge, right? I climbed up and proceeded along it with slow, wobbly steps, eyes constantly sweeping the churning muck beneath me. Every rising bubble and reptilian croak sent me into fight-or-flight mode. By the time I was halfway along the makeshift bridge, it took all my willpower to avoid firing at anything that moved.

Oh, and speaking of which . . . I realized at that moment that I was rocking barely any ammo. I'd expected the stock to be packed full of it, based on the large pouches on both sides, but they were entirely empty. In a show of exceptionally poor firearms handling, the only shells were currently loaded inside the gun. Racking back the weapon's pump-action slide, I looked into the chamber and got a full count: five.

Five shells of dubious quality against one superpowered wild animal.

Panic mode, engage.

I wandered farther along my rotten bridge, scanning the water and clumps of reed for any sign of the beast in question. Despite my best efforts, though, I couldn't spot anything. It crossed my mind that Tekshim had gotten the location wrong, or that the monster had somehow been taken out by other means—another miracle-infused entity, perhaps, or the scavengers that prowled the planet. It wouldn't have been the first time an animal was killed for its valuable components, after all.

But just as I came to the end of the wood, feeling more confident than ever that I wouldn't have to face a titanic energy beast, ripples spread across the water. Black sediment churned up to the surface in vast, billowing clouds. Even the log beneath me began rattling.

Before I could step back or ready my weapons, the water about fifty paces ahead burst up in a dark spray. Then a rigid, dome-like form began cresting the surface. It was small at first, no more than a meter across at its center, but it grew . . . and grew . . . and grew.

Soon, the dome had turned to something resembling a mountain. It was composed of bulbous, bony plates covered in silt and algae, all pockmarked with the scars of past battles.

What the hell are you?

It didn't take me long to get that answer. Within seconds, my mind shifted gears and took in the sight as a unified whole—the rounded, slightly elongated shape, the quilted texture of the plates, the slight ribbing along the edges . . .

It was a turtle. A giant, energy-suffused turtle.

[NEMESIS EVENT]
Corrupted Testudine (BEAST)
CALCULATING . . .
Estimated Kill Points: 183,800

The sheer amount of Kill Points was incredible, though not in a positive way. This brute carried nearly two-thirds of the Kill Point total assigned to Chanzig, who'd been a literal god's chosen warrior. And while I'd doubted the chok'tal's Kill Point-calculating algorithm in the past, I knew it didn't make mistakes of this magnitude. This was a force to be reckoned with.

I looked down and scrambled to shoulder the shotgun, only to notice the water near me parting for some fresh intrusion. When I glanced back up with no shortage of reluctance, I found the face of my foe.

The turtle's head was crisscrossed with dozens of wounds, some fresh and others long since puckered. Both eyes were milky white yet bloodshot. And its mouth, which should've been a cute, gentle curve, was literally overflowing with rows of jagged, mismatched teeth. Several of the larger incisors had already sliced up through the roof of its mouth or down through its jaw.

My finger shook on the shotgun's trigger. "Let's dance."

8

You might assume this is the part where I filled the monster turtle's face with a point-blank volley of crystal shards. If so, you'd be wrong.

Because the moment I squeezed the trigger, nothing happened. Zilch. Rather than hearing a satisfying, supersonic *pop*, I heard the click of a rattling spring, followed by the stomach-dropping *dink* of the shotgun's striker hitting—yet failing to ignite—the chambered shell. With a hammering heart and a dry mouth, I frantically pumped the shotgun to load a fresh round and try again.

As soon as the dud had been ejected, I squeezed again and braced for impact. Again, nothing. At this point, the turtle was just sitting there, studying me with its ghostly eyes. In less than two seconds, I cycled through the rest of the shells . . . or should I say duds. Not a single one went off. In the end, I found myself surrounded by a bunch of useless ammo and holding what might as well have been a wood-and-metal club.

At that pivotal moment, the turtle went into murder mode. It surged forward on cement-like legs, wrenching its jaws open to swallow me whole as it barreled closer. Suddenly I was staring down an absolute phalanx of chipped, rot-infested teeth that numbered in the hundreds. A tongue made of scar tissue and corded muscle lashed out to snatch me off the log.

Almost without conscious thought, I activated Overclock and Indomitable. The rush of power was borderline euphoric—until the tongue hit me, that is. Its coarse, bloated length whipped around my torso, pinning my arms to my sides and easily yanking me into the air. Then the muscles constricted, squeezing me until I felt my ribs straining to crack. Pasty saliva that smelled of decaying meat oozed down my legs.

The turtle lumbered closer, mouth still extended and tongue fixing me in place like a trophy. This might not seem significant to you, but it was. See, it takes a certain degree of intelligence to enjoy "toying" with prey.

Most turtles and near-turtle species lack that kind of higher thought. Like most other simple creatures, they enjoy gobbling up whatever they can find as fast as they can find it. But not this beast. It was taking its sweet time, literally tasting me and my fear.

The turtle's tongue squeezed again, this time sending rockets of pain down my arms. Overcome by the rush of burning nerves, I let go of the shotgun. It clattered to the log below and slid into the muck.

"Aw, shit," I muttered, glancing down to see if I still had the hammer affixed to my belt. No such luck—the tongue's bulk obscured anything beyond my collarbone. "This isn't . . . playing . . . fair!"

To nobody's surprise, the turtle didn't give a damn about my protests. It stomped closer and closer, jaws further widening in anticipation of its meal.

I desperately searched for a way out. Mind Cascade was an option, but I didn't want to chance it. I'd already seen the repercussions of trying to invade a mildly crazed animal's mind in a dangerous position. Even if I managed to reach the root of the turtle's mind unscathed and affect it at the source, there was no telling what it would do to me. There was a chance it would drop me, but also an equal chance of it tensing its muscles out of fear and crushing me into paste.

Then an insane thought struck me.

Telekinesis.

It had worked under pressure with Thirmen, then with Chanzig. In fact, adrenaline seemed to heighten its impact. Drawing on my memories of those encounters, I blocked out the turtle's presence and sank deep into my mind. The hammer was easily located—a buzzing, solid mass of quantum energy—but it was also fixed in the turtle's grasp against my leg. Even with the upgrade to Telekinesis 2, which tangibly improved my mind-matter connection and command over particles, I knew it was fruitless. Nothing short of a hydraulic crane would be able to remove it.

Still, my mind continued sweeping outward, searching for anything that might be of use. Rocks, twigs, water . . . all of it was utterly useless in my situation. But then, like a flash of divine intervention, I sensed something familiar. Something that might be *just* crazy enough to work.

Focusing harder than ever, I established a link between my consciousness and one of the dud shells below. They were small, and thus easily controlled—even more so with the upgraded ability. With a blast of willpower, I yanked up on the shell and thrust it toward the turtle's mouth.

The shell clattered against rows of teeth, its link with my mind flickering each time it made impact. If this was going to work, I needed to move fast. No time (or room) for half-measures. Once I'd maneuvered the shell into the back of the turtle's mouth, keeping it firmly fixed against a tumor-laden uvula, I pulled the trigger.

Well, sort of.

My mind *was* the trigger.

Drawing on my reserves of mental power, I injected a push of energy into the tiny striker portion at the back of the shell. A vicious *kood* sound echoed from the turtle's mouth, followed by a spray of glinting shrapnel and a puff of black smoke.

The turtle reared back, slamming me against the log and loosing a blood-curdling shriek. By the time it had resecured its tongue grip and lifted me back up, the effects of the shell's detonation were clear. Blood drained in long, thin rivulets through the monster's teeth, filling the water below with red clouds. Charred flesh hung in strips from the roof of its mouth.

But the turtle wasn't deterred by the damage. In fact, it seemed more pissed off and energized than before. Its tongue ratcheted around me like a vise, sending fresh spurts of pain through my kidney and spleen. My lower ribs shattered like dry kindling.

Even still, I refused to let the turtle be the only one who took advantage of the agony. Keeping my eyes open this time, I glared at the turtle and formed a new, stronger link with the next shell. Midway through the turtle's mad charge toward me, I thrust the dud straight under its tongue and triggered the striker.

Once again, there was a supersonic crack and a wisp of smoke. Strands of tongue snapped, smoldering tendons flopped out over the turtle's lower jaw like rubber bands stretched beyond their limit. There was an instant reduction in the tongue's power. Enough for me to draw half a breath, anyway.

This time around, though, the shock didn't seem to set in. The turtle surged through the torment and came running at me like a living storm. Murky water and shattered driftwood filled the air in the creature's wake.

Shit.

In a profoundly ballsy move, I played my final hand by trying to pick up two shells at once. Whether due to my recent Rank Point investment or my overwhelming terror, I managed to "glue" the shells together and lift them as a unified whole. Just as the tongue began retracting like a winch toward waiting fangs, I tucked the pair of shells into the same spot as before and set them off.

The combined force of the blasts set my ears ringing. Smoke and misted blood came bursting out toward me. Before I could even see the damage, the tongue lost all its force and dropped me into the muck.

I landed with a hard splash, relieved to find I was only in water up to my waist. Not so relieving was the fact that the sludge beneath me began to devour my boots. It took a monumental effort to jar my foot loose, let alone begin wading back toward the log.

Then there was the turtle. It loomed far, far above me, its mottled underbelly covered with a horde of leech-like insects and other parasites. Saliva-laden blood came down like an unholy rain all around me . . . followed by entire clumps of tissue.

When I managed to trudge back a few steps, I saw just how effectively I'd nailed my target. The turtle's tongue lay floundering in the water to my side, almost entirely disconnected aside from a narrow strand of flesh pinched between its teeth. The muscles were firing at random, sending the tip thrashing through the murk like a blind eel.

This was the time to strike. Unfastening the hammer from my belt, I pushed through the muck and toward one of the turtle's deformed, scaly legs. The one nearest to me looked like a veritable tree trunk. Unlike most docile turtles, this variety had skin that resembled boiled leather. Even with the help of my upgrades, I doubted I could pierce its armored coating.

While trying to work around this new problem, however, the turtle evidently noticed my change in location. It responded by lifting up like a wild stallion and letting out a hideous roar. The undersides of its shriveled, cracked feet blotted out all light, hanging above me like the waiting blades of a guillotine. And that comparison isn't just for dramatic effect—the infected nails at the ends of both claws looked capable of severing my torso with ease.

Just as it moved to slam downward, instinct took over. I rolled backward through the muck, nearly drowning myself in the process. I came up sputtering and covered in rancid silt, desperate to avoid both the oncoming ground-pound and vomiting.

The turtle's front legs slammed into the water less than three paces away, slapping me with a sulfur-smelling tsunami. Before I knew it, I was thrashing under the surface, fighting to rise through churning waves.

I rose just as the turtle launched its follow-up attack. With all the (non-)control of a rabid dog, the beast whipped its head from side to side, raking its fang-pierced snout through the muck and snapping at anything it encountered. I tumbled backward, scrambling away from the bloodlust-fueled frenzy.

Just in time, too. The turtle managed to snatch a sunken log from the exact place I'd just been. It lifted its prize as easily as if it were a ball of cotton, then crunched clean through it with a sickening *klop*. The mangled halves of the log crashed down on either side of me.

My blood ran cold. How the hell was I going to knock this thing's jaws out of commission for good, let alone kill it? I didn't even want to think about its battering-ram legs, which could probably kill me with an accidental nudge.

Once again, Mind Cascade was on the table, but something in me begged to avoid using it. It was too raw, too unpredictable in its outcomes. If the turtle decided to go on a rampage due to my mental meddling, there was a very, very high chance I'd wind up stomped beneath its feet.

Then there was the underbelly, which seemed relatively thin, on account of all the bloodsuckers gathered along it. But getting to the underbelly wouldn't be easy. And even if I did manage to bruise it by throwing the hammer straight up—there was no way I'd be able to reach it via melee combat—the turtle would have me in a horrible spot. The instant it felt a twinge of pain beneath it, it would surely respond by dropping back to the muck and crushing me.

No, I had to go with my killer instincts. The head was *always* the prime target. It was the most exposed, not to mention crowded with varying "soft" spots that even the lowliest hammer could destroy. I was far from an expert on turtle physiology, so I didn't know if I could crack the skull open, but I *did* know that most eyeballs had a direct route to the brain. A bundle of supercharged nerves that had evolved to deliver searing pain the instant something threatened them.

"Alright, Mr. Shell," I said gruffly, raising my hammer before me like a legendary warrior. "We've had our fun, but this has got to stop."

The turtle responded by loosing a vicious growl and plowing forward. I rolled to the side several times, unable to see anything beyond swirls of dirty water and decaying plant matter. But you'd better believe I *felt* it when the turtle's legs ripped through the sediment just behind me. The impact nearly broke my ankles.

I spun around, momentarily surprised I was even alive. The turtle had managed to charge straight past me. Whether due to its bloated size or corrupted vision, it didn't seem to notice that it had lost sight of its prey.

Even so, it didn't take the beast long to notice the issue. It began wildly biting at the water all around it, simultaneously hammering the muck with its claws and screeching in turn.

None of that rage mattered to me, though. My attention had drifted to the very back of the turtle, where I spotted a bulbous, spike-laden tail writhing in agitation. Unlike the rest of its body, the turtle kept the tail more or less stationary. It was so long that it resembled a lizard's. The effects of unstable energy, I guessed.

The important detail, however, was how deeply it extended into the water. In my eyes, it wasn't a body part, but rather a ramp. A way to scale the creature and gain access to that precious, jelly-filled head.

While the turtle busied itself with a lethal temper tantrum, I hauled ass through the quicksand-like waters and toward the waiting ramp. With every passing second, I feared the beast would spin around or otherwise skewer me with its tail. I drew hard on the power of Overclock, straining my muscles to their limits as the turtle's roaring rose to deafening levels.

Just three paces from my target, the turtle noticed something was amiss. Maybe it sensed the small waves caused by my movement, or maybe it had just exhausted itself and decided to switch up its tactics. To this day, I have no clue.

Not that the reason mattered, of course—the results were the same. The turtle abruptly reared up again, pivoting slightly at the peak toward me. The tail whipped away, and before I could put two and two together, foul water drizzled down on me from the looming claws.

There was nowhere to go. If I rolled back, it would still catch me. If I rolled to the side, it would gobble me up with those horrid jaws. My only path was forward.

Drawing in a labored breath, I forced my legs onward, carrying me directly under the turtle's bulk. The shadows around me shrank as the beast began its next slam. In the instant before impact, I shut my eyes and froze up, waiting for death.

The claws struck mud like a hydrogen bomb. I was thrown forward and under the water, but to my shock, there was no serious damage. The worst I'd taken was a spray of wooden shrapnel caused by yet another exploding log.

Upon bursting through the surface, I immediately made a beeline for that damn tail. It was straight ahead, waggling as though trying to taunt me. Overhead, the mass of parasites affixed to the turtle's underbelly squirmed and zipped about. There was also quite a colony forming on the genitals, though we won't get into that.

Once again, the turtle carried out a vicious, toothy assault on the water behind me. I just kept moving, praying I'd emerge before my enemy decided to take my advice and press its whole body down on me.

A fresh wave of vigor came over me as I neared the edge of the shell. A few more steps, and I'd be taking the tail highway all the way to Hammer City. But before I could get out from beneath the turtle, my foot slammed into something. A log, probably. I went down hard, hissing and cursing . . . and managed to bump the turtle's back-left leg in the process.

For an instant, everything stopped. I half-knelt, half-stood in the water, eyes wide as I sensed the turtle's complete lack of motion. But when I saw its dense thigh muscles tense in anticipation of another move, I didn't need to be told twice. I dove forward just as the turtle did exactly as I'd feared and dropped its body like a sledgehammer.

The resulting shockwave was impressive. Fetid water kicked me from behind, tossing me forward (yet again) into a clump of moldy reeds. But this time around, I wasn't on the defensive anymore. The only way to end this exhausting game of cat and mouse was through bloodshed.

Before the turtle could rise back up, let alone maneuver around to face me, I charged the tail with everything left in my tank. My legs burned as I came within ten paces, then five, then two . . .

At that moment, the turtle began to ascend like a demon summoned from the pits of hell. *Too late, asshole.* I consciously pumped Overclock's force into my legs, then leapt straight toward the only tail region that wasn't infested with spikes. My chest slammed against a patch of armored scales. Even as I grappled to gain purchase on the appendage, I could feel the muscles deep below knotting in preparation for something deadly.

I sprang to my feet, tugging myself up the living slope by using my free hand to grasp at the spikes all around me. Midway to the shell portion, the tail began thrashing back and forth. I was too far up to be affected, though, and kept using the bony barbs as my handholds.

At that moment, the turtle seemed to realize it was in a pickle. It stomped its legs and bit at the air, mobilizing every ounce of its muscle mass to shake off the invader. Even the tail started to whip up and down in wild strikes, which would've sent me tumbling if not for my makeshift poles.

Again, the turtle performed its sink-to-the-mud tactic. It seemed inefficient, if not totally useless . . . until I realized what it was trying to do. Just as I'd suspected at the start of the fight, the beast was intelligent. It was able to plan, to predict, to utilize its environment as a weapon on the fly.

The turtle was trying to drown me.

Inch by inch, the beast descended into the water. The commotion below suggested that it wasn't just dropping, but rather *digging* itself deeper in a conscious attempt to escape. Within seconds, the majority of the tail was submerged. I didn't need to wait around and find out where the strategy would end. Instead, I hurried up the remainder of the tail and onto the shell, then began navigating toward its highest point.

It wasn't easy, to say the least. The quilted texture of the plates—combined with a years-old coating of grime, lichen, and slime—made it nearly impossible to run. Hell, even walking was a challenge. I'd only managed to make it a quarter up the bumpy slope by the time water began splashing over the outer lip of the shell.

I redoubled my efforts, pushing upward despite slipping, falling, stumbling, and generally failing to conquer the slick terrain. When I glanced back, I saw it wasn't fast enough. The water was still surging up through the plates, and by now it was literally nipping at my heels.

With a grunt of pure disdain, I powered through the flood and made it to the very peak of the turtle's shell. Only then did I realize I was breathless, shaking, and completely drained in every sense of the word. Keeping Overclock and Indomitable activated so long was surely eating away at my meager calorie load. Half of me wanted to flop down right there and take a nap. The other half, though, wasn't stupid enough to indulge in that.

That isn't to say that I had a clear plan. Even as I stood there, trembling and trying to maintain a grip on the hammer, the water continued to rise. The shell around me was shrinking, vanishing back under the waves like a collapsing island.

For the briefest moment, I wondered if I could simply trudge back to Tekshim and tell him I'd killed the goddamn thing. If it was under the swamp, who would ever know? But I had a feeling the monk wasn't stupid. And even if he was, I *needed* the KP. Given my own panic, even at the paltry rank of 11, it wasn't hard to see why so many Purifiers turned to cruelty. The threat of imminent death was enough to change anyone from a rational person to a killing machine.

Such reflections circled in my head as I waited, uneasily watching the waters rise to the uppermost point of the shell. If the turtle went any deeper, my feet would be underwater. And if that happened, this fight was over. I'd be dueling the beast on its terms, in its arena. It could take me out simply by surfacing or pulling me into the vacuum formed by its descent.

The instant before the water reached my boots, however, I sensed a familiar rumbling. The turtle pushed up from the muck just as it had done at the beginning of the encounter, but this time with renewed force. The sudden motion threw me forward and nestled me in the waterlogged crevice between two plates.

I fought my way to a standing position, then looked down to see the flailing head of the turtle. Whether it knew my location or not, I couldn't say, but I wouldn't give it the time to readjust and carry out a new plan. With my hammer firmly gripped, I slid down through the plates and jumped onto the beast's comically muscular neck.

As soon as I landed there, the turtle's head thrashing went into overdrive. I straddled it as though it were a colossal horse and held on for dear life, occasionally shifting my legs to avoid getting them jammed between flesh and shell.

Then I began inching forward. With every small bit of progress toward the skull, the turtle's aggression ramped up. It knew exactly what I was planning.

When the turtle slammed its chin down into the muck, I took my shot by lunging forward and hooking my legs into the cupped spots on either side of the head—some form of primitive ears, maybe, or just cranial indentations. Not that it matters.

Once fixed in my rodeo stance and certain I could withstand a few more thrashings, I lifted the hammer with both hands and brought it down on the turtle's skull.

The hammer bounced off as though it had struck concrete. Bone-jarring impacts raced up my forearms and left my wrists aching. I shook out my left hand, hissing through the pain.

What was this thing even *made of*? With Overclock running hard, I should've been able to crack straight through the thing's head. But there was nothing there—not even a bruise or signs of split skin.

Despite that, the blow clearly had *some* impact. The turtle ceased all movement, becoming just as rigid as me. Then it gradually lifted its head as though trying to get a direct look at me.

I dug my heels into the beast's side, remaining in place even as the snout tipped fully vertical and its milky eyes rolled back toward me. The sight was chilling, but it also put an idea in my head. I returned to the prior line of logic I'd had while assessing the beast's head. The eyes were the simplest, most vulnerable point on nearly any animal, and this turtle was no exception.

Inhaling deeply, I reactivated Telekinesis and established a new link with the hammer in my hands. The power of the day's upgrade became evident when I found that I could easily rip the weapon out of my own grasp. Wasting no time, I sent the hammer floating along the ridge of the snout and toward the turtle's left eye.

The farther the hammer flew, the weaker the link became. Not by much, though. If I recalled correctly, the skill let me exert my will up to ten meters, and this was closer to five. Even so, I had to work fast. If the turtle suddenly sprinted away or managed to somehow knock the hammer out of reach, I'd be screwed.

Injecting another burst of mental power, I flipped the hammer so the wooden grip faced the turtle's eye like a lobotomy pick. All of my pent-up rage came flowing forth, strengthening the mental bond and building up within the hammer like a coiled spring. I prepared to drive the point inward, to pop the fluid-filled tissues . . .

But at the last instant, something stopped me.

Tekshim's words came pressing forward from the depths of my mind. *Killing born from wrath will send you to the lowest hells. Killing born from compassion will liberate you.*

In that sliver of a second, I understood that this turtle wasn't an enemy. Not in the same sense as Chanzig or Liura or any of their ilk had been. This was just an animal that had wandered toward something shiny. It had grown attached to the power, to the sense of domination it had been denied as a lowly prey animal. In the turtle's mind, it was fighting for its life. Calling upon reserves of instincts that had been baked into its marrow over billions of years of evolution.

Then another insight sprang up. One that chilled me far more than the first. I understood, in some quiet and inexpressible way, that I could've been this turtle. Rather than being born in Chanzig's laboratory, I could've been born in this system, in this swamp. In that way, the two of us were equals. We'd both been dropped into life without a user's guide or clear direction, and we'd both stumbled across power far beyond what any being should possess.

When this second, more vital realization came over me, something clicked. The turtle's mind was suddenly thrust into my awareness, hovering like a dense, boiling cloud all around me. I could sense its fear, its hatred, its confusion. I also sensed its will to live. It was so powerful that it nearly brought tears to my eyes. And no, I'm not joking.

If you've never been hit with a blast of empathy, you may not understand this at all. I get that. But if you have—if you've seen broken, battered war refugees, or a starving child, or a good man drawing their last breath—you will know exactly how it feels. The urge to express love is driven through your ribcage like a dagger.

Now, you might expect that this is where the turtle and I shared a tender moment. The part where we set aside our feud and had a tea party in the swamp.

Nope.

The turtle suddenly bucked, and with my legs weakened from the heartstring overload, I didn't have the strength to hold on. Before I got my wits about me, I was tumbling down from the head and into the water. My link to the hammer was as thin as fishing line.

Again, I came up sputtering from the muck. The turtle stood over me with pure malice in its eyes, its teeth shedding blood and blackened tissue.

But even as we locked eyes, I sensed the hammer still hovering near its face.

"Sorry," I whispered. "One of us has to go, and it won't be me."

It might've been my imagination, but the turtle seemed to cock its head at that. Almost as though it was curious what I had to say.

It didn't get the chance to ponder. I forced a renewed burst of energy into the hammer—this time driven by sadness, not anger—and drove the grip-end of the hammer straight into the turtle's eye.

Blood gushed from the wound, and the turtle retracted its head toward the cover of its shell. But it was too late. I walked forward on shaking legs, furrowing my brow as I fought to maintain the quantum connection. The hammer continued squirming through the eye socket, ripping through bundles of optical nerves and blood vessels.

Then the hammer touched something spongy, and I knew at once I'd reached the brain. Sparing a final, pitiful glance at my foe, who was gripped by so much pain they'd fallen into spasms, it was clear I had to end this as soon as possible.

I closed my eyes, bolstered the bond, and pumped one last shot of energy into the hammer. Its wooden end ripped straight through the gray matter. The turtle staggered and slumped to one side, but continued to howl as its consciousness shut down.

At some point in the past, I—or maybe the real Dak—had learned that the brain itself didn't feel any pain. It was the central locus of pain, and as such, it didn't have any nerve endings of its own. This gave me the slightest hint of solace as I continued to drive the hammer through the beast's brain. Every so often, I felt its metal head bounce off the inner wall of the skull.

After another twenty or so seconds of heart-wrenching violence, the turtle finally twitched and collapsed to the muck. I did a few more passes with the hammer to ensure the beast was dead, not merely unconscious, then withdrew the weapon from the ruined eye.

It landed back in my grip, bloody and covered in fleshy bits.

While lowering the hammer and rinsing it in the dark water, I got my definitive proof of the turtle's demise.

NEMESIS ENCOUNTER SUCCESSFUL
Kills: 1
Kill Points Awarded: 183,800
Storehouse Time Awarded: 4 Hours

The notification was bittersweet. The Kill Points were wonderful, of course, and part of me wanted to jump for joy at the addition of four whole hours of Storehouse Time, but most of me was just crestfallen. Somehow, some way, I'd developed a bond with the turtle in its last moments. The final blows had made me feel that I was murdering a friend, or at least an innocent creature.

"So long, Mr. Shell," I said quietly, turning away.

Before I could drag myself back up to Tekshim, a weird, humming tone rippled out over the swamp.

I glanced sidelong at the turtle's corpse, though "corpse" was no longer an accurate term. The entire mass of flesh was coming undone, wisping into the air like a million fireflies made of golden light. Stranger still, though, was that the motes didn't disperse. They swirled and condensed as a living storm, spiraling into some compact configuration where the turtle's center had been.

With some trepidation, I moved closer to the lights. They were funneling down and inward, almost as though being drained through a very narrow hole in the swamp floor. When the remainder of the glowing motes vanished in the same spot, I learned why.

Just beneath the water was a marble-sized cube of perfect proportions and smoothness. It had a gold-chrome color, as well as a faint glow that pressed up through the sediment. Wellspring confetti.

I narrowed my eyes, then reached down and retrieved it. The cube was heavier than I'd expected—despite fitting on a fingertip, it weighed nearly as much as my hammer.

Keeping an eye on the blood-stained, melted flesh-infested waters around me, I backed up with my hammer outstretched. I had no idea what the hell was going on anymore, but I'd be damned if anything else in this cursed place took me out.

"On the off chance Tekshim is right about rebirth being real," I said to the cube, keeping my gaze largely confined to the swamp as I retreated to land, "I hope you'll accept my apology for killing your former body, Mr. Shell."

9

When I finally reached the crest of the ridge, I found Tekshim sitting in the lotus position atop a boulder. His size and unshakable poise gave him the distinct appearance of a statue.

But before I'd come within fifty paces of the monk, he opened his eyes and looked straight at me. "Greetings, Dak."

His voice seemed to break a spell I hadn't known I was under. I was struck by the sudden weight of my body, the fatigue of the upgrades draining my inner reserves, and especially the mounting pain from my broken bones. All I could manage was a groan as I slumped against a nearby tree and dropped my hammer to the dirt.

"How was the encounter?" he asked.

I pulled in long, heaving breaths, sliding down until my ass was firmly on the soil. "Thanks . . . for the greeting. Not even a . . . 'Wow, you're alive,' huh?"

Tekshim frowned. "Your survival is obvious. You are standing before me."

"Standing . . . is a strong word." I struggled up to my feet, then moved closer to Tekshim with the golden cube in hand. "What is this? The, uh, turtle turned into it after death."

To my surprise, Tekshim regarded the cube as though it were a common sight. "That, Dak, is the inert form of the Wellspring's miracle."

I turned it over in my hand, skeptical. "Are you saying it was like this before the turtle found it?"

"Perhaps not so ordered in shape, but yes," Tekshim explained. "In its dormant form, the material is highly dense and resistant to damage."

"So, how do we wake it up?"

"That is a question for a later time."

"Oh, come on. A giant turtle can learn how to utilize it, but not me?"

"You saw the consequences of improper application," the monk said, a note of warning in their voice. But their serious demeanor quickly gave way to a smile. "Put such things out of your mind, Dak. What matters is that you have accomplished the Perfection of Power."

"Can't say I feel too powerful right now."

"Power is not held in the body," Tekshim said. "It is a latent force that lies coiled in the mind."

"If you say so."

"You do not trust your own power yet, do you?"

I shook my head. "If that was the first challenge, I'm not sure I'm the guy you're looking for. That was pure luck . . . and the stupidity of an overgrown turtle."

Tekshim's smile broadened. "The most critical aspect of your victory is the execution. The fact that you killed out of mercy, not spite, is what separates a brute from a champion. Even this single act of compassion has strengthened your mind."

I narrowed my eyes. "How do you know it was a mercy killing? Maybe I bashed its head in until it turned to hamburger."

The monk's gaze pierced my damn soul. "I know that you felt its mind, Dak. You sensed its pain."

"But how do you know that?"

"Because I can feel *your* mind," Tekshim said. "This ability lies dormant in all sentient beings. It is difficult to rouse, but once it has been brought to light, it cannot be repressed. Take comfort in your accomplishment."

I nodded up at him wearily, curious yet not wanting to risk another hour-long lecture. Truth be told, I believed Tekshim when he said he could view my mind as I'd viewed the turtle's. I wasn't jazzed about it, though. Glimpsing the turtle's consciousness, even for a moment, had been tremendously painful. I'd never felt such sorrow, such regret—and all for a creature trying to murder me.

If Tekshim's words were valid, and this ability to see another being's mind wasn't just a fluke . . . I had no idea what I'd do. How could I gather up Kill Points and go toe to toe with the Unmade if I felt the agony of every enemy I fought? I'd be constantly drowning in a sea of misery.

"Tek, I've got a question," I said softly. "Have you ever heard of something called Mind Cascade?"

The monk angled his head. "The name does not resonate with me. Why do you ask?"

"It's just . . . it's a, uh, 'skill' I picked up recently. It seems to do the same thing that you're describing. You know, letting me take a peek at someone else's mind. But it's a lot more tangible than what happened with the turtle."

"I see," Tekshim said, nodding sagely. "This is a query best reserved for Scryer Narbu. I'm certain he'll want to speak with you, given your success today. You have, after all, earned your access to the first of the classified teachings."

I retrieved the hammer and lumbered back over to Tekshim, ready for my mercifully legs-free journey back to the monastery.

"What happened to your second weapon?" he asked as he knelt down.

Sighing, I began the long climb back to his skull. "Let's just say you don't need any defective equipment in your armory. I did you a favor."

By the time we'd returned to the monastery's walls, dusk was fully upon us. Teams of monks patrolled the compound's outskirts under a blazing red sky. The coming nightfall didn't concern me, though. Not like it had while I was dodging Chanzig's goons and engaging in guerilla warfare. For the first time in a long, long while, nightfall represented a warm meal and a place to sleep without getting my throat slit.

The inside of the monastery was, to my slight confusion, abuzz with activity. Monks hurried down the various passages and spiral stairwells, filling the floor with constant vibration. All of the braziers and hanging chandeliers had been lit, and there was a strange smell in the air. Not a bad smell—far from it, in fact. It smelled like actual human food.

Tekshim didn't answer any of my questions about the hubbub, though. Instead, he took me straight to the dormitory wing of the main building and deposited me in front of a decidedly small (read: Dak-sized) door. Then he took the strange golden cube I'd earned from my battle.

"Hey, I earned that," I said.

Tekshim grunted. "Scryer Narbu is the sole protector of the Spark's creations. He will speak with you about it." The monk gestured to the door. "In the meantime, I hope your accommodations will prove suitable. Inside, you will find a bath, fresh clothing, and a few other amenities to aid your recovery."

I opened my mouth to ask a question—I had dozens of them—but Tekshim had already started walking off. Any words I might've spoken were lost to the heavy thuds of his feet.

Shrugging, I turned to the room's door. It was far more ornate than I'd expected from a bunch of monks, seemingly formed from a combination of precious metals and aged wood. The central design was that of a thousand-armed deity sitting atop a cloud throne, raining shafts of light down on the countless monks below. Such a precise image could only have been created through laser etching—or by a sentient machine with a flair for creativity, I supposed.

Much as I would've loved to pace the narrow corridor and check out all the door masterpieces, though, I was far more tempted by Tekshim's remarks about bathwater and amenities. A quick sniff-check confirmed that I smelled exactly like the swamp. That is to say, like a strip of rotten meat that had been smoked with sulfur fumes.

I could only hope the monks kept these rooms stocked with industrial-grade soap.

My first challenge was opening the door, which proved far harder than expected in light of my injuries and the general weight of the slab. They must've shaved the thing straight off one of those crystal trees. Once I put my shoulders into it and wedged it open, however, the effort proved more than worthwhile.

Picture the nicest, fanciest suite you've ever stayed in, then multiply that by a factor of ten. Velvet couches, lacquered wooden tables, platinum trim on the walls . . . It was closer to an emperor's summer residence than a monastic cell. Even without windows, the room carried a sense of spaciousness that let me truly *breathe* for the first time in days.

I wandered over to one of the many crystal-studded sofas and plopped down, groaning aloud at the sheer pleasure of the experience.

"Pleasant, is it not?"

The voice behind me reactivated the latent adrenaline in my veins. I popped up with fists raised, eyes wild, only to find Akasha leaning against a marble pillar and tinkering with her peoples' consciousness-cube thing. Her wry grin was clearly in response to my overreaction.

"Can't you let a man *rest*?" I grumbled, settling myself back onto the satin cushions. "Besides, it's bad manners to camp out in someone else's room."

Akasha came over and sat opposite me in a throne-style chair. She kept both hands primly positioned on the cube, much like a queen at a royal banquet. "Who said this was your room?"

"Uh, Tekshim?"

"It's *our* room," she said. "There are separate sleeping quarters."

I turned around and was flabbergasted to find that she was correct. Sure enough, there were five or six other doors branching off this room, which was now revealed to be more of a foyer than the main living space.

"Of course, there's also a chamber with a large bed, if you would prefer to share," Akasha said, her lips quirking up in amusement. "I'm not prone to snoring, you know."

Although she didn't mention it, I was quite sure I'd started blushing at her comment. I couldn't help myself. Even though I intellectually knew Akasha was several thousand years old, thus making her the ultimate cougar, her appearance suggested a far, far more youthful age. And sure, her body had several features that marked her as an alien, but she was humanoid enough to tickle the deeply rooted, lizard-brain parts of my psyche. Despite all odds, she truly was beautiful. She was also the first female to ever suggest sharing a bed with me.

"I, uh . . ."

Akasha waved off my stammering. "It was merely a bit of humor, Dak. I do not sleep. Not often, anyway."

"Oh, right. I knew you were kidding."

"Of course, you did." She smiled. "How was your first trial?"

"You knew I was going to fight that thing, didn't you?"

Akasha nodded. "It took me sixty years of training to be declared ready for the First Perfection. The memory of that encounter is still fresh in my mind."

"You mean, you did it too?"

"Naturally. The Second Perfection, too."

"You knew about the Wayfarers this whole time, then."

"Yes," she said, "I did. What of it?"

"Was it really necessary to keep me out of the loop? Seems like it's important to know how many Unmades are floating around out there."

"I told you what you needed to know at that point in time. Unless we have faced something directly, we will never understand its name or what it means."

"Yeah, but still . . . I think you could've given me a bit more to work with. My head feels like it's going to explode every time Narbu brings up metaphysics."

Akasha hummed. "Such topics will become familiar to you soon enough. Now that you've passed the trial of the First Perfection, the archives are at your disposal."

I leaned farther back and folded my arms. "Yeah, about that. Are you sure reading is really the solution to our problem?"

"I do not understand."

"It's just . . . well, I'm not so sold on the idea that we can beat the Unmade through knowledge. He didn't kick my ass by lecturing from a textbook, after all. In there, inside his domain, it was all brute force."

"Power is nothing without control, Dak."

"You sure about that? I think I could've taken him down if I'd been allowed to bring a few nukes through the portal."

"This training is not purely for your benefit," she said, her voice growing sharper. "As I've told you, I will not guide you along this path unless I'm certain your mind possesses integrity."

"You don't trust me yet?"

"All beings can be trusted until they engage in betrayal. You would not be the first Purifier to lose control of your mind once the fear of death sets in. To become the Purified One, you must overcome that fear. You must see death as part of yourself."

I stared at her for a long while, then nodded. It was clear she wouldn't budge. Still, one question from her earlier remarks circled my mind. "What about the third?"

"Hmm?"

"The Third Perfection. You said you finished the first two—how about number three? Tekshim said Narbu's the only one who's gone past that one."

"So, he is. I . . . departed prior to partaking in it."

I narrowed my eyes. "Why?"

"It is not important, Dak."

But something told me it was. Call it intuition, call it precognition . . . Whatever it's labeled, it was a distinct feeling. Akasha was holding something back from me.

"Did something happen between you and the monks?" I asked hesitantly.

Her smile faded. "That's not your concern."

"So . . . it did?"

"Knowledge of my past will not benefit your future," she said coolly. "There may be a place and time to share such information, but it is not here and now."

I nodded, willing to back down if it meant she'd clue me in later. Pressing her beyond her limits wouldn't turn out well for either of us.

"If you don't mind," I said, rising with hisses of pain, "I'm going to curl up in a bath and rinse myself off. I think I've got an ecosystem growing in my belly button."

Akasha didn't say anything as I stood and walked away, awkwardly trying each of the doors until I located the proper room.

I replayed our interaction over and over again as I sat on the edge of the clawfoot tub, absentmindedly testing the water temperature. Akasha wasn't easily rattled, so what the hell had gone down here? What had been severe enough to make her leave what were, in essence, a home and family built over several thousand years?

Try as I might, nothing came to mind. She had a poker face that rivaled that of the best card sharks on Halcium Beta. With a sigh, I resigned myself to undressing, settling into the steaming tub, and letting my thoughts dissipate like the layer of grime all over my body.

Midway through my soak, however, a disquieting thought occurred. Guide—and by extension Modri and all the other Purifiers in that collective consciousness—saw everything that I saw. That meant they were currently staring down at my junk.

I glanced up at the crystal-dotted ceiling with a grimace. It seemed I couldn't catch a break anywhere, even when "alone."

But the creepy insight also reminded me to check in with my most loyal companion. The one who'd been there since day one, helping me kick ass and take names.

"What's happening?" I asked Modri as I unmuted him.

"*You prick,*" Modri growled—expectedly. "*You really had the gall to keep me hushed for all that time? How 'bout I stuff you in a closet and shut you up for days on end?*"

"It wasn't a day," I said, rolling my eyes. "Consider it me giving a break to your mental tongue. You use it too much."

"*Speakin' of usin' tongues . . .*"

"I don't like where you're going with this."

"*Akasha was—*"

"I *really* don't like this, Modri."

"*Relax, you prude,*" he said, huffing. "*I'm just sayin' that you need to be careful about what you say around her. She's real close with these monks—who, by the way, are some real weirdos. I betcha they've got a sacrifice chamber underground.*"

I smirked. "You know, I was thinking the same thing when I first arrived. But things seem decent. Calm."

"*They just threw you into a hell of a fight with shit for gear!*"

"Yeah, for a trial."

"*Or to get you killed.*"

"What's your brilliant alternative, then? Fly off by myself, try to outrun the Unmade? At least this place knows something about what we're dealing with."

"You heard 'em. They worship the Unmade's species. That don't sound too good."

I scrubbed at my arms with a bar of lavender soap. "Not all Wayfarers are evil, Modri."

"Oh, yeah? Even their precious Throne created a goddamn warzone by saturatin' it with some mumbo-jumbo mind metal. Just like the Unmade did with the chok'tal. Still think either side's good?"

"You're trying to guess the moral alignment of extradimensional gods."

"Bah. I'll judge the monks, then. Seems to me that they're just as greedy as all the scavs on this planet. Tryin' to horde all that golden metal . . . and for what?"

"To keep it away from bad people?"

"Who watches the watchmen, Purifier?"

I massaged my temples to ward off the coming migraine. "You know, Modri, this is my first bath in a long-ass time. My first chance to relax, no less. I did you a favor by taking that hush order away. Don't make me regret it."

"Yeah, yeah," Modri said. *"Fine, I'll take it easy on you. Let's get back to Akasha and how shady she's been."*

"Enough."

"Well, shit, what can I even talk about?"

"The weather, food, and guns. Nothing else."

"Alright, then let's chat about guns. Might as well slap the monks with an attempted murder charge, based on the shotgun they gave you."

I groaned and sank deeper into the tub. "Maybe *you're* the one who needs meditation, not me."

"Oh, wake up. Meditation? Your first task was to go kill a giant turtle so the monastery could stockpile even more of the rift's metal. If you ask me, they're just usin' you as a human errand—"

"We'll come back to this later," I said, hushing Modri and sighing. "Maybe I'll let you back out when you're ready to drop the conspiracies. Maybe."

Just as I leaned back, ready to enjoy whatever dregs of my warm bathwater remained, a knock came at the door.

"Dry yourself off and get dressed," Akasha said. "The feast is waiting."

I sat up straight. "Feast?"

"It means a large gathering of food."

"Thanks for that," I said, cocking a brow. "What exactly am I supposed to wear?"

"It should be on the hanger near you."

Frowning, I turned around and looked at the spot Akasha had indicated. Believe me when I say that I would've preferred to fight ten mega-turtles than wear my assigned costume.

10

Picture, if you will, an obese chicken draped with diamonds, crystal beads, and silk tassels. Now take that picture, replace the fowl head with a human's, and add a pair of long-nosed shoes that might've belonged to a jester in a past life. That about sums up the ceremonial garb I was expected to wear.

"Keep your chin elevated," Akasha said as we walked toward the grand hall. "It's unbecoming of a trainee to look at the ground while moving."

"Easy to say when you've been given normal clothes," I murmured.

Well, in all fairness, Akasha's clothes weren't "normal" either. In fact, they were just as ostentatious as mine, though in a much more positive regard. The monks had supplied her with an elegant, attention-drawing gown that emphasized a plunging neckline and glimmering facial veil. The fact that it was form-fitting didn't help to dissolve my very, *very* confused feelings about Akasha and her attractiveness.

"How long ago did they make this thing?" I asked, pinching one of the absurdly long pleats on my man-skirt. "Feels like they haven't encountered a human in ages."

Akasha smiled. "I knew the man for whom this attire was tailored."

"Oh? Dapper fellow?"

"He was," she said quietly. "Unfortunately, he didn't survive the Second Perfection's trial."

Suddenly, my horrid getup felt more like a funeral suit. "Nothing like wearing a dead man's clothes."

"Mind your words, Dak. It is not as though he perished while wearing it."

"Well, thank Halcius."

"Although he did die about six hours after removing it . . ."

I scowled at her. "Very funny."

"That was not a joke."

"Oh." I gulped hard. "I hope they don't serve me his leftovers."

She delivered a light elbow to my ribs, shutting me up just as we reached the hall's open main doors.

To the monks' credit, they'd done a phenomenal job of dressing the place up. This was my first time setting foot in the place, in fairness, but it was obvious they'd pulled out all the stops for little old me, their guest of honor.

Polished brass braziers lined the room, casting light on an impressive array of tapestries, murals, and statues. Much like the door to my quarters, the main motif was that of god-like beings with tons of arms, eyes, and glowing lights. Arranged in the center of the hall were two gargantuan tables, clearly constructed to fit monks instead of pesky humans. Somewhere around sixty monks sat cross-legged along the outer edges of the tables with their heads bowed in meditation.

At the far end of the hall, raised upon a dais to stand at even height with the monk tables, was one more table. Its tiny size communicated that it had been placed there for Akasha and I.

Scryer Narbu and his four warriors waited behind that table, arranged in a semicircle around a gorgeous vestibule that featured exotic flowers.

"Welcome, cherished ones," Narbu boomed, prompting all the seated monks to open their eyes at once. "This banquet is being held in honor of Purifier Dak's mastery over the First Perfection. It is a time to renew the mind and body in preparation for the coming days."

Rather than clapping, the assembled monks closed their eyes again and let out a collective hum. The digital mechanism that produced their voice allowed them to reach an unparalleled level of harmony. Within seconds, the sound was so uniform and powerful that I felt it pulsing in my chest.

"Approach, cherished ones," Narbu said.

Akasha and I shared a look, then did as the teacher asked. Our long, *long* walk down the velvet carpet, accompanied by the monks' hum, made it feel as though I were approaching the altar for marriage.

Upon reaching the dais, we circled a winding staircase that led up to the table. The height seemed dizzying when I'd finally made it there, but this was helped somewhat by the sight (and smell) of countless dishes that covered the table.

We took our places in high-backed chairs, staring out across the feast and down at the brothers on either side of the hall. It was a strange experience, settling in at such an altitude. It felt as though we were about to dine on the edge of a cliff.

"Feast well," Narbu said from behind us, moving with his entourage to a ramp that led back down to floor level. "Remember to restrain the senses. Taste, touch, smell, and tactile inputs will attempt to hijack your awareness. Be vigilant."

I cocked a brow as Narbu lumbered out of sight, wondering exactly what he'd meant. This *was* my first banquet, true, but I also sensed that it wasn't normal for a host to warn their guests prior to eating. After all, wasn't the whole point of a "feast" to shut off your mind, grab a fork, and stuff yourself silly? Scryer Narbu made it sound like the boiled figs and caramelized vegetables across from me were liable to invade my mind.

Down below, the monks opened their chest panels and began inserting food. Well, food is a poor term here. Their tables were bare aside from bowls of glowing, sparking . . . stuff. Some of the contents burned a fierce blue color, while others were closer to platinum or violet.

"What exactly are they injecting?" I asked Akasha.

She withheld her answer until she'd delicately selected a piece of flatbread and laid it on her plate. "Compounds necessary for survival, of course."

"Such as?"

"Deuterium crystals, polynucleotides . . . and their sacrament." She glanced my way. "Why do you ask?"

"Call it curiosity."

It shouldn't have surprised me that the monks ate such a . . . colorful diet. After all, it would've been tantamount to suicide if their creators had forced biological needs on them—especially given their intended purpose of colonizing planets across the universe. Any lump of barren rock was packed with vital minerals that could support a machine, but organic life . . . well, that was significantly harder to find out in the vast unknown.

The item that jumped out most from Akasha's list, though, was the last one. *Their sacrament.* It had to be the same sacrament Narbu had referenced during our first meeting—that is to say, the psychedelic compound found in the Throne of Radiance's fungus. Sure enough, I saw all of the brothers loading their syringes with dark, bubbling liquid and injecting it ritualistically. Well, *almost* all the brothers. Tekshim just sat there, staring at the sacrament bowls warily . . .

My next observation was jarring enough to make me forget this incident, however. "Akasha, is it just me, or is there no meat on this table?"

"Of course not," she said, as she removed her utensils from a satin bag. "The brothers do not condone the killing of living beings for sustenance."

"I should've figured."

"They say that dead flesh pollutes the mind," she continued. "When working with the deepest recesses of the mind, any disturbance is capable of causing great harm. As such, all the food they have presented was chosen with the utmost care."

"How so?"

Akasha began to look annoyed at my stream of questions. It seemed that even she experienced the pull of hunger in front of so many dishes. Even so, she indulged me. "Your species has largely abandoned traditional frameworks for medicine and well-being, but the monastery has not. Each of the herbs, vegetables, and fruits before you have a specific purpose. They engage various systems in the body and generate vital energy."

"What, uh, systems are we talking about here? Any aphrodisiacs?"

"No, Dak," she said curtly. "Now eat."

So, I did. I ate like a wild animal, focused solely on my plate and cramming as much food as possible into my mouth between gulps of watered-down juice. I ate until any normal person with working vision would've asked me when the baby was due.

Some of the dishes used ingredients prized and cultivated by humanoids—mushrooms, artichokes, onions, that sort of thing—while others relied on vegetables and fruits I'd never seen (and yes, that includes the real Dak's memories). In fact, several components were so alien that I couldn't even form a comparison with more pedestrian fruits and vegetables.

Regardless, the food was excellent—though it's not hard to find just about anything appetizing after subsisting on rations for extended periods of time. I tore my way through breads, soups, braised artichoke-like sprouts, cakes, sandwiches, purees . . . anything put before me soon met a grisly fate in my stomach.

I'll admit, the lack of meat was mildly disappointing, but I also understood the monks' deep aversion to the carnivore lifestyle. If forgoing a perfectly seared steak with creamy dill sauce meant staying on the brothers' good sides, I'd bite the bullet.

When I was finally finished with my gorging session, I dabbed my mouth with a cloth napkin, groaned, and leaned back. Akasha was angled toward me. Even with her blindfold, it was obvious shock had taken root on her entire face.

"Yes?" I asked, breathing shallow around the bowling balls in my stomach.

She pushed her plate back a few inches. "I have never seen a humanoid consume so much food in one sitting."

"You must be impressed."

"That is not the word that rises to the mind."

"So, uh, what do we do now? Wait for the singalong part of the show?"

Akasha's head turned ever so slightly toward the vestibule behind us. "I believe Scryer Narbu has other plans for you."

The tone of her voice made it sound like the teacher was planning to kill me. When I followed her gaze, only to catch sight of Scryer Narbu crouched behind us like some sort of stalking jungle cat, I wondered if this really was the end.

Luckily, Narbu spoke up before the fear of death really sank into my bones. "Purifier Dak, I would request an audience with you."

Stifling a moan from the sheer intestinal overload, I squirmed in my seat to fully face the monk. "Does this 'audience' involve any hard labor or other exercise?"

"Not in the slightest."

"Alright, then," I said, pushing my chair back and giving Akasha a brief nod. "Lead on, Narbu. Just, uh, make sure you're ready for a few extra kilograms on your head."

Scryer Narbu clearly wasn't too amused by my joke, because he insisted that I walk on my own two legs instead of receiving the royal skull-chauffeur treatment. We made quite the odd pair as we navigated the corridors—Narbu with his long, slow strides that spanned a vast distance, and me with my waddling attempts to keep up.

He led me deep, deep into the catacombs of the mountains, though this path was plainly different from the one Tekshim had taken for my first meeting here. We traversed broad, shadowy staircases and stalactite-encrusted passages. Narbu kept to the monk-sized main path, while I was forced to use the crude, human-sized routes that had been hastily added to the right-hand side. The farther we progressed, the quieter everything became. The more haunting, too. It was as though the mountain's core was guarding an ancient secret not meant for mortal ears.

"Mind telling me what this is about?" I asked, speaking for the first time since we left the banquet.

Narbu paused a few steps ahead of me. "Brother Tekshim has informed me that your performance during the trial was admirable."

"Thanks, but I don't see how that relates to this outing."

"You are traversing ground that few have ever seen," Narbu continued, practically ignoring my reply. "I can count on two hands the number of outsiders that have reached this point. Even among the brothers of this order, the number is not much greater."

"Are you taking me to the archives?"

"Hmm?"

"You and Tekshim mentioned that I'd get access to some classified stuff if I mastered the First Perfection."

Scryer Narbu hummed in acknowledgment. "That is an element of this meeting, yes. But there is more to discuss. And given the delicate nature of your situation, I believe it is best to discuss such matters with a degree of privacy."

I hurried to catch up as Narbu resumed his trek. "What do you mean? You don't trust the brothers?"

"I did not say that."

"Akasha, then?"

Narbu didn't counter that one.

"I know you two have some history," I pressed. "Why exactly did she leave this place?"

"You should be wary of gossip, Purifier Dak. It is a slow rot in the mind."

"It's not gossip if it relates to my survival."

Narbu glanced back, his eyes glowing like stars in the darkness. "Nothing about this situation threatens your survival. I urge you, with all the force of your mind, to remove distractions and remain centered. What you are attempting to do here is unprecedented."

"Meaning?"

Again, Narbu stopped. "Do you know how many outsiders have perished attempting the First Perfection's trial?"

"Not a clue."

"One out of every six hundred succeed," he said coldly. "And in regard to the trial of the Second Perfection, that number dwindles to one out of every five thousand."

"You've had five thousand nomads find this place? I didn't know it was so popular."

"Five thousand have arrived in total over the course of countless centuries," Narbu said. "Among them, Akasha was the only being to reach the second milestone."

My steps slowed. "The *only* one?"

"Yes. As you may have sensed, her mind is exponentially more power-ful than yours. Do you understand what I am saying?"

"Spell it out a bit clearer. I'm a little slow because of the food coma."

Narbu grunted. "You are not prepared for these trials, Purifier Dak. Most outsiders spent decades training for their first trial."

"So, why throw me into the deep end?"

"Because we do not have a choice. The chok'tal has forced our hand. If not for its urgency and lethal nature, you, too, would have spent years in preparation. Not only in the art of combat, but in meditation, breath control, energy work. . . . Alas, we do not have that sort of time. As such, our order is placing a great burden upon you."

"So I've noticed."

"I am advising you to drop your foolish ways," Narbu said, the gentle-ness of his voice giving way to a hard edge. "If you do not call upon the full power and restraint of your mind, you will die on this world—or worse, lose your sanity to the chok'tal. There is no room for pointless inquiries or flapping your tongue."

That was enough to shut me up. Narbu had a point—while I was treat-ing this whole situation with a liberal dose of dark humor, the monks and Akasha were biting their nails and praying that I'd get my act together. For all I knew, they had been waiting thousands upon thousands of years for the chance to turn a Purifier into something noble. Something capable of dismantling the Unmade and reversing the vast harms it had brought to this universe. In that sense, the goals of the monastic order were fully in alignment with Modri's. He, too, had dreamed of a world where the chok'tal was used to undo this calamity.

The only way to actualize those visions was to get serious.

"Forgive me," I said quietly. "It's . . . hard to treat things with any degree of gravitas when you've lived a life like mine."

Scryer Narbu nodded slowly. "There is nothing to forgive. You are a product of your conditioning, no more and no less than any other being. Even the brothers here are bound by the constraints of memory, survival, and neural functioning."

"Here I was, thinking a mechanical body would solve all my problems." When Narbu didn't respond, a serious (and very relevant) question came to my mind. "Say, how many times have you tried to turn a Purifier into . . . whatever you're trying to make?"

Narbu came to a halt in front of a tremendous, gold-plated door framed with obsidian. He took hold of the ring-shaped handles, then pushed some kind of crackling energy into them. When their latch gave way, he finally whispered, "It is best not to ask such things, Purifier Dak. Not all answers inspire hope."

His words put a shiver in my spine. I stood there, rigid and baffled, as the large doors swung open. Waiting beyond the threshold was an immaculate, cylindrical archive, its curved walls bursting with tomes, scrolls, and stacked tablets. All of it was lit by the persistent green glow of alien lanterns.

"This is the Radiant Repository," Narbu said, stepping aside to allow me entrance. "It is what will decide the fate of your war against the Unmade."

11

Mere seconds after revealing this grand chamber, Narbu turned to leave.

"Hey, hold up," I called. Surprisingly, he actually did lumber back this time. "Tekshim promised me some answers—from you."

"Regarding?"

"Two things. Morphic Imprints, and that mysterious metal that I brought back from the turtle."

"I am unfamiliar with the first term you used, but I can grasp the meaning you hold in your mind. Let us return to it at a later date, however. It is a complex topic, and many of our records will shed light upon it."

"I feel like I'm learning more about patience than about actually stopping the Unmade," I said, sighing. "Alright, onto the metal, then. Straight answers, please."

Narbu smiled down at me. "We have come to know it as *Dalaya.* In your tongue, the nearest translation is Sparkseed."

"Not sure how I feel about the use of 'seed' to describe interdimensional discharge."

If Narbu got my crass humor, he didn't show it. "It is the lifeblood of our order. A source of seemingly infinite energy."

"That's not possible."

"And how do you know that?"

"Because it's physics," I said, somewhat taken aback that I had to defend such a fundamental building block of thermodynamics to a sentient machine. "Infinite energy would break the universe."

"You presume that the source of its power is derived from this dimension," Narbu countered. "The Unmade, too, violates laws of this universe's physics. Yet the proof of its existence stands before me."

"Alright, fine. Let's pretend for a second that this 'Sparkseed' stuff really does have a never-ending supply of juice. How would I use it?"

"You do not need to ponder such questions at this time, Purifier Dak. Outsiders are not permitted to permanently bond with Sparkseed until they have mastered the Third Perfection."

"Should've seen that coming."

Narbu appraised me with a look that might've been sympathy. "You have seen, with your own eyes, the calamities that result from beings attempting to utilize its power too soon. I do not wish to see this fate befall you."

"Can I be frank with you?"

"You may."

"I'm a little curious why your order has such a stranglehold over the planet's Sparkseed," I said, hoping Narbu wouldn't crush me like an insect for my borderline conspiratorial comments. "I get that it's risky stuff, but the rift produced it without putting your names on it. What gives you the authority to keep it out of decent hands?"

"Ah, I understand. You are alleging that we have a vested interest in controlling the Sparkseed."

"Well," I said, trying to hedge, "that's a tad more . . . direct than I would've preferred. I don't think you have some nefarious agenda or anything like that."

"The truth is, we do have an agenda," Narbu said. "Though it is difficult to convey."

"Try me."

"Some of the Sparkseed, as I have said, is used to bolster the order. Those who have sustained injuries or reached new levels of mastery are granted access to small quantities." To illustrate this, Narbu peeled back one fold of his robes and revealed a long, twisting scar that shone with the brilliance of Sparkseed. "It is both a healing salve and a route to deeper canyons of the mind."

"But it's infinite energy, right? So shouldn't even a pinch be enough?"

"An ant may push on a boulder with endless force, but this will not suffice," Narbu said. "The same holds true for any organism. There is a minimum level of energy required for proper functions. More challenging tasks require more Sparkseed."

"Fair enough," I said, nodding to acknowledge his point. "What about the rest of it, then? I got the impression your order's been stockpiling it for centuries."

"We have."

"Why? Just to keep it away from the untrained?"

"Partially," Narbu said, at length. "The more vital reason, however, is that it will be used in the near future."

"For what?"

"I have told you enough for this particular moment. Rest assured, Purifier Dak, that there is an altruistic intention behind our possession of Sparkseed. Its glory will be used for the betterment of the masses."

The lofty, poetic language in Narbu's explanation simultaneously gave me hope and put me on edge. It was the same "save the universe" tone that had been employed by Chanzig, Markazian, and every other madman throughout history. But how could I even broach pushing back against that? Narbu could literally kill me by sneezing.

"Settle yourself and seek knowledge at your leisure," Narbu said, breaking my train of thought. "You'll find a streamlined guide for recommended texts on the main table, but you are free to read whatever calls to you. One of the brothers will fetch you in a matter of hours."

"At bedtime?"

Narbu smiled. "Not exactly, no."

"Oh, *please* tell me I get at least one night in a comfy bed. Please."

"Remain in the present," Narbu said, wagging a huge finger in rebuke. "Speculation on the future will do nothing except rouse fear."

"I'd have less fear if you just told me what's about to happen."

But, predictably, Narbu was already out the doors and heading back down the stairs into darkness. That left me alone in the round, cavernous chamber, basking in the lanterns' soft glow.

I didn't even know where to begin in this repository. There was no official count on hand, but I wagered the total number of texts numbered in the tens of thousands.

Looking upward, I discovered that, unlike most places in the monastery, I could actually see the ceiling. This was not an insignificant detail—the circular slab that formed a barrier above me stood out as being more than a simple overhead covering. A series of cogs and pulleys ran along its outer edges, suggesting it could be moved.

A thought occurred to me. *Maybe that's how they restrict access to classified materials. The first floor is for the novice texts, and the one beyond that, the advanced ones . . .*

I supposed I'd find that out soon enough. For now, though, I had my hands more than full when it came to studying the materials available to me. Akasha's earlier comments about how long it had taken her to achieve mastery of the first two Perfections made me wonder how long outsiders were supposed to spend with each level of reading material. From the look of it, one could *easily* spend sixty years trying to tackle everything on the ground floor.

But Narbu had been clear: I only had a few hours to find what I needed to know.

Not wishing to waste any more time, I headed to the central table Narbu had described. There, I noted yet another curious detail about the repository: The table wasn't gigantic. Instead, it was perfectly scaled for humanoids, as was the sheet of parchment that contained the reading list.

I frowned and scanned the walls again. Sure enough, despite their vast quantity, all of the texts were appropriately sized for us small folks. I further confirmed this discovery by picking up a tome from a nearby stack and flipping through the pages. The ink, font, and bindings suggested this text was far less than several thousand years old. Additionally, the writing had been done in the common tongue, not the native language of these monks. Clearly, everything around me was a copy.

Was it possible that there were *two* repositories? One for outsiders, and one for the monks themselves? If so, what had they chosen to leave out in the miniature version?

Cool it with the conspiracies, Dak, I told myself, shaking my head and picking up the reading list. *Just open a book and shut up.*

There were only four titles listed on the parchment. In order of their appearance, they were: *A Treatise on Karma, Wayfarers, and the Absolute; Koans for the Direct Path to Realization; Master Yujan's Commentary on Wellsprings;* and *The Doors Between Worlds.*

Listed beside each text's name was a number that, as I soon learned, corresponded to a position on the shelves all around me. After a cursory look at the labeling system, I went off to find *A Treatise on Karma, Wayfarers, and the Absolute.*

It wasn't too difficult, considering the text had been placed front and center on an altar-like stand on the far side of the repository. This was obviously the crown jewel of the order, the foundational text that informed their outlook on life and death.

I picked the tome up with gentle, cautious hands, already concerned what the monks might do to me if they discovered any damage to their precious books. The treatise was relatively thin, but its metallic outer panels and dense pages gave it real heft. I carried it back to the main table, set it down, and settled into the nearest chair for some reading.

While peeling the cover open, I reflected on how ridiculous this felt. Just days ago, I'd been in a fight for life itself against sadistic killers. Now I was getting the schoolboy experience "I" had never actually received. And rather than starting with the basics, I was jumping straight into one of the most esoteric materials ever compiled.

Life is funny like that.

The first few pages were reserved for dedications to various teachers, masters, and warriors that had probably died thousands of years back. Then the meat of the text began. For your sanity and mine, I won't transcribe exactly what was written there (as though I could even recall it). Rather, I'll provide the gist of what I read.

A long, long, *long* time ago—well, actually, scratch that. The text described a time that preceded *this* universe's time, and began at some unknown point in the multiverse's history. This more or less resonated with my understanding of physics, which maintained that time required space to "function." No matter, no space . . . no time. So, anyway, the treatise began by describing this pre-time state in our universe.

In it, there was nothing. Not even "nothing." Just an endless, ageless vacuum that would one day form a container for our universe. A sprawl of undefined potential energy. This void was known as the Absolute (which is also the "soul" of all beings, which makes sense . . . I guess?).

Put shortly, the Absolute was sort of like the "stuff" that comprised every single particle (and lack of particle) in the entire multiverse. It was like clay, or water, or space itself, infinitely changing and without any one true shape. The Absolute was everything from neutron stars to humanoid DNA, and everything in between.

This is where it gets a little interesting. You might be saying to yourself, "Oh, so the Absolute is just a mumbo-jumbo name for quantum particles." But it goes deeper than that. See, ordinary, physical matter is "blind." It doesn't have consciousness, or intelligence, or anything like that. But the Absolute, by contrast, *was* conscious. At least, it contained the potential to exist *as* consciousness. For a brief, easy metaphor, consider this: the Absolute wasn't just the vid on a simscreen; it was also the simscreen itself, the theater, the audience, and the universe that contained that hypothetical theater.

Despite this, the text made it very clear that the Absolute wasn't one gigantic being, like the monotheistic concepts of God. It seemed to suggest the universe was totally absent of *all* individual souls, and that there was only the Absolute. Or, put more scientifically, the Absolute was just a name for the infinite energy of the multiverse appearing in countless forms.

This leads into the discussion of karma. Being a materialist-minded guy, this was the hardest concept for me to choke down. Despite that, what I found was . . . intriguing. Because the Absolute is a synonym for perfect wisdom, perfect intelligence, perfect creativity, it also meant the true nature of everyone's mind was the same thing. That is to say, all beings have the capacity to become a living expression of perfection. A Wayfarer.

The only trouble, as Narbu had pointed out earlier, was that us ignorant beings got confused about reality and how it works. Instead of recognizing ourselves as the Absolute and popping into existence as a Wayfarer, we become identified with labels such as "alive," "human," "conscious," "good," or "bad." We get attached to the temporary form of existence instead of seeing existence as it is. This is a problem, because it causes our minds to get agitated. It also causes the biggest problem of all, which is being born into new, squishy meat bodies (or demon bodies, according to the text) due to us lacking control over rebirth. A Wayfarer, for example, was beyond this ignorance, allowing them to fully tap into the Absolute and direct where they wanted to be reborn.

Karma, then, was the chain of cause and effect that led to us discovering our true nature and getting released from the suffering of rebirth. Good karma makes your mind more radiant, which makes it more likely to recognize the Absolute. Bad karma, naturally, makes your mind more defiled, which makes it *less* likely to recognize the Absolute. So basically, do good things to get good results. Basic stuff.

Finally, I came to the part about Wayfarers. I already knew most of this, so I'll give a super truncated description.

The first category of Wayfarers had mastery over their own radiance and power. They pledged themselves to taking care of all future beings and took up the role of leaders in the multiverse. These, as you've guessed, were the Radiant Wayfarers.

The second category wasn't so rosy. These Wayfarers, which had ascended to enlightenment through "magic" or other foul deeds, became trapped in their personal nightmares. They sought satisfaction through material pleasure, conquest, and domination, eventually losing their sanity. These unsavory beings were termed Defiled Wayfarers. They had an especially nasty habit of preying on universes and trying to feed their appetite with beings' miseries.

There was also one final, *very* important note near the end of the book. Something called a "Primordial Wayfarer." To dumb it down a little, you can pretty much view a Primordial Wayfarer as the grandaddy of all other Wayfarers. While most Wayfarers (especially Radiant Wayfarers) received training from other enlightened beings, Primordial Wayfarers managed to discover their own brilliance and achieve enlightenment on their own. That is to say, they were just *born* as Wayfarers in the infinite dust of the multiverse. Lucky bastards. As the legends go, there's only ever one Primordial Wayfarer per universe at a time. Typically, they pop up in a given universe every few trillion years—and only to re-teach the path to enlightenment when all records of that path have been destroyed or lost. They serve as a spark in the darkness. A spontaneous miracle of perfection.

Shrugging, I set the book aside and went to fetch the next recommended read. The search didn't take long, seeing as the object in question was perhaps the smallest, and certainly shortest, book in the entire repository. It had a cracked, faded green cover, suggesting it had been in circulation for quite a while.

Without further ado, I returned to my table and peeled open *Koans for the Direct Path to Realization*. This text was rather merciful, in that it provided a cursory definition of the word "koan" for an uncultured swine like me.

Koan:
1. A statement, exchange, or question that points to the Absolute, the supreme and abiding nature of reality.
2. A paradoxical gateway to realms of sudden insight.
3. A pointing with no point.

So, almost like a riddle. A string of text designed to break down logic, push a student to the furthest extremes of cognition, and then deliver a flash of understanding that redefined the context of the text itself. Trippy. Drawing on "real Dak's" memories, I found that I had a relatively rich knowledge base when it came to this topic. Maybe that was why I didn't find it so brain-breaking. Plenty of ancient cultures had turned to pithy quotes, jokes, and riddles as ways to convey information that was too cryptic or hard to grasp by the masses. Several of them had even enjoyed creating poems that could drive men to madness.

Anyway, back to the text itself. It was composed of twenty "koans," most of which were utter nonsense upon first reading. I won't bore you with all of them; instead, I'll jot down my top three favorites, or at least the ones that put a tickle in my brain. I've also been kind enough to offer my unsolicited and probably incorrect take on each one.

First up was a short, snappy koan known as *Naked Armor.*

"The wise man is quiet and unarmed.
Skin, air, and a tongue of restraint.
These alone are his armor."

Master Dak's Commentary: Given the monastery's focus on self-defense—not to mention its overflowing armory—I was a bit surprised to see this outwardly nonviolent entry toward the beginning of the book. Even setting that aside, it didn't make much sense at first glance. After a few minutes of half-focused contemplation, however, something stirred in my mind. I got the impression that this koan was extolling the virtues of defense as offense. That is to say, staying quiet, humble, and sharp enough to spot and avoid any danger long ahead of time. Easy to do when you're not infected with a chok'tal. Still, there was some precious meat to pick apart in those three lines. Given my poor impulse control and planning skills, there was something to be said about looking before leaping—and keeping my presence on the down-low. When it came to the skin and air part, I wasn't so sure, but my uneducated guess was that it had to do with relying on one's own body as opposed to fancy weapons and protection.

Next was what I interpreted as a master's remark to a student. This gem was known as *The Changeling.*

"Look upon the field, young one. Trees grow tall and straight. Bushes spring up with beautiful blossoms. Birds crowd the skies. But what is the true form of these temporary shapes? Before trees, there was soil, water, and starlight. Before the soil, there was rock. Before rock, there was space. And what preceded space? When you can answer with the urgency of an animal being hunted, your mind will come to rest."

Master Dak's Commentary: Although I was barely even an amateur in the field of koan studies, this one seemed obvious. Well, intellectually, that is. The actual "aha!" moment probably required a thousand more hours of contemplation. Anyhow, it was plainly a reference to the Absolute.

The master was trying to push the student toward recognizing the ever-changing, faceless expression of reality itself, and in so doing, point toward the student's own nature. Score one for Master Dak.

The last one, easily the most cryptic of the collection, was titled *One's True Face*.

"One Spring evening, Elder Kantreka was visited by Aspirant Hudram.

Aspirant Hudram approached the venerable elder and said, 'Elder, I wish to know my nature. What can you tell me of the Absolute?'

Elden Kantreka assessed the aspirant and replied, 'Come close, and I will tell you.'

Free of hesitation, the aspirant approached the elder. Once they were within the range of one breath, Elder Kantreka drew a knife from their robes and held it to the aspirant's neck.

'Answer this, Aspirant: Who are you? If you make a sound, I will slice your throat from left to right. If you remain silent, I will slice from right to left. Now, tell me, how shall you answer?'

Master Dak's Commentary: As mentioned, this one was pretty damn tough to crack. It best represented the "koanic" approach of throwing a seemingly impossible conundrum at the reader. One's mind naturally wants to gravitate toward a binary answer—give the name, or keep silent—but the solution is obviously neither of those choices. Due to my ignorance, I wasn't able to get this one to fully click or make sense. My best interpretation is that the student's true identity is that of the Absolute, and therefore they can't say or do anything in particular to point to it. Because, as I mentioned, the Absolute doesn't have a fixed form. Therefore, silence and speaking are two sides of one indescribable coin.

Best I've got. Take it or leave it.

The next selection, *Master Yujan's Commentary on Wellsprings*, turned out to be a scroll nestled inside a weathered bronze tube.

After popping out the scroll, I unfurled it and started reading.

This one was a bit less dry, probably because it was a direct transcript of a master's teachings to a student. It was also mercifully short, so I'll include a snippet of its main points here.

Listen intently, dearest pupil. I have come to banish your defilements and deliver you to the end of suffering. My words, once properly understood, will undo a billion births in the hell realms. In one decisive strike, you will be free from creation and destruction.

Within you is tremendous power. Cultivate it well, guard its sanctum, and smooth the pathways through which it shall be expressed. But be mindful, pupil, that this power belongs to nobody. It exists of its own accord. You are merely host to its brilliance. This power is the same force latent within the void. To claim ownership over it is to deny the eminence of reality; to reject it is to sink into realms of apathy. Move with vigor.

Power born of rage, lust, or spite may prove effective for a time, but it will not last. Pupil, imagine a canine that stands behind a metal barrier and barks from sundown to sunset. Eventually, its throat will grow sore and coarse. Its energy will bleed into the wind. Uncontrolled, unmindful, the canine will be too fatigued to fight when its foe finally overcomes the barrier. In this way, you must cultivate the proper source of power and make yourself ready for battle with the defiled.

Compassion is the surest source of power. Driven by goodwill and wholesome intentions toward your fellow beings, you will draw upon an unending stream of energy. You will attain supernatural resolve on your quest to purify the mind. Let the light of the collective Wayfarers guide you.

Wellsprings exist for naught but the deliverance and transcendence of all mortal beings. Listen closely to their calls; heed diligently their warnings. Tilt back your head, open your lips, and drink deeply of the Wellspring's healing waters. It is a river with no bottom.

Focus your mind, Pupil, and call out day and night to be one with its brilliance. With ceaseless effort, unyielding resolve, and determination, you may join the Wellspring and lend your hands to beings across all worlds.

After a few moments of mindful contemplation, I rolled the scroll back up and returned it to its tube. There honestly wasn't much to extract—at least, not much that resonated with me. I got the idea. Wellsprings were amazing hive-minds of Radiant Wayfarers that wanted to help other beings reach enlightenment and stop falling into defilement. Good, great. But far too religious and theoretical a notion for me at that moment.

I then went off in search of the final text, which ostensibly dealt with rifts and gateways, judging by the title's reference to "doors between worlds."

Much like the first text, this one turned out to be a thick, enigmatic tome that carried an air of specialness. But when I plopped it down on the table and flipped it open to the introduction, I felt my mind turning to sludge.

Strange as it was to say, I found myself missing combat. The thrill of the hunt, the elation of victory, even the rush of fear that came with facing death—all of it had become an unexpected drug of choice while I wasn't noticing. Sitting here and working through countless pages of metaphysical lecturing was perhaps the toughest battle I'd faced.

Then an idea hit me. Reaching into my awareness, I called out to Modri.

"Whaddya want?" he grumbled.

"You're reading what I'm reading, right?"

"Don't have a choice. Your eyes are mine."

"Do I have to focus on the words for you to know what it says?"

"Hell no. I've got the mind of a chok'tal, Purifier. One glance, and it's all stored away."

"Right. So, just for fun, let's say I asked you to read and tell me what this stuff is about . . ."

"What's in it for me?"

I paused, tapping my chin in thought. "What do you want?"

"Sex. I ain't been laid in too long."

"Alright, well, that's off the table for now. So, pick again."

"A stiff drink."

"Are you saying you get a buzz from *me* drinking?"

"Duh," Modri said. *"You feel it, I feel it. So, you get good and loaded, and I'll do your bullshit reading assignment for you."*

It wasn't a terrible tradeoff—I myself had a hankering for a drink—but it also wasn't the easiest request to accommodate. I sincerely doubted the monks were boozehounds that kept flasks and kegs in their storerooms.

"First chance I get to suck down a cocktail, I'll drink as much as you want," I said. "But you might have to wait a few days. Deal?"

Modri grumbled a bit, but relented in the end.

And just like that, I was freed from my tedious task. I sat slumped in the chair, keeping each page open a few seconds and staring at it with glazed eyes before flipping onward at Modri's prompting. Within ten minutes, Modri had absorbed several hundred pages' worth of information and compiled it into a brief summary.

"Hot damn," Modri said, whistling. *"That was the most insane thing I've read since . . . well, hell, I dunno when. Bad memory and all that."*

"Well? What'd it say?"

"You want the long version, or the short one?"

"Make it medium," I said. "Probably not the best idea to reduce one of three required texts into a two-sentence snack."

"Whatever you say, boss. So, basically, seems like it was written by the monks as a primer on rituals that open gateways between worlds. There's

good gateways, neutral ones, and bad ones. Anyway, all of 'em start by making contact with a god or some other being from another dimension. Then you chant the words they tell you to chant, build some type of shrine or whatever, make a few sacrifices or do the right song or yadda yadda yadda . . . Point is, they think you open a rift by makin' some type of bond with stuff beyond our universe."

"Wait, wait, wait. So, someone *invited* the Unmade into our universe? You know, by letting him send the chok'tal through the type of gateway I found?"

"Seems like it."

"And the fungus? That, uh, Throne of Radiance?"

"Same deal."

I groaned. "Are there any caveats I ought to know about rifts?"

"Uh, lemme think . . . oh, right. There's a lot that goes into determining the power and duration of these rifts. Think of it as a recipe. Every ingredient matters. I mean, if you buy this bullshit, you gotta consider the seasons, the gravitational flow, the density of dark matter, the rate of cosmic expansion . . . it's a whole barrel of crazy."

"Alright, so scratch that question. What's next?"

"Well, the monks said . . . again . . . that the final goal of all living beings is to become a Radiant Wayfarer themselves. Take up the mantle or whatever. Supposedly it takes quite a few lifetimes."

"Does that mean rebirth is . . . real?"

"How the hell should I know? I'm just reading whatever shit you put in front of me."

"Right. Sorry. Go on."

"That was about it. Get strong, prepare your mind, be on the lookout for bad Wayfarers tryin' to hijack your body and turn your universe into hell. Basically, if you ain't tryin' to become one of these good Wayfarers, you're probably the kind of weak-minded sonofabitch to invite 'em in through a pagan ritual."

I leaned back in the chair. "Based on the human minds I've seen so far, we're screwed."

The problem, of course, was more nuanced than how I'd framed it. I mean, sure, the generally stupid and selfish state of humans *was* an issue if the Defiled Wayfarers planned to invade our universe and take over weak minds, but it went beyond that. Before the rebirth of the human species and the wars and the Hegemony, the elder alien races had served as a bulwark to guard the universe against extradimensional threats. They'd engineered vast machines and set up ingenious defenses to keep sentient life safe against all the terrors they'd personally encountered.

But the age of aliens was over; it was now the age of humanity. And if we didn't start getting our ducks in a row sooner rather than later, we were screwed.

"Oh, one more thing," Modri said, mentioning this with a tone that bordered on regret. *"There were some, uh, pages tucked inside the book. Looks like someone stashed 'em there. And they're . . . strange. Y'know, printed in hydraulic oil or something, not ink. Real squiggly handwriting. Whoever penned 'em was probably hyped up on amphetamines."*

I cocked a brow. "Well?"

"Maybe best if you take a look. I'll give you a rundown of the ones with text, but there's a, uh . . . illustration to look over, too."

Frowning, I thumbed through the pages until I found the yellowed sheets Modri was referring to. There were four sheets in total, three of which had indeed been penned by someone evidently caught in a psychotic episode. It was a wonder Modri could even decipher the text. The fourth sheet was the one with an image on it . . . and it didn't look too reassuring.

It featured a crude illustration of a mountainside—specifically, a fork in the path that ran up a mountainside. The right-hand path was marked by a boulder with a hexagonal rune, while the left-hand path had a tree with red blossoms. Each path was being traveled by a humanoid figure. On the right was a figure enveloped in a glowing, golden aura. On the left . . . I couldn't quite tell. Their only identifying mark was a wreath of shadow.

"Wonder what it is," I said. "You think it's some kind of metaphor? Radiant Wayfarer, Defiled Wayfarer, two paths?"

"Maybe. Either way, weird as hell. Now, you wanna hear about the written ones?"

I shrugged and slid the illustration back into the book. "Hit me."

"One of 'em was an unhinged rant about a Purified One that'll bypass the whole system. No rebirths, no eons of mind training and all that shit. It'll be dumb as a rock, but get the job done somehow."

"So . . . me."

"I dunno. I guess so."

"What exactly are they, uh, 'fated' to do?"

"Take on the Defiled Wayfarers," Modri explained. *"It says this 'Purified One'—goddamn, I hate the idea of chosen ones—is gonna have the right stuff to fight 'em on their turf."*

"What does the right stuff imply?"

"You're really makin' me work for these drinks." Modri sighed. *"They basically said their chosen one is gonna have a sharp mind, a body that's been touched by the Wayfarers, and biology that can handle extreme adaptation. But the most important thing is that they've got no attachments. Nothin' to worry about losin', nothin' to worry about gainin'."*

"Holy shit," I breathed, my chest suddenly tightening. "That's *me*, Modri. It's really me."

"Little egocentric, huh?"

"You don't get it. That's exactly what Akasha and the monks were talking about. I've got a 'pure mind'—it's empty of personal memories and attachments, remember? Then there's the genetic engineering Chanzig did. The fact that my entire body and nervous system were built to accept new inputs. *And* there's the 'Wayfarer touch' part. Hosting a chok'tal is a pretty damn close match to that."

"Huh. I guess you really are onto somethin' there."

"You think?" I said, bristling. "Did it say anything else? Something that can help me with these insane trials?"

"Uh, yeah, there was one last thing . . ."

"Well, spill it."

"You may not like it, chief."

"Then you need to say it."

Modri let out a long, digital breath. *"It says this champion's gonna merge with our universe's Wellspring . . . then absorb and imprison the Unmade. After that, they'll become a god. A god that's gotta swim around in the void for the rest of time, keepin' a lid the Unmade's defiled energy. No way out."*

12

I sat there in silence for a long while, drumming my fingertips on the chair's armrest and inwardly fuming. Modri, wisely, had opted to hush himself and give me the mental space to digest his revelations. But I was in no mood for digestion, or acceptance, or anything else connected to the idea of surrendering to this shitty fate.

Eventually, I decided to reread the manic screed and carefully examine the last sections. Modri's interpretation was surely accurate, but maybe it had missed some critical nuance or caveat that suggested another course of action. To my dismay, it hadn't. Modri had, with a few words, captured the bleak essence of what awaited me. In fact, he'd delivered that news with an unusual softness. He'd tried to protect my feelings and let me down easily.

That truth was both heartwarming and infuriating. Heartwarming because it meant his disembodied consciousness genuinely cared for me, but infuriating because it hadn't gotten into the grislier, more unsettling aspects of what the text said.

Modri's description had highlighted most beings' ultimate fear: death. But the actual text presented a view of reality in which death was the least of my concerns. Sure, it said that I would triumph over the Unmade, but it also said that I'd reach that goal by literally absorbing the Unmade into myself. In effect, the Unmade and I would become a single, eternal being.

For the rest of eternity, I would have to drift in the dark, empty sprawl of the void.

Translation? I would become imprisoned by life itself. Forever.

You might think such a fate isn't so bad—after all, many religions tout eternal life as the end goal—but that's because you haven't *really* considered the implications. Us humanoids tend to get bored with media, food, or even sex if there aren't constant variations in the content. We are creatures of endless seeking. And somewhere deep in our consciousness, we comfort ourselves with the knowledge that one day, we will die, and then we'll get a welcome break from the monotony of existing. We tell ourselves that no matter how bad "being" gets, it will end someday.

I, on the other hand, would *not* have that luxury. The end would never come.

So I sat at the table, the book slammed shut and pushed away, contemplating what the hell I had done to deserve this destiny.

At the start, my greatest fear had been death. Being absorbed by the chok'tal and stuck in its collective consciousness was a horror beyond belief. But now, shockingly, I found myself even more deeply disturbed by the exact opposite of that fate. I truly was damned if I did, damned if I didn't.

Of course, at the time, I hadn't considered what my death meant for the greater part of existence. If I fell in battle, I'd suffer for it—but so would everyone else. If the order was telling the truth, which I sincerely believed, I was their one and only hope to prevent the Unmade from turning our universe into an endless, sadistic playground. By the same token, I was also their sacrificial lamb. I would take on the burden of eternal existence to spare others from the same outcome.

Plus, on some superficial and self-centered level, I found myself dreading the loss of being "me." It didn't matter that I would be reborn after death—what mattered was that I would no longer be Dak. After finding out about my strange birth, I'd initially been depressed. But that depression had rapidly given way to something that I just now appreciated: hope. Hope that I could become somebody great, that I could make a name for myself, that I could be loved and praised as my own individual, regardless of how I came to exist.

If I died and merged with the Unmade, that hope was fruitless. My own individuality meant nothing in the face of a formless god. The moment my mind and body shut down, I would cease to exist as the being that I had just recently started to appreciate.

These miserable thoughts circled until, finally, I heard a series of rumbling footsteps echoing from the nearby passage.

I turned to find Tekshim stepping through the threshold.

"Take me to Narbu," I said curtly. "We need to talk."

Only after speaking did I notice the look on the monk's face. He wasn't wearing his usual coy, almost mischievous smile. Instead, he appeared somber. Regretful, even.

He lifted a delicate finger. "First, Dak, I believe you and I should exchange words."

"About what? Your order's quest to kill me and trap me in eternity?"

"I can understand your anger, your pain. I am sorry you had to learn such information in so impersonal a way."

"All this time, you and Narbu and Akasha and everyone else knew about this. What other bullshit are you hiding from me?"

"Calm your mind. I will explain, but only if you can maintain control."

I stood and circled the chair, trying to breathe normally. After a few minutes of pacing, cursing, and scowling, I deemed myself ready. "Explain."

Tekshim moved to the table and squatted down beside the reading list. "You must promise not to disclose anything I tell you to Scryer Narbu. It is most . . . sensitive."

"I'm a little too busy worrying about eternity to tattle on you."

"Very well," Tekshim said softly. "The writing that contained your destiny was not on the Scryer's prescribed list."

"What do you mean?"

Tekshim gestured to the book. "The materials you found within those pages are not part of *any* collection here. I found them many years ago, while wandering in the forbidden areas of the mountainside. They were in a lockbox that had somehow washed out through an old cistern drain, just waiting on the riverbank."

"Why put them here?"

"Because I felt you had the right to know," Tekshim said. "Some brothers may believe that the goal of universal liberation justifies the obscuration of truth, but I do not. I go against the order in saying such things to you."

I looked up at the monk for a time, trying to gauge the rather human sympathy in his eyes. "You're saying that you risked a lot by putting this here. For me."

"For all Purifiers who have visited our monastery," he corrected.

"Sounds like you don't have as much faith as the others."

"Do not say such things, Dak."

"Well, isn't it true? I saw you skipping out on the sacrament. You don't trust this whole thing entirely either, do you?"

"I have my own path," he said faintly. "That does not make me faithless."

"But it *does* make you concerned . . . just like me."

"For countless centuries, we have worked toward the goal of creating a champion. Yet . . . as time wears on . . . I have observed Scryer Narbu growing impatient. Rash, even. He has concealed more and more from the candidates."

"Well, what else is he concealing?"

"I cannot say. Even this text required great effort for its insertion into the repository. If there are additional secrets, I have not accessed them."

I took shallow breaths, trying to calm myself. "Did Narbu write those pages?"

"I believe so."

"What about the illustration? What is it showing?"

"It is unclear, Dak. But I trust you will make good use of the knowledge."

"Fair enough," I said, crossing my arms. "I suppose I ought to be thanking you. It's not the news I wanted—not in the slightest—but at least you had the nerve to show me the truth."

Tekshim nodded. "For the record, Dak, Akasha did not know about the champion's fate. As I said, such materials are not known to the order at large. I suspect they were placed in the cistern for Scryer Narbu's safe-keeping." He met my gaze seriously. "Akasha has a role to play in all this, I am certain, but it is not the heartless one you imagine."

"Oh." I suddenly felt sheepish, if not ashamed. "I'm . . . sorry I snapped at you. It's just a lot to take in. Especially after what I've been through."

"Your wrath is understandable," Tekshim said gently. "At times, I believe the monks of our order have lost touch with the greatest beauty of humanoids and other organic life: their emotions. The teachings of the Wellspring were delivered for the benefit of all life, and emphasized compassion above everything else. Perhaps our logical minds have dulled this realization."

"Guess that explains why they don't have any qualms about using us Purifiers as living test subjects."

"I know you may view my brethren as evil, but I urge you to look deeply at their intentions. Just as you humanoids are bound by desires of lust and craving, we are bound by the desires of computation. Our order has long acknowledged that the suffering of one being is negligible compared to the possible salvation of infinite beings."

"If I'm being honest, that sounds pretty damn easy to say when you aren't the 'one being' on the chopping block."

"Our order would gladly shoulder that responsibility if we could. As you have observed from the Sparkseed-infused beast, as well as the chok'tal itself, the creations of the Wayfarers were designed to interface with biological life."

"Which is why none of you can achieve the part of the prophecy that revolves around working with the Wayfarers' powers."

Tekshim nodded. "We are able to practice and implement their teachings, but their true glory—the ability to evolve organic life to new heights—is lost on us. Our bodies are advanced, but they are also rigid in design. We cannot become what is required for this task."

After contemplating Tekshim's words for a short while, I nodded. "So, you think it's true, then. You really think I'm the one who will change everything."

"The probabilities suggest this is so."

"If the shoe fits . . ." I muttered, trying and failing to take inspiration from Tekshim. The monks certainly made this fate *sound* noble, but the selfish, human side of me couldn't see it that way. I just felt like a pawn. "Tek, I need to ask one more thing. You might not have an answer."

"Go ahead, dear friend."

"You said Narbu was getting impatient. Rushing things. Why is that?"

Tekshim's gaze darkened—literally. The cobalt spark in his eyes faded to pinpricks of light. "In the fathomless void of the multiverse, universes appear and disappear constantly. Every so often, however, a Wayfarer becomes interested in one particular universe."

"Like the Unmade with ours."

"Yes. The Wayfarers are not the only higher-dimension beings with a keen interest in physical matter, but they are the most ancient. To them, the laws of our reality are merely knots in the fabric of existence."

"So, why hasn't the Unmade untied those knots?"

"It has," Tekshim said. "The rifts it opened to release the chok'tal represent a violation of this dimension's order."

"Doesn't seem to have released any more of them since then."

"Our order has seen to that."

"How?"

"You read the text on how rifts develop," Tekshim said. "Once, there were many cults and societies that derived their power from these sources. For thousands of years, they passed down their foul secrets and indulged in dark rituals."

"You mean . . . that's real? People *actually* worshipped the Unmade?"

"Among other defiled beings, yes. Many cultures did not know what they were doing. All they understood was the transaction. They provided what the entity desired, and the entity provided in return. Food, medicine, euphoria . . . all this and more was dangled before the mortals' hungry minds."

"But if all it takes to open a rift is a ritual, or a mass slaughter or whatever, there should be more chok'tal floating around."

"Such rituals are not so simple, nor so common," Tekshim said darkly, before shaking his head. "I did not exist at the time, but it's said that our order worked extensively to eradicate this defiled knowledge. Our brothers and outsiders traveled from world to world, cleansing any trace of knowledge about dimensions beyond our own."

"What do you mean 'cleansing'? It sounds like the order—"

"That which will not be heard by ears shall be received by flesh. That's what Scryer Narbu used to tell me, anyway." He shrugged. "It wasn't a venture entirely written in blood, Dak. The order spent countless centuries studying, spreading, and practicing the teachings of the Wellspring. This wisdom was, and still is, our best protection against defilement."

The notion of traveling around to stomp out knowledge was brutish, but I understood it. The text regarding rifts had essentially confirmed that ordinary, stupid people were responsible for the Unmade turning this corner of the universe into a free-for-all event. Anything too dangerous to be repressed had to be destroyed.

"Say . . . how much power would the Unmade need to send our slice of the galaxy a chok'tal storm?"

"That depends on many things," Tekshim said. "Our place in the cosmic cycles, the minds of those in the area, the—"

"I'm asking if it can happen again. You said the order stomped out the Unmade's cults and did some rituals of its own to strengthen the fabric of reality—which is all great, by the way—but everything I've seen lately suggests the Unmade isn't getting weaker. Just the opposite."

Tekshim's face soured. "This prophecy has been in motion since the dawn of time. It is what you and I were born to serve. Regardless of our feelings, we must have faith. The end is nigh."

"Tek, with the age of that prophecy, I wouldn't be surprised if the math for the grand finale is a little off. It could take a thousand years for it to happen. Or a million."

"Or a month." His lips quirked with unease. "There are signs, Dak."

"Like . . . ?"

"I am simply describing what the advanced sutras say," he explained. "The position of the stars, the change in the seasons . . . all of reality is crying out in warning. If you fail in your mission, the teachings of the Wellspring will be snuffed out in this region of the cosmos. With the fall of one galaxy, there comes another, and another, and another . . . As more and more beings descend into madness, feeding the Unmade and welcoming it into our dimension, it becomes increasingly likely that this universe will return to eons of defilement. Beings will roam the hells and burning tundra, forever seeking medicine for a disease they have inflicted upon themselves."

Although it was largely implied, not spoken aloud, I understood what Tekshim was so worried about. If there really was a colossal war going on between wisdom and ignorance, peace and violence, this struggle between the Wellspring and the Unmade represented an apocalyptic war. All we really care about as sentient beings is preserving and passing down "good" knowledge—how to tell the truth, how to avoid killing, how to stop plagues.

In the world of "good" knowledge, the teachings of Wayfarers and their Wellspring represented the pinnacle. Even if I couldn't prove it, I had a suspicion that Radiant Wayfarers had been guiding our universe since the dawn of creation. They had served as quiet, gentle parents, leading us deluded mortals away from pain and toward freedom.

The prospect of us losing their knowledge and being cast back into endless cycles of darkness, animal thinking, and superstition was horrifying. This wasn't just about survival; it was about saving the innocence and wisdom of an entire universe. If the plans of the Wellspring (and by extension, I) failed here, the Unmade would someday become this dimension's god. It would say what passed as right and wrong, true and false.

What a hideous idea.

Any way you sliced it, the Unmade was out for the blood of this entire universe. I had a chance to stop it—whether or not I liked my own ending to the story.

"No time to waste, then," I said firmly, pulling on a resolved face that didn't match my dread at all. "Lead the way, Tek."

"Certainly." As before, Tek bent down to allow me to scale his shoulders and reach the perch of his skull. "Ah, and Dak . . . please refrain from considering this when we meet with Scryer Narbu. His mind is powerful. If he glimpses what I have told you . . ."

"Again, your secrets are safe with me."

But as we shuffled back down the stony corridors, I wondered if I'd truly be able to keep my word. How was I supposed to just "block out" my preoccupation with this storm of new information? Death, rebirth, colliding universes, gods . . . each new snippet of destiny was like a hydrogen bomb in my meat-based brain.

Gathering myself and the fractured contents of my mind, I tried to breathe through the confusion. Inhale, exhale, inhale, exhale. The sensations were direct and calming, even if my heart was galloping throughout. I needed to make a plan—if not for my survival, then for my sanity.

After all, ever since the chok'tal invaded my body, I'd been carried forth by one goal or another. Survival had been the driving force, but maybe it was time to branch out. Time to start seeing myself as some integral piece of universal fate.

Besides, it wasn't as though I was irrevocably tied to the wheel of destiny. The monks and their radiance might've seen it that way, but goddammit, I had something none of them had: human gusto. Throughout history, my ancestors had balked at destiny. They had cast aside dogma, rewritten their own fates, and persisted through sheer force of will. There was no reason I couldn't do the same. I could find a way to fix this *and* continue living as myself.

With that realization, some of the fear faded. I could do this. I had to.

Along the way, I took a quick peek at my Status Display. I still had a cool fifteen or so hours until my next rank-up—not an issue *yet*, assuming I was about to receive yet another trial that involved combat. Now, if the Second Perfection's trial didn't require bloodshed . . . I might be in some hot water. But I wasn't overly worried. After all, if I was such a VIP in the eyes of Narbu and his order, they'd surely planned a way to keep me going, if only to fulfill their own desires.

After some ten minutes of strolling around, Tekshim brought us through a large arch and into an adjoining chamber lit by hovering lanterns. It was an oval-shaped space, its walls decorated with scenes of epic battles and mythological happenings that I could barely make out due to their massive scale.

Scryer Narbu waited in the very center of the room, kneeling with his legs tucked beneath him and hands joined in his lap. He didn't turn back as Tekshim brought me within spitting distance.

"Scryer?" Tekshim broached, his nervousness evident even to my human ears. "Purifier Dak is ready, I believe. He has a firm command of the required texts."

Narbu remained silent for nearly a minute. When he finally spoke, his voice was as hard as iron. "Very well. Leave us, Brother."

Tekshim wasted no time in obeying that order. In fact, he seemed relieved to be settling me onto the tiles and scurrying away as fast as possible.

Once Tekshim's footsteps had faded into silence, Narbu turned back and opened his eyes. "It seems that Brother Tekshim thinks highly of your understanding. What do you believe?"

Doing my best to keep my mind focused on anything except what I'd learned, I replied, "Oh, I think I've got a *very* solid grasp."

"Good. You will need it for your next trial."

"Right now?"

Narbu stood and retrieved his log-like walking stick from the nearby shelf. "There is no time except the eternal 'now,' Purifier. But you will learn this soon enough."

I glanced about, trying to locate my next batch of busted equipment. To my relief, there wasn't a janky shotgun anywhere in sight.

"Weapons will not be required," Narbu said, startling me. "Not external weapons, anyway."

"Come again?"

Narbu reached into the folds of his robes and pulled out a cube of Sparkseed. The cube I'd recovered from the turtle, by the looks of it. It looked like a speck of dust between Narbu's oversized fingers.

"Do I have to fight that thing?" I asked.

"The Second Perfection is also known as the Perfection of Control," Narbu explained. "Much like the outsiders who came before you, your only tool for this trial will be the Sparkseed you recovered from your first encounter. It will serve as your armor, weapon, and anchor."

"Anchor?"

Rather than replying, Narbu flicked his fingers open. The Sparkseed didn't fall, but instead broke apart and fanned out to form a dazzling, symmetrical shape reminiscent of a highly magnified snowflake. The thinness of the shape made the Sparkseed look like liquid light.

"This is a mandala," Narbu said. "It is an external representation of your internal state."

I gazed at the creation, spellbound. "Pretty. But what does it do?"

"It is a gateway, of sorts."

"Like the ones Wayfarers make?"

"On a lesser scale, but yes." Narbu rotated the mandala before me, revealing its immaculate, precise design. "By meditating deeply upon the form of the mandala, your consciousness will exit the body and travel through the gateway."

"Uh . . . to where?"

"The Pure Ground," Narbu explained. "It is the seat of your true nature. A world formed from your source energy. Every being possesses their own sanctum, deep within the heart and mind. There, you will be capable of meditating without the interference of the food-flesh formation."

"You mean body."

"A body is nothing but digested food." Narbu reeled the mandala back toward himself, then collapsed it back into the cube. "You may consider the Pure Ground to be your eternal home. It is a space that overflows with the wisdom of the Absolute and its students."

I studied the mandala more closely, intrigued by what Narbu was saying—even if recent experiences made me doubt he was telling me the full truth. From the sound of it, the mandala was some kind of esoteric gateway to my own personal bubble. A vehicle through which I could arrive in a bliss-filled, knowledge-soaked realm detached from time and space.

A beautiful concept, sure, but was it *real*? That remained to be seen. It was entirely possible these monks had been studying their own nature for so long that they'd gone off the deep end.

"So, what exactly is the trial?" I asked. "Forming a mandala? Meditating in the Pure Ground?"

Narbu nodded. "Precisely. But you must heed my warnings, Purifier Dak. Your first entrance into the Pure Ground will not be calm."

"What's that supposed to mean?"

"Birth after birth, you have wandered this universe and others. It has likely been eons since your mind ever touched the Pure Ground. Given your interest in physics, it should come as no surprise that nature does not permit vacuums for long."

I squinted at Narbu, silently urging him to continue.

"The Pure Ground is full of potential energy," Narbu said. "It is the closest you will come to touching the Absolute in your human form. To recognize this, however, you must destroy what has obscured its radiance."

"You lost me."

Narbu just grunted, then paused to reassess his explanation. "During your many lives, you have accrued karma. Some good, some impure. Yet with each evil deed, you have fed a being that dwells deep within your mind. This being is a collection of your own tainted karma."

"Wait, wait. You're telling me that all the shi—sorry, *bad*—things I've done gave birth to a new creature? And it's . . . inside me?"

"It is within your Pure Ground, more accurately. It feeds off the pain, fear, and guilt that is pushed out of your awareness and into the subconscious. Until you have vanquished this being, you will be unable to connect to your Pure Ground using normal consciousness."

I nodded slowly, starting to grasp what Narbu was saying. My next trial consisted of two parts: first, forming the mandala . . . and second, traveling *through* that mandala and killing the bad-karma monster that lived beyond the barrier. The entire thing was batshit, but I found myself strangely excited to put the concepts to the test.

"Does this 'thing' have a name?" I asked. "Karma Beast, maybe?"

Narbu considered it for a moment. "Translated from our tongue, these beings are known as Accretions. The runoff of countless past lives and echoes of misery."

"Accretions," I said, tasting the name. "Not bad."

After studying me for a prolonged moment, Narbu extended his hand and sent the Sparkseed cube drifting across the tiles.

It hovered before me, spinning in slow, smooth revolutions.

"Steady your mind," Narbu said. "It is time to harness the power of Sparkseed."

13

Gazing at the golden enigma hovering before me, I was struck by a sense of danger. It wasn't the heart-pumping, muscle-tensing variety associated with running into a rifle-wielding enemy, but something quieter, more insidious.

Maybe I should've had more reverence for the Sparkseed cube. After all, it had been produced by one of the "good" Wayfarers, ostensibly to aid the universe in defending itself. But at the same time, it was still a creation of Wayfarers. And the only Wayfarer I'd run into up to that point was the Unmade.

Viewed through that cynical lens, the cube in front of me was functionally no different from the chok'tal inside my nervous system. Like the chok'tal, Sparkseed was a mysterious, physics-defying creation that had been pushed into our universe through a rift. It was also capable of fusing with one's body and calling upon eldritch power. All I could do was hope that *this* Spark's creations were benevolent.

With no shortage of hesitation, I reached out and cupped the cube in my hands. The instant I made contact, the cube stopped spinning and dropped with its familiar, inexplicable weight.

"Good," Narbu said, walking around me in a wide circle. "Now reach out toward the Sparkseed with your mind. View its particles as an extension of your physical body."

It was easier said than done. My mind groped at it through Telekinesis, but there simply wasn't an opening. Unlike most objects I manipulated through the same skill, the Sparkseed cube was nearly impossible to "grasp" on account of its density. Even on a quantum level, it was as tightly packed as concrete. In contrast, ordinary Telekinesis targets had a quantum structure full of gaps, and their loose particles buzzed about like gnats above still water.

Without a handhold, some way to dig my mental claws in and assert control, my mind lost its edge. After several minutes of straining and grunting, I found myself besieged by the mother of all migraines. Sweat streamed down my cheeks.

"Force will not suffice," Narbu said, his voice so patronizing I wanted to square up with him. "You must seek assimilation, not domination. You will achieve nothing if you continue to view the Sparkseed as something beyond yourself."

I bristled at his flowery words, only to realize that he might be right. Up until now, I *had* viewed Telekinesis targets as part of myself, but only to achieve a particular aim. I'd handled them like temporary tools by flooding their quantum form with energy and controlling it for a time. Here, that wouldn't fly.

Again, I reached out with the tendrils of my mind. Once again, they were met by the impenetrable mesh of the Sparkseed. But there was something new this time: a faint "glow" to the material, a taste of the energy contained within its molecular bonds. Curious about this new development, I began running the gaze of Telekinesis up and down my own body. Sure enough, the same glow was present. That gave me an idea—one that Narbu verbalized mere seconds later.

"Good," he said. "Experience the lack of division between your own body and the Sparkseed. It is only your conceptual mind that creates separation."

I frowned at him. "Is the Sparkseed alive? It's glowing with the same energy as I am."

"All things are alive," Narbu replied. "The chok'tal within you, too, resonates with this energy."

"But the chok'tal is conscious. The Sparkseed isn't."

"How do you know that?"

"Because the chok'tal can think," I said. "The Sparkseed is just . . . stuff."

"This perception, once again, stems from deluded consciousness. Rocks, trees, space, air . . . all of it holds the vital essence of reality."

"I dunno about that. My Telekinesis skill makes a difference between animate and inanimate objects, and the Unmade programmed that difference."

"A program is only as intelligent as its designer." Narbu paused before me. "You are beginning to break down the barriers of your mind. Reach farther. Perceive that there is no distinction between living and unliving. If you can do this, the Sparkseed will conform to your will . . . along with the rest of the universe."

Narbu's words sounded like utter nonsense, but I still redoubled my efforts to understand what he was hinting at. If Sparkseed truly was alive, and I managed to tame it . . . there would be nothing preventing me from applying Telekinesis to "animate" objects.

Viewed from that angle, the Sparkseed was like a gateway drug for the mind. It danced on the borders of living and unliving, conscious and unconscious. It was a training device that, if mastered, would open the door to unthinkable power. Power that the Unmade likely hadn't even assumed us stupid mortals were capable of wielding.

This idea gave me the courage to try again. Closing my eyes this time, I extended my mind back toward the Sparkseed. Rather than seeking an opening in its quantum form, however, I just caressed it. I felt the nooks and crannies of its shape. The instant I did this, it was as though the glue holding the Sparkseed together began to dissolve. The strange material drifted outward in sympathy with my mind, expanding and loosening as it did so.

At a certain point, there was no longer a sense of duality present. There wasn't a mind reaching toward an external object—there was a single dance, a union of mind and matter. Before I knew it, the Sparkseed was assuming the shape of my mental field. Its fizzling quantum foam had become the tangible expression of my will. Emboldened by the display, I started arranging it into new and strange shapes. It assumed each form with far less effort than that required to manipulate inanimate matter.

"Well done," Narbu said, prompting me to open my eyes.

Just as I'd expected, the Sparkseed was no longer fixed in a cuboid arrangement. Instead, it was circling around me in wide, glowing halos, much like a living set of armor.

"The hardest task is complete," Narbu continued. "Your next goal is to form your mandala."

Keeping most of my attention on maintaining the marvelous Sparkseed display, I asked, "How?"

"There is no special effort required."

Puzzled and slightly annoyed by the non-explanation, I began experimenting with different techniques to form something akin to what Narbu had made. My first attempt, which involved flattening and extending the Sparkseed into a mandala-ish shape, ended in abject failure. Too much mental strain resulted in the Sparkseed collapsing back into a cube form that bounced off the tiles.

Next, I played around with forming a mental image of a beautiful mandala and then expressing it through the Sparkseed. This method got me a bit farther than the first, but the resulting shape was asymmetrical, flimsy, and obviously unstable. It, too, dissolved after several seconds.

"You are trying too hard," Narbu said. "Allow the mind to be at rest."

I glared at him. "If I rest my mind, it'll turn back into a cube."

"How do you know this? Is it the truth, or simply the voice of your egoic consciousness?"

"It's what I feel."

Narbu gave a great, heaving sigh, much like a parent trying to get a point across to their kid. "A mandala is not a particular shape, Purifier Dak. It is a living representation of the mind. It cannot be imagined, created, or forced into being. You must allow the mind to project its own shape without interference."

I stared at him for a time, blinking with plain annoyance, but eventually decided to test out his awful advice upon realizing he wouldn't be giving any further pointers. After recollecting my mind and slipping back into the quantum link, I repeated something I'd done earlier in the session: letting the Sparkseed come to *me*.

Much like before, the Sparkseed seemed to sense my lack of manipulation and relaxed in turn. It flowed out like a jellyfish, saturating my mental space with golden light. But this time around, I took my foot even further off the pedal. From here on out, the Sparkseed would determine its own course of action. I took on the role of a detached observer.

Second by second, I felt my control lessening, slipping off the glowing material like hands upon oiled metal. Soon enough, the Sparkseed was acting completely of its own accord. It flared out to new limits as though gauging my reaction, yet upon realizing I didn't push back, it condensed to a more reasonable shape and began . . . organizing.

There may be better words for the Sparkseed's behavior, but I think that one conveys the point well enough. The Sparkseed arranged itself into clean, symmetrical lines, branching out from a central axis to form various struts that resembled the spokes of a wheel. I watched in pure amazement, trying my best to, well, *not* try to do anything.

Before I knew it, the Sparkseed mandala was complete. I opened my eyes to find a flawless, stunningly beautiful configuration that my conscious mind could never have envisioned. It was roughly rectangular, though crisscrossed by various lines and sharp angles that all fed into the center.

"Damn," I whispered, watching the last details emerge as I willfully slowed my breathing and relaxed into the experience. "Is *that* my mind?"

"A visual manifestation of it, yes," Narbu said. "Maintain your concentration, but do not inject any effort."

Again, I can't express to you the insane paradox that is "try to avoid trying."

"Sit upright yet relaxed," he continued. He waited until I'd done so. "Now gaze into the center of the mandala, preventing the eyes from straining as you do so. Exclude all other objects from your visual field."

It wasn't easy—far from it—but after several minutes of trying, I managed to find a sweet spot somewhere between effort and total laziness. My gaze was unfocused, yet not quite blurry. It was as though I saw everything in a flat, two-dimensional presentation, devoid of anything that might snag my attention and pull it toward a specific object. Even so, the mandala (and in particular, its dazzling center) occupied my consciousness.

Narbu didn't speak after that. He just stood behind the mandala, observing me and nodding every so often I presumably reached some new milestone.

Minutes ticked by, and by, and by . . . and despite the lack of mind-blowing sensations or visual appearances, I found myself undisturbed. Not even bored. Then, at a mark I'd place somewhere around an hour, a curious shift occurred.

Time and space seemed to vanish. Not in a visual sense, mind you, but in a more abstract way. It felt like I was no longer being carried down the river of linear time. No longer bound by the rigid confines of physical space. There was nothing in existence except the mandala. It expanded to fill my entire consciousness, growing stronger and more vibrant even as my mind quieted.

Suddenly, with zero warning, all thoughts ceased. Flatline.

Part of my mind rebelled at this new silence, but even that resistance was acknowledged as nothing more than the flickering of neurons. Every drop of tension in my body boiled off until I sensed myself as empty space.

Gradually, the beautiful lines and intersections of the mandala began expanding beyond the edges of my vision. It seemed that way, anyhow, until I realized what was *really* happening: The mandala was pulling me inward. The mandala's elegant design stretched and warped around me as though it were the inner lining of a black hole. My entire body was filled with warm, pulsing energy, melting my flesh and bones until they were nothing but streams of flickering sensations.

Still, I kept my cool. Narbu knew what he was doing—probably. Breath by steady breath, I moved deeper into the mandala's epicenter.

But the slow advance didn't last long. Within seconds, I felt as though I was being rocketed forward. The mandala's center was always one step ahead of me, shrinking back even as I moved toward it at exponentially higher speeds.

Before long the mandala's lines were nothing but a glowing blur around me. They twisted and stretched, coiling ever inward toward the pit of the singularity.

In an instant that literally took my breath away, I slipped *through* the center.

The dazzling sight was replaced by blackness, and the wild rush of emotions and physical inputs faded to a sense of utter weightlessness. Just as when I had gone through Chanzig's gateway, it felt—for a mere moment—that I had abandoned my body.

Yet as I'd expected (and hoped), the world trickled back in a stream of individual elements. First was vision, which revealed a fog-shrouded, void-like space stretching to the furthest horizons of infinity. Infinite pinpricks of light that resembled stars hung overhead.

Next was sensation. My body emerged from the formless expanse in a wash of pins and needles, congealing into a presence that I innately recognized as my own. Upon glancing down, I found that I had a humanoid form made from golden light. I lifted a hand and rotated it, transfixed by the airy, almost bubbly quality to the feeling of the pseudo-limb. If I looked closely enough, I could actually see *through* the "flesh."

Hearing came soon after, filling my sensory world with long, ethereal notes like a wind chime's. They arose from nowhere in particular.

Taste and smell were conspicuously absent, though I supposed I didn't need them here. I hadn't come all this way to attend a banquet.

The last sensory experience, which I hadn't even considered as such until reading one of the repository's texts, was mental activity. It rolled in as a collection of scattered thoughts and opinions about my new situation. *Weird* was the prevailing description my mind produced.

Studied in this mystical yet detached environment, it became immediately obvious that the mind was, in fact, just another sense organ. The ear's job was to hear, the tongue's was to taste, and the mind's was to think. This understanding didn't come through words, but as a recognition of what was true. These damn monks really *did* have consciousness figured out. Then again, I suppose it's easy to grasp the subtleties of existence when you have hundreds of thousands of years for analysis.

Once the mind-blowingness of this new environment wore off, however, I was back to baseline. Back to the task-oriented mode of asking, "What the hell am I doing here?"

After a few moments, snippets of the "real" world and its demands leaked back into my mind. *Pure Ground. Trial. And what was that other thing?*

I stood there, wracking my brain and tapping my opaque chin like an idiot, until the answer presented itself—not as a thought, but as a presence materializing in the distance.

Gnarled limbs rose up from the fog, followed by masses of scorched flesh and twisting bone nubs. The sky overhead darkened and filled with ash. Biting winds swept through the void. As more and more of the corrupted figure clawed its way out of the ground, the environment around me soured into a blighted hellscape.

When the mist around my foe began to disperse, I got my first good look at them. They towered far above me like a mountain of pustule-covered skin and black veins, completely featureless aside from a skewed set of three eyes and crooked arms where their chest should've been. Every inch of their bulk writhed with misshapen, half-digested bodies squirming just under the surface.

[NEMESIS EVENT]
Accretion (UNKNOWN)
CALCULATING . . .
Estimated Kill Points: 704,600

"We have waited for you," the Accretion howled through drooling mouths. Its voice emerged like the agonized squeals of infants. "Come forth and let us feed."

14

I'd seen some ugly sons of bitches before, but this Accretion took the cake of dishonor. Just looking at it made me want to vomit—assuming I *could* vomit, given my semi-corporeal form. But the nastiness of the Accretion went beyond a basic level of disgust.

See, what made it so horrid was that it was a living mirror of my own existence. Not my existence in this form, perhaps, but *all* of my existence. Every birth, every death, every incarnation I'd experienced throughout the multiverse.

You might think this perspective is a little too spiritual, or that I'm merely being poetic. But I'd urge you to reconsider. For starters, I felt an unmistakable sense of kinship with the entity. It was as familiar to me as my own body, regardless of our differences in appearance and mental states.

More than that, given how accurate the knowledge of Narbu and the other monks had been up until this point, I had no reason to doubt that they'd told the truth when it came to this creature's nature. The Accretion was a product of everything tainted, neglected, and rotted within me. It was a living heap of all the miseries I'd shoved under the carpet of my conscious mind.

Staring at the Accretion, I found myself overwhelmed by the power of that karmic residue. The air itself felt charged with a potent cocktail of fear and guilt and dread and hatred. That last was the predominant note. Prickly, seething hatred. The kind of hatred you might feel upon seeing your home planet nuked from orbit.

When the creature began slithering closer, a strange paralysis overtook me. All the feelings I'd kept bottled up, brewing amid a sea of adrenaline and bloodshed, came bursting out of my chest in a tidal wave. It took all my strength to avoid collapsing to my knees and sobbing like a child.

But somehow, some way, I held on through my quivering limbs and churning gut. Muscle memory came roaring back with a vengeance.

Weapons, I thought to myself, trying to guide the rational part of my mind like a shepherd. *First step is always to get weapons.*

I glanced about, scanning the fog in all directions for something lethal. To my dismay, there was nothing. All I had at my disposal were my fists, legs, and mind. In light of the Accretion's overwhelming size, the latter would be my best bet.

In a matter of seconds, the beast would be upon me. I made use of the precious pre-slaughter time by experimenting with my mental command over the environment. Yet for all my grunting and wishing, the most I managed was turning my right hand into a blade-like point. Whether it was made of Sparkseed or some other essence, I couldn't say. All I knew was that it would have to do.

When the Accretion came within five meters of me, a plethora of bony, twitching appendages fanned out from its spine. Their spider-like appearance took me back to my first fight in the jungle caverns. They weren't good flashbacks.

At the exact instant I sprang forward with my dagger-hand extended, the Accretion's appendages darted toward me. I rolled to the side just in time to avoid being turned into a shish kebab, then came up on one knee, panting.

The sudden exhaustion puzzled me. I hadn't taken more than a few steps since entering this place, and already I was winded. Obviously, the Accretion was affecting me more than I'd expected. Even as I stood, readying myself for the next joust, I felt the strength bleeding out of my limbs. The overpowering aura of fear was turning solid muscle into jelly.

Desperate to recoup some power, I called upon Overclock. Nothing happened.

"What the hell?" I whispered.

There was no time to analyze my lack of powers, though. The Accretion tensed for another volley of thrusts. I leapt back in time to see the first of the spinal spears dig into the ground where I'd been standing. The follow-up strikes, though, weren't so easily dodged.

One ripped straight through my left leg, flooding me with pain that was somehow even worse than in the physical world. Another tore through my right shoulder and slammed me straight to the ground.

I was pinned. No matter how much I yanked at the appendage, it kept me firmly rooted, allowing the Accretion to casually drift closer. Its hideous eyes and mouths worked in feverish cycles as it sensed my desperation. Bile dribbled down its scar-encrusted folds.

Recalling my earlier skill, however, I pushed all my focus into my right hand. Again, the fingers slid together and formed a crude blade. I wasted no time in slashing at the appendage. The instant the blade met the Accretion's spear, black smog erupted from the wound and blossomed out across my face.

I kept hacking away, blind and coughing, until I felt the pressure ease. The Accretion let out a murderous screech somewhere in the haze. When the smog dispersed, I saw its appendage whipping through the air, shriveled and bleeding more fumes. But not *all* of the appendage was there. Its tip was still embedded in my shoulder, keeping me nailed to the firmament.

"This . . . is gonna suck," I wheezed.

Driven by the fear of imminent death, I set aside my reservations and rolled the right side of my torso skyward. The Sparkseed-flesh around my wound widened and tore as I slid off the spike. I screamed in pain and began crawling backward, gritting my teeth against the worst of the agony.

To my horror, the Accretion's mouths opened wide at my cries. Thin, wispy strands of *something* coalesced in the air and flowed into its waiting maws.

Holy shit, I thought as I struggled back to my feet. *It's literally drinking my pain.*

This theory was cemented an instant later, when the Accretion's veins began swelling and pulsing with motes of dark purple energy. Pus drained out of its pores in sickly yellow beads.

Another shape came flashing toward me through the fog. I sidestepped and slid back, narrowly dodging the Accretion's strike. Once the attack had passed me, however, I realized that it hadn't been carried out using the same appendages on its back. Instead, the creature was making use of a new weapon: a long, squirming rope of intestines connected to its stomach.

The blood-soaked coil thrashed behind me, snapping at the ground in search of prey. I didn't give it the chance to retract or change targets. Dashing over to it, I used my blade-hand to slice clean through the guts.

Again, black smog misted the air. The portion of the intestines still connected to the Accretion shrank back and vanished, leaving behind a trail of frothy, pinkish blood. The section I'd severed immediately shriveled in on itself and began flaking away to dust.

A small victory, but a damn good one. The Accretion's avalanche of distress lightened just a shade.

Seizing the momentary break, I sprinted forward and rolled through a lightning-fast barrage of stabs from the appendages. The Accretion's roiling flesh lay before me. Without so much as a shred of hesitation, I jumped straight at the diseased skin. On the way down, I thrust the hand-blade outward. It bit deeply into the Accretion, sinking farther and farther until the base of my wrist touched flesh.

The creature's innards burned my hand as though it were hydrochloric acid. I ripped it free, cursing and snarling all the while. The skin from my fingers to my forearm had blistered from a light, golden tone to something closer to copper.

At that moment, it became even clearer that this wasn't a normal encounter. Every attempt to damage the beast carried a risk of accidental self-harm, and every hit scored on *me* provided a stream of fresh energy. Even as I drew back, trying not to lose my footing on the mound of pudgy, fluid-filled skin, I sensed the Accretion soaking up my recent pain. Every grunt that escaped my lips turned to vapor and drifted up toward its eager mouths.

There had to be a trick to this. Some method of fighting that would turn an impossible fight into something challenging, yet fair. Otherwise, Narbu wouldn't have sent me in. Not with so much riding on me as their future champion.

The mind, I thought, panicked. *The mind has to be the key.*

It was the only "weapon" I'd been given for this trial, and all of Narbu's emphasis on its hidden strength now seemed like obvious clues as to my path forward. I called upon the first thing I'd sensed upon seeing the Accretion: my mental bond with it. If this beast really was a part of me, I could theoretically manipulate it in the same way I'd controlled Sparkseed. I likely couldn't tap into Telekinesis here, but my hand-blade indicated I *could* control the environment using my mind.

With a deep breath, I shut my eyes and probed the space before me. The Accretion's mental signature was impossible to miss: a brutish, diseased presence occupying the air in all directions. Relying on the same mental muscles I'd used to alter my body, I reached out and tried to grasp the Accretion. Tried to absorb it into myself.

It was fruitless. Each time I sank my mind into the Accretion's hurricane of corruption, another pulse of pain and terror electrocuted me. There was no way into the madness. Not without losing myself to it.

I didn't get a chance to try again, though. Midway through my analysis, the Accretion unleashed yet another ability. The same pores that had leaked pus now began venting noxious fumes. Billowing yellow clouds erupted toward me like lava from a volcanic eruption.

Genius or not, I knew it was a bad idea to stay anywhere close to that shit. I was proven right in the worst way possible when, during my attempt to descend the rubbery flesh, the edge of the fumes licked my back. Searing pain blossomed up and down my spine. It took a monumental effort to resist crying out and further nourishing the Accretion.

Spurred on by the torment, I leapt back down to ground level and came up from a well-executed roll. I spun back to find the Accretion bulging in preparation for some new horror.

In a display that was both astonishing and sickening, the scar tissue running up and down the center of its body split open like the doors of a living gate. A flood of blood, pus, and mucus spilled forth.

I took a few steps back, tensing in anticipation, but the surge didn't come anywhere close to me. It pooled around the creature and drained away, leaving behind a dark, cavernous rift that had formerly been a stomach.

"Nice going," I called, smirking. "Guess you didn't have the *guts* to fight me. Get it? Guts?"

The Accretion's twitching flesh-flaps pulled even farther apart. "Feast, my children."

Suddenly, wet, emaciated bodies came surging out of the Accretion's torso. There were dozens of them, maybe hundreds, all shimmering with splotches of afterbirth. As they tumbled over one another in a wave of flesh, they let out ear-piercing shrieks.

I readied my hand-blade again, but I knew it wouldn't be enough. There were too many of them, and from the looks of it, there was no hope of using something like fear or self-preservation instincts to drive them off. Unlike normal soldiers, these things couldn't be intimidated or routed. They were mindless, ravenous beasts.

Now it made sense why the Accretion's Kill Point value had been so high. I wasn't fighting one being—I was fighting a hive mind. As the horde of red-soaked automatons drew nearer, I was hit by one more startling realization:

These were all *me*.

Sure, they were different heights and genders and even species, but I sensed my innate bond with them. These . . . things were all clones of the countless incarnations I'd had throughout the multiverse. At one time—maybe ten years ago, maybe a trillion—I had been all of these creatures. This seemed even more probable when I noticed animals and nameless abominations parading out of the Accretion's stomach hole. I'd been born as, and died as, everything before me.

This disturbing insight also jump-started a new theory. Perhaps I hadn't been able to attack the Accretion using my mind because of its concentrated energy. Each of the pitiful beings shambling toward me represented part of that collective. Viewed from that angle, my mind assault on the Accretion had been akin to jumping into a vat full of man-eating insects and trying to tame the swarm from the inside. Whether or not the Accretion had any resonance with my mind due to our shared identities, it didn't matter. I'd overwhelmed myself with a rash approach.

In contrast, each of these minions had to have less defenses against my willpower. After all, they were the individual molecules that comprised the Accretion. On their own, they were nothing. That also meant they were vulnerable.

Backpedaling to outpace the charging wretches, I projected my mind out and toward their ranks. Much like the Accretion, unsurprisingly, their natures consisted of dark, tainted energy. That was the bad news. The *good* news was that as I'd expected, their mental manifestations were much weaker. Whereas the Accretion's presence had been a dense, impenetrable fortress, the presence belonging to these creatures was raggedy and more open to a direct assault.

I injected the full force of my mind into the weakest foe—a tall, spastic man running at the front of the pack. For an instant, I felt our shared bond, and then I slid straight past his defenses. The man stopped mid-stride and locked eyes with me.

I was in.

With another push of energy, I felt my mental aura descend into the particles of his being. My willpower infused every cell, every drop of blood, every subatomic flicker. Rather than injuring or draining me, the new connection filled me with energy. It was as though the wretch had become my personal battery.

Now, the horde was nearly upon me. They loomed in a wall of thrashing arms and lolling tongues. I didn't pay it any mind. This was it—the breakthrough I needed. Keeping my eyes trained on the mind-locked man, I experimented by willing him to lift his right arm. Sure enough, he obeyed like a puppet with its strings being yanked about.

Lifting an arm wouldn't do much, of course. Nor would most of the basic actions my new lackey could perform. The Accretion's power was tremendous, and the wretch would be crushed in a matter of seconds if it turned on its master. No, I needed to think more creatively.

More out of desperation than ingenuity, I mirrored what I'd done with the Sparkseed. I probed the quantum form of the man until I was not only immersed in it, but part of it. Every drop of his energy felt like my own. Despite our distance in geographical terms, it was as though we occupied the same mental space.

Then, with one bold and ill-considered shift, I dissolved the man. A flash of blinding light burned away the arena's darkness, causing every wretch to stop, turn, and stare at the spectacle. Even the Accretion shut its infected eyes and recoiled.

My body tingled with fresh power. Looking down at my hands, I found that their glow had increased by orders of magnitude. It took little more than a wishful thought to turn both hands into impressive-looking, scythe-like blades. Another thought shifted them into spears.

"Oh, yeah," I said under my breath, grinning at the wretches as their dead comrade's light faded and they all turned back to me. "It's go time."

Emboldened and now brimming with vital energy, I began seizing each of the minions' minds using the same tactic. With each act of mental assault and dissolution, my power swelled at an exponential rate. Soon I was tearing through clumps of two, three, and even four wretches at a time, igniting their bodies and devouring their essence in fractions of a second.

Before long, the arena was a forest of blazing light. I felt like the embodiment of a nuclear blast. The rush was absolutely euphoric, if not intoxicating. It felt as though I could use my bare hands to rip through steel.

"You feed, we feed." The Accretion's tortured voice broke through my concentration as the last of the wretches' lights dwindled. "We are the same. And we will devour you."

In response, I just smiled. Then I began walking forward, both hands extended to the sides and formed into the crescent curves of sickles. Even with my mind unfocused, I could *see* my own power boiling around me in golden waves.

When I'd come within fifty paces of the Accretion, I squinted and attempted another mental attack on its form. Once again, however, its presence was still beyond my reach. It pushed back against me with a flood of burning pain.

No matter, though. I'd absorbed enough energy to finish this fight. It wasn't a hope, but a definite conclusion that echoed through my skull.

Until the Accretion switched up its tactics, that is.

Countless pincers made of bone and cartilage jutted out through its skin, surrounding it like a bony phalanx. Then, to my horror, the pincers angled downward and pushed against the firmament. The Accretion rose on its new "legs," which were entirely too spider-like.

Before I could think of a counterstrategy, the Accretion thundered toward me. There was nowhere to go; several of its pincers twitched in the air, ready to catch me if I moved left or right. Behind wasn't an option, either, since the new aracho-Accretion moved at nearly three times my own sprinting speed.

The ground pulsed beneath me as it drew nearer . . . nearer . . . nearer. Panic chewed through my fresh confidence. Yet in those final seconds before impact, a strange calmness quelled everything else. A single idea rose in my mind. A single intention.

And just like that, brilliant, gleaming wings sprouted from my back. I rose high above the Accretion, neither ecstatic nor concerned. Even as I hovered directly above the abomination, I found myself possessed by an unshakable steadiness I'd never experienced. It felt as though I'd tripped and fallen into the mind of an immortal god. A Spark, even. Nothing could harm me.

That same calm, pitiless energy sent me diving straight for the Accretion's cluster of eyes without a hint of fear. The beast lifted its gaze at the last moment, but by then, it was too late.

Every pincer that came my way was severed as quickly as it came rushing forth. My sickle-shaped hands chewed through everything the Accretion threw at me: spines, globs of bile, spurts of dark fumes. All of it burned away before my radiance.

When I came within spitting distance of my enemy, I joined my hands in a praying motion and slashed straight down at the grotesque face. The curves of both sickles ripped clean through eyes, teeth, and tendons, clouding the air with foul smog.

But I didn't pull away. The pain was nothing but a tickle running up and down my body. With the sickles still embedded in the Accretion, charring the rotten flesh beneath, I called upon a deeper reserve of strength. My hands carved even farther into the beast. Blood and white discharge sprayed past me. Squeals and screeches flowed from its countless mouths.

Even as the Accretion squirmed and weakened, however, the stillness remained. There was no hatred in my task. No cruelty. This was, as Narbu and Tekshim had described it, a noble kill.

When the sickles bit through a hard shell that might've been a skull, I intuitively moved into the final phase of my attack. By channeling my focus out of the body and into the mind, I discovered that I now had a clear opening. Gone was the hellish barrier that had previously prevented my infiltration attempts.

Mentally, I sensed my will slithering into the cavernous space at the core of the Accretion. Pulsing around me were the black, spiteful walls of its consciousness, and just ahead was the nexus of the chaos. To my surprise, it wasn't some dead and twisted heart. Instead, it was the same essence I'd perceived within myself. The same locus of awareness.

That's its true nature, I thought to myself, the wisdom of the repository's texts suddenly clicking in place. *It wasn't born this way. It fell into ignorance.*

Seeing its essential form, which was no different than my own, I understood what I had to do. It was just like taming Sparkseed. Instead of resisting it, trying to destroy it, I had to merge with it. I had to acknowledge it as a part of me that had been forgotten.

With a burst of crackling energy, I used my mind to pierce the very center of the Accretion. There was a flash of brilliant light, then . . . silence. A static expanse. Once again, I found myself drifting through that timeless void that had preceded the Pure Ground.

NEMESIS ENCOUNTER SUCCESSFUL
Kills: 1
Kill Points Awarded: 704,600
Storehouse Time Awarded: 12 Hours, 20 Minutes

RANK-UP AVAILABLE: RANK 12

15

When I opened my eyes—my real, physical eyes—the meditation hall was exactly as I remembered it. All of my body's aches, pains, and random itches returned in a heartbeat, but strangely enough, there wasn't a single indication I'd suffered an injury in the fight. Hell, there wasn't even any adrenaline or sense of danger left over. The mandala was gone, as was any trace of the Pure Ground and the slaughter that had taken place there. If I hadn't known any better, I'd have assumed I was waking up from a split-second dream.

"Well done," Narbu said, circling back around me and sitting down in the lotus posture. "You have achieved mastery of the Second Perfection."

I took a few well-deserved seconds to rub my face. "Well, that sure was something."

"I am sure you performed admirably."

Narbu's demeanor was relatively normal—at least, as normal as a mecha-monk's can get—but there was a sly edge to his voice. It didn't entail surprise, exactly, but something warmer. After a moment of reflection, it hit me: he was proud.

"Did you drug me?" I asked.

"Certainly not," Narbu said. "What you experienced was nothing more than the projections of your own mind."

"But there was real pain," I said, becoming curiously heated despite my lack of wounds or overall current suffering. "Tell me what that mandala really is."

"A gateway, as I described."

"But it's a *real* gateway, isn't it?"

"I do not grasp your meaning."

I sighed. "I thought you were being poetic. But that mandala . . . it really sucked me in. And it *really* made me fight that thing."

"And?"

"It's just too much. I feel like my brain's about to snap."

"This is normal, considering the strain of the trial. It will fade after a brief respite."

"But that isn't what I'm concerned about," I said curtly. "You just showed me a window to another dimension, and that rebirth is probably real, and that . . . well, that that *thing* was lurking inside of me."

"Ah. You are troubled by what you've perceived. It threatens your perception of reality."

Said in such a light, disarming way, I had to concede that Narbu was right. Even though I couldn't personally frame my inner state, that was *exactly* what had happened. Up until that point, my genetic host's memories—counterfeit or otherwise—had provided a neat, workable set of tools with which to understand life. The chok'tal and the Unmade had certainly thrown a wrench in my metaphysical understanding of the universe, but even those elements had eventually been incorporated into my larger understanding of "how things worked."

The Pure Ground, however, shattered my prim and proper hold on reality. It sparked a cataclysmic shift in my confidence about how much I really understood the fundamental laws of my own dimension. Of course, it wasn't just about the Pure Ground; it was about what the Pure Ground represented.

One day, one mandala, and one encounter were all it had taken to shove my logical mind off the rails. What other sanity-breaking secrets were nestled in the universe, waiting to spring out and surprise me? How could I be certain of anything anymore?

Narbu seemed to sense this distress. His eyes softened, and he bowed his head slightly as he gathered his thoughts. "In our order, we call this process 'disenchantment.' For some, it is dull and gradual—for others, rapid and painful. Through this process, we shed our false concepts about reality. We learn to adopt reality itself as our new framework."

"But that's just it—I don't know what reality is, anymore. I mean, I thought I did, but now . . ."

"Now you are falling over a cliff. Your biological, human side cries out, urging you to grab any vines or ropes within reach."

"Yeah," I said, somewhat surprised he'd managed to intuit my situation so easily. "That's exactly it."

Narbu nodded. "In order to complete this journey, you must let go of your handholds. Reality is an endless mystery. It cannot be understood and told through crude, dualistic tools such as language."

"What's wrong with language?"

"It is the root of all defilements." Upon noticing my confusion, he elaborated. "By terming an object beautiful, I have given rise to ugliness. By giving you a name, I have denied all that you might become in another form."

I didn't understand most of what he was talking about, but I also wasn't in any sort of mood to receive an exegesis session after that slog of a battle. As such, I just nodded along and tried to look pensive.

"It is a great deed, slaying the Accretion," Narbu said at last. "Many do not survive the attempt. They are consumed by their karmic residue, dragged into the hells."

I swallowed hard. "You mean . . . you *really* can die from that thing?"

Again, Narbu offered one of his famous wise-master nods. "Those who lose their minds during the encounter never return to their bodies. Sometimes it is immediate, other times after a significant delay . . . but invariably, death must follow. There is no sense in preserving a hollow shell."

The prospect of having been killed and abandoning my body was frightening, but not nearly as much as the related consequence—that is, being dragged into a literal hell dimension by the Accretion. Ordinarily, I'd have poked at Narbu with more questions about the mechanics of life, death, and reincarnation, but it was too much. Too raw, maybe. Some aspect of me already knew that he was telling the truth about all this rebirth mumbo-jumbo. Whether the Pure Ground was real or not, the experience itself had been strikingly, vividly authentic. While there, I'd personally verified everything the repository had told me about past lives and mental powers.

I didn't know what I craved more—to understand how it all functioned, or to have never learned a thing. Sometimes ignorance really is bliss.

"I've got a question you might not be able to answer," I said.

Narbu lifted his chin, waiting expectantly.

"Since all of that took place in the Pure Ground, or my mind, or wherever it was . . . does that mean Purifiers can earn points from simulated enemies?"

He considered the question for a time. "We experimented with such optimistic solutions in the beginning. Alas, the chok'tal is able to distinguish the real from the virtual."

"But the Accretion was—"

"Alive," Narbu cut in. "It possessed a core of reality, just like you or any other sentient being. Although the environment of your trial was not grounded in physical matter, it was still a struggle for life itself. The chok'tal realized this."

"Not bad," I said, whistling. "Not bad at all. Almost makes it worth having to fight that thing." Thinking further on the concept, though, a new query bubbled up. "You monks clearly have some kind of telekinetic hardware . . . but I only have Telekinesis because I chose that upgrade. So, how'd you know I would have it?"

"That is a query for the Wellspring."

"You're saying that *they* knew I'd have it?"

"Of course."

I blanched. "What would've happened to me if I'd come here without it? I can't imagine that fight would've even been possible without some basic grasp of mental powers."

Narbu eyed me with a placid expression. "Your mind is overburdened with questions, Purifier Dak. I believe it is time for your rest."

"Right. Rest." No matter how perturbed I was about this predestination business, the prospect of getting a few hours of decent sleep was enough to jar me out of my rut. "Do I get to keep that Sparkseed, by the way?"

"Only after the Third Perfection has been mastered."

"So, the classified repository texts *and* the Sparkseed are earned by conquering the next trial? What the hell's my reward for surviving this one?"

"A soft bed and solace," Narbu said with a thin smile. "Go on your way, Purifier Dak. Allow the mind to rest in the repose of nonexistence."

"That might just be the creepiest framing of sleep I've ever heard."

Per usual, Narbu was content to let me have the last word. He simply closed his eyes and sank into his meditative practice, either oblivious to my presence or hoping I'd piss off if he ignored me long enough. I was sharp enough to take the hint.

The long, meandering journey back to my quarters was rife with speculation. The perplexing sameness of the monastery's interior spaces led to plenty of aimless wandering and backtracking, which in turn led to rumination.

I should've been elated at my recent victory, especially given the ludicrous amount of Kill Points it had yielded, but I wasn't. Although my life was more secure than ever due to a guaranteed rank-up and Storehouse Time buffer hours, my existential fate was far less certain. The conversation with Narbu, instead of reassuring me, had merely planted more seeds of doubt.

How much did he *really* know about me? Obviously, he'd accessed the forbidden sutra that Tekshim had smuggled my way, but there had to be more. The sutra hadn't spoken of the "champion" requiring Telekinesis, after all. The longer I spent in this place, the more convinced I became that I wasn't some lucky candidate able to jump through their hoops—I was a victim of cosmic grooming. Narbu had known my role in this whole thing long before I ever met him on the compound's front steps. Tekshim, too, had sensed it.

The most pressing question now was . . . had Akasha known? Although she'd *claimed* she had no knowledge of the prophecy's details, how could I be certain she was telling me the truth? For all I knew, perhaps she'd been sent out of the monastery with the express purpose of locating me. Perhaps she'd gone to elaborate lengths to put herself in the right place, at the right time, to intercept me on my Chanzig-killing quest.

That was dipping hard into conspiracy territory, though. My mind recoiled from taking any of those scenarios too seriously. If I really believed Akasha was gaslighting me, helping orchestrate some grand prophecy on the behalf of a questionable monastic order, I had no idea what I'd do. No idea what it would do to *me*, even.

Regardless of how much I resented it, I was at the mercy of others for the foreseeable future. I had to trust their intentions were pure and their words were at least somewhat genuine. Otherwise, madness would soon follow. Then death.

When I came within sight of the door to my quarters, I leaned against the wall and took a cursory glance at my Status Display to ensure everything was on track.

STATUS DISPLAY
PURIFIER RANK: 11
RANK-UP AVAILABLE: RANK 12 (409,600 KP required)

Kill Points: 888,400
Genofacturing Points: 27,340

Rank Points: 0

Rank Time: 9 Hours, 41 Minutes, 10 Seconds
Storehouse Time: 22 Hours, 20 Minutes, 0 Seconds

Anima: 320%
Dominion: 0/4

From the looks of it, I still had enough time to catch a full night of sleep and rank-up in the morning without risking even a bit of Storehouse Time. And speaking of Storehouse Time, goddamn. I now officially had a full "normal day" worth of accumulated time to serve as insurance. Once I triggered tomorrow morning's sweet, sweet rank-up, I'd technically have forty-four hours to achieve my next milestone.

Forty-four hours of guaranteed existence may not seem like much, especially when you're a sentient being that expects to enjoy several decades or centuries of life, but in my shoes, it was an absolute windfall. Those forty-four measly hours were enough to ease the burden that had weighed on me ever since the chok'tal appeared.

After closing the Status Display, I approached the door and reached out to open it. No need. The door swung open, revealing a spry-looking Akasha in bright white robes.

"Uh . . . hello?" I said.

She stepped aside to allow me entrance. "You engaged in combat."

"Nice to see you too," I said, as I moved inside.

Akasha closed the door and glanced back at me. "Were you not?"

"Another trial," I said, sighing. "The Second Perfection."

"Just as I sensed, then."

I narrowed my eyes. "Sensed? You mean, you can tell what I did just using your mind?" Upon reflecting on that for a moment, however, I realized how stupid a question it was. "Of course, you can."

"The stench of one's Accretion is impossible to miss."

"You're telling me." I shuffled over to the sofa and sprawled out along it. "Speaking of which . . . why didn't you warn me about that? You said you'd mastered the Second Perfection."

"I have."

"So?"

"It is not my place to disrupt the order's regimen," she explained. "I did not know you would be undertaking the challenge so soon, but even if I had, I would not have spoken. Scryer Narbu decides when each initiate is ready."

"Seems silence is a way of life for you."

Akasha's head slowly swiveled in my direction. "What is meant by that remark?"

"Forget it," I said, semi-regretful I'd spoken so far out of turn. "Just been a long day."

"I sense the turbulence of your mind."

"Well, that tends to happen when your karmic mirror is trying to dissolve you in stomach acid."

"It extends deeper than your encounter." She moved closer, then perched on the edge of the sofa. "You are troubled by me."

"What? No. Of course not."

Her blindfold scrunched as she examined me, presumably scanning every layer of my brain using some hyper-advanced mental technique.

"Can we just sleep?" I said. "It'd do us both some good."

She pursed her lips. "You do not trust me."

"Right now, I don't trust much of anything."

"Your faith in the holy task has been dulled," Akasha said quietly. "By what?"

"Let's talk about it tomorrow."

"Was sparing your life insufficient to prove my loyalty? Our fates are intertwined, Dak. I have sacrificed every tenet of my beliefs to take this chance with you."

"Akasha, you're reading way too much into this."

Light throbbed behind the blindfold, chilling my blood. The last time I'd seen her use that power, she'd vaporized Chanzig.

"I see it," she said in a strange, distant tone. "I see your fear, your hesitation. You are concealing something."

"Listen—"

"You interpret my composure as coldness." As she spoke, she continued to lean closer and closer, mirroring the manner in which her words drilled into my chest. It felt as though she was cutting back layer upon layer of skin in an effort to reach my core. "You assume that my silence is betrayal. But you do not understand the pain of losing your entire world. You do not grasp what molded me into the being you now perceive." She paused, her brows losing a touch of their prior tension. "Or perhaps you *cannot* grasp it. Your human mind has evolved with a very narrow conception of what it means to be dedicated and honest. What do you know of sacrifice?"

"Alright, that's enough," I said sharply, sitting up and pulling away from her. "Where the hell is all this coming from?"

"Your own mind. You have filled it with fear, doubt, and misery, and now you cast its contents upon me."

"Oh, bullshit. I'm just sick of being treated like a prop."

"Every being has its burdens."

"Not like mine!" I snapped. "To this order, I'm just a weapon. I'm a tool. If I die, they'll just replace me."

"It isn't true, Dak. A Purifier with a conscience is not so easy to—"

"Exactly. I'm valuable, but only because I check the right boxes. But I'm a *person*, dammit. I didn't come here to compete for Narbu's affection, much less his starring role in the apocalypse."

For a long, awkward while, Akasha just sat there facing me. As it so often happened, I couldn't discern a thing on her face. More than ever before, she appeared to me as a stone bastion of wisdom, a humanoid-shaped expression of cold and unfeeling knowledge.

But what she did next shattered that impression.

Before I knew it, Akasha's hand rested atop mine. It was surprisingly tender and warm.

"I see the light within you," she whispered, "and so long as it remains pure, I will not allow it to dim or be snuffed out. This is my vow to you."

I didn't know what to say. Not at first, anyhow. I just stared at her with parted lips and trembling hands, trying to determine where this abrupt compassion had come from. It was such a drastic shift from her attitude in past days, which had more or less been focused on reminding me how easily she could kill me if and when I "went bad." For the first time in seemingly ever, she was showing care for me as a being. Not as a Purifier, but a being. And in light of all she'd experienced due to the Unmade—not to mention her thousands of years of life, which had surely been saturated with backstabbing and death—it meant more than I could comprehend.

"Thanks," I said quietly, still in a partial daze from the whirlwind of emotions. "I think it's, uh . . . time to sleep now."

This time, she didn't stop me. She remained on the sofa as I stood and headed into my personal room, her eyeless gaze burning into my back all the while.

Even when I'd showered off, changed, and slipped under the bed's thick velvet covers, I found myself still envisioning the tender curves of Akasha's face. My hands buzzed with the phantom pressure of her touch.

I still didn't know if I could trust her, particularly when it came to matters of destiny and service to the order, but one thing was abundantly clear as I drifted off to sleep:

Feelings make everything messy.

16

Five and a half hours of dreamless sleep later, I awoke to a chamber just as lightless as when I'd conked out—which made sense, considering there weren't any damn windows in the room. My Status Display was my only indication of the passage of time.

The feeling of sheer energy I had upon waking, though, made me triple-check the time listed there. It felt as though I'd slept for two whole days, only to receive an intravenous amphetamine drip just before opening my eyes. Not since merging with the chok'tal had I felt such a complete, pervasive sense of well-being in the body.

Seeing as I still had about four hours left on my Rank Timer, I opted to do something rare: relax. Today was virtually guaranteed to be just as brutal as yesterday, after all. A little de-stressing and deep breathing were just what the proverbial doctor ordered.

After just ten minutes of that, though, I felt an unpleasant gnawing in my chest. I had to *move*. Had to make use of this torrent of energy. The urge was so strong that it forced me out of my cozy bed, over to the closet, and into a set of loose yet breathable cotton clothing.

Akasha was already wide awake and sitting contemplatively on one of the living area's chairs when I emerged. The smooth, controlled rhythm of her abdominal movements suggested she was practicing some esoteric breathing technique.

I did my best to tiptoe around her, hoping I could raid the nearby pantry for something premade and calorically dense, but it was to no avail.

Her brows rose before I'd made it halfway across the room. "You've woken early."

"And you've . . . not slept," I said, puzzled.

"An hour is sufficient for sleep. Provided the body and mind are in harmony, that is."

"Well, I'm not there just yet."

She nodded toward the door that led to the main hallway. "You should spend these hours with great prudence. Just after dawn, our next trial begins."

"*Our?*"

"Yes. I spoke with Scryer Narbu this morning. He has permitted me to attempt the trial of the Third Perfection."

"Oh." I nodded, then stumbled upon an unsavory possibility. "This trial's not a duel to the death between outsiders, is it?"

Akasha just frowned at my dark humor. "The monks have prepared a spread to break the night's fast. You may find it in the main hall."

"You can just call it breakfast, you know."

"Too much talking, Dak," she said, resuming her rigid posture, "and not enough preparation. Do not take the Perfection of Insight lightly."

Somewhat humbled by the woman's biting tone, I headed out of the living quarters and into the monastic hallways. Clearly, Akasha was sparing no effort in readying herself for the day's events. Whether she'd attempted it or not, I had no idea, but the underlying message was obvious enough: *it will not be easy.*

Of course, I didn't need an alien's somber meditation display to tell me that. This was, after all, the fabled Third Perfection—the final edition of what Tekshim had referred to as the Lower Perfections. That *was* a big deal. Beating this trial granted ample access to the monastery's most precious texts, yes, but it also offered something much grander and more worthy of safeguarding through the brutal gauntlet: permanent merging with a clump of Sparkseed.

Despite all my sharp-tongued comments and snark, it wasn't lost on me that Sparkseed was downright deadly in the wrong—or even right—hands. Much like enriched plutonium rods, the substance carried a massive risk of chaos and bloodshed from simple mistakes, let alone active employment as a weapon.

This being the case, it logically followed that the order had gone to great lengths in ensuring only the worthy survived. Narbu wouldn't have to spook me with statistics about how many outsiders and foolish monks had perished trying to master it. My imagination filled in the blanks. After all, if mastering this Perfection and being endowed with a Sparkseed bond was common, the galaxy would've been jam-packed with mind-warriors that wielded golden light and healed themselves at will. At the very least, rumors of such individuals would've been widespread.

As we all know, that's not how things worked in my neck of the 'verse.

Put bluntly, this trial was designed to weed out the runts. There was no room for consolation prizes or half-measures. Either I succeeded and gained access to the tools I needed in my fight against the Unmade, or I failed—which led to the equally unpalatable fates of annihilation-style death *or* rebirth in an even shittier dimension.

Faced with these prospects, you might imagine I threw myself into a rigorous, hours-long training program that pushed my mind and body to their limits. Yeah, not a chance. Taxing myself prior to the trial felt akin to sprinting in preparation for a marathon. It *sounded* right, at least on some intuitive level, but it was just a way to burn out faster when push came to shove. Besides, if I wound up dying during the trial, it would make the morning's sweating and stressing feel like one last kick in the ass from fate. Sort of like getting hit by a hover-tram while coming home from a rough day at the office. I'd rather just take the hover-tram to the face at dawn and skip the paperwork.

Anyhow, I decided to make a beeline for the terraces and reset my overworked brain with some fresh air.

Outside, it was warm and clear. The surrounding fields, forests, and mountains had been painted in the rusty tones of dawn. If not for the looming trial and my general chok'tal woes, it would've been a lovely setting for a hike and maybe a small picnic. Of course, what I needed right now wasn't a day of leisurely activities. More than anything, I just needed the space and time to clear my head.

Everything that had happened in recent days—indeed, since acquiring the chok'tal—only served to scramble my mind and dissolve whatever footing I'd once thought I had. It's not so easy to live up to high standards, train under stressful conditions, and view yourself as a reincarnated god-slaying champion when you aren't even certain what you are.

Akasha and the monks had absurdly long lifespans, and perhaps that explained why they were so indifferent to my struggle. Their refusal to take things slow and steady wasn't exactly callous, but rather misguided. In their nearly immortal eyes, there probably wasn't much in the universe capable of surprising them, let alone confusing them to the point of a mental breakdown. But humans didn't work that way—especially not *this* human. Between my test-tube origin story and age, which was somewhere around that of an ordinary toddler, there was little about me that lent itself to embracing a starring role as the order's chosen one.

As I strolled along the soaring walkways and ancient ramparts of the monastery's outer rings, though, my thoughts shifted to more grounded matters. Akasha, for starters. I still had no idea how to conceive of her gesture from the previous night. Women, particularly alien women, were not my strong suit.

This being the case, I did something risky: I turned to my resident expert.

"You there?" I asked, hoping Modri wouldn't be too pissy about his recent hushings.

To my surprise, Modri was quick to pop up. *"Always."*

"What have you been up t—" I stopped. "Bad question, I guess."

"It's all good. Same shit as ever. Just sittin' around, existin', waitin' to see how far you get on this quest."

"Yeah, that's about what I figured."

"So, what's the deal? You need somethin' from me?"

Unlike prior conversations, there wasn't any resentment in his tone. This struck me as odd for two reasons. First, he was *always* in a mood. And second, he had every right to be snarky. Despite my best intentions, I'd been treating him like a toy that I only brought only when I was bored. After all he'd done for me—albeit with mixed results—he deserved better than that.

"You seem . . . content," I said.

"You're wonderin' why I'm talkin' all nice-like."

"Yeah, that's one way to put it."

"I've . . . well, I've been thinkin' lately."

"Oh?" I said, approaching the edge of an obsidian balcony and sitting down to admire the blazing horizon. "Do tell."

"Guess I just, uh, misjudged you or whatever. Always thought you were soft, spoiled, a little dumb. But you've been dealt a shitty hand."

"That's an understatement."

"Just lemme talk, alright?" When I mimicked zipping my lips shut, he continued. *"I dunno about any of this junk about rebirth or Accretion or Pure Grounds or whatnot, but it seems real clear that you're the best chance we've got to get outta here."*

"Out of where?"

"Here." Realizing it didn't clarify anything, Modri elaborated. *"If you take out the Unmade, maybe we'll finally get a lick of freedom. Oblivion. Whatever."*

"If you believe the monks, you'll probably just be born somewhere else."

"Don't give a damn either way. Anything's better than sittin' around forever."

"Finally decided to become my cheerleader, then?"

Modri growled. *"All I'm sayin' is, you're doin' good. Y'know, all things considered. And I dunno how much help I'll be when it comes to all this mind shit, but I'll do my best. Better than havin' you listen to these nutjobs twenty-four-seven."*

"Still convinced guns can fix everything, huh?"

"That Accretion sonofabitch woulda gone down nice and easy with a frag round to the skull."

I shrugged. "We can agree on that."

"Alright, enough softie chat," he grumbled. *"What'd you call me up for?"*

"A woman."

"Where?"

"No, it's—" I sighed. "It's about Akasha."

"Bit of an age gap, but good choice nonetheless."

"Oh, screw you. You get what I mean."

"Nah, not really," Modri said. *"She put a hand on you and said some more of her witchy alien talk. So, what's the question?"*

"That's just it. Something's different about her, but I can't figure it out."

"Do you need to? She's an alien. An old-ass alien."

"I just . . . aw, Halcius, this is awkward. I don't have any experience with women, okay? So, I just need your take on things. Do you think she was *really* making a move on me?"

"Maybe she was impregnatin' your soul or somethin' like that."

"Helpful."

"Hey, what the hell do I know? She ain't a normal woman, Purifier. I know normal women. This one girl back on—"

"I'll stop you right there. Just . . . give me your honest opinion. Was that a platonic touch, or did it mean something more?"

"Platonic touch? The fuck is that?"

I rolled my eyes. "Was it friendly, or romantic?"

"You want my honest take?"

"That's why I called you up."

"Alright. You ask me, I think she might be gettin' on your good side to fuck you over."

My stomach dropped. I didn't know what I'd expected Modri to say, being the maverick he was, but *that* wasn't it.

"What the hell do you mean?"

"You're sharper than that, Purifier. C'mon, now. From the jump, she made it damn clear that she doesn't care what happens to you. For her, this whole damn thing's about gettin' revenge on the Unmade and wipin' out every chok'tal in the 'verse. Now she's suddenly tryin' to buddy up, play it soft and gentle-like? I ain't buyin' it."

"She could've killed me back on Kagu-9."

"And why didn't she? To take you here, to her monk buddies."

"So what?"

"That's my point. I dunno. It's just a hunch, I guess. Seems mighty suspicious that she'd show her big ol' heart the night before you're going out for this trial."

"What exactly are you saying? You think she's trying to brainwash me or something?"

Modri gave a noncommittal grunt. *"All I'm sayin' is, keep your eyes open. Neither of us knows what these weirdos really* want *in the end. Or what they'll do to you to keep you in-line."*

"Weren't you pushing for me to hook up with her like, a day ago?"

"Nothin' wrong with a little sleepin' with the enemy."

All I could do was groan. "Thanks. Your 'advice' has somehow twisted my head even farther around."

"That's what I'm here for." After a brief chuckle and then a more somber pause, Modri added, *"I'm always on your team, Purifier. Not just 'cause I'm forced to be—hell, that's a big part of it—but 'cause we're brothers in arms. You watch my six, I watch yours."*

I stared out at the sunlit fields, nodding absently. "I appreciate it more than you know."

"So, uh . . . are you gonna hush me again?"

"Considering I'm about to undergo a high-stakes trial with Akasha, your sworn frenemy? You bet I am."

He let out a bitter laugh. *"Oh, you fu—"*

Just like that, I sentenced Modri to another stint in hush-jail. Then I continued to sit there, watching my myriad thoughts about life and death tumble about like dead leaves on the wind. For all his brashness and "quirky" outlooks, Modri was still the closest thing I had to a friend. His counsel was valuable, even if it wasn't always what I wanted to hear. He had a way of cutting through bullshit and seeing the truth—or at least, some drunkard's version of it. Sometimes that was just what I needed.

Here and now, though, I hoped he hadn't dropped a truth bomb on me. Although Akasha wasn't nearly as close to me as Modri, both in physical and emotional regards, she was still an ally I had come to trust with my life. We'd endured bruises, defeats, and victories at one another's side. Moreover, we shared the strange yet intimate bond of having had our lives ruined by the Unmade.

But was that really enough? What if Modri was right, and I was just indulging in the naïveté of a clone who'd never developed street smarts? When viewed from the right angle, it seemed obvious that she was taking advantage of me. Perhaps *using* me was more accurate. Either way, the repercussions were the same: If it turned out that she was just an exceptionally skilled manipulator, a sleeper agent who'd been tasked with securing my participation in the order's prophecy, it would break me.

Eventually, I got up and proceeded to the lower terraces. Sitting in one spot and thinking too much wasn't doing my mental health any good. Once I'd reached a stone bench with a nice view of the southern forests, I plopped down and decided to go through with my rank-up. I had *plenty* of Storehouse Time to hedge any scheduling mistakes, but it was best to be proactive and avoid dipping into that reservoir.

STATUS DISPLAY
PURIFIER RANK: 11
RANK-UP AVAILABLE: RANK 12 (409,600 KP required)

Kill Points: 888,400
Genofacturing Points: 27,340

Rank Points: 0

Rank Time: 2 Hours, 39 Minutes, 4 Seconds
Storehouse Time: 22 Hours, 20 Minutes, 0 Seconds

Anima: 320%
Dominion: 0/4

Naturally, I triggered the rank-up. Then I took another glance at the Status Display to see if there were any major changes.

STATUS DISPLAY
PURIFIER RANK: 12
RANK-UP NOT AVAILABLE (819,200 KP required)

Kill Points: 0
Genofacturing Points: 506,140

Rank Points: 1

Rank Time: 21 Hours, 59 Minutes, 56 Seconds
Storehouse Time: 22 Hours, 20 Minutes, 0 Seconds

Anima: 340%
Dominion: 0/5

As it turned out, there were several. The most obvious was my staggering amount of Genofacturing Points, which would surely come in handy for crafting the Kill Point-boosting tonics I'd had my eye on—not to mention a new set of sweet, sweet gear. By Halcius, I missed high-powered assault rifles.

Next was my Anima, which had jumped (predictably) another 20 percent. Nothing major. And last, but not least, I'd finally gained another Dominion point. Then again, that didn't mean much to me—not yet, anyhow. Any situation where I'd need to activate five powers at once was probably too far gone to be salvageable.

That was the good news. The *bad* news, as you might've guessed, was the absurd Kill Point requirement for Rank 13. Granted, I'd just gotten nearly that amount from one kill, but that had been an exceptional situation. The odds of farming nearly a million KP from assorted animals, Sparkseed-corrupted or not, were frighteningly low. But maybe the monks had a plan for that.

Not wanting to dwell too long on my daunting task, I switched to the task of assigning the Rank Point. Narbu's assurance that I'd be able to further train my mental faculties made it a fairly easy choice. Telekinesis had already saved my ass several times, and its description of the third and final rank—which promised a "strong" quantum link—was too tempting to ignore.

Without another moment's hesitation, I acquired the ultimate form of Telekinesis.

My next Rank Point was already spoken for, of course. The instant I hit Rank 13, I'd throw that point straight into Soaring Death. Wings, baby. Wings.

I closed the Status Display, leaned back, and drank in a long breath of morning air. Things were good. Placid. But before I could enjoy the moment *too* much, I noticed a flash in the sky far, far above me. It was brief, much like a shooting star, and faded before I could get a look at it. At that moment, I didn't think much of it. But I urge you to remember it.

Because that was the flash that changed everything.

Had I focused more on that puny flash, I might've understood what it *really* was. Might've even been able to prevent the catastrophe that followed. But alas, my focus was stolen by a familiar voice calling my name.

I turned to find Akasha, who'd switched out her snow-white robes for a set of black leather armor and what appeared to be a pelt-based cloak. Sheathed at her side was a long, thin blade reminiscent of a rapier. In one instant, the strange flash was forgotten.

"I hope you're ready," she said, approaching me with a thin smile that vanished as soon as I'd turned around. "Though it appears you are not."

For several moments, I just opened and closed my mouth, trying to stammer out a reply. It was virtually impossible to take her seriously when she looked like a dragon-slaying maiden straight out of some leisure-sim game.

Finally, I gathered my wits. "What are you wearing?"

"Armor."

"I'm aware it's armor. But . . . what is *that* armor?"

"It is a traditional set gifted to outsiders," she said, sounding somewhat offended by my tone. "To be precise, it is *my* armor set. The monks refurbished it in honor of my return."

"Guess they don't crank out any new models, huh?"

Akasha grimaced. "It will fulfill its intended purpose."

"Why are you wearing it now?"

"The trial, of course."

"Wait—the trial is starting *now*?"

My "joke" about having to duel Akasha to the death suddenly felt far too feasible.

"The parting ceremony is set to begin, yes," she said gravely, gesturing to something down below.

I leaned over the terrace's edge to find a contingent of monks gathered at the main gates, all kneeling in the same manner as when I'd first arrived. Scryer Narbu and Brother Tekshim stood proudly in the center of the gathering.

Akasha nudged a large cloth bag against my arm, drawing my attention. "I suspected you might squander your time. As such, I assumed the role of preparations myself."

Squinting, I took the bag from her. It was *heavy*. Much heavier than she'd implied by holding it as though it were a sack of feathers.

"What is this?" I asked.

"Rations and armor," she explained. "The latter may not provide comfort, but it will protect your flesh."

I stared down at the bag with disgust, not the least bit excited to look inside. "Great. More costumes."

"*Armor*, not a costume."

Smirking, I let the bag drop to my waist and walked past her. "Call it what you like. I'm not putting this on until I need it."

17

Within ten minutes, we were standing at the front gates with Narbu and his assembled crowd. The feeling in the air was uneasy, charged, as though we were fresh-faced soldiers being sent off to a war we couldn't imagine. This impression was only deepened by the somber look on every monk's face. Only Narbu, the wisest yet most detached of the brothers, managed to retain an uplifting expression.

"The time has come for the trial of the Third Perfection . . . the Perfection of Insight," he said, his voice's vibrations nearly dissolving me on account of how loudly and theatrically he addressed the audience. "On this day, reality itself will decide if you have achieved mastery of the Lower Perfections. Your mind and its karma will aid you—or destroy you."

I watched Narbu carefully as he spoke, trying to decipher the exact cause of his cheery mood. Was it an ordinary part of the sending-off ceremony for everyone who attempted the trial, or was it something special, prepared just for me? I'd seen the same glee in his eyes every time I took a step toward my destiny as the order's champion. Perhaps this was the moment his centuries of effort and struggle led up to. The moment when my triumph became his.

At my side, Akasha stood and listened with clear reverence. She nodded sharply at the conclusion of each sentence, much like a sparrow jabbing its beak into the soil for fat worms. Regardless of my own feelings and fears, she was plainly invested in this spectacle.

It made sense, I supposed. She'd already told me about her prior failure to master the Third Perfection. Although I didn't know how or why she hadn't gone the full distance, it wasn't hard to imagine that a strict perfectionist like her might've been itching to finish the job ever since she left the planet. This was her chance to redeem the past.

Of course, that also led me down new avenues of thought while Narbu's speech continued—most of them caused by Modri's fearmongering. What *was* Akasha's role in all this? Was she some sort of sacred teacher for me? A guardian angel? If she really was somehow involved with the monastery's prophecy, what did it matter if she mastered all the Perfections on her own?

I didn't know, and wasn't sure I wanted to.

"Your task is specific," Narbu went on, drawing my focus. "It begins with this. The key to the sacrament."

He knelt down before us, then opened his massive palm to reveal two small satchels. Akasha and I shared a look before approaching, retrieving our respective bag, and stepping back.

I jangled the satchel a little in my grip, but I didn't get much info from it. The thing felt light, almost empty. My only "clue" as to its contents was the sound of soft shushing as *stuff* collided and shuffled around.

Akasha's glare put a stop to my investigation.

"With the sacrament's key in hand, you will make your way to the spine of the Scholar's Ascent." Narbu turned to the mountain range behind the monastery, gesturing up at a precarious, snow-capped peak that dazzled in the sunlight. "There, you will consume the sacrament and commune with the Throne. Should you survive, your trial will be considered complete." His gaze swiveled toward Akasha. "Remember your fated path. Let your steps be true, and heed the voice of the Absolute."

It took me a moment to put the pieces together. Once I did, my stomach lurched.

He wanted us to climb, without maps or bougie survival gear, to one of the highest elevation points in the entire region. He *then* wanted us to consume whatever the hell was in the satchels so we could directly interface with the Throne and its dormant radiance (AKA, I guess, the Wellspring). To some, this description might sound like a fantastic time. A hike and merging with a godhead—what could be better? But I was too sharp to think that way. Already, I detected the inherent danger of this trial.

Like I mentioned before, the order wouldn't have designed an easy, relaxing task to serve as its final test of power and mental control. Instead, they'd have put together a hellish gauntlet that surpassed all the challenges that had preceded it. Narbu's simple and straightforward instructions put me on edge. What was he hiding?

Before my mind could cobble together an answer, Scryer Narbu clapped, and the gathered monks began humming their ethereal song. All around us, heads bowed and hands joined in prayer.

Akasha turned to me and nodded, signaling that we'd been dismissed. That was that.

We turned and headed off into the fields, following the thin, overgrown game trail that looped around the monastery's walls and extended to the base of the mountains. Before long we were completely immersed in an ocean of tall red grass, our vision restricted to the sky and the soaring peaks ahead.

Neither of us spoke for a good while—which isn't to say it was quiet by any means. Between the omnipresent rustle of the fields, the chittering of hidden insects, and our boots scraping over dusty soil, it felt as though there was hardly any space for words.

That didn't stop my mind from engaging in spirited discussions with itself, however. I still had no idea what to make of Akasha and her sketchy connections to the order. Kilometer by kilometer, more half-baked conspiracy theories swelled up for analysis. What if Akasha had already passed this trial, and had only been sent as my escort to ensure I followed some vital step in the prophecy? What if Akasha's people had *created* the robotic monks? What if . . .

The thoughts went on and on, dimming every so often when I actively reminded myself to keep calm. Even though the hypothetical scenarios I cooked up were frightening, even nauseating, they were also just that—hypothetical. When I looked at the actual reality of my situation, it was considerably less urgent. All that *really* existed around me were trees, mountains, clouds, and dirt. If there was a master plan being hatched under my nose, I'd deal with it when the time came.

Until then, my task was clear. One foot in front of the other.

Time wore on in a gradual, silent procession, its passage marked only by the overhead passage of the system's star. Well, that and the change in scenery. At some point—one which I cannot specify, due to the gradient nature of the terrain—we rose out of the fields and into the low, wooded foothills ringing the mountain range.

Up here, the air was fresh and slightly brisk. Towering trees surrounded us on all sides, obscuring both the grass far below and the peaks high above. Our only real guide was a trail that had been stamped into the soil over countless years of pilgrimages. Occasionally, this trail veered into steep switchbacks or took us past overlooks that allowed us to gauge our progress. Always in silence, of course. Akasha was deep in contemplation about . . . something . . . and I was out of breath more often than not.

Before I knew it, our shadows had stretched into long tails at our backs. The sky turned to a clear, dark blue in anticipation of dusk. Weird birdsongs filled the darkening forest.

"We should stop and make camp," Akasha said at last.

I struggled up the last of a rocky rise, panting as I came to her side. "Here?"

"It is as good a place as any." She glanced around, her gaze eventually settling on a relatively clear expanse of granite protected by an overhang. "Do you know how to construct a fire?"

"Do we need one?"

Akasha nodded. "Even the foothills grow frigid in the darkness. My body will compensate, but yours may not."

"I can tough it out. I'm not too keen on attracting whatever the hell dwells in these woods."

"As you wish." She moved over to the designated spot, dropped her bags, and sat down with prim posture. "Perhaps we should work on your meditation technique."

Scrunching up my face, I moved over to her and dropped my own gear in an unceremonious heap. Then I flopped down on the rock and let all the breath drain out of my body. After countless hours of putting one foot in front of the other, navigating streams and branches and stones, exhaustion slammed into me with a vengeance.

"I appreciate the gesture," I said, groaning, "but I think I'd prefer a nap."

"Rest is—"

"Poison for the mind," I cut in. "I get it."

Akasha grimaced. "No. Rest is aversion to fatigue. It is a cousin of death."

"Death sounds pretty relaxing right about now."

For several minutes, Akasha just studied me, her lips shifting with obvious annoyance. Then she straightened and cleared her throat. "You may not have chosen this course, but it is your karmic fruit. The only decision is whether to embrace the suffering or flee from it. The first option will send you to the lowest hells . . . while the latter will liberate you."

"Now you sound like Narbu."

"Because he teaches the dharma of the Wellspring," she said. "The Great Way. Such teachings are rare, and vanish from the many worlds on a regular basis."

"Yeah, well, if rebirth is real, maybe I can catch it on the next cycle."

Akasha's nostrils flared. "It is a blessing, not a guarantee, to practice the dharma of the awakened ones. Why do you insist on making light of your duty?"

"We've been over this."

"We have, and I showed you compassion. But my patience is not infinite, Dak."

That lit a fire under me. Anger swelled in my chest, red-hot and pulsing. I sat up and glared straight at Akasha.

"*Your* patience?" I growled. "Do you have any idea what it's like, trying to live up to the expectations of beings that have existed for millions of years? To have your whole life stripped away, only to be thrown into an even deeper pit when you try to figure it out? I'm sure you don't. And you never will."

Akasha's face relaxed by degrees. "You see your life as punishment. I see it as a miracle."

"Get real."

"It is the truth. You've been touched by a powerful being. Defiled or not, such an event is incalculably precious. If you succeed in this quest, you will purify the minds of countless beings."

"My quest to die for enlightenment, right?"

A genuine flash of concern moved across her face. "I do not understand."

"Oh, come off it. That's what the order wants. They expect me to beat the Unmade, die, and spend the rest of eternity trapped inside . . . something. The whole goddamn thing is already written. It doesn't matter what I do, does it?"

"I . . ." Her lips tightened. "It doesn't . . ."

Suddenly, the situation flipped. I sensed in Akasha the same floundering, mind-breaking confusion that had overcome me in the repository. She wasn't surprised at having been caught; she was just surprised.

"How did you learn this?" she whispered.

"That's not important," I said, quieter now. "The real question is, did you know?"

"Of course not."

"Don't lie to me, Akasha. Please."

"I didn't know." The rapid rise and fall of her chest backed up her words.

"But you had to know *something*, right? None of this was accidental. When you brought me here, it was—"

"An attempt to atone," she interjected.

I frowned. "Huh?"

"You are correct, in a limited sense. I did not bring you to this world through chance. It was an attempt to tame a Purifier's mind, yes, but not purely for my own comfort."

"I'm more confused than ever."

Akasha drew a deep breath, staring out at the shadowed woods as she did so. "My first journey to this world was far from coincidental. As I explained to you, I had been hunting and destroying the chok'tal for many years with the aid of my people's artifact. On one occasion, the artifact sensed a strong, corrupted presence emanating from this planet. I followed the signal to its source—at least, as near as I could get. Even the artifact is not precise enough to locate one being's presence beyond a radius of several hundred kilometers."

"Okay," I said, nodding and somewhat encouraged by the seeds of an explanation. "So, you came to this world to find a chok'tal, but couldn't pinpoint it."

"Yes," she said, nodding in turn. "During my search, I encountered the monastery and its order. I told them of my purpose, and was relieved when I discovered that they shared my ambitions to rid the universe of the Unmade's scourge. They offered training of the mind, and I readily accepted."

"No offense, but that's more or less what I'd already gathered. Well, except the way you found the planet, anyhow."

She raised a hand, urging silence. I obeyed. "It eventually became apparent that the monastic order was not disclosing the entire truth, however. There were several areas I could not enter. Strange auras that interrupted my meditation. Whispers among trusted brothers. For decades upon decades, I trusted their explanations. Until I no longer could."

I scooted closer as the tension built.

"Several days before I was due to attempt this very trial, Scryer Narbu summoned me. He explained that he had something of vital importance to reveal. Given all I had learned and my dutiful nature, I was eager to follow him." Her face darkened, though it had little to do with the waning daylight around us. "Scryer Narbu unsealed a chamber at the center of the monastery. Inside, I found what had originally drawn me to this world."

My eyes went wide. "A chok'tal?"

"More than that," she said quietly. "The order had been training a Purifier for countless years. Through ritual combat and painstaking calculations, they were able to create a champion with power I had never seen."

"Oh, shit."

She nodded. "Upon seeing the Purifier, my training dissolved. I could not maintain evenness of mind, nor an attitude of discernment and restraint. Before I could stop myself, I went forth and slew the Purifier."

Akasha lowered her head, drowning in some unknown memory. I didn't have the heart (or the breath) to butt in.

"Scryer Narbu was furious," she said finally. "Even so, he had compassion for my rash behavior. He forced me to hear of the order's grand design—a project to remake a Purifier's mind, to use them as a weapon against their creator. In his eyes, it was vital that I agreed with the aims of their prophecy."

"This Purifier . . ." I said, choosing my words delicately. "Were they evil?"

She shook her head. "My last memory of that being is their smile. I claimed their life before I had learned anything about them. Gripped by rage, I saw nothing more than the face of the destroyers that had ravaged my world." After a brief pause, she looked away. "Scryer Narbu begged me to help rebuild what I had decimated. He stated that I had a role to play in this journey, and that there was no other end to this miserable cycle. But I could not bear his words. I was overwhelmed by the sense of betrayal. For centuries, I had called these brothers my family. I had trusted in their teachings, their hearts, their truths. But no longer could I abide their plans. I left the same night."

"And you wandered," I said with as much tact as possible. "You wandered until you found . . . me."

Akasha gazed skyward, her lips churning with repressed emotion. "I did not want to believe that the order was correct. It felt wrong, even heretical, to conceive of a Purifier that could restore dignity to this fallen universe. Yet within you, I sensed the portents the order had described. The prophetic signs were too obvious to ignore."

"So, you delivered me to them," I said, more in shock than anger. "You used me as a replacement for the Purifier you killed."

Her head snapped toward me. "Not a replacement," she said quickly. "I see now that you were always meant to take up the mantle. In hindsight, I understand why Narbu did not exile me . . . why he was far from dismayed by the death of their prior champion."

"You think that Purifier was just a training run?"

"Perhaps. When we arrived yesterday, it was as though the Scryer had already seen it in a vision. Your presence was no surprise to him."

"Yeah," I said faintly, "I noticed that, too."

"I seek your forgiveness, Dak. I did not mean to deceive you."

"Thanks." I swallowed past the lump in my throat. "I just wish you would've told me on your own."

"That is the danger of prophecy. By learning of its course, one may destroy that which has not yet come to pass."

"You believe in it, then," I said. "You really do think I'm the one."

"It is possible."

"What about the enlightenment thing? Did you know I have to die? That they expect me to be trapped inside some kind of superorganism?"

She shook her head fiercely. "Scryer Narbu told me only of your destiny to reach enlightenment. He said nothing of the method through which this might occur."

"But . . . do you believe it? Do you think I'll really have to die for this to work?"

"If I knew, I would tell you. But as I have said, the threads of destiny are slick with blood. If you have learned this information through your own channels, it is impossible to say how the future might be altered."

"That's what I'm thinking, too," I said, sliding even closer as a chill breeze swept through the forest. "If I'm being honest, selfish or not, I want to find a way to make it out alive. Even if that *does* make me just another humanoid."

"It is part of a sentient being's nature," she said in a strangely gentle tone. "That was why I comforted you last night, Dak. You've . . . changed my perception."

"Oh? How so?"

"When I slew the order's Purifier, I saw the chok'tal and their hosts as nothing but abominations. What I failed to realize was that despite their situation, there was still a sentient being within them. Where there is sentience, there is hope." She looked at me sidelong. "Still, it is not easy to show tenderness to you."

"Because of what the Unmade did to your people."

She bobbed her head about, indicating that I was *almost* there, but not quite. "Do you know why my people wore these blindfolds, Dak?"

"Maybe 'cause your eyes are lasers?"

"We blamed ourselves for the appearance of the Unmade. It was our desire to see beyond the veils of reality . . . to know that which mortals were not meant to know. We hid our defiled sight to restrain the passions." She sighed. "Now I believe that our blindness did more than take away temptation. It robbed us of sight, of empathy." Looking toward me, she said, "If I open my heart to you—if I truly see you as an innocent being with the potential of an awakened one—I am overcome by the guilt of what I have done."

"You shouldn't think that way."

"Perhaps I should," she whispered. "I claimed the lives of every Purifier I encountered. They were not sentient beings to me, but akin to insects. Rodents. Now that I have seen the light of the Absolute in you, I must acknowledge that it also existed within them."

"That's different," I said hotly, surprised to be defending her Purifier-killing practices. "You said it yourself, Akasha. They went off the deep end. They were killing for sport."

"And what was I doing? Their deaths gave me great satisfaction."

"It's . . . not the same."

"In the eyes of Scryer Narbu, it is. I cannot disagree with his conclusion. To take life in anger, no matter how justified, is unskillful. It leaves stains upon the mind."

I scoffed. "If we use that logic, then it was also *bad* to have saved me from Chanzig."

Akasha lowered her head. "All I know, with certainty, is that I am glad to have brought you here. The order sees a clear course for you. Even if they are not forthcoming . . . even if they view your body's death as necessary . . . they are acting out of compassion. They will not let the evils of this world overcome you."

"Maybe," I said, picking up and tossing away the twigs around my boots. "Where I'm from, letting someone die for you isn't very kind."

"You presume this life is the only one."

"It's the only one I can prove. I can feel it, taste it, hear it. Rebirth? Who knows?"

She gave a soft smile in the fading light. "Allow me to expand upon what I told you last night, Dak. No matter where your course leads, or what hells you come across, I will be with you. I will not close my heart. Even if it entails the destruction of my own mind and body, I will not draw your blood, for I have seen that the Spark's wisdom resides in you. I must have faith that it will overcome the evils that claimed your brethren. Your fate is mine. Your karma is mine."

I stared at her for a moment, trying to make out her muddy features as the gloom thickened and smudged the details around me. Even in that faint light, I saw the tender, vulnerable aspect she had worked to suppress for so long. I saw the quiver in her lips. I've never been one to believe in "miracles," but what else could explain the seismic shift in her mind? To go from hunting down and eliminating Purifiers to pledging your very existence to one . . . it was unthinkable.

"That means more than you know," I said, barely above a whisper.

She looked away, but stole a few glances while wearing a shy, awkward smile. "Perhaps it is what my people would have wanted. To see something good emerge from so much pain."

"I'm sure they're proud of you."

"It is my hope," she said. "One day, if such a thing ever becomes possible, I will release them from their cube. Then they can speak freely about how I have fared."

Even Akasha's voice bore the weight of her responsibility. The weight of caring for an entire species, an entire legacy that only lived on through her. Such a burden would've driven most humanoids insane long ago.

"You can't think too much about that," I said, resting a tentative hand on her knee. She looked down at it, but otherwise gave no reaction. "Your people wanted you to survive and pass on their history. You've done that. You do it every day by getting up and breathing."

"That is not enough to repay their sacrifice."

"Sacrifice? Akasha, look at me." She did. "They chose to upload their minds to that cube, and they chose *you* to stay in the real world and take care of them. If you ask me, it was selfish."

Her breathing grew heavier. "They did it for noble reasons. They—"

I raised a hand, cutting her off. "Whatever reasons you give, it doesn't change reality. They abandoned you to this fate. And when they did that, they surrendered any right to judge you. What you do in this world, this life . . . it's your decision. So, if you want to help me, I'll gladly accept it—but don't do it out of guilt. You don't owe your people anything."

She nodded absently for a few moments, then said, "You humans have a very peculiar sense of individual freedom."

"I wouldn't call myself a spokesman for your average human. Especially given . . . well, you know. Everything."

Akasha lifted her chin and angled toward me. In the gathering dusk, which was now thick enough to obscure everything but the silhouette of her head, I felt as though we'd locked eyes. Impossible, I know, on account of her blindfold, but still. There was a firm yet unspoken link between us. This was cemented when I felt her hand press atop mine.

Without conscious thought, I found myself drifting closer to her. Her face, in turn, moved toward mine. Soon I felt her warm breath on my cheek, then the slight static of skin about to meet skin, and—

A twig cracked in the nearby brush.

Both of us went on instant alert, jerking back with bated breath and scanning our surroundings.

There wasn't much to see, given the exponentially thickening darkness, but it wasn't hard to locate the origin of the noise. More and more foliage rustled, snapped, and swished on the other side of the trail, each sound drawing incrementally nearer. Ordinarily, I'd have assumed it was just an animal scouring for food. This wasn't ordinary, though. The footfalls were too heavy, too clumsy, and they approached with the gait of a bipedal creature. A humanoid, to be precise.

Akasha's hand slipped off of mine and drifted toward her waist, where she kept some sort of small blade I'd seen intermittently during our trek.

"Wait," I whispered, squinting into the shadows in hopes my eyes would adjust. "Let's not overreact just yet."

Akasha said nothing, but her hand went to her lap.

A few seconds later, there was a new sound: a voice. Though faint at first, the speaker's words gradually pressed through the forest until they were plainly audible. They were speaking in the common tongue . . . and humanoid, it seemed.

". . . much farther," the newcomer—a gravel-voiced man—said. "These maps aren't worth the damn pixels they're made of."

"I said we should stop in the basin," another man replied, his tone higher and more trepid.

"We *know*," a third man said in an imperious, borderline disgusted tone befitting royalty. "Have you not heard of a deadline, Sekris?"

"Of course, I have," the second man, Sekris, huffed back. "This armor's rented by the day. How could I forget?"

"You forgot the last rendezvous point," the first man growled.

"Well, that was different . . . I—"

The third man groaned. "Oh, shut *up*. You're both insufferable."

Akasha and I sat perfectly still as the three men drew nearer, their voices and footsteps placing them at less than a hundred paces away. The urge to stand, find a decent spot, and prepare an ambush was strong, but the logical part of me knew that was just a carryover impulse from my time on Kagu-9. Not every humanoid was a threat. Most of the universe, I told myself, was probably half-decent.

Soon enough, dim, pale lights illuminated the foliage ahead of us, carving out the shapes of massive fronds and tangled thorn bushes. The three wanderers were on a direct collision course with our "camp."

Again, Akasha's hand went to her hip.

"Just hold on," I whispered, grabbing her wrist before she could do anything rash. "They might be friendly."

Before Akasha could reply, the overgrowth across the trail shifted and parted. The silhouettes of all three men came into view, though they obviously didn't see us in turn. Three humans. As I'd gauged from their conversation, they were all wearing armor. What I hadn't expected, though, were the clunky, gadget-laden assault rifles slung over their shoulders and nestled in their arms. Their massive rucksacks and half-face masks didn't put me at ease, either.

Suddenly, one of the men stopped short and pointed his rifle directly at me, blinding me in a wash of silver light. Neon blue boxes sprang up around all three men in turn.

Armed Stranger (HUMANOID) (3)
CALCULATING . . .
Estimated Kill Points: 36,600

18

Within a microsecond, I was primed for battle, adrenaline pumping and legs tensing in preparation for an all-out charge. Akasha's hand went darting for her blade.

But this proved unnecessary.

"For fuck's sake, Sekris," the third man hissed, immediately slapping down the barrel of his comrade's rifle. Blackness reigned as my vision struggled to readjust. "What the hell are you thinking? You could've killed them."

Despite the obvious danger of the situation, the man's rebuke took some of the steam out of me. Akasha, too, seemed to settle, though her hand didn't retreat from the folds of her cloak. We shared an uneasy glance.

"I'm terribly sorry," the same man said, striding forth with his rifle slung over his shoulder. "My *companion* has grown somewhat twitchy in recent days. These are dangerous wilds, as I'm sure you've observed."

I cocked a brow while studying Sekris, who was currently receiving a tongue-lashing from the burlier man in their group. "We certainly have."

The third man, who was about halfway to us, stopped on the trail. "My name is Oklen Fir, and these are my comrades, Sekris and Jalvar. May . . . I approach?"

Though I kept my gaze trained on Oklen, I sensed Akasha looking at me out of the corner of my eye. I was just as wary as her, but I resisted showing that in any form. Weakness tended to breed trouble in situations like this.

"Mind telling us why you're here?" I asked. "And what you need the guns for?"

Oklen hefted his rifle, simultaneously offering a dramatic scoff that suggested his rifle was nothing more than a toy. "This old thing? Ah, well, it's for protection. Terribly aggressive local fauna and whatnot." He glanced back at his companions. "As for why we're here . . . we're surveyors."

I squinted. "Surveyors?"

"That's right. We've been hired by the Melku-Tan Corporation to inspect this region and provide a report on its precious metal content. Just contractors, you see—no corporate lackeys here—so we're keen to get it done as soon as possible."

Again, Akasha and I exchanged a look. There wasn't much expressed in the look, but plenty was said nonetheless. The tension in her face, revealed by the indirect glow of the men's flashlights, all but confirmed that she didn't trust a word out of these people. I, on the other hand, wasn't so cynical. The strangers seemed opportunistic, even a bit dimwitted, but they didn't have the same stench of evil or malice or fanaticism that had characterized Chanzig's forces.

This being the case, it felt like the perfect time to practice that "compassion" schtick I'd heard so much about in the monastery. For all I knew, these men were exactly like us—tired, confused, and hoping to avoid being murdered in the woods.

"Where are you headed?" I asked.

"Hard to explain," Oklen said, almost apologetically. "You see, we have a large number of mineral vein and fracking sites to visit, but they're not arranged in a linear fashion. As such, we're . . . roaming, you might say. We're currently heading to a site along the mountain ridge. Assuming we can locate it."

My internal alarms remained deactivated. Minute by minute, it seemed more obvious that these men weren't killers—just greedy freelancers working for yet another mega-corporation with an interest in the planet's more "exotic" metals. Not much different from any other humanoids on this world, I supposed. After all, Akasha and the monks had already described the somewhat volatile situation related to the extraction of Sparkseed. Viewed through that lens, it made perfect sense that three men wandering through the forest would be packing high-powered weapons and bulky armor for their own defense.

"Forgive me for being direct," I said with a quick glance at Akasha, "but is there something we can help you with? We're on our own course."

Oklen moved a tad closer, prompting Akasha's arm to move deeper into her cloak. He either didn't notice or didn't care. "Ah, how exciting. Where are you headed?"

"Up," Akasha said flatly.

He nodded. "I . . . see. How pleasant. Well, we didn't expect to encounter anybody here, but we're certainly overjoyed to discover you aren't dangerous. Aren't we, gentlemen?" He looked back at his companions, both of whom offered distracted nods. Returning his attention to us, he continued, "Now that we've run into one another, what do you say about establishing a small camp? We have lights, heating coils, food, and even rough shelters. We'd be happy to share."

Before I could speak, Akasha butted in. "Why?"

Although Oklen appeared somewhat taken aback by this—through his eyes, at least, considering his mouth was concealed by the dark half-mask—he quickly recovered and gave a charming laugh. "We've found it important to enjoy the numerical advantage of groups whenever possible. There's quite a culture of camaraderie on this world, you see. Hospitality, you might say."

Subconsciously, I wasn't certain it was a great idea to be sharing a sleeping space with armed men we'd just met. Again, I considered that fear to be a holdover from my past troubles. Oklen's explanation made sense, and I had the feeling that he'd have simply gunned me down already if he wanted any valuables—or Akasha. Instead, he'd put his neck on the line by walking over and keeping his weapon slung back. It had to count for something.

"That . . . sounds reasonable," I said at last, ignoring the pointed looks Akasha shot my way. "We'd be happy to share the site for the evening, though we don't have much . . . well, any . . . food on us."

"Not a problem at all," Oklen said. "We'll share our rations. Our treat."

And with that, the HUD's blue boxes disappeared.

ENCOUNTER FAILED

For once, I was glad to see that message.

The three men wasted no time in joining us beneath the overhang. With speed that spoke to plenty of nights in the field, they plopped down their rucksacks, dumped out the vital contents, and turned to the task of deploying the essentials: namely, a central heating coil for cooking and military-grade pop-up tents. They worked in tandem as a well-oiled team, pausing intermittently only to bicker or criticize one another.

Meanwhile, Akasha and I just rested up against the rock, studying them and their strange dynamic. Akasha was most certainly pissed at me, but that could be dealt with later. It wasn't like there was any hope of resuming our hot-and-heavy connection tonight.

This being the case, I turned my full attention to getting a read on these guys. It wasn't that I didn't trust them, but rather I was interested in prying information out of them. They might know if there'd been a Hegemony presence in the system, for example, or where to find overgrown beasties for Kill Point farming.

Oklen was plainly the leader, barking out orders whenever Sekris or Jalvar appeared devoid of a task. He was right in the middle of the group, size-wise, lacking Jalvar's towering bulk and dwarfing Sekris' rail-thin, stunted frame. It seemed obvious that he'd risen to a leadership role not through force, but through cutting wit, charisma, and his highborn accent, which marked him as *some* sort of Hegemony citizen. Not a capital world inhabitant, maybe, but close.

Curiously enough, all three men were bald. Well, it *seemed* curious, until Oklen himself directly addressed the issue. He must've noticed me staring at his barren scalp, which gleamed in the light of Jalvar's freshly activated heating coil. Rubbing his head and laughing, he said, "Gene scrapers. Can never be too careful."

In all honesty, I had no idea what the hell that meant, but I just nodded and smiled anyway. I was in no mood to interrogate the men or draw excessive attention to us. After all, we'd just been given free access to heat, shelter, blankets, and food. Time to shut up and be happy.

Within a half-hour, full dark had arrived. We all sat in a circle around the pulsing coil, basking in its waves of dry, stale heat. Its reddish glow gave form to the rock beneath us, the mottled wall of the overhang, and, most importantly, the faces of the three men.

In what I took to be a friendly gesture, they'd removed their half-masks. Of course, it was also possible that they'd simply removed them to eat and drink. Whatever the case, I was glad to get a decent look at them. The eyes are often touted as the windows to the soul, but in my experience, the mouth is what you want to watch. Plenty of suppressed emotion winds up spilling out through the quirk of one's lips.

Yet for all my analysis, I couldn't detect anything nefarious there, either. The three men had gaunt, stubble-coated cheeks, indicating they'd spent the last few weeks doing little more than navigating the treacherous wilderness and marking locations for their employer.

"There we go," Sekris said, greedily rubbing his hands together and plucking the strips of mystery meat off the coil's top plate. He was practically salivating as he divvied up the charred, sizzling-fat portions, which were then stuffed inside flatbread and passed around the group with a flask of carbonated water. "Best meat this side of the Eurondes Belt, lemme tell you."

Jalvar grunted as he bit into his meal. "He tells that to everyone."

I nodded gratefully at Sekris as he handed off a portion for Akasha and I. When I passed the food to Akasha, though, her reaction was considerably more muted. She still didn't trust these strangers—not entirely surprising, given her social skills' decay in Chanzig's custody.

"So, where are you from?" Oklen asked me.

"Halcium Beta," I lied, trying to conceal my poor poker face with a bite of mystery meat. It was better than I'd anticipated.

Oklen's eyes lit up. "Really? A highborn, then?" He elbowed Jalvar. "See that? I told you he was highborn. Purple eyes . . . never lie."

"Is it true that they've got fountains of liquid gold over there?" Sekris asked.

I took another bite and chewed at length. "Wouldn't know. I moved on a long time ago."

"A wanderer, just like us," Oklen said with a smile. "And what about your . . . friend?"

All eyes turned to Akasha, but she refused to cede an inch of ground. Her face resembled a slate carving.

"She's, uh, a traveling sage," I explained awkwardly. "I'm an archaeologist. We're looking for . . . ruins."

Oklen's warm smile didn't budge. "Religious ruins, I presume? Since your companion is a sage, after all."

"Yeah. Religious ruins."

"How marvelous." He set down his food and leaned over his knees, eyes gleaming with the heating coil's light. "Have you visited Aunor-2? There's been a lot of commotion there lately." Oklen must've noticed my puzzlement, because he quickly explained, "The other planet in the system. You know, the permawar one with the mechanized defenses. Supposedly a high-end ship crashed there the other day. It's big news among the scavenger packs."

My throat tensed, though it had nothing to do with the too-large chunk of mystery meat I'd bitten off. They were referring to *our* ship, which had previously been Chanzig's. It seemed word of its presence had spread like wildfire. And if these random surveyors knew about it, chances were good that the Hegemony also did.

"Haven't heard of it," I said quietly. "We tend to keep our heads down."

Oklen grunted in assent. "Preaching to the choir, friend. These can be dangerous parts, between the lunatics and the beasts. But my, oh, my, is it rich in resources. How much scandium did we find in the last zone, Jav?"

"Three tons," Jalvar grumbled.

"A princely amount!"

"Enough to eat good for a few months," Sekris added, under his breath.

Oklen shot him a glare, but soon returned his focus to me. "So, how did you arrive here? A private vessel, or one of the ferries that docks in a hub city?"

Taking a sip of water, I worked to prepare my answer. "A ferry."

"Which one?"

"I can't remember," I said, glancing at Akasha for backup I knew wouldn't arrive. "We haven't been here long. We'll probably move on soon, anyhow."

Oklen nodded. "What about the monastery in this valley?"

"Huh?" I asked, hoping my eyes didn't widen too much.

"The monastery. Since you're seeking out religious ruins, it might be of interest to you. Well, they're not *ruins*, per se, but . . ."

"No," I said, "we haven't been."

After that, there was silence for a time. We all sat in our worlds, chewing the rubbery mystery meat, sipping water, and staring at our laps. All except Akasha, that is. She sat with both food and drink untouched, head lowered as though in meditation.

Eventually, Oklen broke the stillness. "You haven't happened to have seen anything . . . weird around these parts, have you?"

I swallowed hard. "How do you mean?"

"Well, it's just . . . there have been some rumors of strange things taking place. Some sort of man with an alien parasite in him. Very powerful, very dangerous."

At this point, my mouth went completely dry. Aside from the monks, we hadn't encountered another sentient being capable of using language. How the hell would three random surveyors have found out there was a Purifier on the planet? Even if they didn't know anything directly, and had only heard the information from a third or fourth-hand source, it still indicated there was a leak somewhere.

"Can't say I have," I said, doing my best to appear baffled. "Where'd you hear that?"

"Oh, just around."

"Around where?"

Oklen's lip twitched. Just a touch, but enough to turn my stomach. "Never mind. It's really not important, is it? We'll be safe as a group."

Again, I looked over at Akasha, but what caught my attention had nothing to do with her—and everything to do with Oklen. In the corner of my vision, I saw his hand flick in a cutting motion. Then I spotted Sekris' subtle nod.

"Uh, just a moment," Sekris said, rising and fishing some sort of device out of his thigh pocket. "I think it's our boss. Corporate life calls. You know how it is . . ."

I watched him with mounting interest as he stepped out of the illuminated circle and into the darkness of the forest beyond.

Oklen shifted his head and waved, presumably to draw my focus. "He'll be back in a moment. Terribly rude, but he *is* our communications liaison, so . . ."

This time, I didn't need to look at Akasha. She shifted in her seat, "accidentally" nudging me with her elbow. It conveyed a clear message, though I'm not sure how. Maybe it was our time in combat together, or maybe the intuition I'd honed in the monastery. Whatever the case, I easily picked up on her intentions. I was in the same boat.

Oklen evidently detected the same shift. He tried a wonky smile, then said, "Everything okay? You look a little—"

Akasha stood like a lightning bolt and whipped her arm outward. In a flash of shadow and steel, a dagger rocketed over the heating coil and buried itself in Oklen's throat.

Instantly, neon blue boxes surrounded the three men—including Sekris, whose own frame was distant and muddied by the darkness.

Oklen Fir (HUMANOID)
Jalvar (HUMANOID)
Sekris (HUMANOID)
CALCULATING . . .
Estimated Kill Points: 63,800

To my surprise, the system counted Oklen as still alive. Not for long, though. Within half a second of the dagger piercing his throat, he began sputtering blood, clawing at the wound, and slumped out of his seat. He pitched forward and grilled his own face on the heating coil as Jalvar struggled to wrench his sidearm out of a polymer holster.

I wouldn't give the burly bastard that chance. Lunging out of my seat, I plowed into Jalvar and took him to the dirt. The smell of burning eyebrows and sizzling flesh filled the darkness as we flopped about, grunting and huffing and throwing wild punches.

An armored knee caught me in the hip. I bit down on the pain, fighting to get a clean grip on Jalvar's neck as he squirmed beneath me. Between his slick armor and bulging muscles, it wasn't an easy task. Even after triggering Overclock, it was clear his strength outmatched mine by a factor of two or more. Every thump of blood moving through his carotid artery felt like a gunshot.

"Move," Akasha ordered from just behind me.

I didn't know what she was planning, but I couldn't afford to ask. Already, Jalvar was slipping out of my grasp and winding up for a vicious counterattack. I sprang off his chestplate and rolled onto the soil.

The instant I was clear, a triplet of ear-splitting, high-powered rifle shots rang out. I glanced back to find Akasha framed in the coil's light, one of the "surveyor's" weapons expertly tucked against her shoulder.

When I looked over at Jalvar, I found little more than an armored body and a half-erased head. The remnants of his brain matter and skull were plastered all over the foliage.

"Goddamn," I hissed. "Some warning next time?"

Akasha shrugged. "I asked you to move."

I blinked at her, bewildered, until the sound of hurried footsteps drew our combined attention.

Shit. The third guy.

He was fleeing somewhere in the deep of night, running so fast and fiercely that his breaths were as audible as the rustling branches. Every so often, he let out a strangled, panicked whine that reminded me of a dying animal.

"We shouldn't follow," I told Akasha, who was busy lifting the rifle and taking aim through the holographic scope. "If there's—"

She cut me off by firing two rounds in quick succession.

A second later came the sound of something heavy thudding to the forest floor. Then there was silence. Bleak, haunting silence.

ENCOUNTER FAILED

Even as I got to my feet, brushing away the soil and ensuring I wasn't spattered in blood, I resented the chok'tal's messages. Sure, Akasha had done the heavy lifting—maybe all of it—but the lack of combined credit for kills was beginning to feel like a serious oversight. Additionally, the shift in Kill Points hadn't gone unnoticed. When we first encountered the trio, they'd been set to award me a measly 36,000 Kill Points. In this second, more visible engagement, they'd been worth about 30,000 Kill Points more. As a group. Clearly detail, especially of the visual sort, had a role to play in dictating the worth of an opponent's death. Another bug in the system, if you asked me.

Not that it was worth dissecting at the moment. As it stood, we were surrounded by three bodies and their now unclaimed gear. The first order of business was figuring out who we'd just killed . . . then *why* we'd killed them. I knew in my heart that we hadn't been wrong to take them down— there really was something shady that had put us both on edge in seconds—but if pressed for an answer, I'd have been lost for words.

"You humans are too cordial," Akasha said, as she lowered the rifle.

I rolled my eyes. "How was I supposed to know they were up to no good?"

"If you'd asked for my insights, I would have said as much."

"Well, it's water under the bridge now." I took another look at Jalvar's corpse, half-expecting the monstrous thing to rise and strangle me. "What do you think they were? Mercenaries?"

She shook her head. "Too disorganized. However, I have a theory."

Without explaining further, Akasha proceeded into the darkness, roughly in the direction she'd been aiming when she took down Sekris. All I could do was stand there like a fool, tapping my foot and trying to catch my breath. She eventually returned with a small, rectangular device in hand: a tablet.

A Hegemony ops-tablet, to be precise.

"It is encrypted," she said, "but I believe its presence is enough to confirm my suspicions."

I took the tablet from her hands, turning it over and inspecting it with dread. "Holy shit. These guys were working for the Hegemony."

"So it seems."

"I thought you said the ship would crash on the permawar planet."

"It did, but I am certain they are examining both worlds in the system to be thorough," Akasha said. "Your presence on this world could be nothing more than speculation to them."

"Maybe. Only question is, what now?"

"We need to leave this place."

"I'm inclined to agree." I glanced up warily, searching the night sky for anything that might indicate a low-altitude surveillance ship. It seemed clear, but then again, the Hegemony had stealth technology. "We need to warn Narbu and the others."

Akasha shook her head. "If we return, we risk leaving a trail for their forces."

"Wait, you think we should keep going? With the Hegemony combing the ground for us?"

"They are not looking for *us*," she said, moving back to the heating coil and stripping anything useful from Oklen's corpse. "The only detail in the Hegemony's possession is your nature—that of a Purifier. Beyond that, all is speculation."

"But if their liaison managed to transmit how we look . . ."

"We *cannot* turn back," Akasha said sharply. "Without attaining the Third Perfection, there is no hope of overcoming the Unmade. We may die in the ascent, Dak, but it is preferable to what will occur if we abandon this task."

Her tone brooked no disagreement, and I wasn't in any mood to put up a fight. Even if I resented the idea of being forced along my destined path, it was hard to dispute her argument against returning to the monastery. At least in the dense woods, we had a good chance of evading any Hegemony patrols. The same couldn't be said for the vast swath of open fields that lined our way back.

"Fine," I said with a huff. "Help me take what we can: food, water, weapons. The monks probably wouldn't approve, but too bad. From here on out, I'm doing things my way."

19

Upon leaving the campsite a half-hour later, our selection of gear was decidedly more robust. Akasha and I had each looted a rucksack, a rifle, climbing gear (very handy for the coming stretch), and as many bricks of rations or pressurized water as we could carry. Under ordinary conditions, we wouldn't have needed most of it. Traveling to the Scholar's Ascent, undergoing the trial, and making the journey back was estimated to take just over a day.

Seeing as we now had clear confirmation of the Hegemony's presence in the system, however, there was no telling how long we'd be stranded in the great outdoors.

Part of me wanted to tuck in my tail, head to the nearest hub city, and catch one of those ferries straight off the planet. The Hegemony hadn't started its dragnet operations on the surface, after all, and there was a good chance we'd be able to flee without triggering any alarms due to our identities.

The other part of me, though, saw the value of Akasha's logic. If we turned back now, we'd lose our access to the fruits of the Third Perfection. I had no way of verifying whether it was actually a necessary part of my long-foretold victory, but thus far, every Perfection had given me a valuable insight into myself and the world at large. It wasn't hard to imagine that this last trial would induce a similarly profound shift in my consciousness.

In fact, I considered while following Akasha and her pilfered light through the darkness, I'd actually come to see my mental journey as its own intrinsic reward. It wasn't an expected change—upon first contact with the monks, I'd viewed them as needlessly confusing, even deranged—but it was now impossible to deny. All of the order's formerly incomprehensible lessons had crystalized into real, practical knowledge.

Maybe that was just the price of becoming my own person. Being grown in a lab and treated like a tool by my creator had stripped much of the "majesty" out of life. Without even knowing it, my mind had turned to a hungry pit. It was starved of meaning, of purpose, of wonder.

The monastery and its lessons had started to satisfy the pit. Each leap in consciousness had made me feel more alive, more connected to the unspeakable strangeness of reality. In turn, it had also brought about further resentment of those who wasted their lives on acquiring wealth and inflicting pain on others.

Even in the shadow of imminent death, I found myself grasping at that which was beyond the petty concerns of the mortal world. I craved knowledge of that which was eternal, perfect, unchanging. There were plenty of religions that could've spoon-fed me their premade answers to those kinds of existential questions, but I didn't want any of them. I'd spent enough time being lied to by prophets and zealots. It was time to figure out reality on my own terms.

After all, if rebirth *was* real, it was logical to assume that I hadn't actually been "born" in Chanzig's laboratory. Instead, going by the repository's information on the subject, it meant I'd been born millions or billions of times—not always as a human, but as insects, as aliens, as machines, as anything that existed throughout the vast cosmos.

What if this really was a rare chance to sort through the tangled web of karma that had led to my birth as Dak? What if, through whatever bizarre strain of luck, I'd been fortunate enough to come across Akasha and the monks as part of my mind's journey? Destined or not, everything I'd learned resonated deep in my heart . . . almost as though I was relearning a half-forgotten lullaby. What that lullaby was, I couldn't say. Still, I had this precise mind and body at my disposal to continue the investigation.

The farther we trekked into the blackness, the firmer my resolve became. I *would* conquer this trial. I *would* perfect my mind and body. I *would* take responsibility for my fate, regardless of how or why I'd come into this universe.

Part of that responsibility was kicking the shit out of the Unmade.

The night wore on, stars slowly revolving through the lattice of branches overhead. Gradually, almost imperceptibly, the forest thinned into clusters of tall, scraggly saplings. Rock replaced the soil underfoot. Before I knew it, we were trudging up steep, zigzagging paths and threading between cracked boulders. Freezing winds buffeted my shirt and stung the flesh beneath. Every so often, we took turns slipping into harnesses and using grappling claws to scale nearly vertical ascents, trading off the role of climber and belayer.

Eventually, we stopped to rest at another overhang. This one was more bowl-shaped, meaning we could completely conceal ourselves beneath the rock lip and set up the heating coil without betraying ourselves to overhead observers.

Moonlight revealed the true extent of our climb. Unbeknownst to me, we'd ascended several hundred meters, turning the land below into a relatively flat and distant sprawl. Here and there, we spotted guttering campfires and the momentary flashes of explosives.

"How many do you think are working with the Hegemony?" I asked, plopping down beside Akasha to drink from my stolen canteen.

"I do not know," she said, "though I doubt it's many. This world has always been a breeding ground for conflict."

I nodded. "Probably depends on whether the Hegemony was willing to pay more than the other guys."

"They almost assuredly are."

"You really think the Hegemony's that interested in a Purifier? I mean, Modri and Chanzig said they were, but who knows?"

Akasha considered the question for a long while. "I have not had many encounters with the Hegemony, but I know of their ambitions. It is just as Jekra Modri stated. There is not a single power in this universe that would pass up the opportunity to harness the chok'tal."

"Yeah, well, I think Modri taught them a lesson about getting overconfident."

"Death is nothing to them," she said faintly. "The escape of Jekra Modri may have claimed lives, but it also proved the worth of a Purifier. They have surely studied the evidence left behind by his actions."

"What's that supposed to mean?"

"They will be more prepared when they encounter their next Purifier."

I shivered a bit at the idea, but my prevailing mood was one of curiosity. All this talk of the Hegemony and their chok'tal ambitions raised questions about an organization far more involved in my life.

"How did they keep the Purifier alive?" I asked.

Akasha glanced at me. "I do not understand."

"The order. You said they'd kept a Purifier in the monastery for a long time . . . but Purifiers expire pretty quick without things to kill. So, how they'd keep the Purifier alive, ranking up?"

"With blood."

"Well, obviously. But *whose* blood?"

"I do not know," she said at length. "Such questions did not seem important at the time."

"They feel important now."

"You worry that their ethics are compromised."

I narrowed my eyes at her, trying to extract the gist of what she was getting at. When I'd first raised the question, I hadn't been thinking about the order's ethics (or lack thereof) whatsoever. The more I reflected on it, the more I realized Akasha was right. I *did* have concerns about their moral compass. The order was outwardly diligent in its attitude to compassion, and yet . . . the Kill Points had to come from somewhere. Narbu had already confirmed that hallucinatory or virtual enemies didn't count for Purifiers, so what had they been feeding to their prior champion? The only reasonable answer was life. Warm, beating-hearted life.

"I think they're an order built on secrecy," I said at last. "Even Tekshim and the others don't know what's being hidden at the top."

"There's no malice in them, Dak."

"I know."

In truth, however, I *didn't* know. Since my arrival, my impression of the order hadn't improved in the transparency department. To me, an outsider, it seemed like yet another hierarchy that hoarded power and knowledge at the expense of those on the bottom rungs. Worse, it wasn't above outright lying to those it had deemed useful in its shadowy plans. History has shown, time and time again, that the worst crimes were committed by those with a radical vision and a disregard for those standing in their way.

"Maybe we should sleep," I said eventually. "We can—"

"Share a sleeping bag," she interjected.

I blinked at her. "Yeah. To conserve warmth, I guess."

A smile crept across her face, though I wasn't sure if it indicated she was joking or merely enjoying my discomfort.

"There's no time for sleep," she said. "You still need to accrue Kill Points."

Strangely enough, I'd nearly forgotten about that oh-so-important requirement. A quick exercise in mental math assured me that I still had about ten hours on the clock.

"What's your plan?" I asked. "Shoot down a few cloaked Hegemony ships?"

Akasha switched off the heating coil, letting our overhang fade into darkness. "The area is plentiful in wild beasts."

"Which you think I should hunt . . . in the dark . . . while Hegemony scouts are prowling."

"You'll need to dispatch them either way. The path to the Scholar's Ascent is rife with dens and caves, and it is probable that the way has been left untouched for many centuries."

"Great. Plenty of time for all the furry, fanged monstrosities to experience a surge in population growth."

"Precisely," Akasha said, not catching a single iota of my sarcasm. "I'm certain any travelers in the area will appreciate such a culling."

"Bold of you to assume any travelers wander up here."

"I know of at least two."

"Hah, very funny," I said, with a grimace. "So, are we heading out now?"

She leaned back against the rock and took a sip from her canteen. "You are. I'll stay, center my mind, and prepare for the ritual." When I visibly balked at the idea, she smiled. "It's only for your benefit, Dak. If I ventured at your side, every foe would be vanquished before you even saw them."

I smirked and turned away. "Suit yourself."

"Oh, and Dak," she said hastily, making me glance back, "be sure to mind your steps. Scryer Narbu told me that each of us will know which path is ours. It is important you follow your prescribed path, and no other."

"Wait . . . we're splitting up?"

"Only near the summit. I'll guide you when it's time to do so. The moment you get a feeling you are near your destiny . . . return to this camp. Go no farther."

It was a strange, cryptic set of instructions, but who was I to refuse? If for no other reason than to make Akasha feel better, I readily agreed. Then I set out to hunt.

Twenty minutes later, I grumbled under my breath as I picked my way up the haphazard slopes. Whereas the mountain had seemed dead and barren while I journeyed with Akasha, it now felt threatening, almost predatory. Every time pebbles skittered down the steep trail toward me, I tensed up and brought Oklen's rifle to my shoulder. Invariably, the barrel-mounted flashlight would reveal nothing more than a small lizard or mollusk-like creature, neither of which were worth a single Kill Point.

All of a sudden, though, things changed. Mid-step, familiar forms emerged from the darkness, even if I couldn't consciously tell how or why they were familiar. I lifted the beam of my flashlight and studied what lay before me.

Sure enough, it was a fork in the path. One that tickled the déjà vu lobe in my brain. To the left was a path marked by a boulder with a faded-yet-still-visible rune in the shape of a hexagon. To the right, a shriveled tree with dying, semi-frozen blossoms. The scene was a *perfect* recreation of the illustration Tekshim had shown me.

Where the hell do they lead?

I waffled for a moment, wondering if I should go right, left, or just haul ass back to camp. Well, I immediately tossed out option three. I *needed* Kill Points, and I didn't feel like telling Akasha about the total insanity of Narbu's "artwork" just yet. She'd undoubtedly take away whatever choice I had left in the matter. My logical side told me I ought to go right, as it had been the "Radiant" path, according to the illustration. But I've never been one for common sense. No, it had to be the left-hand path. I wanted to know what deep, dark shit was hiding up there. Hell, maybe the path was even "destined" to be Akasha's, but I didn't care anymore. Narbu had been playing games with my fate since day one. It was time to even the score.

Steeling my nerves, I resettled the rifle's sling and went left. Within a few minutes, things started getting spooky. Mainly because I knew this was a spot Narbu had marked as an extreme no-go zone in his psychotic drawing session. Time for some friendly chat to take the edge off.

"How are things in, uh, wherever you are?" I asked, mentally toggling Modri's speech permission as I did so.

"*Peachy,*" he replied without missing a beat. "*I really am your booty call, huh?*"

"Not familiar with the term."

"*You bring me out when you're feelin' lonely. Or just scared shitless, I guess. Seems you're a little of both right now.*"

"Wouldn't you be?"

"*Guess so. Not 'cause of the dark or takin' the evil path, though. Nah, you've got bigger problems.*"

It didn't take a genius to guess what he meant. "You mean the Hegemony."

"*Obviously.*"

"Think you can help me out? You used to be one of their grunts, so you probably know a fair amount about their tactics, right?"

"*I was a reformer, not a goddamn grunt.*"

"All the better."

"*Listen, these guys don't fuck around. If they're already hirin' advance observers, you're too late. You shoulda called me up the second you found that tablet."*

"What do you mean, too late?"

"Standard procedure for operations. They hire a buncha locals, have 'em map out all the spots their target might be hidin'. Once they've got their 'hot zones' map loaded up, they'll come down like the worst damn storm you ever seen."

"They don't even know if I'm here."

"Doesn't take a genius to work it out. They probably locked down that permawar world and combed the wreckage while you were still playin' monkey in the damn trees."

"There's no way they were that fast . . . is there?"

Modri scoffed. *"Guess you don't got a clue how fast the Hegemony's pinches are. They've got the best tech in the 'verse. If you've got a target on your head, they'll launch when you take a breath and be there before you let it out. And you, my friend, have a big-ass target on your noggin."*

"Thanks for the reassurance," I said, sighing. "Alright, let's get real. Even if they did find the wreckage, it doesn't mean they'll know I'm *here.*"

"Like I said, that conclusion don't take a genius. It's the only civilized world in the system. And since there were no bodies, and one escape capsule missin' . . ."

"Shit. You really think they're going to bring the rain down on this world?"

"All I can say is, you're lucky you're a damn Purifier. If you were just some insurgent trash, they'd have ashed the whole planet without a thought."

Reflecting on Modri's words, I scaled the next rise and resumed my hike. "Can't say I feel too lucky right now."

"What you and Blue Babe need to do is get the hell into orbit on one of those ferry things. Might already be too late, but if you go now—"

"We can't," I cut in. "You heard her."

"She's livin' in her own world. Plus, after what I just heard, it seems she ain't got a great track record with keepin' Purifiers alive here . . ."

"Well, I just so happen to believe she's right. We *need* to finish the trial."

Modri groaned. *"Alright, listen. If you insist on bein' a dumbass, the best you can do is stay frosty. You see anybody—and I mean anybody—you drop 'em without a second thought. Don't go usin' any of your upgrades unless you've got cover from air cams. And most importantly . . . don't say my name, or Hegemony, or 'Purifier' out loud anymore. You'd be damn surprised how sensitive their surveillance shit is."*

"Oh, please. Now you're just spouting propaganda. You don't have to hype up their tech anymore, you know. You're dead."

"Suit yourself, chief. Go on and say one of the forbidden words. Say it real loud. We'll count how long it takes for a gunship to scoop your scrawny ass up."

Although Modri's warning felt like a ludicrous example of exaggeration, I still wasn't stupid enough to try my luck. Dead or not, Modri *had* been a special forces operative for the Hegemony. I'd never forgive myself if I got captured or killed due to deliberately disregarding his advice.

This being the case, I grunted in assent and pushed on.

Before long, I could see my breath misting in the moonlight. The last of the vegetation dwindled, giving way to steep formations of rock and frost. If I hadn't encountered any beasts on my trek through the wooded parts, what were the odds of finding them up here? I didn't know, but I also didn't want to let my guard down and get jumped by a pack of rabid elk.

Maybe Akasha had been right about this being a bountiful hunting spot, but wrong about the time. If the local critters were diurnal, it made sense why I hadn't spotted any. They'd be too busy napping or chewing on the day's collection of scraps. The other possibility was that the mountain's inhabitants weren't ground dwellers. This high up, it seemed likely that the dominant species was something with wings.

Whatever the case, I neither saw nor heard anything as I drew closer and closer to the summit. In hindsight, this was probably a bad idea. Akasha hadn't told me to avoid the Scholar's Ascent, per se, but she also hadn't instructed me to wander down a path I had no business wandering. In fact, she'd expressly warned against it. Even so, sticking around a little longer to finish my hunt seemed a lot better than trudging downhill in the dark, shivering, sniffling, and bitter about the failed search. Besides, I wanted to know why the hell Narbu had seen fit to illustrate this path as a "bad" one. So far, it was a bunch of nothing. Akasha was going to grill and scold me either way, so why not go the full distance and make the tongue-lashing worth it?

"Say," I told Modri, keeping my voice low in case any predators were lurking, "you think anything's holed up in these caves?"

To illustrate my point, I squinted at a series of pitch-black holes lining the nearest ridge.

"I wouldn't go pokin' around," Modri growled.

"Why? Afraid of a little fight?"

"You asked, I answered. Caves are never good."

"Yeah, but maybe—"

Something cracked under my boot.

I angled the rifle's flashlight down, only to freeze when I recognized what I'd crushed: a thin, curved bone covered in bits of icy meat. Something had picked it nearly clean, and recently.

There wasn't even time to be afraid. The instant I stepped off the bone halves, a tremor worked through the rock beneath me. I swung the flashlight's beam about in total disarray, tracking the wobble of pebbles and the microscopic cracks worming underfoot.

"I bet it's a spider," Modri quipped.

"Not helpful," I said through gritted teeth. "In fact, worse than not helpful."

Suddenly, the "boulder" a few paces to my left wrenched upward as though launched by an underground geyser. I leapt back and shone the light in its general direction. To my horror, the boulder was hovering in midair—and held aloft by a cluster of dense, spore-infected tendrils. The appendages ran deep into some sort of pit that had been dug out beneath the boulder, a fact I only realized when a larger, more disturbing mass of flesh rose up in front of the tendrils.

It was something like a squid, though its dozens of eyes, mushroom-like growths, and festering skin tipped the scale closer to "living nightmare."

Strangely enough, the thing didn't attack. It just hovered there, studying me.

I wasn't about to waste my golden opportunity. Shouldering the rifle, I lined up my shots and slipped my finger over the trigger.

My HUD lit up in response.

Subterranean Menace (BEAST)
CALCULATING . . .
Estimated Kill Points: 31,000

"Well, Modri," I said, as the beast loosed an ear-stabbing screech, "at least it wasn't a spider."

20

I fired four semi-automatic shots before the so-called "Subterranean Menace" could make a move. Each round slammed into its head-torso, spraying the rock with dead, pulpy skin and puffs of dark blood. One or two bullets even caught the thing right in its eye clusters.

Still, the menace didn't back down. If anything, I only succeeded in pissing it off further. This point was made clear when its torn-off flesh, which lay scattered before me, began writhing and bubbling. Liquefied rock streamed under my flashlight's beam like molten silver.

Acid blood. Goddamn acid blood.

I hopped backward, narrowly dodging one of the menace's tendrils. The length of rotten muscle—which I now realized to be several times longer than what I'd observed—whipped across the stone, filling the darkness with sparks. My flashlight exposed the culprit: cracked, yellowy talons of bone that ran all along the tendril's length.

I dropped to a crouch and let off another volley, this time peppering the upper part of the menace's face. Assuming it was more animal than fungus, it had to have a center to its nervous system. An operating center. Being a humanoid myself, I figured the brain would be in the usual spot.

Wrong. When the blood and muzzle flashes faded, there was a ragged, leaking hole where the creature's "forehead" had once been. But that was it. No brain matter, no skull. Just meat.

The menace responded by slashing at me with a handful of tendrils. I rolled beneath the first swing, but the second caught me right in the back. Before I knew it, I was lying on my chest and groaning through the throb of broken ribs. Pain raced up my spine, almost but not quite blotting out the sudden chill of my insides being exposed to the mountain's night air. When I instinctively reached back, my fingers came away bloody.

Once again, the menace reared back in my peripheral vision. I flopped backward, bringing the rifle to bear and dumping countless shots into its face. Meanwhile, I toggled Indomitable to start blunting the pain and sealing me back up.

The bullets slowed the menace, but only momentarily. Even as its blood steamed in the frigid air, the beast redoubled its efforts to skewer and eat me. Tendrils came surging out of the pit, thrusting like elastic knives at the stone around me. More sparks and mica chips lit up the darkness.

Fortunately, the menace's bloodlust was to my advantage. It was so lost in its personal murder-quest that it didn't notice me shuffle backward, get to my feet, and start running like hell down the mountain.

Cowardly? Maybe. But any creature that could survive half a magazine's worth of ammunition to the face was above my paygrade. Purifier or not, I wasn't gonna tango with that *thing*.

Sadly, the thing had other plans.

Before I'd made it ten paces, the sound of muscle rippling and snapping filled the air. A length of steel-hard tissue coiled around both my legs in an instant. Once again, I took a nasty spill downslope, slamming my already-cracked ribs into a patch of mottled rock. This time around, my chin also took the blow. At least, I think it did. There's a gap in my memory after the tendrils grabbing me. The next thing I knew, I was being dragged back up the slope, the sling-affixed rifle scraping along with me.

By that point, though, it was already too late. Despite pushing my arms to the breaking point, repeatedly trying and failing to grab the rifle for a last-minute surprise, the menace had me. I spun around to find myself just a few meters from the edge of the beast's pit. Its head loomed over me, fangs twisted into a shockingly expressive smile as if in celebration.

I braced my entire body, ready for the inevitable wombo-combo of teeth and acid to strip me down to the bone—but it didn't come. Instead, the tendrils yanked my legs clean over the edge of the pit. With a hammering heart, I clawed at the dirt and stone, all concern for my fingers gone in an instant. Primal fear drove me. It drove me through the pain of my nails shattering, then the pain of the delicate bones cracking. Yet for all my struggling, I was tugged down just the same. The menace wrapped my entire body in tendrils and lowered me into its black, humid domain with the control of a doting mother, completely oblivious to my screams.

After almost a minute of steady descent, though, my lungs gave out. I felt like a hare in the clutches of a fox—immobile, paralyzed with fear, trying to balance the survival drive with my body's depleting energy.

My terror worsened when the menace lowered the boulder above, blotting out the night sky and blinding me inside this hellish tunnel.

All my fighting, all my resisting . . . and it had come to this. There was no help coming. By the time Akasha even realized something was wrong, I'd be nothing but a morsel inside the menace's gut. If I was lucky, maybe she'd eventually track down this place and avenge me. Not that it mattered. Soon enough I'd be dead, forgotten, just another stupid humanoid who'd wandered too far up the mountain.

The worst part of my fate was the silence. Because the chok'tal more or less shut off in combat situations, I couldn't converse with Modri in my final moments. It would've been nice to hear a friendly voice while being ripped apart.

Hell, I couldn't even see anything. The descent's almost tangible darkness functioned like an executioner's blindfold, upping my tension to unbearable levels. At least with vision, I could—

Wait a damn second.

Amazingly, Nocturnal—the upgrade I'd purchased and written off as useless—now had a role. Well, okay, I'd previously used it to decent effect, but this was what it had *really* been designed for. Mentally switching on the power, I stared into the formless black ahead and waited.

After a few seconds of transitory flickering, my vision gained *some* clarity. Not much, and not nearly enough to let me aim at anything beyond a few meters, but it was better than nothing. Now I could see the texture of the tunnel: its gelatinous outer layer, its teeth-chiseled curves, its haphazard recesses and alcoves that served as hoarding spots for shattered bones.

Part of my mind wondered how I could see anything—was it an amplification of the tunnel's faint ambient light, or some other visual system entirely?—but the majority of it was focused on freeing my ass.

I still had the rifle, but it was sandwiched against my chest and half-drained of ammo. I had Mind Cascade, but wasn't yet desperate enough to use it against this nightmarish creature and its diseased inner world.

My last option was "old faithful," also known as Telekinesis. A spark of joy leapt up in my chest when I remembered its recent advancement to the third and final tier. Plus, I'd just bested my Accretion—that had to count for something, right? Well, I sure as hell hoped so.

Closing my eyes, I activated Telekinesis and began probing the space around me. To my surprise, I didn't encounter the vague and empty landscape I associated with the power. In its stead was a vibrant, almost overwhelming sprawl, a flurry of energy and consciousness. Not a single space was devoid of that incredible power. In fact, there was no "space" at all. Even the formerly empty terrain between objects was revealed as an ocean of latent potential.

You might compare it to staring up at the sky. In daylight, it's clear, empty. But come nightfall, a vast network of lights.

There were no actual lights in my awareness, of course, but the idea is poetic enough to paint the picture. It was certainly enough to temporarily stun me. My last use of Telekinesis had been prior to both the power's third rank *and* the unlocking of the mandala. Although I couldn't prove it, I had a hunch that both changes had combined to radically transform the power's characteristics.

For a while I just let my awareness drift out, dancing among and probing the effervescent beauty. There seemed to be no true "center" to me or my mind. Every single point was its own center, its own locus of awareness.

But before long, I understood that this wasn't the time to putz around. I was on a collision course with a gruesome end. Gathering my semi-scattered awareness, I began to perceive myself as a humming core. Well, it wasn't *me*, I realized, but rather a tangible expression of where I placed my attention. To test this theory, I sent my awareness forth until it met the densely packed energy of the tunnel wall. Then I turned "myself" around and absorbed the sight of my physical body and the tendrils locked around me, all of which appeared as a blob of chaotic brilliance.

It was equal parts mesmerizing and frightening. Whereas I'd previously been controlling Telekinesis from a fixed point, extending my will toward external objects and manipulating them from the control room that was my skull, I had now collapsed the borders between "me" and "my will."

In essence, I had *become* my willpower, my awareness.

The most practical effect of this shift was in the power's force application. Before, I'd felt my willpower dim and finally crack when I moved it too far away from my body. That same decay-over-distance factor was still present, but it had been vastly reduced. Eager to check another hypothesis, I drifted up toward the boulder atop the tunnel. My body continued to descend below me, a fading blot of light among other, lesser lights.

Yet despite that distance, I could still feel everything around "me." It was as though I'd managed to uncouple mind and body, roaming about with the mind while the body stayed at home. Unfortunately, that new capability didn't change very much on a strength level. After locating a loose stone just a few meters below the boulder, I gave it a mental tug. It didn't budge.

When I repeated the test on a stone about ten meters from my body, though, it *did* come popping out. That gave me a good baseline for Telekinesis' new constraints. It wasn't the miraculous, planet-crushing power I'd have liked for the situation, but it would have to do.

Guiding my awareness downward, I probed for the bottom of the tunnel. It extended farther than I'd imagined possible. With every meter I descended, the terrain became darker, hazier, almost as though glimpsed through a growing fog. This had nothing to do with the actual light, and everything to do with the distance from my body.

Still, I was eventually able to hit *something* solid. Not quite stone, but far from empty air. As the tendrils continued to lower my body, this sensory information solidified into certainty. I was being lowered into a forest of teeth, flesh, and roiling fluids.

The moment I got a clear picture of that terrain, fear came roaring back into awareness. Telekinesis's range and strength both instantly shrank to half their former glory. Some deeper, quieter part of my mind inherently understood the relationship. Fear choked the power of the mind. Pain and doubt, I guessed, would act similarly.

Keep it together, I told myself. *Stay calm to stay alive.*

I pulled the focal point of Telekinesis back to my body, examining the tendrils for any sign of weakness. Maybe the creature's brain was distributed throughout its limbs. The structure of the fungus-and-flesh combo was too dense to penetrate, though, so such a guess didn't help me much. Even still . . . I noticed something new. Something curious.

The bag Narbu had given me was still affixed to my belt. Affixed to my hip, more accurately, due to the menace's tendrils sandwiching it in place. But its placement wasn't important. What *was* important was the area where the tendrils touched the bag.

The quantum microscope of Telekinesis revealed extensive damage to the menace's flesh. It resembled burns—chemical burns, to be precise. Everywhere the tendrils made contact with the bag, there were sores, boils, oozing pus.

What the hell was in that bag? I'd carried it on my hip since we left the monastery, but I hadn't felt so much as a tingle through the fabric of my pants. If it was really that caustic, it should've chewed halfway to my thigh bones by that moment. Clearly it contained something that left human flesh untouched, but ravaged this thing.

Was this the third trial? I had no idea, but it seemed as likely a theory as any other. Why else would Narbu have given us a bag full of something that targeted this particular creature?

Driven by a fresh spurt of hope, I plunged my awareness into the bag and prodded around. The structure of its contents was loose, vibrant . . . *Flowers*, I realized after a moment. The conclusion arose as unprompted and intuitively as every prior insight. Somehow, some way, I just *knew* what I was examining. Even as I rested in the quantum void between the flowers, I sensed their oils seeping out of crushed petals, bleeding through the bag, and chewing into the menace's flesh.

This gave me an idea. Employing the same strategy I'd used on the corrupted turtle—telekinetically gripping two things at once, that is—I grasped both sides of the cloth bag and began tugging in opposite directions. Immense pain rippled through my forehead as I diverted more and more energy to the task. Before long, I could sense my body shaking, warm rivulets of blood flowing from my nostrils. Muscles spasmed in the tendril's clutches.

Then, like a dam breaking, the tension gave way to release. The bag split open down the center, causing the bag's potent mash of plant matter and oils to press directly against the menace.

A hideous shriek filled the tunnel. The sound was grating enough to ricochet through my skull, instantly canceling Telekinesis and returning me to normal perception. With Nocturnal's visual aid, I saw the tendrils squirming beneath me. But I didn't need my eyes to confirm that. Already, the tendrils were loosening around my torso, growing slack and twitching in cycles as the burning flowers did their work.

"That's right," I hissed, struggling to uncoil my limbs from the tangle of mutated flesh. "Just let me down nice and easy . . ."

To its credit, the menace *did* let me down. With one strong, collective spasm, the tendrils lost the remainder of their strength and released me. Unfortunately, I had again been "released" in a manner that echoed my situation with the forest sloths—that is to say, with total disregard for my existence.

For what seemed like the millionth time, I slid back into free fall. Each of my frantic attempts to call up Telekinesis and get a readout of the environment ended in total failure, as did any effort to latch onto the branch-like tendrils past which I plummeted. All I knew was darkness, motion, pain, and the hot rush of dead air on my face.

Just before impact, though, Telekinesis returned a faint afterimage of the terrain.

It was hard, spiky, and less than a second away.

"Oh, motherfu—"

My head slammed against stone, and consciousness lapsed into black, humming static.

Sometime later—time sure does get wonky, given enough concussions—I discovered I wasn't dead. Vaguely disappointing, given the whole-body agony to which I awoke. It felt as though the universe had grabbed its largest, heaviest meat tenderizer and gone to town on every muscle I knew (and even a few I didn't). And as for my head, well, one can only imagine. Take the pain of stubbing your toe on a wooden chair's leg, shift it to the cranial area, and loop it until you want to bash your own brains in. Then you might have a taste of my first waking moments.

Strangely enough, though, the pain didn't last. Within a matter of seconds, every ache, throb, and jolt had faded into a buttery sense of well-being. My limbs became filled with a low-intensity buzzing, much like the aftereffect of a good massage. Well, I've never had a massage, but one can imagine, right?

Anyhow, the point is, I went from battered to good as new (or better) in no time at all. A small miracle, surpassed only by what I saw when I tentatively lifted my eyelids.

I'd expected to find a nightmarish den full of bodies and weird, bubbling fluids, but the reality was just the opposite. The floor beneath me was not made of tissue, but rather the dense, intricate threads of a massive carpet, all heated to perfection and given form by a series of lanterns hanging overhead.

Taken aback by the sudden jump in scenery, I sat up and glanced about. My newly repaired body didn't protest. This chamber had similar dimensions to the menace's tunnel—the same cylindrical shape, the same "ceiling" receding into blackness—but it was less, well . . . monstrous.

The gilded, masterfully polished walls reminded me of the monastery's most sacred areas. And come to think of it, so did the lanterns and the fragrant hints of incense in the air. Standing up, I tested a hunch that had started to form. Yep. Just as I'd predicted, the rug was a chamber-wide depiction of some epic mythological event. Probably the climax of a battle that featured centrally in the order's cosmology.

Far as I could tell, the battle was being waged between a huge, shape-less void and an army of golden humanoids. Various critters and species marched alongside the latter, their claws and fangs and spears angled toward the void's overwhelming ranks.

The closer I looked, the more details I saw. Everything from spilled intestines to the whites of individual warriors' eyes had been painstakingly woven into the scene—further proof that the monks were responsible. No organic being's hands could've created something so precise.

I wanted to stick around, exploring the enormous rug all day, but a faint tickle in the back of my mind vetoed that plan. It was a rather curious phenomenon. Deep down, I knew none of this was right. I'd been about to die. I'd been falling into an abomination's belly. I'd been separated from Akasha, probably lost to the ravages of time.

So, why the hell was I here?

This *very* logical question kept slipping away, though. Each time I shifted my attention to it, some new sight or sound would barrel into con-sciousness, redirecting me from my task. And although I *should've* noted this as the first sign that something was off, I didn't. Most distressing of all was that I saw this all happening at the forefront of my mind—but still stopped giving a damn.

Curious, I tested my neural link with Modri. Nothing came back.

After a time, though, whatever scraps of concern I had were nuked by a feeling of unshakable tranquility. It was the same lightness that had swept over my body, though translated to the mental plane. By the time my brain really started lapping up the happy juices, I wasn't bothered by anything. Torture? Bring it on. Imprisonment? Sure. Death? Well, okay.

In this haze of delight, I sought out the chamber's only door and began moving down the hallways. I wandered as I pleased, more skipping than walking. At some point, a voice caught my attention. It wasn't saying any-thing I could understand, but it had a light, melodic quality that reminded me of a lullaby.

I traced the voice to a small chamber at the top of a stairwell. Its thick obsidian door was ajar, allowing the beautiful chant to trickle out like wind through a keyhole.

Peering through the divide, I saw a figure standing before a wall of burning candles. Though his back was turned to me, their white robes—not to mention incredible size—identified him as a monk. It seemed impossible that such beautiful sounds could emerge from a machine, but at that moment, I was beyond poking holes in the experience. When my curiosity finally overtook me, I stepped into the room as though exploring some new region of a dream world.

The monk's height threw off my sense of scale. It took several minutes of spirited walking to reach the center of the chamber, at which point the monk ceased his chanting and turned back to look at me.

"Greetings," I said. "I . . . think I'm lost."

The monk studied me for a long time, then bowed his head. "It has been many, many years since one of flesh and bone entered this place."

This was where the first pang of doubt crept in. This monk spoke as if I'd fallen out of space and decided to pop into their monastery unannounced. Surely Narbu, Tekshim, or one of the others would've spread word of my presence. Even if they hadn't, weren't the monks able to sense latent powers, and especially Purifiers? That sure was how it had seemed.

Still, I decided not to grill the poor monk too much. I was interrupting their session; the least I could do was remain light and cordial.

"My name is Dak," I explained. "The Scryer sent me here for a trial. The Third Perfection's trial, that is. But now—"

"You find yourself in a shifting maze," the monk finished. "Nothing is as solid as it ought to be."

"Yeah. Exactly. The last thing I knew, I was fighting some kind of fungus creature. And now . . . well, now I don't know what's going on."

The monk nodded in understanding, then gestured for me to approach. So, I did. As I neared the wall of candles, the monk turned away and headed to a nearby altar.

At least, it appeared to be an altar. Vaguely pyramidal in shape, its panels were caked in gold leaf and rows of sparkling diamonds. Exotic flowers, twisting ivory horns, strands of beads, and dozens of other expensive trinkets had been draped over the altar's edges.

"Pretty," I said, as we drew close. "Is this how I complete the trial? Touch the pyramid or something?"

The monk slowed to a stop, then gazed longingly at the altar. "Not exactly. Still, I believe it is what you require."

"Huh?"

"I have not heard of the name you use, but I know of your true nature. Presuming you *are* the one, of course."

"What, a Purifier? Yeah, that'd be me." Finally, a drop of normalcy. I smiled at the monk. "Is the Scholar's Ascent some kind of separate monastery? I thought Narbu would've put out a PSA for this prophecy stuff."

"This is not the Scholar's Ascent."

I squinted at him. "What do you mean? I followed the path up here."

"Your steps have led you astray," the monk said absently, as he stepped up to the altar. "Though perhaps there is no such thing as astray. Right, wrong . . . here, there . . . In the end, destiny cares not. It is strange, however . . . we always foresaw the blue seer walking this path."

Blue seer. The name stopped me in my tracks. He was referring to Akasha. Suddenly, my mind flashed back to what Tekshim had shown me: Narbu's illustration of the paths. It all made sense. In hindsight, it was so obvious. The figure on the left—the one with the dark aura—had been draped in white robes and marked by silver hair. Which made *me* the figure depicted on the right-hand path. The path that probably led to the *true* summit, and not this false summit.

That could only mean one thing . . . Narbu had banked on me going right to some other fate, and Akasha going left and meeting the menace. He'd tried to kill her.

"If this isn't the Scholar's Ascent, where the hell am I?" I whispered.

"This is a forgotten place. A mausoleum."

The tiny hairs up and down my arms stood at attention. "I don't understand."

"No, you do not . . . but you will."

"Is this a riddle or something? One of Narbu's tricks?"

"Scryer Narbu holds no sway here." The monk began fiddling with the altar panels' various locks. "Not since he painted these walls with our blood."

21

Fear came spurting up through my awareness like an oil geyser. The monk had delivered the words in a bleak, passionless tone that left no ambiguity as to his meaning. Unlike this was a *serious* case of something being lost in translation, I'd just had my entire world shredded to bits.

"Painted . . . the walls . . . with your blood?" I whispered.

The monk undid another lock, then turned and gave me a polite nod.

"Please tell me you're referring to some hideous interior design choices."

"You will grasp the reality of things soon enough, Purifier."

"Screw that. You monks have been saying that since I arrived, and all I've gotten are more questions. If you know something about Narbu, you need to tell me. *Now.*"

My little outburst prompted the monk to angle himself toward me and lock eyes. The notch in my throat bobbed painfully. It was clear that if this titan didn't want to surrender answers, there was nothing I could do to change that decision.

"I am not like the Betraying Oracle," the monk growled. "I have promised reality, and I will reveal it to you."

"Betraying Oracle?"

"Scryer Narbu. It is how we regard him in this strange place."

The monk's mention of *strange* sent another flicker through my mind. Deep down, I still knew this was all wrong. Everything from the menace's disappearance to Modri's absence confirmed that this place was not "normal"—not in the same way you or I would use the description, anyhow. But for better or worse, I had to keep it copacetic and carry on chatting with this monk. He was my only source of information in here. Besides, if he knew something about Narbu—especially something treacherous related to fucking with my sense of reality—it was worth far more than a speedy escape.

"Got it," I said, nodding calmly. "Narbu, the Betraying Oracle."

The monk undid a final latch, resting his hands on the altar's main panels. "In order to comprehend Narbu's sins, you must know what drove him to cruelty."

"Can you at least tell me what this place is before we dive in?"

The monk held my gaze for a moment, utterly unreadable, then relented. "In days long past, this *was* the order's monastery. It was our original settlement, chosen by the sharpest mind aboard our vessel."

"So . . . this used to be the order's home."

"Yes."

"What caused the move?"

"This is where simple explanations will not suffice," the monk said, returning his attention to the altar and manipulating the strange, glowing runes that appeared upon its panels. "Your mind is guarded, but I can see through the cracks."

"People have said that a lot lately."

Undeterred by my flippant response, the monk continued as though I hadn't spoken. "I see the prophecy Narbu revealed to you."

"He didn't exactly *reveal* it. One of the other monks slipped me the truth. Seems he's been trying to hide the outcome of my hard work."

"He has been trying to sell you a falsehood. A naïve fantasy peddled to your humanoid consciousness."

"Spell it out, please. Are you saying I *don't* wind up being consumed by the Wellspring?"

"You do not." Just as I began to sigh in relief, the monk held up a finger. "Your fate is not so merciful, Purifier. Observe."

More unsettled than ever, I watched in silence as the top corners of the altar unfurled like a golden flower. A beam of brilliant light lanced straight up through the central gap. Well, it resembled light. The true nature of the beam became obvious when it split into a crackling, kaleidoscopic fountain of Sparkseed particles. Each of the motes seemed to possess its own volition, dancing about and interlocking with others to form fractal-like impressions that dissolved as soon as they'd emerged.

Seconds later, however, a ripple passed through the erratic cloud. Starting from the center and fanning out to the edges of the mass, the shockwave imbued the entire thing with some semblance of order. Not just order, I soon understood. There was a grand design baked into the energy. A creative vision in which each mote of Sparkseed had its proper place.

The golden storm swirled around us until it had formed a cylinder with towering walls, effectively hemming us in. This didn't concern me, though. I was too awestruck by the majesty of the process. Before my very eyes, a masterpiece was taking shape. Due to its rounded shape and general massiveness, though, I couldn't tell precisely what that masterpiece was. I spun in place, overwhelmed, as a three-sixty mural materialized out of nothingness. Details came in chunks: a rendition of a battle, a cluster of stars, a face . . .

The charge in the air faded, leaving behind a few zipping particles desperate to squeeze into their allotted place or fill in a scene's final details.

"Holy shit," I said with a whistle, slowly revolving to take in the display's full glory.

There had to be millions of years of history "etched" upon the mural. Even without a clear beginning or end point—largely due to the cylinder's edgeless, looping design—there was a story being told here. A story of empires, bloodshed, and—

My blood ran cold when I noticed the overarching motif for the scene that faced me. Woven into every row, column, and border patch were . . . chok'tals. They weren't silver here, but they sure as shit had the same unmistakable slug shape. Several of them were wriggling down the throats of what I took to be alien victims.

"What is this?" I whispered.

"In our tongue, this work is titled *The Divine and Immutable Path of the Purified One*." The monk stepped to my side. "It was a joint creation by our order."

"But how could you see this . . . this . . . ?" Lost for words, I settled for waving my arms at the all-encompassing creation.

"Before the Throne sank into its long slumber, we held rituals of communion. When the forests between worlds were thin, we would gather in the sacred spaces and call out for guidance. We would bask in the Wellspring's wisdom, join our minds with it, seek perfection through it. One day, our entire meditation circle was overcome by a vision of terrifying intensity."

"The Throne showed *this* to you?"

Nodding, the monk said, "A divine vision from the Radiant Wayfarers, or perhaps the essence of the Wellspring itself. It was burned into the mind of every being who witnessed it. We worked tirelessly to preserve it in a permanent medium and store it for the coming ages."

"Did you know what it was showing?"

"No. It took centuries to decipher its meaning." The monk approached the mural and traced a finger over one of its countless vignettes. "This vision, this work, became the bedrock of our order. We did not need words to grasp the Wellspring's plan for us."

"Stopping the Unmade, right?"

The monk hummed in approval. "The Radiant Wayfarers knew their kin would bring suffering to infinite beings. In us, a group of lowly sentient beings, they saw a chance to avoid such a fate. To the Wayfarers, we were shepherds of this realm. Teachers."

"For the 'chosen' Purifier. I've heard all this before."

"Perhaps, but you have not arranged the pieces," the monk said sharply. "Listen, Purifier, and listen well. The Wayfarers knew that our minds were unsullied by biological drives. We could act without lust, or envy, or hatred."

"Again, already heard it. Can you *please* just explain what the hell is going on with the mural?"

The monk glared at me for a moment, almost as though preparing to smack me through a wall or two. In the end, though, they inclined their head and stepped back. "As you desire, Purifier. Let us proceed in the proper order."

He turned to a panel on my left, strategically using his body to obscure what I presumed was the final area of the storyline. This revealed, logically enough, the beginning panel. Compared to most of the other scenes, this one was quiet, sparse. A single planet hovered on a backdrop of matte gold. Just above the planet, though, was a large spiral. Coils of chaotic energy snaked out from the figure and descended toward the world below.

"That's the Unmade, isn't it?" I said. "The rift, I mean. The one it used to dump chok'tals onto Akasha's planet."

The monk looked at me strangely upon hearing the name *Akasha*, but didn't comment on it. "Yes. This moment represents a breach in the fabric of reality. The same as every cycle."

I squinted. "What do you mean, every cycle?"

"This is not the first universe the Defiled Wayfarers have preyed upon. It is not even the first time they have tormented ours."

"None of you monks thought to mention that before now?"

"It is accepted as the way of things," the monk said. "In every cycle, these Wayfarers find a way to whisper their defilements to sentient beings and begin infecting their minds. Likewise, however, the Wellsprings speaks to those who are ready. They forever seek the end of the Defiled Wayfarers' madness."

"But have the Defiled Wayfarers ever *lost* in a cycle?"

"If our prophecy comes to fruition, they may."

Acid popped in my stomach. By now, it was clear that *nobody* understood Defiled Wayfarers. Nobody had a secret bullet to stop them, or some fantastic mumbo-machine to lock them in an eternal prison. The way this monk spoke of it, I got the impression that these Wayfarers were an accepted evil in the fabric of existence. No matter what anybody did, they would come back again . . . and again . . . and again. Even if I succeeded, it seemed statistically likely that these bastards would just spring up in the next universal cycle.

"Always chok'tal?" I asked with a grimace.

The monk looked at me quizzically.

"I mean, has the Unmade always 'invaded' with the chok'tal? Is it his gimmick?"

"No. This is his first cycle."

"How do you know it'll work, then? Your whole order's prophecy is based on the idea that you're turning his weapon against him. He made the weapon, though. What if he's already got a work-around?"

"Our prophecies are not wishful thinking," the monk said sternly. "They are paths forged by the Wellspring. Solutions to unsolvable problems. If they had been calculated by sentient minds, there would be room for doubt. But one cannot doubt the very source of all wisdom."

I crossed my arms and lifted a brow. "Let's see about that. What comes next in your glorious prophecy?"

Rather than answering, the monk gestured to the next panel on the right. This one depicted total anarchy. The same planet was still featured centrally, but now it was emitting chok'tal streams in all directions, much like the spokes of a wheel. These chok'tal highways wove through what appeared to be an artistic rendition of the local galaxy, skewering planets that contained countless numbers of creatures, ships, and machines.

This panel, I understood in a flash. It was clearly a recreation of the chok'tal and its path of annihilation. The monk must've sensed my certainty, because he wasted no time in moving along and pointing to the following panel.

Now, this was where things got interesting. Or horrifying, from my perspective.

The panel was bisected, presenting a different scene on each half. On the left-hand side, a celestial sphere with a thousand arms presided over a crowd of humanoid machines. Clearly the Wellspring and its congregation of monks.

On the right-hand side was another celestial figure, but unlike its counterpart, this one was more hideous than majestic. Tendrils, teeth, and horns jutted out from its shadowy body. The Unmade. Mirroring the left-hand image, this Wayfarer was also presiding over something: a vat. Specifically, a vat used for cloning and genetic acceleration. This last detail wouldn't have been obvious to most people, given the mural's high degree of "creative liberty," but it was plain as day to me.

Equally plain were the figures arranged in a ritual-like circle around the vat. The first was a blue-skinned woman covered in robes and strange markings. Akasha. The second was a white-hooded man bearing scalpels. Markazian. And the third . . .

"The Shattered Lord," the monk said, startling me. "Here, he breathes life into his creation."

"I knew him as Chanzig," I said coldly.

"Look here."

The monk pointed to a smaller sub-panel situated at the bottom of the mural—at my eye level, no less. In it, Chanzig—AKA the Shattered Lord— stood atop Akasha's home planet. His hand was outstretched, just a hair's width from touching a strange circle.

"Is that a gateway to the Unmade's dimension?" I asked. "From what I know, he tried to go through it and ended up losing his mind. And his body, I guess."

"Just so." The monk nodded in satisfaction, then shifted to the next panel. "The death of the Shattered Lord."

Here, my mood further descended. The panel didn't show Chanzig as a man, but rather as I'd fought him in his fragile dreamscape: a dark, lumbering giant that walked among the stars. In the first vignette, Chanzig sat defiantly atop a glimmering throne . . . within a very familiar tower. In the next, two humanoids—an armored warrior and a blue-skinned woman in robes—appeared to be scaling the tower. The third vignette depicted the epic clash, which ended with the woman destroying Chanzig in a flash of light. Streams of dark, mysterious energy poured out of the dead emperor's body and into the armored man. Into *me*.

"The Wayfarers showed you everything here?" I said, in a quiet voice.

"Every particle of it."

I didn't know what to say, let alone think. Throughout my time in the monastery, Narbu and his monks had possessed an uncanny talent for analyzing me. They'd also made a number of batshit-insane predictions that hadn't seemed at all feasible in a universe devoid of fate. Yet how could I make sense of *this*? No amount of lucky guessing explained the details present within the mural. Although I hadn't received an official timeline, I suspected that all of this had been made well before Akasha's birth. Magic or not, this was *spooky*.

"Come," the monk said, shepherding me toward the next panel with his massive hand. "You must see the remainder of the journey."

I pushed back against their palm. "Why are you showing me this?"

The monk didn't answer. Instead, they waited until my displeasure turned to morbid curiosity. It didn't take long. Much as I resented everything to do with prophecies and omens, there was something real here. Something that might help me avoid the fate Narbu had engineered.

The following panel was initially hard to interpret. It had been separated into three roughly equal sections, all joined by a central ring.

"This is the rise of the Purified One," the monk explained. "Each of their trials brings them closer to ascendence." He then gestured to each of the three sections in a clockwise motion.

The first showed the same armored warrior preparing to square off with a gigantic, deformed turtle. Clutched in his raised hands were what appeared to be—honest to goddamn Halcius—a shotgun and a hammer.

The second featured my showdown with the Accretion, which had been rendered here as a mass of writhing bodies.

Then there was the third and final section, which might as well have been subtitled "you are here." In this image, I was ripping the heart out of a colossal, twisting beast I recognized as the menace. Only . . . that hadn't happened. I was either staring into my own future, or locating the point where I'd gone off the rails of destiny. Hell, if I went by the monks' logic, maybe the mere act of *seeing* this mural had irrevocably changed my course.

The monk then directed my attention to the central hub connecting all of the sections. Within it, I sat in the cross-legged lotus position often favored by the monks. My eyes were closed yet emitting ripples of light, and my entire body was surrounded by a raging aura.

"What is that?" I asked. "What's it saying?"

"After completing their trials, the Purified One speaks directly to the Wellspring. They call it out of its slumber and receive instructions on how to defeat the Unmade."

That stirred up plenty of questions, but I was content to hold them back until I'd finished this grim gallery viewing. It was hard to know if I ought to jump for joy or break down weeping without knowing the end of the tale.

As expected, the monk hastily moved to the penultimate panel. Just as with the last one, the image was divided into three panes. The difference here, though, was that the sections told a linear story. The three panes had been stacked upon one another, clearly drawing the eyes downward. Each row depicted a different battle, but they all shared two things: my presence in combat, and a monstrous creature that presided over the encounters.

I squinted at the creature. With each battle, its murky aura seemed less and less distinct. By the third pane, it was nearly nonexistent.

"What's going on here?" I asked.

"These are the battles expected of the Purified One," the monk said. He pointed to the uppermost row, which depicted a fierce battle between me and a crimson-armored warrior in a sprawling laboratory. "First, they end the life of the Duplicitous Contender." His finger drifted to the second pane, a brawl with a crowned brute in the space between hundreds of planets. "Then they slay the Addled Regent." He then directed my attention to the third and final scene, which depicted a tremendous, serpent-like creature preparing to bite me in half. "Finally, they destroy the Sun Eater. With each victory, the power of the Purified One increases. Their mind gains insights into the Unmade's nature."

"Does the Unmade have its own champion? Seems like if you're trying to shape me into one, he'd be doing the same thing."

"All sentient beings, given enough defilements in the mind, are champions of Wayfarers like the Unmade. Their offerings . . . their sacrifices . . . each sin weakens the barrier between our worlds."

"You mean to tell me there's a universal scale between good and evil?"

"Such a model would be too simplistic, but let us say this: There is power behind every intention, every action. Every universe is nothing more than the combined thoughts of the sentient beings who exist there. If the virtues of the Radiant Wayfarers protect a universe, then their absence damns it."

It all seemed a tad fantastical and anthropocentric, but rather than getting into a verbal sparring match, I turned my thoughts inward. If this monk was telling the truth, there were massive implications I couldn't even begin to grasp. What if he was right, and this universe's slow death-by-the Unmade was its own fault? What if humanity's savagery and greed had been the very things that led the Unmade to our doorstep, much like the smell of blood luring a predator?

All along, I'd assumed Purifiers and chok'tal were the Unmade's weapons of conquest. But now, it seemed they were closer to the Unmade's highly coveted emissaries in this fallen playground. They formed a vital supply line to a reservoir that *we*, the pitiful mortals, had been filling since the dawn of civilization. The Unmade wasn't a conqueror, but instead a parasite that had an appetite for our moral failures.

Rather than make me resent humanity, though, it only stoked my anger toward Narbu. There was no way he hadn't known all of this. My mind, my body, my future—all of it was being spent on paying back the sins of a universe that I hadn't asked to join.

It was all too much for me. As such, I shrugged and turned toward the last panel. This time, the monk didn't hurry to point out anything. He remained at my side, stoic and motionless, as I pondered the nightmare before me.

The scene at the top of the panel was surprisingly rosy, given what came below. In it, I stood triumphantly atop the Unmade's corpse, my fist raised to deliver a killing blow. That was where the good news ended. In the next image, I was falling head over heels into some sort of abyss. After that was an illustration of my body being stretched, ripped apart, and glued back together using dark, roiling energy. And finally, as the cherry atop this miserable sundae, I was portrayed as the Unmade's replacement. Countless creatures knelt before me, their arms raised and mouths agape in agony. The kingdom around them was one of incessant pain.

"I don't understand," I said, staring at the panel with furrowed brows. "It doesn't make—"

"This is your fate," the monk said in a quiet yet stern tone. "You will slay the Unmade, but your mind will be overcome by its sins. The same hatred that flows through its veins will become part of you. In that moment, you will become a Defiled Wayfarer."

"That can't be true. I don't give a fuck about its powers."

"There is no choice in the matter of seizing power. There is a karmic cost to every action."

"What does that even mean?"

"To kill an insect is a pity, but to kill a Wayfarer is a sin worthy of rebirth in the hells. Any being that slays one, defiled or otherwise, receives this consequence tenfold."

"Listen, I'm done with being afraid of karma. There's no proof to any of this. Skip the religion and show me the evidence."

"Karma is just a word, Purifier," the monk explained calmly. "Physics easily teaches that there is a reaction to every action. Your mind is not developed enough to see the threads of karma, but they exist."

"Even *if* that's true, it doesn't add up. The Unmade is *evil*. Killing that son of a bitch is a favor to the universe."

"It does not matter. A Wayfarer is a Wayfarer. When we take life, we also take on every evil that dwelt in the victim's mind. And with your mind, given its rawness, there is no hope of mitigating the outcome."

I couldn't believe what I was hearing. All this work, all this effort, and I was *still* fated to wind up paying for my "crimes" eternally—to save the very same people who'd been feeding the Unmade for millennia? Sensing my control slipping, I did my best to breathe slowly and get my emotions in check.

"What exactly is the outcome?" I asked.

The monk looked at the panel for a time. "You will emerge victorious, but the Unmade's karmic fruit will ripen and fester within you. They will corrupt your weakened mind. As such, you will be reborn in an instant. Mired in the defilements, you will unconsciously give birth to a new dimension. A new realm. In this realm, you will be the god of all things."

I pondered the monk's description. "That doesn't sound *too* bad. It's more or less what I found out from that contraband book. Not quite the same as heaven, I guess, but—"

"You do not understand," the monk cut in. "You will not be a merciful god. Any memory of goodness, of this world, will be burned out of your mind."

"Meaning?"

"Your dimension is destined to be a hell realm. A world of endless torture and pain. In this place, the words of the awakened ones will never be allowed to flourish. Trillions will die in your infinite prison. Even you will be shackled by your own wickedness, doomed to die, reincarnate, and die again until the end of time." My mouth dropped, but the monk pressed on. "You must grasp, Purifier, that this is the best possible outcome."

When I found the wherewithal to finally speak, my words emerged in gasps. "Best. Possible. Outcome? What the *fuck* are you talking about!?"

The monk wandered around the mural's inner circle, running a hand across the Sparkseed design of my future. "Our order's purpose was to carry out the vision of the Radiant Wayfarers in this universe, and in particular, the Wellspring they have formed in fellowship. They have seen true reality, and they know what is good and proper for the long-term virtue of this universe . . . and all others. They would not have presented this course unless the alternatives were unthinkable."

"You don't know that. There has to be another way."

"That was what Narbu, the Betraying Oracle, also believed."

"Maybe he's right."

The monk studied me for a while, cobalt eyes piercing my very soul. "What did Scryer Narbu tell you about our homeworld? About our origins?"

"That you all came from another planet to seek enlightenment for the universe."

"That is true . . . to a point. But he leaves out his own scheming. His distaste for the prophecy presented by the Wellspring."

"Go on."

"He, like you, believed that this course was barbaric. He believed that through determination and focus, he could reach through the veil and see beyond even the Wellspring's wisdom. In his arrogant mind, this would bring about a different course. A better course."

"Did he find it?"

"An alternative, yes," the monk said, "but not a bloodless one. He was blinded by his own fervor, his own aspirations. He spent over three hundred years in meditation . . . never pausing, never faltering. By the time he emerged from his ritual, his name had nearly been forgotten."

"That didn't answer my question."

The monk raised a finger, urging patience. "The instant he awoke, he summoned the entire order. Elders and novices alike sat in rapt attention, all prepared to hear the oracle's great insights. But alas, they were not well received."

"Why not?"

"Narbu's plan involved less death among sentient beings, to be sure, but it also guaranteed the downfall of the Radiant Wayfarers and their teachings." The monk turned away. "Although some brothers saw the wisdom of this new direction, the majority were not swayed—including the elders. He was rebuked for his foolishness, and that was thought to be the end of it."

A knot began forming deep in my stomach. "I'm guessing that *wasn't* the end of it."

"No," the monk said, his voice touched by a note that might've been regret in a less mechanical being. "Narbu could not abide by the elders' decision. In his mind, he was an integral part of a new prophecy. This gave him the justification he required to advance his ambitions . . . regardless of the cost."

"Shit. This is where the blood painting comes in, isn't it?"

"Narbu did not act immediately. He bided his time, lurking for years, then decades, then centuries. One fateful day, while my brothers and I were engaged in a mass ritual, he carried out his aims. With a weapon most foul, he defiled our bodies. Next, he buried this place and its sins deep beneath the soil. Only then did he trek down to the foot of the mountains and begin constructing his own monastery. All in service of his own prophecy."

"But there are still monks that—"

"Their minds were tampered with," the monk said. "Memories were erased, altered. None of them can recall what Narbu did to the missing brothers."

For nearly ten seconds I just stood there, trying and failing to process what this monk was telling me. It seemed so absurd, so unthinkable. Narbu didn't seem capable of killing anything without cause, especially his own brothers in the order. But how else could I explain this mural? For the first time in ages, everything being told to me made sense. There was no hidden information, no "wait and see," no misdirection.

Well, except for one tiny, crucial detail.

"So," I said, struggling to find the right words for such a strange question, "if he killed you all, how are we talking right now?"

With a snap of his fingers, the monk dispelled the entire mural. A storm of molten Sparkseed flowed upward, swirled together above my head, and drained back into the altar. Once the last mote had vanished, the altar resealed.

"What did you see upon arriving here?" the monk asked.

"That doesn't answer anything about why you're alive."

"Bear with me, Purifier. It will make answering your query easier."

I scratched my head, wondering if it was a trick question. "There was some kind of . . ." I paused, realizing how damn difficult it was to remember anything about what had preceded this moment. "There was a fungal creature. A menace. I don't know. It looked like the Throne up on the peak . . . only a lot worse."

The monk nodded. "Among our order, this organism was originally known as the *junarra-gol.* 'That Which Feasts on the Mind.'"

"Catchy name," I said bitterly. "I'll stick with menace."

"The junnara-gol was little more than a nuisance when our order first arrived on this world. It kept to itself, only devouring those who willingly gave their bodies to it. It was revered by the locals as a source of wisdom, but our elders disagreed."

"So, what changed?"

"In time, Oracle Narbu discovered that the junnara-gol was sentient. Its hunger for the rift involved energy, yes, but not that of radioactivity. Instead, it hungered for mental energy. Over time, and due to its complex fungal structure, it accrued vast reservoirs of power."

Frowning, I patted the leaking bag on my hip. "Is that why Narbu gave me these flowers? To get some sort of sap out of it?"

Again, the monk nodded. "When the junnara-gol's remarkable qualities were discovered, the elders began using it for rituals with organic beings. They termed it the Throne of Radiance. Those wishing to master the Third Perfection were tasked with scaling the Scholar's Ascent, finding the junnara-gol's root, and draining its vital fluid. This fluid would then be mixed with the sacred flower, creating a potent concoction sure to guarantee visions beneath the light of the rift."

"What you're saying, then, is that this . . . menace thing . . . really *does* contain the fluid . . . the order uses to trip its ass off."

"I am unfamiliar with the expression, but your mind indicates that it understands the intention. The junnara-gol, for countless centuries, was a source of overwhelming knowledge and insight."

"Right . . . so Narbu's plan was for me to reach the Scholar's Ascent and use this flower to make a psychoactive drug. The sacrament or whatever."

"For the first half of the trial, yes," the monk said. "It was believed that those who brewed the sacrament and consumed it beneath the rift would recognize the Absolute in their own minds. It was a crucial part of our prophecy for the Purified One. The moment at which their mind's potential came alive."

I hummed in understanding, calling to mind the third trial's illustration on the mural. "This is all helpful, but it doesn't explain how the hell you're dead and still talking to me."

"What we did not realize, in those early days, was that the junnara-gol was more intelligent . . . and insidious . . . than appearances suggested. You see, it was not interested merely in mental energy. In particular, it was drawn to corrupted karma."

"Again with the karma . . ."

The monk lifted a hand to call for silence. "Narbu recognized these qualities. Quietly, always with the silent precision of a lynx, he fed the junnara-gol's appetite. He allowed its roots and spores to encroach on the monastery. When it came time to enact his fatal plan, he sealed us inside our chamber. We were powerless against the junnara-gol's hunger."

"Hold on. You're saying Narbu killed you all using the fungus!?"

"Death would be a mercy. The junnara-gol has flourished in this tainted place, absorbing the residue of dead minds and feeding on the remains of those who have not yet expired."

My mouth suddenly went dry. "What do you mean, absorbing the residue of dead minds?"

"In many ways, the junnara-gol is similar to your chok'tal. Many elders believed, in fact, that the junnara-gol learned how to consume consciousness from its contact with the Unmade."

"How would it have any contact with them?"

"None can say, Purifier. But it stands to reason. If the junnara-gol could siphon the energy of radiance, it could also siphon it from less wholesome sources."

"Alright, fair enough," I said in exasperation. "Now lay it out for me. What the fuck is going on?"

Out of nowhere, the monk's eyes darkened. "Such a pity. I'd hoped you would understand your predicament by now. It is always unsavory to explain such things to newcomers."

"Newcomers? How many—"

"The junnara-gol has lured thousands of victims here since the days of Narbu's crime. Even now, it still devours the bodies and minds of those who should have died centuries ago. It keeps them alive, nourishing them even as it drains every memory, hope, and fear from awareness. All I have managed, during my thousands of years of enslavement here, is to manifest this dream environment for the comfort of the bewildered."

Although I *heard* the monk's words, not a single one of them registered as holding any sense. It was like sitting through a storm of babble. But some deeper, unconscious part of me began to grasp what was happening here. My only comparison to the feeling in my gut would be that of waking up in a triage center, dazed and aching, only to discover that your legs had both been amputated.

"Are you saying we're . . . being eaten . . . right now?" I whispered.

The monk glanced away. "One molecule at a time."

"Well, get me *out!*"

"As I said, Purifier, I am powerless in this realm. The only purpose of this world, this beautiful place, is to provide guidance to the beings trapped in the junnara-gol's nightmare. I cannot release you from this place any more than I can release myself."

I started pacing in circles, heart thundering and lungs shrinking. "This can't be happening."

"There is one note of solace," the monk said, his voice as impassive as ever. "If you truly are destined to become the Purified One, you will awaken. If you are not, of course, you will die here with the rest of us."

A flicker of hope burned away the fears. I rounded on the monk, fists clenched and jaw set in unshakable determination. "You mean, I'm fated to get out of here?"

"Measured against the elders' prophecy—the very same one that I have immortalized in the mural—you are already beyond the bounds of destiny. Narbu has ensured that. From this point on, none can say what will happen."

"But . . . you said the Purified One will wake up."

"The Purified One is not bound by the laws of cause and effect," the monk explained. "They are expected to kill a Wayfarer . . . The meddling of the junnara-gol is nothing to them."

"Well, how do I do it, then?"

"That is a question for the Purified One themselves."

I rolled my eyes. "Very helpful."

"Promise me one thing, Purifier." I glanced at the monk with weariness and nodded for him to continue. "If you truly are the Purified One . . . if you escape from this wretched place and slay the junnara-gol . . . I implore you to put an end to Narbu and his scheming. You cannot afford to follow his twisted path, whether or not this moment was predestined by it. Reality itself cannot afford this. His actions will plunge countless worlds into unyielding darkness." He straightened to the tune of clanking joints. "If you heed my words, I can perish knowing I have fulfilled my duty. I will have altered the course of Narbu's madness."

A pregnant silence followed as the two of us held one another's gaze. In the monk's cold, mechanical eyes, I saw the weight of infinite possible futures. The torment of holding this broken nightmare together.

"Yeah, alright," I said quietly. "*When* I get out, I'll do it. For you . . . and for your brothers."

With that, I had a goal. A path to survival. Now I just had to do the impossible work of pursuing it.

22

Right about now, you're probably scratching your head and trying to make sense out of this long, convoluted string of events. How do I know that? Because I lived through all of this. You might think you're mighty confused while trying to plod through this tale, but imagine actually living it.

In the interest of showing you mercy I never received, and also to prepare you for the coming madness, I'm going to offer a truncated rundown of the entire situation. Wellsprings, Wayfarers, the Unmade, the monks . . . all of it. Here we go.

Beneath our usual, boring physical reality, there's a bubbling void made of pure potential. The void is self-aware, however, as it's literally made of the Absolute. It's not easy to define the Absolute, but at its core, it's the "living spark" that you see in the eyes of sentient creatures. Wise, compassionate radiance.

Rarely, a mortal being manages to skyrocket their mind straight into the void and shed their physical body. These are called Wayfarers, or awakened ones, or any other name a particular culture chooses. Masters of physical (and mental) existence.

Some of these beings were lucky enough to study the Absolute within their own minds. They used its power to teach sentient beings how to love one another, build harmonious societies, and so on and so forth. *Other* Wayfarers weren't so pleasant, and fell into states of varying insanity due to lack of radiance. These "bad" beings, consequently, made it their personal mission to treat the multiverse as a five-course buffet of pain and fear.

Somehow, some way, an alien civilization established contact with a hive-mind of "good" Wayfarers, known as a Wellspring, and downloaded its collective teachings. They then packaged these teachings into inorganic beings and shipped them across the universe to learn more.

As you might've guessed, these inorganic beings were the monks. A bunch of them landed here, on this planet. They began hearing new messages from the Wellspring via the "Throne of Radiance"—a gigantic hunk of fungus capable of transmitting messages between our universe and the Wellspring in the form of psychedelic trips. The Throne eventually ended up spitting out a prophecy related to little old me. A prophecy related to stopping one of the "bad," or Defiled, Wayfarers. Yes, the Unmade.

Only problem, of course, was that the prophecy's solution involved retraining one of the Unmade's own champions. To that end, the order began accepting humanoids and tutoring them, all in hopes that one of them would turn out to be their "chosen one." The downside to this prophecy was that, even in the best-case scenario, trillions would die. As you might imagine, not all of the monks thought this was swell.

One monk in particular, a fellow known as Narbu, tried to find an alternate route through isolation and doubling down on the drugs. And he did—after a fashion. Narbu's "new and improved" plan made quite a stir, though for all the wrong reasons. With his aspirations mocked and cast aside, Narbu decided the only logical solution was to murder all the contrarian monks, set up his own monastery, and begin educating a new generation of brothers for use in his *own* prophecy.

This went swimmingly, until the actual "chosen one" appeared on their doorstep for training. Through some combination of happenstance, lies, and sheer bad luck, the "chosen one" ended up at the bottom of a long, dark pit, being devoured by a mind-eating fungus with a taste for monks. Not that he knew much about the reality of things, of course, seeing as his mind was trapped in psychedelic purgatory with a ghost.

Complicated, right? Believe me, I know.

This stripped-down version of recent happenings was more or less what ran through my mind as I paced around the chamber, trying to scrounge up a single iota of comprehension. Thus far, my experience on this world had been one long, twisting experience of deception. Everyone seemed to have their own agenda, their own "destiny," their own way to redirect me toward whatever goal they perceived as most favorable.

Hell, I was doubting my own sanity so much that I no longer knew if I was in a hallucinatory dreamworld. What if this was yet another of Narbu's tricks? Was I still on the predestined course I'd seen in the mural, or was I waist-deep in someone else's triple-backstabbing plan?

I had no answers to questions of that sort. Yet as I wandered about, muttering to myself and racking my brain for ways out of the nightmare,

I found that I didn't give a damn about answers anymore. Ever since birth (literally), I'd been running around in circles, asking this person and that to tell me who I was and what I needed. Nobody's reply had captured the full story. The more I poked, prodded, and pulled at the threads of my existence, the more I understood a terrifying truth: Everyone was just as goddamn confused as me.

That realization, as flippant as it sounds, smashed through the last walls of my panic. A cool breeze of peace moved through me, and I came to a stop mid-stride. There was glorious freedom in embracing the absurd. In abandoning the quest for certainty.

Down here, stuck in ghost-land, it didn't matter whose prophecy was right, whose course was better, whose training regimen would give me what. All that mattered was surviving—not for anyone else, but for me. *Only* me. For too long, I'd run around with the burdens of galactic destiny and sages on my back. Each time push came to shove, I'd been stomped under the heels of those who saw me as an instrument above an individual.

Well, fuck that. Nobody else would—or even could—guarantee my fate. As always, it came down to me, myself, and I.

And I *refused* to die here.

After some intense brainstorming, I came up with a list of plans for Operation Escape from Madness. The first plan, which I naïvely hoped would work through the power of love or some other emotional magic, involved sitting cross-legged and conjuring a mental image of sunny fields. Honestly, I have no idea what I was expecting from that one. My only prize for that long, sustained effort was a pounding headache from furrowing my brow so much.

Next, I tried the brute-force method of punching a wall. If this place really was just a "simulation" generated by a monk's willpower, maybe I could jar myself out of the dream and back into reality through pain. No dice there. All I succeeded in doing was putting a smirk on the resident monk, who seemed more amused than intrigued.

I then moved on to a tactic I more or less knew wouldn't work: relying on my chok'tal powers. Just as before, nothing happened. It felt as though I could dimly discern the chok'tal's consciousness, but couldn't access it.

My fourth tactic was . . . unconventional. I figured that if I'd "woken up" in this place, I might be able to "sleep out" of it too. After all, drifting off to sleep brought you into a liminal state where fantasy and reality seemed to blur. Unfortunately, I'd never mastered the art of forcing myself to sleep.

The best I managed was a fitful, terror-stricken bout of napping, which I suspect was actually caused by holding my breath to the point of blacking out. It didn't catapult me back to the waking world.

That left my fifth and final plan, which was easily the boldest of the bunch. Murdering myself. It was a tried-and-true strategy I'd employed in my own life (that is to say, not in the original Dak's memories), and tended to bring about a swift end to any dreams gone south.

Of course, there were risks involved. Once you became lucid in a dream, you were comforted by the knowledge that whatever you did was more or less irrelevant. Whether you pitched yourself off a cliff or ran headfirst into a monster's jaws, you were guaranteed to wake up in your bed, safe and sound—if a bit sweaty. Here, though, there was no such certainty. Although I wasn't an expert, I knew there had to be shades of difference between a self-manifested dream and a superorganism's hallucinatory prison. If I killed myself here, it might well be the end. Or not, if rebirth was actually a feature of reality.

Either way, it wasn't a risk-free tactic. That meant I had to do something I truly, truly hated, especially given my newfound resolve to *not* rely on anybody else. With shameful, dragging steps, I returned to the monk.

"What happens if I kill myself in here?" I asked.

The monk smiled at me. "It is unknown. I have never felt the urge to destroy myself."

"I don't want to *destroy* myself, just get out of here."

"Several have tried," the monk said. "I do not know what became of them. I remain here in tranquility, spreading the sacred light of wisdom."

I groaned. "Yes, yes, very noble. But take a step back. You just said people have done it. What happened to their . . . spirits, or whatever? Did they stick around?"

"They vanished."

"You mean, died? Or just left?"

"Such distinctions are difficult to make."

"Useful," I said, frowning. "If I do this, and I *don't* wake up, I'll spend the rest of my existence haunting you here."

"You will not be able. The moment death occurs, you will already be immersed in your new birth."

"Yeah, yeah, yeah."

I shook my head and wandered off, intent on finding something lethal that could end my life with minimal suffering. The search was extensive, but the results lackluster. Whether by design or simple happenstance, the only serviceable item for my task was a long, thin length of metal protruding from a brazier.

Survival instincts flared up as I inspected the sword-like fixture. To do this properly (in other words, without blinding pain), I'd need to slam my head down at *just* the right angle to skewer my eyeball. Assuming biology was the same here as in the real world, it would be enough to pop my brainstem and induce instant death. Nagging doubts, of course, began to chip away at my confidence in the idea. What if I missed? What if I chickened out and hit my cheek? What if there was no death here, but rather an infinite procession of ever-worsening outcomes?

Screw it. Better to die with gusto than as a shriveled corpse-turned-buffet for the junnara-gol.

Gathering my courage before logic could gain any traction, I took a final breath and slammed my left eye down on the spike. There was a squelching sound, a jolt of blistering pain, and then . . . nothing. Well, almost nothing. The sensations of my body and ordinary, thinking mind faded into the ether, leaving behind a murky void. Prior to learning from the monks, I would've called it oblivion. Now, however, I had a higher vantage point. "I" was still present in the void, still clearly comprehending its presence. That meant there was still *something*. It wasn't true death. Not yet, anyway.

Bit by bit, a new world took form around me. Light came in dim, drifting patches, and sounds emerged as strangled bleats.

Oh, shit, I thought, struggling to even perceive the words as they arose. *Did I just* actually *kill myself? Am I about to be reborn?*

For better or worse, that didn't seem very likely. The fact that I could even think as "myself," with all of Dak's memories and quirks, seemed to support that. Furthermore, each returning sensation seemed to land precisely where it had been prior to the spike-face incident, reconstructing the solidity of my "normal" body. Soon enough, my weight, height, and general orientation were back to baseline levels. The air, too, felt more like an open space than a womb—which I figured I would've inhabited if I'd been reborn.

At a point I couldn't quite identify, the chaotic sensations of the environment settled into something my brain could term "semi-real." I found myself in a dark, humid tunnel lined with walls that *breathed*. Even through my boots, I sensed a pronounced heartbeat pulsing up from the floor. This entire place was alive . . . and defiled.

Don't ask me how I knew that, because I couldn't (and still can't) say. All I knew was that its corruption jumped out at me with flashing red alarms. There was something sickly about it, something that hung in the air and colored the very atoms around me.

Before long, I gained the ability to move my body. I lifted both hands, one at a time, and studied them closely. Both were completely black. Not due to shadow—faint, ruddy light pressed through the intestine-like walls around me—but rather due to their nature. Compared to the world around me, my flesh was an absence. A pure void.

As mists swirled in the passage ahead, I called upon my chok'tal powers to see if they were back online. Again, nothing. For that, I was strangely glad. The chok'tal had become something of a barometer for reality. Anytime I was in a dream or some other form of "altered existence," I couldn't summon its presence or power. By the same token, I had hope that its reappearance would confirm that I'd come back to full reality.

For now, though, I knew that I wasn't fully out of the woods. I was still in some crossover state between the waking world and the hallucination. A secondary, deeper level of the junnara-gol's nightmare, maybe? I quickly discarded that fear. This had to be *closer* to reality, not farther down. The mural-guarding monk had been operating a dream within a dream to avoid panicking newcomers. Given the hellish appearance of this new place, it seemed logical to assume that I'd just accessed the "raw experience" formerly concealed by the monk's pleasant distortions.

In other words, I'd checked out of the tutorial area. This was the real deal, horrors and all.

With that comforting thought, I set off to find a way out. As I moved down the passage, which seemed to snake about and twist of its own accord, more and more sensory details trickled in. Much like eyes adjusting to an influx of light, the various sounds, shapes, and feelings were hazy at first, but gradually became clearer.

What I'd taken to be a whispering breeze was soon revealed to be a chorus of screams. The voices were distinct yet melting together: men, women, children, aliens. It seemed to echo from within the walls themselves.

Next, the forms along the walls came alive with vivid clarity. No longer did I see bumps, ridges, bones, or patches of tissue. Now I saw a collage of naked, emaciated bodies, all contorted and anchored in place by invisible hands. I wandered up to a skeletal man and waved a hand in front of his milk-white, bloody eyes, but all I received was more pitiful shrieking. Every few seconds, a fresh spasm moved through his back and snapped his limbs into a new configuration.

After stepping back, though, I saw that he was one of numberless victims. Holes in the walls that had previously been a few centimeters wide were now gaping, cavernous spaces piled with mindless humanoids. The ceiling peeled back to reveal a canyon made of thrashing limbs.

It's just like the Accretion, I thought to myself, shutting my eyes against the ever-expanding display of miseries. *Only this thing hasn't just been drinking up my pain—it's been wringing it out of everyone here.*

I forced myself to concentrate, hoping I might remember how I'd overcome the Accretion. If these beasts shared some aspect of their nature, there might be a common theme to their behavior, or some pattern I could exploit. But before I could explore that line of thinking too far, the sound of scrabbling claws echoed from the depths of the tunnel.

Whirling around, I stared in the direction of the noise's origin. All I saw were more bodies squirming in a bank of fog. Only . . . there *was* something there. The longer I gazed that way, the more certain I became. There was a presence lurking in the fog. A presence that was *very* interested in me.

Abruptly, words made of patchwork, stitched-together voices slithered into my mind. *"You . . . do not . . . sleep."*

My eyes widened as I stared at the lurking shadow.

"You . . . must . . . sleep."

Shrinking back a few steps, I hardened my hands into fists at my side.

"Sleep . . . so we . . . may feed."

"Alright, that's enough of that," I said flatly.

The junnara-gol must've decided it was growing bored with talking, too, because it surged forward without missing a beat. All I saw was a tangle of flailing legs, smog, and decay—and that was all the confirmation I needed.

Just as the junnara-gol unleashed a hair-raising screech, I turned to the closest wall of tissue and punched. My fist crashed through several layers of cartilage and fluid, then began burrowing outward, stretching the gruesome material to its breaking point. The junnara-gol's cries grew even louder, but I didn't dare turn back. If it fed on defiled energy, the last thing I wanted to do was give it a free meal—especially if there was no way out.

The gibbering and clawing came nearer and nearer. I leaned my whole body into the strike, fist quivering as it tore through successively tougher sheets of tissue. By now the resistance was rubbery and strained, much like an overfilled waterskin. This was *it.* There was no plan B, no last-ditch miracle plan hiding up my sleeve.

I'd broken out of the monk's dreamscape, and now I'd break out of the junnara-gol's mental clutches. That, or die pathetically.

Second by second, grunt by grunt, my fist powered through the organic barrier. My entire body burned with the exertion. No matter how hard I pushed, the junnara-gol's nightmare pushed back twice as hard.

Before I knew it, the junnara-gol's murmuring overtook my own heartbeat in my ears. Creeping threads of darkness spooled across the floor below me and wriggled between my legs. The presence of death itself hung heavy at my back.

Then the junnara-gol's mouth opened—a fact I only learned when I felt the press of its teeth against my back.

This was it. Make-or-break time. Calling upon my reserves of pent-up fear, spite, and frustration, I put every possible drop of mental fuel behind my fist. Sweat prickled on my forehead. Aches carved up and down my wrist like cracks forming in a wooden beam.

Hot breath washed over me as the junnara-gol's mouth widened, and—

Skrich.

My fist tore straight through the back lining of the wall. Before I'd hardly even sensed the cool, spacious void around my fingers, though, the dream began to collapse. Liquefied streams of light, dazzling and chromatic, burst through the breach in a rainbow flood. The junnara-gol shrieked and shrank back. I, meanwhile, withdrew my fist and stared into the heart of the rift.

It was indescribable. Utterly beyond any concept the ordinary mind can grasp. If I had to use one word, it would be "blinding"—in every sense of the word. Blinding to the eyes, to the ears, to thought. In that instant, I saw what underpins the fabric of reality. The maelstrom that rages across time and space.

Although I didn't realize it at the time, I now understand why the creature's lair was built upon this void-like foundation. Regardless of how it took form in this universe, the junnara-gol wasn't a native of our physical dimension. Its body—or rather, its fungal colony—was just the tip of an eldritch iceberg. A visible manifestation of a creature that had no physical shape. The fungus was merely its colony, its medium to interact with the universe. I suspect that, much like the Unmade and other immaterial terrors, it had first stumbled across our world through curiosity. And just like the Unmade, it stayed because of its hunger.

None of this went through my mind in the moment, of course. I was too busy being overwhelmed by the light of eternity.

* * *

I can't say what happened to my body in the seconds right after perceiving that light. It's a blank spot in my memory. Either I never experienced it, or I did, and it was so insane I shoved it into subconsciousness.

Whatever the case, I had a gnarly bout of déjà vu when I returned to awareness. Once again, I was immobile, wracked with pain, staring into the darkness of my eyelids, and overcome by the sensation of waking up from a long and confusing fever dream. Dreams upon dreams. With my luck, I'd probably only succeeded in burrowing even farther into the junnara-gol's hallucination. *How many more tissue-walls would I need to punch?*

As I lay there, barely breathing, I decided I didn't care. I'd rip open every junnara-gol wall in existence if it meant returning to the waking world and settling the score. My anger assured me of that. Maybe it was fortunate that Narbu had deceived me. I mean, sure, he *was* the reason I'd even run into the junnara-gol, but he was also a source of disdain. Him and his lies were a steady stream of fuel for the nuclear fission in my chest.

Even if it was the last thing I did, I *would* get out of this place and have my vengeance.

This time around, however, there was a sense of stability to the experience. The pains didn't flicker or vanish. When I managed to pry my eyelids open, I was strangely delighted by the fact that I was in a real, seemingly physical world of dread.

Though I was facedown, my body wasn't exactly flat. Instead, it was held aloft by a twisting network of vines, gill-covered mushroom caps, and sinew. A crown of wilted tendrils brushed my scalp and hung past my brow—destroyed by my breakout plan, I guessed. The floor below was similar to the walls; it writhed and squelched just inches from my face, churning the pools of dark, steaming sludge that had pooled in its craters.

That wasn't the nastiest part of the floor, though. Woven into the mesh-like beads were hundreds upon hundreds of corpses, all in varying states of decomposition or fungi-fication. Everything from animal skeletons to bloated humanoids to . . . robotic monk parts . . . had been cobbled together with the junnara-gol's mushrooms to form a sickening tapestry. The assimilation was so thorough that it soon became impossible to distinguish the fungus from its victims.

Summoning the energy to lift my aching neck, I found that the walls were equally corrupted and strewn with decay. The unholy mass ascended in all directions, covering the interior of the tunnel I'd fallen down so long ago.

Or had it been? In truth, I had no idea how much time had passed between the first fight and now. Hallucinations were funny like that. The fact that I wasn't dead, of course, suggested I hadn't been underground long enough to activate the chok'tal's host-death program.

The chok'tal. Merely thinking of that wonderful, terrible parasite was enough to shift my mind back into gear.

Wasting no time, I called upon Modri.

"Holy *fuck!*"

His scream nearly killed me via shock. Seeing as how we were trapped in the junnara-gol's funhouse, however, I couldn't reply out loud. Better to switch to a mental conversation.

Would you shut the hell up? We're in a— I paused, a grin erupting upon my bloodied face. *You can hear me! I can hear you!*

"*You're tellin' me! This whole thing has taken a first-class trip out of reality.*"

We can talk about that later.

"*Did you hear that sonofabitch!? Narbu's a—*"

I said, we'll talk about it later. Right now, we have to survive.

"Fair enough," Modri said, instantly dropping back to a reasonable voice. The perks of being a disembodied consciousness with eternity to learn emotional management, I guess. "*That upgrade that gives you claws and fangs sure woulda been nice here.*"

Helpful, Modri. Very helpful.

"*Well, shit, what do you expect me to do? Call in orbital bombardment?*"

Use your chok'tal brain.

"*Huh. Guess you could— Hey. Hold up. How the hell're you talkin' to me?*"

With my mind?

"*Nah, it ain't that. We're only able to talk when you're out of combat, Purifier.*"

Slowly, despite the fog in my battered head, I understood what he meant. *The encounter ended?*

"*You musta gotten an encounter failed message. Probably were too loopy to know it.*"

Yeah, maybe. Or I'm still dreaming.

Modri sighed. "*I'm real, alright. Listen, this might make it easier for you. It doesn't see you as a threat. Might be able to get yourself free, find another tunnel out of here.*"

Yeah, I said, hyping myself up with Modri's words, *you're right. Let's see how this goes.*

My first order of business was to check my remaining time. All strategies were worthless until I knew exactly how long I had to implement them.

Given my surroundings, though, I didn't feel comfortable pulling up the full Status Display. There wasn't much I could do to defend myself if the junnara-gol *did* decide to attack, but I still refused to let myself die due to checking a virtual menu. This being the case, I flexed a cognitive muscle I hadn't used since my first day with the chok'tal. Instead of pulling up the entire display, I was able to summon my key metrics on the left-hand side of the HUD.

Rank Time: 0 Hours, 0 Minutes, 0 Seconds
Storehouse Time: 17 Hours, 37 Minutes, 4 Seconds
RANK-UP NOT AVAILABLE

Shit.

A rush of fear pumped through my head and down into my gurgling bowels. I'd started chewing into Storehouse Time. I'd *actually* done it. It was something I'd known was possible on a theoretical level, but never truly considered.

Until now, I'd seen the Rank Time as a hard stop. Anytime I had less than five hours left on the clock, I started to get sweaty palms. Less than three hours, and I was shitting bricks. But now, thanks to the junnara-gol's long sleep, I was well past the red line. I was dipping into the coffers. Borrowing time from death itself.

"Don't stare at it," Modri growled. *"Won't help, only hurt."*

He was probably right, but it was hard to take advice from someone who'd been killed by the same timer. I couldn't let that happen. I wouldn't. It was time to bust out of here, and fast.

Glancing about, I saw no sign of the rifle. It was possible that it was wedged beneath me, buried in the living shell the junnara-gol had grown around my body, but unlikely. A few blasts of Telekinesis suggested it wasn't anywhere in reach—and certainly nowhere I could reach with enough mental power to retrieve it.

Oh, and I couldn't even make use of Telekinesis here. Although it had become my universal problem-solving power, it had one glaring flaw: the inability to work with animate matter. This is especially troublesome when you're imprisoned in a dungeon made of animate matter.

Briefly, I toyed with trying to extract bones or other bits of digested bodies. Another failure. Most of the "workable" bits were too far for my mental strength (or lack thereof), and those within range were pinned under literal tons of fungus. Just like me.

Then I turned to my clothes. Theoretically, I could rip my garments off and use them as garrotes, but then I'd just be naked and at the mercy of an angry fungal colony. A fungal colony still very capable of tossing me back into a hallucination, no less.

No, I had to be cautious. Subtle. Some might even say . . . unorthodox.

Several meters away, enshrined in a tangle of twitching growths, was what appeared to be the junnara-gol's central stalk. Long, shuddering contractions moved through its calcified plates, and the flesh beneath was practically glowing with energized capillary webs. If there was one thing I knew about plants (and I guess fungi, by extension), it was that they relied on their roots to shuffle nutrients around. Severing the main channel should be enough to kill it—eventually, that is.

Only problem, as you've probably guessed, was my distance from that stalk. I had nothing to stab from a distance, nothing to throw, and nothing in my bag of upgrade tricks capable of causing that kind of damage. Well, aside from Mind Cascade . . . and I wasn't feeling bold enough to try that out on another creature holding me in its grip, given the sloth's volatile reaction.

That left one solution. If the mountain wouldn't come to me, I'd go to the mountain.

Squirming around in my earthy prison, I got a decent feel for the density of the junnara-gol's grip. The upper half of my body was relatively free, while my right leg was pinned around the thigh area. As such, my calves and foot were totally numb—so numb, in fact, that I hadn't even known they were numb until I tried to move them. There was a good chance the lack of circulation had started killing the tissue long ago.

Modri, I said mentally, already dreading both possible answers to this question, *how long would it take for me to heal from, say, catastrophic damage to my body?*

"How catastrophic are you talkin' about?"

Oh, I dunno. Pretend I had my leg ripped off.

"With 340% Anima? Probably under a day, assumin' you didn't bust up anything else. But it— Whoa, whoa, whoa. Why are you askin' that?"

I'm already dipping into Storehouse Time. The way I see it, I either keep twiddling my thumbs and wind up as Purifier jerky . . . or I get myself out. By any means necessary.

"You aren't gonna rip your own damn leg off."

How do you know?

"You ain't that kinda man. I've seen 'em, worked with 'em, even killed 'em. But that ain't you, Purifier. You'll get halfway and pass out."

I scoffed. *Oh, yeah? Just watch me.*

"Nope. Don't even think about it. Tearin' off your leg makes for a real bad pissin' contest."

It's not a pissing contest. It's survival.

"Alright, pup, calm down and listen to a man who's lost more limbs than a forgetful cannibal. You might—might—get yourself free, but shock's a real pain in the ass. It takes you to lights-out land real quick, no matter how tough you are. Then there's the blood loss. You'll probably pass out 'fore you get a tourniquet ready, let alone on the leg. Sure, you could try to cauterize the bleedin' stump, but that's no easy task without heat."

I listened to Modri's warnings with a clear, sober mind, nodding along with each very practical point. He was right, after all. During my scant existence, the years of which I could count on one hand, I'd been subjected to very little in the way of self-imposed pain. Even amp-sticks had been too grating on the throat for me to enjoy smoking them. The odds of me being able to suck down a breath, grit my teeth, and rip my leg off one bit of stringy flesh at a time were laughably small.

Which was why I had to do it.

In recent days, and especially recent hours, I'd grown jaded as hell with everyone defining the boundaries of who I was and what role I played in the universe's destiny. Each person had a different and often contradictory vision of my capabilities and limitations. To some, I was the Messiah. To others, a fearsome blight. Beneath all of that, though, I was just me. Just Dak. I had to learn who that was, whether through joy or pain.

It was time to see what I was made of. Literally.

Firmly digging my palms into the biomass on either side of me, I heaved like I'd never heaved before. Aside from dislocating *something* in my left leg—which still felt pain, mind you—I was in the same terrible situation. I let myself sag, drew a breath, and tried again. This time, there was a distinct and anus-puckering *pop* in my right ankle.

I slumped back down, my face red and streaked with sweat. This was going to be a long, dreadful affair.

Five minutes of shoving later, I felt something wet seeping through my pants. Blood. I savored the moment, certain I would never again be so joyous about damage to my body. Then it was back to shoving. With each push, my torso extended farther and farther from the fungus. My left leg (the good one) had taken a fair beating in the effort, and would probably need a few hours of healing on its own.

"Had enough yet?" Modri prodded.

I scowled. *Just getting started.*

"Give it a rest, Purifier. You ain't cut out for this."

Something about his sentiment lit a powder keg in my chest. He was right—I wasn't cut out for this. I wasn't cut out for anything I'd been asked to do in the preceding days. I'd been thrown into this meat grinder without so much as a word of consolation.

All my pain, all my frustration, came bursting out in a spirited push that threatened to pop the blood vessels in my forehead. My eyes bulged and my jaw locked. I'd either get out now or die from the strain. Either way, it was better than listening to Modri's shit-talking.

When my arms began to quiver, though, I knew it was over. Legs didn't just rip off. They needed to be sliced, crushed, or—

That's it. Before I could gather the good sense to stop myself, I began putting the horrid thought into action. *Just weaken the tissue . . .*

After shifting a hand to the fungal mound above me, I gritted my teeth and diverted all my strength to twisting at the hip. All my wriggling, grunting, and shoving must've done something, because I was able to rotate far more than before. I put this extra leverage to work by rolling back and forth like a beast death-rolling its prey to . . . well, death.

Twist by twist, my body rotated. All except my left leg, that is. But that was the point. Soon I could feel bands of sinew gliding over the biomass, their fibers splintering with each pass. After a few more test rolls, I determined that the leg was more or less detached. Enough to soak my shirt with blood, anyway.

And now, I mentally told Modri, *it's time for the conclusion of tonight's event.*

In a spectacular display of both stupidity and courage, I repeated my first mega-heave using the fungus below. My body began sliding out of its prison—and kept sliding. If not for the junnara-gol's dormant presence, I would've been howling for joy. A shit-eating grin appeared on my face as I reached the floor and began tugging myself along using roots.

Abruptly, I flopped forward and into a puddle of foul fungus-juice. I swiped away the mess, then rolled out to figure out what had happened. To my surprise, I'd succeeded. I was completely out of the junnara-gol's grip.

Of course, that also meant I was now missing a leg. Part of it, at least. I lifted the twitching remains of my right leg into the air. There was still a thigh—mostly—that ended in a bloody tuft of dangling muscle strands. My shattered femur protruded like a flag of victory. It would hurt like no tomorrow when proper blood flow resumed and the adrenaline wore off, but until then, I had a few minutes of freedom to keep myself alive.

"You stupid, stupid man," Modri groaned. "*Get your shirt off.*"

I stared at the leg as blood began pumping out in weak spurts. *Oh, come on,* I thought-told him. *At least buy me dinner first.*

"*No time for jokes, shithead. You've got no idea what might be in this fungus. Could be an anti-clottin' compound, could be the kind of bacteria that rots your balls off.*"

That's not a thing.

"*Wanna bet your balls on it?*"

On second thought, maybe it *was* time to get serious.

I hurried to peel my shirt off, wringing out as much sweat, blood, and unidentified liquid as possible. Modri began instructing me on how to form the tourniquet, but I knew enough to help myself there. After tearing off an entire sleeve, I wrapped the fabric around my thigh's midpoint and pulled it tight. I even tied a nice bow for good measure.

"*The hell are you doin'?*" Modri said. "*Right now, you've got a snug fit. You need to fully choke the flow. Take a look around.*" Nothing popped out during my cursory sweep of the nearby fungus. Not to me, anyway. "*Bone. Your bone.*"

Huh?

"*Snap the rest of your thigh bone off and thread it into the tourniquet. Only way to get a proper seal.*"

I swallowed the bulge in my throat and stared at my protruding femur.

This won't hurt, right? I asked mentally.

"*Might be the worst pain you've ever had.*"

I was hoping you'd lie to me.

23

Out of genuine concern for those with weak stomachs, I'll skip right to the part where I got a chunk of my femur wrapped up tight in the tourniquet's knot. Following Modri's advice, I gave the bone a few spirited twists to fully cut off the blood flow.

The effects were nearly immediate—in a visual sense, that is. The budding red pool beneath my leg stabilized in shape, no longer expanding to overflow into the surrounding floor craters. That being said, I was several minutes too late to avoid tingling extremities and a drunken veil over my perceptions. Each time I shifted or glanced about, it felt as though someone delivered a punishing whack to my inner ear.

"*You hear me?*" Modri asked.

His words came to me like an alarm in deep sleep. I jolted upright, eyes flashing open, only to find I was still slumped against the same knob of fungus. I hadn't even known I drifted off.

Yeah, I'm up, I mentally said. *You think there's some kind of narcoleptic gas in here?*

"*It's called hypovolemic shock, Purifier.*"

Huh?

"*Loss of vital fluids. Explains why you keep passin' out, and why you've got to stop doin' that.*"

Oh, forgive me. I was too busy dealing with a brain that's shutting down mid-thought.

"*Yeah, yeah, yeah. Just kill this thing so we can climb on out.*"

I glanced over at the junnara-gol's central stalk, scanning its calcium-based armor to identify angles of attack. The thick, chalky panels separated and rejoined each time the fungus "breathed," or shuttled nutrients, or did whatever overgrown vegetation did. During some of the fiercer contractions, the plates bulged outward far enough to reveal the flesh I'd seen previously.

Its texture was something between mushroom gills and human sinew. As before, streaks of bright energy swam up and down its patches.

Modri gave a warning grunt. "*What's your plan? Stab it? Shoot it?*"

Nope. I'm gonna beat it to death.

"*You're gonna do* what?"

That thing royally fucked up my evening. It's had thousands of years to eat minds, or souls, or whatever they are. On top of all that, it's Narbu's pet. So, you'd better believe I'm going to enjoy ripping it apart, spore by spore.

"*Uh-huh. While dyin' from blood loss.*"

Yep. Then you'll never be able to call me soft again.

"*Why? 'Cause you'll be dead, or—*"

I hushed Modri. Yes, he was probably my best resource down here—if I passed out, I *needed* someone to manually wake me—but he was also a detriment to my focus. To take down the junnara-gol, I'd need every ounce of mental energy, confidence, and strength I could muster. Once I started ripping out handfuls of fungus guts, it would be on me in a flash. Saddling myself with Modri's critical remarks prior to the brawl would only hurt my odds.

Setting my gaze on the stalk, I leaned forward and began tugging myself closer to the grotesque sprawl. The junnara-gol loomed over me, beneath me, all around me, silently welcoming such a pitiful challenge.

After sliding through a final trench of goop, I came face to face with the stalk's quilted outer plates. I watched them impassively, tracking their rises and falls as sweat formed ribbons on my neck. *You can do this,* I told myself, though the junnara-gol's shuddering took the gusto out of my pep talk.

I wasn't ready for this. Modri knew it, I knew it—hell, Akasha definitely knew it. Still, I had to try.

Pulling in a deep breath, I shut my eyes and visualized my mandala. Intricate lines extended through the blackness of the mind, swirling and interlocking to form the proper pattern. When the shape came together in earnest, I didn't even think of the junnara-gol or severed legs. The blazing symbol of my own mind, my own seed of Primordial Wisdom, burned away everything except awareness. Even the rogue thoughts that sprang up to undermine my focus were destroyed. I remained in that quiet, blinding place for several minutes, continually pulling myself toward the mandala's light as I'd learned to do with Narbu.

At last, my eyes opened again. The mandala was gone, naturally, but it had taken all of my terror on its way out. All that lingered was the calm, cold fury of a man about to unleash terrible justice on those who deserved it.

I thrust my hands toward the junnara-gol, wedging both into the shared gap between two of its exterior panels with palms facing out. Once I'd gotten a good grip on the calcified edges, I snarled and wrenched them apart.

Fungal flesh ripped with the sound of corn losing its husk. The two panels hung loosely by their base fibers, exposing the network of capillaries and other critical bits they'd formerly concealed.

I stared into the soft, pulpy heart of my foe, grinning like a madman at the fact that the junnara-gol hadn't detected me.

Given my luck, it should come as no surprise that this was the same moment the junnara-gol awakened.

An enormous neon box surrounded the junnara-gol, extending beyond my vision in all directions and glitching in an attempt to render the creature in its entirety. Then a bone-rattling tremor moved through the chamber, prompting gigantic vines and other mutated limbs to peel off the walls and descend toward me like a living forest.

[ENCOUNTER DESIGNATION CHANGED: NEMESIS EVENT]
[COMBATANT DESIGNATION CHANGED: NAME UPDATED]
[Subterranean Menace is now Junnara-gol]

[NEMESIS EVENT]
Junnara-gol (UNKNOWN)
CALCULATING . . .
Estimated Kill Points: 239,500

Rather than frighten me, the high Kill Points sent a surge of crackling bloodlust through my chest. Before, when the chok'tal had only been able to visually identify the beast's size and capabilities, the same creature had only been set to award 31,000 Kill Points. Being subjected to its hidden yet most lethal threat, hallucinations, had ratcheted that number up to more agreeable levels. At the very least, I now felt I was getting some buck for my bang.

Wasting no time, I dug my hands straight into the junnara-gol's stalk. Milky, glowing fluid gushed out like blood as I grasped fibrous arteries and tugged them open. Anytime my fingers found something beating or otherwise squirming, I crushed it to a pulp. Within seconds, I was up to the elbows in junnara-gol flesh, clawing and punching and snapping anything within reach.

Certified badass—until I noticed my foe wasn't as damaged as it should've been.

Overhead, the junnara-gol's tendrils continued to descend at the same slow, agonizing speed. If it was terrified for its life, or even experiencing mild discomfort, it didn't show it.

This pushed me to work harder and nastier. I toggled on Overclock and Indomitable—both of which I'd disabled during the amputation for blood pressure purposes—and resumed my crusade of chaos. Before long, I was raking away like a rabid canine, slashing away every trace of fungus or fluid. The stalk's core resembled a giant, half-chewed piece of fruit.

Even so, the tendrils kept coming.

Deeper into the stalk, just behind a thin layer of roots and tissue, something glimmered. I hurried to dig at it. Well before I'd reached the shiny doodad, however, I understood what it was. *Sparkseed.* It wasn't just the color, but the mental warble it emitted in close proximity.

What the hell was it doing here? Up until now, I'd assumed Sparkseed leeched into the soil around the monastery and ended up in waterways. That certainly explained how it had spread across the planet's surface and corrupted the basin-dwelling creatures.

But the junnara-gol wasn't anywhere near a water source. It wasn't even near soil. Either it had gone a long, long way to get a taste, or someone had delivered this meal.

I didn't have time to analyze that, though. The more I shredded the stalk's inner walls, the more Sparkseed glinted. What had started as a scattering of golden flakes was now a highway of thick, marbled veins.

The tendrils' shadows danced over my forearms, hitting me with yet another much-needed dose of pressure. *Think, Dak, think.* Acting on instinct, I stared into the Sparkseed-infused fungus and tried to assert my mental control. The plan ceased an instant later, when biting pain lanced through my forehead. I cried out and slumped forward, only to realize I didn't move. Neither did my arms. The junnara-gol's flesh had hardened around me, and was now creeping—one small, silvery root at a time— toward my face.

For whatever reason, the Sparkseed was beyond my control. Maybe Narbu had helped me the first time, or maybe I'd been working with "non-bonded" Sparkseed. If the latter theory was true, I was in trouble. How could I hope to defeat a psychedelic fungal colony with a metric ton of *bonded* Sparkseed running through its body?

The answer was, I couldn't. With both arms pinned, one leg out of commission, and the other scrabbling desperately on fungus beneath me, my death was closer to an overconfident hunter's demise than the sacrifice of a martyr.

I shut my eyes, wincing as the tendrils brushed my head like a doting mother.

Reach within. The voice sent my heart on a gallop. It wasn't mine, yet it also wasn't Modri's, or Guide's, or even Narbu's. It *sounded* like me, but . . . it couldn't be. It was strong and confident, utterly decisive in its recommendation. *Reveal that which is defiled to the light.*

It even used the awkward vocabulary of a Wayfarer.

I glanced around the darkness of my mind's eye, waiting to see if the junnara-gol or an evil spirit or anything else would pop and exclaim, *"Hah! It was just my voice all along!"*

It didn't. Taking the place of that expectation was a deep, wordless certainty that simply *knew* what I had to do.

Mind Cascade.

Now, you surely recall me saying that I'd absolutely, categorically rejected the idea of using that upgrade on any alien and unpredictable beasts. Well, that was before the insane suddenly seemed feasible. Mind Cascade was volatile, to say the least, but it was also my last hope of inflicting death on either of us. Given what the junnara-gol did to its victims, I was almost rooting for the creature to freak out, cause a cave-in, and pancake me under a boulder. Taking down the junnara-gol with the same attack would just be icing on the cake.

As I triggered Mind Cascade and sank into its ethereal expanse, though, a sense of eerie stillness rained down. Unlike the first time I'd used it, nothing about this felt reckless or overwhelming. In fact, it felt as if—for the first time in a long, long while—my mind and body were in perfect alignment. Put simply, the heart and the head were on the same page. I didn't feel powerless or vulnerable or out of place in the shifting void. Not even the swirling, defiled energy all around me could pierce my determination.

Part of this newfound comfort was surely from Telekinesis, which seemed to hone *all* of my mental abilities, but the other part was new, inexplicable. It was tied to the strange voice, but what exactly was the voice? When examined, it revealed nothing but my own mind.

Scattered around my disembodied presence were tall, twisting pillars that I innately recognized as defiled. A dense haze pooled around and between them. The junnara-gol circled me in that murk, its presence marked by an infected red glow.

I watched everything with total coolness, more interested in the firmness of this experience than my actual enemy. It was night and day compared to my fight with the sloth. Back then, my mind and its incessant whirling had nearly spelled my doom. Here, though, my thoughts were more akin to a burbling stream than a waterfall. My emotions were muted, slippery things suspended in an ocean of pure resolve.

Lastly, the dimension itself was more stable. Before, my mind's eye had struggled to perceive even the faint outline of my enemy. Not anymore. The junnara-gol was a sharp, tangible presence in my periphery.

I latched onto that presence and sharpened it with concentration, excluding anything that wouldn't help me identify my quarry. This included the faint impression of a physical body, as well as its accompanying sense organs. Each time a fear, itch, or memory surfaced in consciousness, my attention snapped right back to the junnara-gol without getting bogged down in self-reflective thought loops. There was no time wasted by grappling with whatever distraction appeared, nor was there even a smidge of doubt regarding whether I was meditating "the right way." Instead of trying to tame the mind, I was watching it tame itself. Automatic course correction, baby.

This laser-focused lock came in handy when the junnara-gol moved in for the kill. My mind remained at ease, entirely relaxed, as the pulsing red glow moved through the fog behind me. Twenty meters, fifteen, ten . . . I could sense its position down to the millimeter.

At three meters away, it lunged.

I spun at the last second, snatched the junnara-gol's presence by its throat, and held it high.

Squirming in my grasp was a shadowy, chameleon-like being with the legs of a crab and the head of a humanoid. Even as my grip tightened, the creature thrashed and tried to needle me. No such luck. Its limbs were thick and impossibly dark, almost like solid spears of ink. They slashed straight through the airy form of my mind-made arm.

The junnara-gol's face shifted with impressive rapidity. One moment it was a young woman's, the next an aging alien. Each time I tried to deeply examine a face's features, it changed to something new and more tortured. By the time I unfurled my ribcage—a more confident recreation of what I'd done to the sloth—the faces were blurring to the point of visual static.

Radiance burst forth from my heart in the form of long, jagged glass shards. The junnara-gol lifted its clacking legs to deflect the energy, but it was fruitless. My light vaporized its limbs in a spray of dark steam and howls.

The beast recoiled, but I didn't loosen my grip. Instead, I pressed the shards of radiance even deeper into its central mass. It was a slow, painful affair trying to overpower the junnara-gol's strength, with the radiance penetrating flesh a centimeter at a time. Anger began to flower, but my mind turned on this emotion and nullified it.

There was no room for wrath here—only calmness.

This became clear a moment later, when the junnara-gol suddenly flared with dark energy and surged closer. My hand didn't budge. As a result, the junnara-gol succeeded only in impaling itself on my radiance.

A blinding mixture of white light and red flashes began pouring from the wound. Sensations of burning and stinging bubbled up, and once again, my mind packed them far away from center-stage consciousness. I couldn't afford to slip up here, even for a moment. The junnara-gol's energy, despite its weakened state, was still powerful enough to tear my mind apart at the root. It wasn't a theory, but rather one of those instinctive truths I understood as well as my own need for oxygen. This was a war for existence, and the junnara-gol wouldn't surrender easily.

Another tidal wave of energy blasted outward, but unlike the prior one, it didn't harm me. It didn't even try. Rather, it condensed in spherical clouds all around the junnara-gol, whose mind-made body had now gone limp. Despite that, I could still feel its presence. It wasn't dead, but it no longer inhabited the dark shell in my grasp.

After a moment's hesitation, I dropped the corpse and studied the clouds of energy. Sure enough, *they* were the new epicenter of the junnara-gol's mind. The mutant corpse was nothing but a sloughed-off skin, a set of cracked armor.

I gazed at the nearest of the energy clouds, preparing to dispel it with a supercharged blast of radiance. Just as my focus came to a fever pitch, though, the cloud split open down the center and blanketed me in a wave of fog.

This part might be a tad hard to explain using fickle tools like words (yes, even compared to what's already happened), so bear with me. At the moment these experiences actually occurred, I had no idea what was happening. I've couched the following paragraphs in brief, retrospective explanations and metaphors to give you the orientation I was denied.

The air thinned almost instantly, but the sight to which I returned wasn't quite the same. "I" found myself standing on a verdant, craggy mountainside bursting with red flowers. Only . . . it wasn't "me." It was someone else's body, someone else's mind. Despite that, there was no fear—indeed, no reaction of any kind—to the fact that I was now inhabiting a stranger's existence. That was probably because everything I termed as me, Dak Korasa, was absent. My memories, my opinions, my judgments, my likes and dislikes. I mean, even the tone of the "thinking voice" in this being's mind was completely different from my own. Again, I didn't even realize that at the time, because there was no "me" to contrast the stranger's experiences with mine.

Does that make sense? No? Alright, well, try this metaphor on for size. It felt as though I were in a dream, living out the life of a dream character with zero connection to me in the real world. A king dreaming of being a beggar, or a soldier dreaming of being his enemy. Every thought, movement, and choice seems completely normal and rational to you . . . *in the context* of being that dream character. Only upon waking and remembering your true identity do you understand you were existing in a stranger's shoes.

For the purpose of simplicity, I'll maintain the first-person perspective, describing speech and actions as though I did them. But, you know, I didn't. The experiences experienced *themselves.*

Now, back to the mountainside. I was walking up the long, twisting path that led to the Sage's Ascent. A very ancient path. It was a stormy day, though still bright enough for pleasant travel, and the Ascent towered like a jutting demon's fang just ahead. My six arms and four triple-jointed legs made easy work of the steep rises comprising the path.

At twenty-three years old, I was one of the oldest females in the clan. By extension, I was also one of the wisest and most cherished. Geriatric life wasn't a walk in the park, however. Already, my organs were aching. Sleep came more often and lasted longer. Within a year's time, this body would fail and be called back to the Wayfarers' Grove.

Like the sages before me, I had made this climb to finish my life with dignity. It was a challenge, yes, but also the greatest moment of a sage's life. The culmination of a lifetime's worth of divination, contemplation, and exploring the limits of the mind. My entire clan had seen me off, showering me with garlands and holy tinctures.

I would not let them down. For my clan—those who had birthed me, clothed me, fed me—nothing was too great a sacrifice. I could only hope that my meager wisdom contributed to the Throne of Radiance, nourishing those who came long after me through the fungal sacrament.

Cresting the next ridge, I saw it. The Throne of Radiance claimed the entire mountaintop, its spores and vines extended as though in welcome. The sacrament's pungent odor, that of blood mingling with soil, traveled swiftly on the breeze.

Pride swelled in my heart at the very sight of it. For thousands of years, it had been the guiding presence for my clan. A window into other worlds, other futures. My earliest memories as a girl involved drinking the bitter brew and falling into an ocean of radiance.

Within the clan itself, there were rumors that the Steel Scholars would soon arrive: hulking, fearless entities that had traveled across the stars to continue turning the wheels of destiny on this planet. Several of my predecessors had feared the machines and their wrath. They'd claimed, in their sacramental visions, the Steel Scholars brought death and fire to our world. They were wrong. I had seen the truth of it in my own visions.

The Steel Scholars would elevate our people from prey to masters of reality. They would share their secrets, and in turn, we would teach them about the Throne of Radiance. Together, we would overcome the Unmade and usher in an age of unending peace.

I moved closer to the Throne, spreading my arms wide to mimic the organism's gestures. Euphoria warmed my chest.

Drink of my wisdom, and drink deeply, I thought, as the first tendrils snaked toward my head. *Let my memories awaken the radiance within the Steel Scholars. Through this, I am complete. May the countless worlds dwell in everlasting joy.*

Everything went black.

For a single, confusing instant, I was Dak again. Just as the seed of a confused thought began to sprout, though, my mind went launching into another "remote viewing" experience.

My head moved through tufts of fog, but I hardly felt anything. In fact, this entire inner experience was considerably "quieter" than the one that had preceded it. There were hardly any thoughts, any shreds of narrative to lend context to the moment. Still, the situation became clear enough when the fog parted.

I was standing atop the Sage's Ascent—no, wait, the Scholar's Ascent. That's right. We'd changed the name months ago, just after exterminating the last of this world's corrupted fanatics. With six arms and four legs, even their bodies had suggested the extent of their defilement. If not for the sap they'd extracted from the Throne of Radiance, they'd likely have devolved into demonic hordes. But even that sacrament, a divine and wise brew, had not been enough to save their minds.

I'd seen their downfall from the moment we arrived on this world. It was inevitable, really. Their bodies were too tainted by greed and sexual desire, their lives too short to properly contemplate radiance and escape rebirth—let alone understand the Unmade. No, it was good that I'd given them a dignified death. Their minds had nourished my brothers and shown us the proper path.

Still, the Throne of Radiance troubled me. Its flesh was fading, its sap drying and diluting. No matter how much we brewed, it did not produce further revelations. The elders claimed it was because we had seen enough. Now that the path of the Purified One had been revealed, even immortalized as a mural, there was no further need for glimpses of the higher dimensions.

But what did my foolish brothers know? They were weak and timid, still haunted by the tragedies on the homeworld. So haunted, in fact, that they'd purged their own memories of everything prior to arriving on this world. They'd chosen blissful ignorance over faith in the Absolute. They all assumed I had done the same.

I hadn't, of course. I couldn't. Not at such a vital junction in the prophecy. The others were blind, viewing this world as newborns, so the holy tasks ahead fell to *me*. Each night, my mind was stricken by the homeworld and the terrors that had happened there. The devastation the Unmade had wrought.

Such memories brought defilement into the mind, but they were necessary evils. I needed to confront what my brothers had hidden from. I needed to continue engineering the prophecy, reshaping it, steering it away from the dangerous outcome my brothers had deemed optimal in their apathy.

And to do that, I required the Throne's sap. It wasn't yet strong enough to shape the flow of reality, but it would be. All it needed was more blood, more energy.

Over the past decades, I had come to this place under the cover of night, sacrificing lesser animals and humanoids to study the effects. True to my expectations, higher forms of consciousness yielded more potent sap. Not only that, though—it created miracles. One particular being, an outsider seeking to learn our ways, had caused a marked change in the Throne. Just days after consuming the humanoid, golden flecks had appeared within the organism's stalk and roots. Unlike the sap, which quickly spoiled, these flecks were stable, malleable, and . . . alive.

The next logical step was to supply the Throne with even better nutrition.

Bending down, I reached into the soil, gripped one of the Throne's roots, and tugged upward. By now, the Throne and I were so intimate that it did not startle. My hand came away with a massive clod of earth, spores, and hair-like threads. Most important, however, was the pulsing vein that ran down its center.

This place is no longer sanctified ground, Radiant One, I thought as I stroked the withered vines. *I shall provide you with a better dwelling. A home beneath the monastery of my bloated, spineless order. There, we will reclaim your glory.*

The sound of cracking footsteps drew my focus.

Wrapping the severed root in my robes, I turned to find another elder approaching through the fog.

"Oracle Narbu, what are you doing here at this hour?"

"Contemplation, Scryer," I said. "Please excuse me. I must fetch water from the deep cisterns."

Again, the vision ceased without warning.

A new experience exploded into awareness, this time predominantly colored by two sensations: pain and fear.

All around me, my brothers perished. Tendrils and teeth mutilated their bodies. Every panel of the floor, walls, and ceiling had been claimed by the Throne of Radiance's creeping flesh. Only . . . it was not the Throne any longer. It was something horrible, something devised in the mind of the mad. Only the Wellspring could explain how a forgotten, withered plant had turned into this brutish creation.

How long had we been trapped in this hall? I couldn't say. My body had long since become paralyzed, and now I felt little more than the creature devouring me.

On the far side of the hall, a handful of brothers with still-working limbs pounded on the towering doors. Not that it mattered much. It was clear they'd been barred shut—and also clear who had barred them. There had been a marked change in Oracle Narbu in recent years. He'd grown colder, more aloof. More eager to challenge the elders and the prophecy they'd received so long ago.

Most importantly, he had been making more and more unscheduled visits to the cisterns just below this hall. He'd claimed responsibility for maintenance duties and warned us away from wandering its depths. Perhaps I should not have been so surprised when the floor burst open and ushered in the creature.

I shut my eyes, aware of each pixel winking out one at a time as vines burrowed into my logic nets.

May radiance prevail, I thought. *May the prophecy not be derailed by this sin.*

Another flash, and another experience began.

I sure as hell hoped I'd get breakfast after this. I didn't mind one-on-one time with Scryer Narbu, but we'd been walking for sixteen hours in these damn mountains. He said it was because us humanoid outsiders were squishier. We needed hard labor to detach from our bodies and enter our awareness. That was well and good, but it didn't stop my mind from incessantly complaining.

It was my fourth year on this world. I'd come here on the advice on a friend, an anthropologist that studied cultures of "transcendent wisdom." My mind was certainly calmer than it had been on arrival, but I wasn't anywhere near the levels of power I'd first been promised. After all, these monks were making some major claims. They said I had the seed of radiance in me. The potential to shape the universe by contributing to its destiny.

There'd been a few other outsiders, but most didn't tend to stick around long. Seeing as I never actually saw any of them leave, I figured they packed their bags and left in the middle of the night via one of the nearby settlement's ferries. Weird, to put it mildly. I mean, the monastery was harsh, but it was also a *monastery* run by harsh machines. Harshness was part of the package.

"Come, Tordra," Narbu said, waving me closer as he approached some kind of pit. "It is time to gaze into the Throne of Radiance itself."

Nodding dutifully, I stepped beside him and gazed down into the depths. The walls were blanketed with some kind of thick, diseased-looking fungus.

"Scryer, what is—"

Something struck my back, and suddenly I was falling, screaming, begging for—

Once more, the experience dissolved into blackness.

I tried to catch my breath, to ground myself as Dak in that fleeting moment, but there was no chance. Even as I recalled my name, a gust of mental energy shoved me into the next vision, and I was back to being someone else.

The time for the next migration had come. If left purely up to me, I'd have likely allowed the organism to continue growing and absorbing minds, but it was not my decision. This was the will of the Absolute.

As I wandered through the cistern, admiring the organism's impressive growth and scale, I thought back to the first time I'd done this process. Back when the organism had been known as the junnara-gol, perched high atop the mountain. In those days, it had been so weak, so drained of vital essence. By pruning it and transporting it to the cistern, I'd given it rebirth. I'd spared the healthiest flesh and allowed it to grow stronger.

Now it was time to repeat the process, once again following the instructions I'd received through the sacrament. The first step was to locate and clip a potent stalk, or at least a root bulb. As glorious as it would've been to transport the entire colony, it wasn't feasible anymore. The organism's stunning rate of expansion, paired with the defilements it had absorbed from the dying, meant it was no longer suitable for divination purposes. Its sap was potent, but wicked—far too wicked for the minds of my prophecy's outsiders.

In a few short years, *she* would arrive on our world. Later would come the Purifier. I would still have centuries to prepare for the latter's coming, but I could not afford to squander my time. Each day was a chance to further the aims of the Absolute in this failing world. A chance to transcend this fickle reality.

I moved down the long, thin strip of stone that spanned the cistern. Millions of golden flecks were suspended in the water below. Sparkseed. Beautiful Sparkseed. The metallic particles had formed like dewdrops on the organism's roots soon after the death of my brothers. Even as I watched, the pale, dangling roots descending from the ceiling beaded with golden energy.

It's better this way, I thought. *At least in death, you are redeemed. You are no longer impeding the course of destiny, but instead aiding it.*

The loss of the old monastery occasionally ached, but I did not indulge such useless feelings. The prophecy had required their deaths—not only to teach the true path, but also to nourish the beasts of these lands for the Purified One. They required challenging foes and bloodshed to advance, after all. This was the only way to evolve their physical forms in time.

At the very back of the cistern, the Sparkseed-infused water flowed toward a drainage canal. It would then cascade down through the mountain, spilling out into the river, plains, and forests. A wonderful cycle, indeed.

Midway down the stone strip, I spied a robust column of fungus that seemed to act like a nexus. Thousands of smaller roots and tendrils branched off its central stalk. This was it. The exact specimen I'd seen in my vision.

When I brought you here, I promised you a better dwelling, I told its consciousness. *I have fulfilled this promise and allowed you to thrive in isolation. Now I return with a promise of similar glory. What was once your grave shall become your womb.*

The experience vanished without a trace (again), plunging me into the murky darkness of Mind Cascade's arena. Something was different, though. This time, my ordinary consciousness was present. I knew I was Dak, and that I was deep in the junnara-gol's lair, and that I'd used Mind Cascade, and that I'd been cycling through what seemed to be regurgitated memories from the creature's victims . . .

I drifted in the void for a while, confident there was something important to extract from all of that. Something on the tip of my tongue, but just out of reach.

Then it exploded in my awareness.

Narbu.

The son of a bitch was even more insidious than the ghostly monk had suggested. He'd wiped out an entire race of indigenous people because they weren't "worthy" of the junnara-gol's power, only to appropriate the organism for himself and his own prideful uses. Then he'd proceeded to "offer" living beings of all types to his pet . . . solely to brew more potent sap mixtures and explore the higher dimensions' prophecies. Outsiders, locals, animals—how many had he sacrificed for his own ambitions?

Sure, he'd also committed fratricide en masse by killing the other monks, but I didn't feel as much sympathy for them. They'd all been equally guilty of genocide and weaponizing a formerly benevolent (or at least neutral) organism.

The real kicker, however, came when my frazzled mind finally understood the implications of that last vision. Narbu had gone down into the cistern—the bottom of the old monastery, and where I was physically dying right now—and taken a clipping of the junnara-gol for a second round of relocation. Somewhere that had to do with graves and wombs, apparently? That meant there was a bigger, more fucked-up fungal node lurking *somewhere* on this planet. And from how it had sounded, Narbu had big plans for his reborn obsession.

Then there was Sparkseed. All this time, I'd bought Narbu's explanation that it was simply a byproduct of the world's radiance. Now I knew better. It was closer to ashes than a miracle. How many monks and outsiders had been slaughtered just to flood the world's water supply with Sparkseed steroids?

Wait, I thought, another nagging connection rising to the surface, *why would he need so many animals with Sparkseed in them?*

I pondered the question for a moment, more concerned with a clear answer than returning to my body, only to come up empty-handed. There had to be some connection between the Sparkseed beasts, the junnara-gol, and Narbu's "new and improved" prophecy, but it wasn't obvious. What I could say with certainty, though, was that I *needed* a showdown with Narbu. I needed answers. I was owed that much.

Hoping for a smoother exit than the first time I'd used the ability, I toggled off Mind Cascade.

Nothing happened.

I frowned, then tried again. Nada. I kept drifting in the void, completely alone now that the junnara-gol and its clouds of memories had vanished. Confusion quickly turned to fear—fear I couldn't dispel using the calm, decisive mind I'd had earlier.

Then I noticed the fog at my feet receding. It thinned and dispersed into nothingness, gradually darkening the void until it felt as though I'd been buried alive in a tomb. The blackness sloshed around me and trickled into my mind. Everything grew sluggish, hazy. Not a single sensation related to my body remained. Even my awareness seemed to spiral in on itself, keenly aware of my mental capabilities throttling down and solidifying like molasses.

Holy shit, I realized at length. *I'm dying.*

24

None of the texts in the Radiant Repository had discussed my particular situation, but I had a hunch that dying inside the collapsing mind of the junnara-gol was *not* recommended for an optimal rebirth. Although I was still agnostic on the matter, it shifted further and further into awareness as my brain's mental storm quieted. Soon enough, nothing else existed. It was just me, the void, and my whirling thoughts about what was coming.

As such, I'll lay out what happened in a few pages, but you ought to know that this inner turmoil lasted what felt like hours. When you're facing death, every minute of that turmoil feels urgent.

Part of me *wanted* to believe in rebirth. If nothing else, I sometimes felt I deserved a second shot at the game of life. It was hard to think of a worse (or at least, more unfair) starting position than Chanzig's cloning vat. That position had only gotten worse when I understood the insane web of secrets, crimes, coverups, prophecies, and expectations it involved.

The larger part of me, however, balked at the idea. Some of that dislike was theoretical—I'd never seen anything substantial about human consciousness surviving beyond death—while most was grounded in far more personal concerns.

For starters, living was overrated. Living as a body that could be tortured, mutilated, or killed, to be more precise. Ever since my birth, I'd been abused or targeted through no fault of my own. I'd been created by a vicious man with no regard for others . . . and now I was dying because of a vicious machine with no regard for others. With all that in context, you can understand why I wasn't fully onboard about hopping back into the venom-infested pool of life. Assholes though they were, Narbu was right to say that the birth, aging, and death were suffering. Where was the chocolate filling to this experience?

Of course, this angle assumed I had a choice in the matter. Narbu (and indeed, all of the monastic texts) had suggested a different story. In their eyes, rebirth wasn't a marvelous gift from the heavens. It was a punishment one imposed on themselves. A natural consequence of defiling one's relationship to their inner Absolute until they became trapped in a body made of flesh. Unlike the dogma of the Halcius Hegemony, in which life was a sacred blessing bestowed by a creator to its underlings, this account of things lined up fairly closely with my own experience.

After all, Halcius had never come to me in the pre-existential womb and *asked* me if I'd like to join the world. I hadn't been invoiced for birth. Everything from animals to humanoids to extradimensional beings seemed to be united in one thing: the confusion of realizing you exist, and then wondering what the hell to do with that knowledge.

Accepting the monks' view as truth, though, unsettled me just as much as rejecting it in favor of oblivion. You might presume that was because it validated Narbu and his insanity, but it wasn't. While floating through the void, examining the gallery of memories I'd experienced in my brief existence, I found there was a defining theme. In each memory, I was a victim. An underdog. Everything I did (no matter how brutal or bloody) was vindicated by the cruelty of my oppressors. It was a compelling story, and one that often seemed true enough to let me feel "virtuous." I mean, come on—I was just doing what any normal, ethical person would've done, or at least *wish* they'd done.

But that whole narrative fell apart in the doctrine of the Absolute. In *this* view of reality, I deserved the exact birth I received because of deeds done in prior lives. If that was true, what kind of monster had I been before this life? How could I feel justified using violence to get out of a problem I might've created through the same behavior?

This line of logic popped the bubble of my back-and-forth mental dialogue.

A clear, crisp voice, much like the one that had guided me during the junnara-gol encounter, spoke up at the forefront of my awareness.

Through my own deeds, I have built this fallen world. Through my own deeds, I will liberate it.

Suddenly, the question of rebirth didn't matter to me. Everything felt *right*. Of course, I was stuck here, dying, speculating about my fate. Through my own actions, I'd been led here. Nothing else would've made sense. There was no magical force coming to rescue me or punish me.

It was just me.

My karma, my fate. My destiny.

Blissful calmness settled over my mind. If I died, I died. Okay. If I was reborn, I was reborn. Even if I found myself in the womb of a demon, thrown out into the worst possible universe in the worst possible moment of history, I would embrace it. I would bring purity to a world of defilement. I'd be a candle in infinite darkness.

The thoughts weren't just metaphorical. Through no effort of my own, a bright, piercing light flowed from the center of my presence. The light carved its way through jagged black brambles, revealing a slender path that stretched on endlessly.

Before I could even try to move forward, a figure wreathed in faint golden energy appeared far along the path. White robes, blue skin, silvery hair . . .

"Come this way, Dak," Akasha whispered, her voice somehow easily crossing the vast distance between us. "The path is fraught with terrors, but you are the Absolute. Your mere presence burns away the delusions of life and death. You cannot be broken."

The voice wasn't Akasha's—in fact, it was far closer to my own "inner strength" speaker—but it belonged to her nonetheless. *She, too, is the Absolute*, I thought in that same voice.

The light of her aura blinded me. It was too pure, too welcoming.

Even so, I reached out with a hand that felt unworthy. My fingers stretched closer, closer . . .

Thwack.

Pain crackled across my cheek, instantly shuttling me back to the waking world. My first taste of normalcy was a chok'tal update, projected into the darkness behind my eyelids.

[COMBATANT DESIGNATION CHANGED: NAME UPDATED]
[Junnara-gol is now Junnara-gol Colony Node 1]

NEMESIS ENCOUNTER SUCCESSFUL
Kills: 1
Kill Points Awarded: 239,500
Storehouse Time Awarded: 4 Hours, 10 Minutes

Colony node?

That could only mean one thing—and it was a thing I didn't fully grasp until much, much later. The fact that the system had identified this foe as a "node" meant I hadn't killed the true junnara-gol. I'd killed a *part* of it, a small cluster of a much larger and more pervasive organism. That meant two things: first, these roots probably spanned most of the planet, and second, there would be a nasty fight on the horizon.

None of this occurred to me at that moment, but it might clear up some of the confusion about such a strange message. Anyway, back to waking up.

I wrenched my eyes open, equal parts euphoric about the Storehouse Time and pissed off about being struck, only to find myself stretched out across Akasha's lap. She stared down at me with a grimace and a hand still half-open from the slap. Her face and robes were smeared with the junnara-gol's dark fluids, not to mention bright blood I'd leaked.

"You . . . saved me," I said, jaw trembling from the abrupt return to physical reality.

"Narrowly," she said. None of the bitterness in her brow or lips had faded. "What were you thinking? I warned you to stay on your path. I *warned* you!"

"N-No," I slurred. "You . . . from the . . . rebirth."

She watched me for a while longer, nostrils flared and chest heaving, then seemed to grasp that I was in no cognitive shape to have such a serious conversation. Especially not with the risk of bleeding out in the junnara-gol's den still on the table.

Akasha shifted as though preparing to sling me over her shoulder, then wriggled her knees back and let me flop over into the fungus soup. Ignoring my groans, she approached the junnara-gol's shredded stalk, pulled out her own satchel of special flowers, and began mixing its contents into what remained of the sap.

"Stop," I managed, fear mounting in my chest. "'Kasha . . . no."

Again, she paid me no mind. Her attention was reserved for the junnara-gol and its sap, which was now bubbling from its contact with the flowers. When the bubbling subsided, she used the vial to scoop up as much of the tainted brew as possible. Finally, she capped the vial and returned to me.

Even with a pounding heart, I struggled to keep my eyes open and control my tingling lips. "Bad . . . bad sap. Don't drink. Please."

Akasha studied the vial, then tucked it in her robes. "We can't let its wisdom go to waste."

"Wisdom!? The—"

"You destroyed its core," she said fiercely. "This colony is magnitudes larger than the Throne of Radiance. Do you have *any* idea how many beings sacrificed their minds to it? How many eons of contemplation it contains?" When I let out a pained groan in response, she shook her head. "Of course, you don't. To you, this was just another kill. To us, to the order itself, this was a living expression of destiny."

"Just . . . listen . . . me, 'Kasha . . ."

"There's no time. Once brewed, the heartsap will only remain potent for a few hours. I must consume it without delay."

Unable to express myself in any coherent manner, I settled for barking, "Throne!"

Akasha glowered at me, then sighed. "We don't have time to reach the Throne of Radiance. There are cycles to the stars, Dak. Cycles to the moons. Cycles that influence rituals such as this. The opportunity for insight is waning rapidly." She barely repressed a snarl. "It may already be too late for me to awaken the wisdom of my ancestors."

"It's . . . *tainted.*"

"Enough," she snapped. "Our only hope now is this colony's heartsap. Pray that its age and power have made it potent enough to compensate."

Every fiber of my flesh screamed out in warning, but it didn't make a lick of difference. Akasha was too zealous to hear me out—not that I was capable of saying anything worth hearing. My only course of action was to get that vial and smash it before we reached her chosen ritual grounds, even if she killed me for it. Confident in my brash plan, I rolled myself toward Akasha, reached out, and—

Konk.

When I came back to consciousness and felt the throbbing lump on the back of my skull, I assumed I'd passed out for a second or two. But even without opening my eyes, I quickly detected how much had changed in my environment: frigid air in place of humid, motion in place of stillness, wind in place of silence. Then there was the crunch of gravel, almost as though I was being dragged . . . *Hold on.* I *was* being dragged.

Cracking open my eyes for what felt like the millionth time in recent days, I was confronted by an open field of stars. Purplish predawn light pressed in from the left border of my vision. It was almost daybreak. How long *had* I been out this time? And more importantly, how the hell had I wound up here?

While waiting for my mind and body to reconnect, I pulled up the full Status Display to see how my time and Kill Point quota were looking.

STATUS DISPLAY
PURIFIER RANK: 12
RANK-UP NOT AVAILABLE (819,200 KP required)

Kill Points: 239,500
Genofacturing Points: 506,140

Rank Points: 0

Rank Time: 0 Hours, 0 Minutes, 0 Seconds
Storehouse Time: 11 Hours, 29 Minutes, 31 Seconds

Anima: 340%
Dominion: 0/5

I wasn't even halfway to my goal, and continued to sink deeper in time debt despite an infusion of four Storehouse hours. Not a fantastic situation. That being said, the numbers didn't cause much concern. The pain gripping my body made death feel like a welcome alternative to carrying on with this little game.

What *did* concern me was what I'd experienced in the junnara-gol's mind. Every vignette had offered me a piece of a puzzle, even if I had no idea what the puzzle depicted. Maybe I didn't need one. It was clear that Narbu's aspirations went far beyond anything I could've imagined. How much farther, well . . . that remained to be seen. I couldn't afford to put anything past a man who'd given up his body, homeworld, brothers, and conscience in pursuit of a singular goal.

Akasha didn't seem to grasp that danger. She was too blinded by her quest for wisdom, for atonement of one kind or another. Judging by the way she spoke of Narbu, she still perceived him as the same noble, devoted monk that had spent his life seeking universal enlightenment. She couldn't see how far he'd fallen, nor how fanatical his vision had become. Then again, how could she? I'd only glimpsed that bitter truth through the junnara-gol's fracturing mind.

Just before I closed the Status Display, ready to try my hand at a second round of warning Akasha, something caught my eye: a new notification beside the Upgrades tab.

More confused than intrigued, I selected the box.

*[**Mind Cascade**] NEURAL BRIDGE ESTABLISHED*

*Through skillful application of this Morphic Imprint, you have established a functioning neural bridge with **Mind Cascade**. This ability is now modifiable with Rank Points, and is catalogued under the **Mutation** tree along with its associated description and upgrade requirements.*

Huh. This was . . . new. I thought of calling up Modri for his input, but between the kerfuffle with Akasha, and his general ignorance on Morphic Imprint topics, I stepped back from that idea. Instead, I quickly tabbed over to Mutation and scanned the list. My new addition was obvious.

Mind Cascade (REQ Rank 10): Triggers a sudden release of repressed mental impressions, often causing disorientation or madness. (1/3)

Despite my present circumstances and growing laundry list of assholes to deal with, *this* brief string of text occupied my entire focus. This was major. So major it took me several moments to understand why.

See, up until now I had assumed my Upgrades tab gave me access to powers the Unmade had "programmed" into its chok'tal army. That is to say, things such as Telekinesis and Overclock were features of the experience that any Purifier could learn and use. In contrast, Morphic Imprints had appeared more like bugs that allowed a Purifier to go beyond their intended boundaries. This shift, though, suggested a more modular (and surely chaotic) picture of chok'tal powers.

Through some unknown mechanism, Mind Cascade had been converted from a Morphic Imprint to a "normal" ability. An ability sanctioned by the system, even. The "neural bridge established" message suggested that the change was due to my recent usage of Mind Cascade—after all, every skill and movement is improved through strengthening neural connections—but I couldn't pinpoint exactly what had prompted the change.

I could fret about that later, however. The key takeaway was that the chok'tal didn't just enhance Purifiers—it *learned* from them. Its neural connectivity and powers weren't entirely fixed, but instead a dynamic expression of their host. *Hosts*, rather. If my theory was accurate, every ability stored in the chok'tal had once been a Morphic Imprint created by a Purifier. Morphic Imprints that were then practiced, honed, and saved in the chok'tal as normal abilities. That meant that at some point, every power I had—from Silence to Telekinesis, and everything in between—had been *invented* by an individual Purifier.

Well, Chanzig hadn't exactly been a Purifier, but he'd been touched by the Unmade all the same. Now his breakthrough resided in me. The only question was, how powerful could it become through ranking up? Where was the limit to power?

An excellent question . . . at a terrible time.

Determined to get through to Akasha, I closed the Status Display and lifted my head. To my surprise, I was cocooned in some kind of blanket that had been tied shut with rope and bracing sticks. Akasha marched ahead of me with a rifle slung over one shoulder and my blanket's knotted end over the other, dragging me up a rocky, ice-veined path. A high one, no less. On either side of the precarious ascent were glacial ravines and, farther down, black marshes and forests. All of it looked so tiny, so fragile. Just as it had from the perspective of the six-armed alien in the junnara-gol's vision.

Night was fast retreating, leaving the lowlands blanketed in thick, clumping fog. An ominous sign for this ominous mess.

"Akasha, you need to believe me," I said through a parched throat, thrilled that my brain could once again express coherent sentences. "Narbu isn't what you think. He's using the monks. Using us."

Akasha glanced over her shoulder, but kept walking. "You're awake. I thought the climb would have brought you back to consciousness."

"Well, I'm here now. And—"

"Is the chok'tal sated enough to keep you alive?" Dumbfounded by her question, I waited until she continued. "If it is not, you should rest and recover your mind. You may hunt while I consume the sacrament."

"Did you hear a word I just said?"

"Your mind was damaged by the organism," she said coldly. "Guard yourself against these delusions, or they may become permanent."

"They aren't *delusions*, dammit. I looked into that thing's mind. I saw its memories, its past lives. Whatever they were, Narbu was in them. He's a murderer, Akasha."

"There is a reason I counseled you to stay on the main path. Your mind wasn't prepared to encounter such an ancient being."

I growled through my teeth. "Why do you think it was hidden all the way down in those ruins?"

"They were not ruins, Dak. They were the organism's dwelling. Surely you understand why it would protect itself against such an incursion into its home."

"Oh, kill me *now*," I hissed. "Akasha, listen. I didn't go anywhere near that place. It grabbed me on the surface, pulled me down, and started trying to dissolve me into a memory soup—just like Narbu did to the old monks! And he was trying to do the same damn thing to you."

"Be calm, Dak."

"You think I'm crazy, but I'm *not*. There used to be a monastery there. There used to be monks. Narbu killed them all to brew better drugs and craft a new prophecy."

Akasha didn't reply this time. It made sense, I guessed—as my words echoed down into the valleys, I acknowledged just how insane I actually sounded. Akasha didn't know anything about the monks, or the junnara-gol, or the slaughter, or the batshit thoughts that had coursed through Narbu's mind for thousands of years. Considering the profound weakness still wracking my body, there was no chance to pull the old "shake her into her senses" tactic.

To get *anywhere* with stopping Akasha, I had to play along, at least for the time being. If I could get her to lower her guard, I'd have a better shot at getting my point across. She might not be able or willing to absorb everything I had to say, but she didn't need to. All that mattered was ensuring she didn't drink the sap.

Thus, as Akasha dragged me along under a bruised sky, I devoted the lion's share of my mental power to discerning the magic words. There had to be some string of language capable of cutting through her dogmatism and revealing the danger at hand. Some line of argument that, delivered with the right confidence, could pull her back from the brink of Narbu's influence.

Try as I might, however, I hadn't come up with a damn thing by the time Akasha tugged me to the back of a low cave.

She came to my side and undid the ropes, then feverishly began plucking things out of her rucksack and arranging them on the frost-freckled stone floor: a woven prayer mat, carved trinkets, waterskins.

While she worked, I craned my neck around and stared at her. "I think I'm feeling better."

She pressed on with her task in silence.

"Much better, in fact," I said, adding a faux sigh of contentment to sell it. "What *really* happened in that pit is coming back to me now. Guess I was pretty rattled for a while."

"Do you really think your mind is so opaque to me?" Akasha asked faintly.

I shrugged the blanket off my arms and chest, then blinked at her. "What do you mean by that?"

"I know you are concerned," she said with a note of quiet sincerity, continuing to diligently set up her ritual space. "When I found you, I sensed your frail connection to this life. I sensed your pain and anguish. Almost any being would be scarred by the experience of making contact with such an organism."

"Akasha, it's—"

"No," she cut in. "You don't understand the rarity of this moment, Dak. You don't know what it's like, waiting centuries to actualize the potential of the mind for the sake of your slaughtered people. You don't know how many beings suffered to bring about the wisdom of the sacrament." She took the vial of flower-sap brew from her robes, then cradled it in her palms. "This heartsap is my chance to become what I am meant to be."

"I'm not asking you to give up on the ritual. I'm asking you to postpone it."

"There is no other time for action. You may not be able to sense it, but the cycles are in motion. Defilement is overcoming wisdom. If I lose this chance, I may never have access to the Wellspring again."

"Just a few days." I groaned. "I *need* to talk with Narbu before you do anything. I'm begging."

Akasha looked my way, shook her head slowly, and knelt on the prayer mat.

"Don't do this, Akasha."

"The ritual space is secure," she said, back perfectly straight and face angled toward the gray light outside. "My mind is prepared. The brew may be potent, but I am ready. If I am not, I have wasted my years in this body, and I will accept my failing—regardless of the consequences." She turned to face me. "You should know, Dak, that you cannot stop me. You'll have to kill me."

Though the blindfold blocked access to her eyes, I felt a chill run down my spine that indicated we were holding one another's gaze. I had no doubt in my mind that she meant every word she'd said. Her faith burned like an inferno, and she was more than ready to become a martyr if needed.

I wasn't ready to let her do that, however.

When she went to unseal the vial, I sprang out of my blanket swaddling. Tried to, anyhow. By some stroke of genius, I'd forgotten about the part where I ripped my leg off. This resulted in me throwing myself about a meter, then slamming my chin and chest into the stone floor.

Akasha didn't flinch. She just sat there, eyeing me pitifully as I tried to regather my breath. Then, evidently deciding I was finished with my theatrics, she turned back away from me.

In that moment, I spotted a thin, reddish line running down the side of her left arm. Blistery patches had cropped up all around the wound. *The junnara-gol*, I thought. It must've scratched her while she wasn't paying attention. Considering her lack of other injuries and the relatively small size of this one, it seemed likely that the junnara-gol had done this intentionally. Assuming the organism was even capable of conscious thought, naturally. The more I studied the red line, the more likely it seemed. Her behavior had never been so rash, so ignorant of obvious dangers. It was possible that Narbu's rhetoric alone had gotten her fired up, but I doubted that. This urge to defy common sense was too foreign to her. It had to be a product of the junnara-gol's toxins.

Good luck explaining all of that to *her*, of course.

My only remaining option was Telekinesis, which could hopefully pluck the vial from her hands and smash it. I'd have to be quick, though. Quick and subtle. The moment she understood my plan, she'd tighten her grip and resist me. In my current state, I was in no shape to duke it out for mental control.

Because of this, I let Akasha think the battle was over. I sagged slightly, panting into the stone and pretending I wasn't watching her loosen the stopper. Just before she got it free, I shut my eyes, pushed my focus into the quantum sea that formed the glass vial, and exerted control. One blast of spirited willpower—all I could afford—sent the vial flying from her hands.

I opened my eyes just as Akasha startled. The vial rocketed toward the cave's mouth, glinting in midair. She leapt up and dove after it . . . only to fall flat on her stomach with claw-like hands extended. Her face was that of a mother watching their child stumble over a cliff.

The vial came down hard on the stone outside the cave. A high ring confirmed the glass had shattered. I allowed myself a thin smile as the sap mixture drained out in a dark blot, spreading into the snow and sizzling.

"*No!*" Akasha roared, scrambling toward the mess on hands and knees. She began pawing at the mound of glass and fluid, trying in vain to gather it in her palms and lick what was left.

I watched her with a strange impression of sadness. Even if she *was* under the influence of Narbu's propaganda and the junnara-gol's mind-warping chemicals, this desperation still had its roots in personal and long-suffered guilt. Guilt over the fate of her people, over her own self-imposed duties, over failing to stop a force that no mortal could even comprehend. My intervention might've saved her from a terrible experience, but it also denied her the salvation she believed she needed.

Eventually, it became too much to handle. There was no usable sap left in the snow—the remnants were just frozen droplets—but Akasha continued to shovel glass and bits of ice into her mouth, chewing despite the streams of blood running down her chin.

With a weary sigh, I looked at my leg to find a way to stand. It had grown a bit while I was passed out in the junnara-gol lair and on the mountainside, but it was nowhere near a return to full functionality. In its present form, it resembled an infant foot growing out of my knee. To counteract this, I pulled the thickest bracing stick from Akasha's makeshift blanket-sled and tucked it under my arm. There. Now, I at least had a walking stick to help me guide my intoxicated, delusional companion down a murder mountain.

With the best limping gait I could manage, I exited the cave and went to Akasha's side. The snow beneath her was a slush of blood and crystalized fluid.

"It's gone," she said weakly, her lacerated hands shaking palms-up on her lap. "My last chance to redeem my people, and you've stolen it from me."

"It couldn't be done this way," I said, as I leaned on the stick. "Shouldn't be, anyway."

"You speak as if you know."

"Akasha, come on. Let's get the hell away from this place and—"

The rest of my words vanished in a chorus of deep, droning hums that moved over the mountains like a shockwave. Both Akasha and I froze and regarded one another, then cast our united gaze about in search of the source. The sound remained somewhat constant in volume and tone, but its otherworldly resonance made it difficult to trace.

Finally, I spotted something far in the distance. Just up the path, crowning a final, snow-encrusted rise, was a distortion in the air. Snowflakes hung in place and slowly spun, forming a dome of glimmering pinpoints.

"The Throne," Akasha said in a breathy voice.

"Does it usually make noise?"

"No."

Just then, I noticed a line of deep, erratic prints running up the snow on a different part of the mountainside. There had to be hundreds of impressions, and the fact that I could plainly distinguish each one at this distance told me they hadn't been formed by humans.

"Let's go there," I said in a voice devoid of passion. "I've got some feedback on their *music.*"

25

We made an odd couple heading up the last of the mountain—me with my walking stick and mutant proto-leg, and Akasha with her bloodstained face and hands. No words were exchanged along the way.

I used the brief silence to consider what I would discuss with Narbu. Oddly enough, in spite of everything I've learned about him and his convoluted schemes, I still couldn't decide on a single word to say. It's hard to rip someone apart when you're not sure what they've actually done.

Maybe I didn't need the "right" words, though. My anger would be enough. It drove me and my stick up the final ascent at breakneck speed, missing limb and cutting winds be damned. Every jolt of pain was oil for the fire that burned in my ribcage. By the time I'd reached the final cliff, where the collective hum was so loud it throbbed in my ears, I was far ahead of Akasha.

I gritted my teeth, slid my walking stick through the back of my belt, and began hauling myself up on frozen handholds. Meter by meter, I ascended the icy rise. My mind settled in the hideous orchestra formed by the combination of heartbeats, ethereal humming, and ice cracking below my grip.

I'm coming for you, I thought, my body on pissed-off machine mode. *You assholes messed with the wrong asshole.*

Finally, my hand slipped over the top edge and groped at powdery snow. This was it. The meeting I'd been owed for so long.

I pulled myself up the remainder of the way, intentionally averting my gaze from the Throne itself to avoid any "surprises" that might cause me to lose my grip and fall to the rocks below. Once I was entirely on flat ground, though, I settled myself on the walking stick and looked outward.

Sitting cross-legged with his back to me was Scryer Narbu. He faced the heap of ice-choked vines, roots, and spores that comprised the Throne of

Radiance, as did the countless other monks who'd formed rows on his left and right. The levitating-snow dome covered the entire gathering like a chapel.

"Just as it was foretold," Narbu said, standing and slowly revolving to face me. "Somewhat later than I expected, but what matters is that you've come." His head tilted slightly, suggesting he'd noticed something new and unexpected. "Your . . . leg . . ."

"Yeah. My leg."

"Where have you been?" Narbu demanded, stalking toward me with such speed that the other monks ceased their collective hum. "What have you done, Purifier?"

"Oh, not much. I just uncovered your dirty little secrets. All of them."

The moment I said this, Narbu ceased his walk forward. "You don't know what you're meddling with. Too much ignorance in your mind. Too much doubt." He glanced away. "No matter. The hour of destiny is at hand, and all these pests of defilement will be burned away in the light of your nature."

I leaned on the walking stick, confused by how quickly he'd reverted back to normalcy after my bombshell. "Didn't you hear me? I know what you did to the locals, and the monks, and the outsiders. I even know what you tried to do to Akasha. You won't deceive me anymore."

"*Tried* to do?" he asked, with a sudden hint of concern.

In an excellent display of timing, Akasha's hand rose past the cliff's edge and clapped the snow behind me. She then pulled herself up and over, stood, and locked eyes with Narbu. A face and neck painted with rivers of frozen blood gave her the appearance of a demon.

"This cannot be," Narbu whispered to himself, taking a reflexive step back and cocking his head in disbelief. "My vision was clear, unblemished . . ."

His discomfort went down like a fine glass of honey wine. "That's right, Narbu. She's here with me, not dead in the old monastery."

"You don't understand," he hissed, much to the alarm of the monks in attendance. "If one piece is out of place, they are all in disarray. Something has interfered with the karmic threads."

"Oh, go to hell. Just because she's alive doesn't mean there are occult forces on our side."

Akasha moved past me with quivering lips. "Narbu? What's the meaning of these words?"

"He was trying to kill you," I said flatly. "If I'd taken this path instead of yours, you probably would be."

She glanced at me, jaw working, then kept appraising Narbu. "It's impossible. Tell him the true way of things, Scryer."

Narbu was silent for a long while. At last, he said, "Enough of this talk. This has to be *finished.* The winds of destiny do not wait. They whisper, whisper, whisper . . ."

"What's the rush?" I said. "Tell us what this is all about, and maybe I won't kill you. I probably will, but maybe not."

"Dak—"

I lifted a hand to silence her. "I want to know what he has to say. What could possibly justify any of this?"

"The fate of countless worlds," Narbu growled.

"Forget that. Let's talk about the fates of the people you slaughtered. Your own brothers. If you ask me, you're looking just as bad as the Unmade."

The monks sitting behind Narbu began to stir. Several rose from their places in the gathering, murmuring to one another and moving nearer.

Narbu whirled around. "*Sit.*"

His followers obeyed. All except Tekshim, that is. The curious monk remained standing even as his brothers tugged at his robe.

"What are they talking about, Scryer?"

"Be seated and silence yourself," Narbu said. "This does not concern you."

I limped closer on my walking stick. "Oh, but I think it does. Any one of these monks could've wound up in the same spot as the ones I saw down in that monastery." I looked directly at Tekshim. "He killed them all using this fungus, Tek. The junnara-gol took their memories."

"Do *not* speak that foul name," Narbu boomed.

"Tell the dead not to use it."

Narbu looked back at the heart of the fungal colony. In a clipped, almost manic cadence, he said, "Perhaps this is one final ploy by the Unmade . . . its last act of tampering with destiny."

"Scryer, I don't understand any of this," Akasha said shakily.

"Set your mind at ease, Sister," he replied. "Soon, all will be made right. The Throne will be restored . . . and this passing darkness will be repelled."

Akasha lifted her shaking, bloodstained hands to reveal the last smears of fungal sap. "I've done what was asked of me."

The last of Narbu's faux composure evaporated, plucking the brightness from his cobalt eyes. He slowly looked my way. "She has consumed the sacrament?"

"I . . . I took what I could," she said in a faltering voice. "When—"

Narbu's eyes flared, and he extended a spear-like finger toward Aka-sha. "*Nadra.*" The word, issued like a bullet, echoed down into the lowest valleys with a rumble I'd never heard in his usual speech.

For a moment, I was too confused to react. He'd spoken as though reciting a spell or praising the name of some dead god, yet it hadn't done anything. Then I saw Akasha in my periphery. She'd collapsed to the snow in an unmoving heap, her rifle still tightly slung across her back. My first instinct was to scream, to charge Narbu and end his miserable existence, but I stopped myself. That moment of reflective pausing—ironically, something the monks had probably taught me—gave me enough time to realize Akasha wasn't dead. Her back rose and fell in long, deep cycles. Was she . . . asleep? In a coma? I couldn't quite tell.

"What the hell did you just do?" I seethed. "If you've hurt her, I'll—"

Narbu stepped toward me. "She's merely unconscious. Restrain your tongue and mind, Purifier. There's no room for error on the precipice of fate."

"You've lost your goddamn mind."

"I've not *lost* anything. I've *shed* things. I've shed fear, pain, doubt, loneliness, guilt. I've shed that which stands in the way of this holy mis-sion." He studied Akasha's prone form. "How much of the sacrament has she consumed?"

Much as I wanted to rip him a new rump-hole, I was struck by the genuine worry in his voice. Maybe I was misinterpreting this—the part related to Akasha, anyway.

I gave a weak shrug. "Not much. A few drops. I smashed the vial of it."

"Good," Narbu said, pacing back and forth feverishly. "Good, good. Very good . . ."

"Alright, enough of the cult shtick. What's going on? And how the ever-living Halcius did you knock her out with one word?"

He raised a hand to demand silence, then asked a question of his own with burning urgency. "How did you discover that cursed place?"

"Call it luck."

"This is not a game, Purifier!"

"You sure about that? Because it seems like one—to you, I mean. How else could you massacre the same beings you called your brothers? How could you betray everything you've ever stood for? Hell, at this point, I *hope* you've gone insane and are playing a game. Any other alternative means you're worth being killed right now."

"It is called the Path of Paradox for a reason. Now speak with truth, Purifier, and speak swiftly. How did you come to enter that place?"

"It was me, Scryer," Tekshim breathed. His fellow brothers kept their bodies seated and heads bowed as per Narbu's order, but even the most steadfast among them were beginning to watch with furtive glances. "I revealed to him my concerns. The things I'd discovered near the left side of the mountain path. I—I didn't know there was anything there."

Narbu rounded on Tekshim like a rabid beast. "You have no idea how much you have undone!"

"Leave him be," I said through clenched jaws. "This is between *us*. All Tek did was point me toward the truth . . . and that's more than you'll ever get credit for."

But Narbu didn't seem interested in listening to me. He continued facing Tekshim, hydraulic hand joints cycling in agitation. "How pitiful, to have wasted this blessed path and divine form on doubt."

"It isn't doubt, Scryer. It is my conviction."

"It's your headstrong nature. Your flaw. Did I not tell you this was the outcome of denying the sacrament?"

"Scryer, I—"

"Spare me your words. I know of your insolence. I have known for some time. Still, I did not foresee such weakness taking root among my own order. Among the flimsy minds of the outsiders, perhaps, but not the order. You fill me with disdain."

"He deserved to know his fate in the prophecy," Tekshim said, plainly rife with shame he had no business feeling. "Deception is wrong, Scryer. You taught us this."

"*Wrong*?" Narbu exploded. "I have seen that which is *wrong* in this world, Brother—and it lingers in my mind each day. You and the others cannot possibly imagine such defilement, let alone bear it. You chose to scurry for the shelter of ignorance, for the paradise of rebirth. You cast your memories of those dark days into the pits of oblivion. So do not speak to me of what is *wrong*, Brother Tekshim. Each step along this path has been carved out and conquered to prevent something so horrible you cannot even imagine it."

Nobody spoke after Narbu's outburst, though that had very little to do with what he'd actually said. The larger reason for our silence was the rustle of fabric on snow.

Glancing sidelong, I was momentarily elated to find Akasha stirring. Trying to get up. Only . . . it wasn't quite right. There was something uncanny about her brief, spastic movements. They weren't random enough to be seizures, nor controlled enough to pass for normal muscle responses. It was as though Akasha's body had been hijacked by a large, frustrated insect trying to burrow out of her skin.

"Brothers," Narbu called, hurriedly moving up and down the ranks of monks, "now is the time to remake this world! The moment you have spent eons preparing for! Lift the sacrament, consume it without hesitation, and proceed boldly into the expanse of the void. We have forged this destiny, and now it shall forge you."

Tekshim resisted, but the others—despite a few uneasy glances—eventually relented, each lifting their respective clay pot off the snow before them and working the stoppers free. Within seconds, the flower-sap brew's earthy odor suffused the air.

I wobbled ambivalently on the walking stick, my mind screaming for me to run to Akasha and murder Narbu with equal haste. The utterly bonkers nature of the situation didn't make that choice any easier. If I didn't render aid to my blue companion, there was a very real chance of death, especially given the subzero temperatures up here. On the other hand, Narbu had gone just full speed ahead with actualizing his mysterious master plan . . . and that spelled trouble. At this point, I put *nothing* past the defiled monk.

In the end, I loosed a frustrated growl and threw myself toward Akasha. Crawling over, I braced her shaking arms and tried to help her up. She didn't seem to *want* to move, though. She remained on her hands and knees, face obscured by hair and hanging flaps of clothing. Strange, almost autonomous energy thumped under her skin. When I felt something like a human finger trace my palm despite the fabric between us, I jerked back.

"Akasha?" I whispered. "Are you—"

"Get away from her, Purifier," Narbu shouted. "There is nothing to be done for her now. We must hurry . . . hurry to the shores of transcendence."

I glared at Narbu. "What did you do to her?"

He didn't listen. He was too busy moving about the monks, muttering and encouraging them in turn as they peeled back their chest panels and "drank" the clay pots' contents. Even as I observed at a distance, the normally clear fluid surrounding their brains darkened to the color of swamp water, suggesting the brew was more potent than ever before. Billowing tassels of sap soon concealed every trace of gray matter.

Only Tekshim—good, dependable Tekshim—held off on partaking. He watched his brothers in a haze of bafflement and terror, occasionally trying to snap them out of Narbu's prophetic trance to no avail. Whether due to their ritualized sap consumption or simply complacency, none of them seemed willing to go against the master's orders.

I couldn't attend to that, though. Akasha's sudden descent into wet, strangled coughing drew my full attention. I scrambled back over to her and placed my hands on her back. The convulsions were like miniature explosions along her spine.

"Do *not* touch her," Narbu roared upon seeing me. "She is not the woman you know. She is—"

The Scryer's voice faltered in the face of soft, almost private laughter. My heart sank when I realized it was coming from Akasha. She wasn't the type to laugh—and especially not like this. It had the breathless giddiness of a child, or someone who'd just lost all contact with reality. Akasha seemed to be the latter. She huffed into the snow, bloody hands flexing and releasing in rhythmic cycles. Her entire body shuddered.

Although my first instinct was to grab and shake her until the light of sanity reappeared, I stopped myself. There was a good chance this was Narbu's doing, and given the ease with which he'd commanded her to lose consciousness, I couldn't risk giving him another reason to tamper with her mind.

This impression changed when I caught sight of Narbu's demeanor. He stared at Akasha with unbridled tension, watching her movements the same way a prey animal might try to anticipate a predator's course of action. In short, he was frightened of her. If he *had* put this whole thing in motion, it was no longer under his control.

That gave me all the reason I needed to crawl backward once again.

"Whatever you see, hear, or feel, Purifier," Narbu said in a warning tone, "do not touch her. If you treat the manifestation as real, it will *become* real."

I scrambled to my feet. "What are you talking about? You did this to her!"

"No. I tried to save her, to spare her from this. This horror would not have occurred if you both"—he looked at Tekshim, then back at me—"had trusted in my divine vision. Now the only path is written in blood." He beckoned me closer with a curled finger. "Come close and prepare yourself. This is the razor's edge of destiny. One miscalculation, and it will all be for naught."

Trusting Narbu was the last thing on my daily agenda, but it was less daunting than the prospect of ignoring his words and bringing about something unthinkably terrible—not only for the universe, but for Akasha herself. I had to believe he wasn't the sadistic tyrant I'd been shown. I *wanted* to believe it.

Scowling, I braced myself on the walking stick and limped toward Narbu. Akasha's madness and agitation worsened as I crossed the snow.

When I reached the halfway mark to the Throne of Radiance, Narbu spun to face it, lifted a hand, and exerted some kind of telekinetic force over the fungus. Akasha's golden cube—the very same one that contained her peoples' collective consciousness—lifted from the center of the brambles. It was anchored by a thick, corded stalk that connected it to the heart of the fungal colony.

I halted, jarred by the sudden sight, only to grow even more jarred when the cube kept rising . . . and rising . . . and rising. Its primary stalk seemed limitless, stretching higher and higher until the cube had vanished into the thin clouds above, then stretching farther. Soon, the stalk's base began widening to form a mound-like base. This base only expanded as the stalk rose. The stone and ice surrounding the Throne of Radiance shattered with the dull, skittering crack of a glacier in motion. Even as I stood there, mouth agape and eyes wide, the Throne ripped through the mountaintop and shed its stone covering like molted skin.

"Do not fear, Brothers!" Narbu shouted, boosting his voice above the waterfall-esque din using digital amplification. "Allow the void to take you! Fill it with your light! The light of existence, of the Absolute itself!"

To my astonishment, the rows of monks sat completely still as the Throne of Radiance crept toward them. Vines exploded through the ice in a widening radius, and masses of surfacing fungus displaced ship-sized chunks of stone everywhere I looked. I let out a panicked cry just before the Throne reached the first of the brothers, but it was much too late.

The fungus washed over the monks in a violent, thrashing tidal wave, spearing through eye sockets and blossoming through brain chambers in a matter of seconds. Only Tekshim, the wisest of the bunch, had the foresight to sprint away from the horror and toward me. The mountaintop's sundering was so ferocious I couldn't discern the mega-monk's pounding steps.

"We must leave this place," Tekshim told me as he bent down. "Climb atop my back. I will take you and Sister Akasha to safety."

I looked back at the blue-skinned woman, who'd somehow managed to stand despite the constant spasms. With her arms at her sides and head cocked at a severe angle, she looked like a member of the living dead. My only solace was that she'd left the loaded rifle on the snow.

"Not until we've finished with Narbu," I shouted back to Tekshim.

"We cannot succeed, Dak. I can't say what Scryer Narbu is doing, but his machinations run deep. Please heed my words. I beg of you."

Tekshim was probably right. Logically, I knew that. But some part of me—the part that had beelined for Chanzig's tower, eager for answers—couldn't leave until I'd figured out the meaning behind the madness. Bizarre or not, this situation was the epicenter of universal destiny. I could feel that much in my marrow.

Another piece of the puzzle became evident when I glanced in Narbu's direction. At first, I thought he too had been swallowed by the Throne, given his absence. The fungus had more or less claimed the entire mountaintop, and was now oozing out of the slope below on all sides. It crossed my mind that Narbu had sacrificed himself to the fungus, allowing it to spread beneath the entire planet. Then I spotted his eyes and mouth amid the roiling beast.

In a mind-warping display, Narbu "swam" to the forefront of the colony until his head and torso were plainly visible. Although I understood he wasn't the literal face of the Throne, my brain had trouble accepting that. It was as though he, the cube, and the fungus itself constituted one organism with a coherent sense of identity.

"Purifier, Brother Tekshim, approach," Narbu said, his voice twisted into disparate tones reminiscent of a ship's failing AI navigator. "We do not wish to consume you against your wishes, but we will do what we must for the integrity of existence."

Strangely enough, this fungus-monk-cube hybrid was exactly what I'd call an affront to the "integrity of existence." It was so hideous, so corrupted, that I found myself *glad* to have Narbu's face as a visual reference point. Without that help, I don't know where I would've looked to address it.

"What . . . the living *fuck* . . . is happening?" I yelled.

Narbu (or at least, the hive mind calling itself "we") began to answer, but he was cut off by the sounds coming from behind Tekshim and I.

I turned to find Akasha staggering forward. Each movement was sloppy and chaotic, as if her limbs were all controlled by distinct muscles incapable of coordination. Her mouth was stretched wide open, and it emitted a voice that sounded nothing like her own.

"Yes, Scryer Narbu," she said in patchy, zigzagging tones, "they're owed an explanation for your bad behavior."

All I could was manage was staring at her. Despite the voice's horrid dissonance and unnatural rhythm, there was something familiar buried in the words. Something that itched the deep recesses of my memory. I'd heard that voice before, but I couldn't recall where . . .

"Sister?" Tekshim whispered, leaning closer.

"Sister Akasha isn't available right now," she gurgled back.

Narbu flexed his new fungal limbs, attempting to erect a vine-and-spore barrier between us and Akasha. "Move *away* from her."

"What have you done?" Tekshim raged, seizing Narbu's flesh and ripping it out of his path. "You've broken her!"

Despite Narbu's best efforts, he couldn't stop Tekshim. Each wall of plant matter and diseased flesh was torn apart as quickly as it was built. By the time Narbu realized this and began diverting massive amounts of fungus to the wall, Tekshim had already broken through. He raced toward Akasha with his palms outstretched and held low, surely trying to scoop her up and get her to safety.

He never got a chance.

One of Narbu's chitin-tipped tendrils speared through Tekshim's chest, spewing brain matter out through his back and lifting his body clean off the ground. I cried out and shambled forward, but it was more a reflex than a hope I could save him. The tendril held him aloft for a moment, letting the mixture of vital fluids, tissue, and wire-like sensory probes drain down his legs.

Flooded with a torrent of rage, I instantly activated Telekinesis and thrust my willpower into Akasha's discarded rifle. More specifically, I took control of its barrel and trigger. It was far from me—about twice the distance I'd experienced with prior attempts—but there wasn't shred of hesitation to compete for my focus. Instinct guided me as I hurriedly aimed the weapon at Narbu's face and locked the trigger down.

[NEMESIS EVENT]
Narbu / Throne of Radiance (UNKNOWN)
CALCULATING . . .
Estimated Kill Points: 3,407,800

The mountaintop came alive with the supersonic *whump-whump-whump* of automatic rifle fire. I kept my willpower tethered in place, eyes shut and body trembling as I resisted the weapon's urge to recoil straight over the side of the cliff. By the time the magazine was dry, I sensed a thin, warm trail of blood running from my nose to my lips.

Panting, I opened my eyes and looked through Narbu's hastily assembled fungus maze. The bullets had mostly hit their mark, peppering his eyes, mouth, and brain chamber in a remarkably tight grouping. There had to be fifteen holes drilled into the bastard.

Despite that, his eyes snapped open with the same fervor. Sap and other gelatinous secretions flowed to the wounds and filled them in. Even the brain chamber, the highest-priority target, was untouched aside from a few pockmarks.

"You're an abomination," I said, as I fiercely wiped away my blood. "The monks were never anything to you, were they? They were just your batteries for this . . . this . . . *thing.*"

Narbu looked to Akasha, who wore a lopsided smile, then back to me. "They were our brothers. For thousands of years, they served at our side. Now they exist within us, and as us."

"Except Tekshim, you son of a bitch."

"Do not speak of what you do not know. Tekshim was not merely a member of the order—he was our brother. Our *blood* brother, ripped from our mother's womb. What would you know of destroying your own kin, tainting your own karma, for the benefit of beings you will never meet? We have made our sacrifice. Now you must make yours."

My lips quivered as I studied Narbu, unable to find even one word in response. How was it possible for one being to have descended so far? To have forsaken everything and everyone, right down to his only brother?

"It pains us to have done this, but perhaps it is better this way," Narbu said at length. "He will not have to witness such profound . . . defilement."

"You'll die for this."

"Calm yourself." He used a tendril to indicate Akasha. "It is feeding on your anger. We cannot join you with the Throne until you have released this poison."

"Oh, is that right?" I shouted, tapping into the fresh geysers of hatred exploding through my chest. "Well, in that case, fuck you, fuck you again, and fuck you a third time, just for good measure! For the record, her name isn't *it*—it's Akasha! I—"

"This is becoming . . . interesting," Akasha said, before falling into another laughing fit. "Just a moment. I'll slip into something more comfortable. Or perhaps . . . slip *out.*"

Though I had no idea what was happening, Narbu instantly retracted all of his fungal body, clearing what remained of the mountaintop. Now with a direct line of sight, I saw Akasha quaking like a pressurized canister about to pop.

Awed by the sight, I hardly noticed the *ENCOUNTER FAILED* message. Even the system seemed to realize Narbu wasn't my biggest problem anymore.

Akasha's neck bulged in three spots. Her skin loosened and sagged over her muscles and bones. Then a thin line emerged at her forehead, running down the entirety of her body and perfectly bisecting it. Before I could take a step in her direction, I froze at the sound of skin splitting like cheap fabric.

Both halves of Akasha's skin suddenly separated, peeling outward like a gruesome flower in bloom. Only it wasn't *just* the skin. Her entire body bisected down that central seam. Clothing, muscle, bone, veins—all of it flapped outward to reveal an anatomically impossible inner cavity where her organs ought to be. Even her ribs fanned out to form a wiry clamshell shape.

Strangely enough, though, her severed blindfold remained fixed to both halves of her face as though held there by adhesives . . . or something else. Behind the fabric, all around her exposed brain matter, were the metallic bands and studs of cybernetic implants.

I didn't think of those implants right then, however. My mind was completely blank by this point. Between the fungal colony, Tekshim's death, and now *this*, I was too rattled to know what was real. Hell, maybe I'd never escaped the junnara-gol, and had hallucinated this entire experience.

But deep down, I knew that was too good to be true. This experience was too visceral to be anything except reality.

Still, the temptation to view it all as a nightmare didn't fade. It only grew stronger when *something* began stirring inside Akasha's open body, heralding its arrival with black mist, dribbling blood, and whispers just at the edge of my awareness.

"Purifier," Narbu said quietly, "we urge you to come this way."

I didn't move. Partially because I despised Narbu, but mostly because I couldn't. I was transfixed by the violation of physical laws taking place before my very eyes.

The churning, slithering shape inside Akasha gradually expanded, then toppled out onto the snow like an overgrown placenta, still connected to its "mother's" body via an umbilical cord. The mound of bloody, rubbery flesh steamed in the subzero conditions. Just as I began to get a feel for its infant-like shape, however, the creature deftly stood.

Second by second, in what I can only describe as a time-defying optical illusion, the creature grew from a curio to an adult humanoid. By the time I rubbed my eyes to ensure I was seeing clearly, its final shape had crystallized.

The being—evidently male—had a skinless, emaciated body that might as well have been the embodiment of torture. Nails, studs, knives, glass shards, and pins had been driven into every inch of raw, jerky-like muscles and blackened tendons. Patches of frost had already begun spreading across its open flesh. As for its head, well, it was covered by a soiled burlap sack overflowing with maggots and roaches. It was far taller than Akasha, whose body remained bisected, quivering, but still upright through some sort of magic. Still connected by its umbilical cord, too.

"Ah, much better," the stranger said. "It's time to explain a few things with plain language, monk. Dak and I have been waiting long enough."

Stripped of Akasha's influence, I recognized their voice immediately.

The Unmade.

26

Everything is so . . . tangible," the Unmade said, flexing its bloody, skeletal fingers with disturbingly human curiosity. Narbu tried to say something, but I didn't have the attention for it. The Unmade tilted its eyeless head in my direction. "Perhaps I should apologize to you, Dak, for my rudeness upon entering my domain. You see, things are very different there. What passes as one millisecond in this world is half a trillion years in mine. Why . . . it's almost enough to drive one to madness."

It took a monumental act of will to summon words. "Is she dead?"

The Unmade let his infected hand drop back to his side. "I haven't decided yet."

Although my entire body boiled with rage—both at the Unmade for, well, *everything*, and at Narbu for his role in this disaster—the rational side of me made a curious observation. The Unmade spoke with a total lack of emotional affect. Not one of the countless blades, spikes, or pincers driven into his flesh gave him any outward trouble.

"What are you waiting for?" the Unmade said to Narbu with the contented evenness of a sedative addict. "We both know the truth behind all these games. The only one who doesn't is Dak. Now, will you enlighten him, or should I?"

For the first time since the Unmade's arrival, I looked at the fungal monk. Even with his new and improved mega-body and divine levels of power, he was more rattled than ever before. The tiny spark in his eyes danced about in what must've constituted digital panic.

Common sense told me I ought to bullrush the Unmade and kill him for what he'd done to me, to Akasha, to the universe at large. He was, after all, the only known solution to the chok'tal preparing to kill me in a few hours. But I couldn't do it.

As they say, the enemy of my enemy is my friend. The Unmade, for all his terror, was a temporary ally that gave me leverage over Narbu. The Scryer wouldn't be willing to do anything rash after spending thousands of years imagining, crafting, and implementing a prophecy for universal salvation.

I, on the other hand, had no such reservations. From where I stood, the vast majority of outcomes ended with me trapped in one form of eternal suffering or another. At least the Unmade's promise of death and imprisonment inside the chok'tal had been honest from the start. I'd made my peace with it.

"Yeah, what he said," I told Narbu. "You've been dodging my questions every chance you get. Now you're going to answer them all in *complete* detail."

The Unmade glanced at me. "Such fire. This is why I enjoy your existence, Dak. It has given me great pleasure so far."

I scowled in response, then moved the focus back to Narbu. "Are you going to spill, or are we going to rip you apart, quark by quark?"

"We must trust in the prophecy," Narbu said in a quiet, clipped tone. "The prophecy is guided by wisdom . . . We are guided by the Absolute . . ."

"Your prophecy is over," I yelled.

"*Our* prophecy," the Unmade corrected.

Narbu's eyes dimmed. "What?"

The Unmade turned to face me, then lifted a finger. Rusty coils of barbed wire burst from the ice around me. In under a second, I was surrounded by the hellish birdcage. So surrounded, in fact, that I couldn't move a muscle without slicing myself open. This might explain why I remained perfectly still as the Unmade summoned the finishing touch: a short, thin rod of steel that began hovering a hair's width from my left eyeball.

"Tell him the truth, or I'll kill him and explain it myself," the Unmade informed Narbu dispassionately. "Don't worry, Scryer. I'll fill in all the missing dots when you're finished. There's no point in ruining the suspense now."

Narbu's supercharged eyes swiveled from me to the Unmade, then back again. It didn't take long for him to realize he was outgunned. Without any sign of exertion, he recalled the last of his tendrils and spore nodes.

"We have not been entirely honest with you, Dak," he said, in what may be the universe's largest understatement. "We have . . . concealed certain facets of the order's nature and origin for the benefit of your mind. Now, it seems, the truth of all things must be spoken. If this is what the prophecy requires, we will not refuse the call."

"All I hear is more talking," I said, keenly aware of the brain-popping metal rod hovering before my eye.

The Unmade's only response was to circle my cage.

"We told you that we were ignorant of our birthplace, but this was not true," Narbu said at length. "Long ago, we were born as a mortal, organic being in an empire that sought universal enlightenment. Their aspiration was one of benevolence: a universe devoid of cruelty, ignorance, and greed. In those days, it was a beautiful empire. It was the seed of something unspeakably profound."

"Just you wait," the Unmade whispered. "You won't believe the twists to the tale."

Narbu waited a long while before proceeding. "We were oracles to the empress and her court. It was a sacred duty, an honor. Upon reaching our hundredth year of existence, we all received the great liberation. Our minds were severed from the flesh and placed in the shells you have come to call our forms."

"Just say it normally," I sighed. "You had your brains removed and put in robot bodies."

Narbu ignored me. "As oracles, we were expected to commune with and interpret a will far beyond our own—that of the Wellspring. Our universe's Wellspring contained the minds of infinite Radiant Wayfarers, all working to achieve the same goal as our empire. In that sense, we were its emissaries, its translators." He looked away, seemingly . . . ashamed? "Oracles were supplied with anything that would clarify the Wellspring's divine guidance and help our empire actualize it. We filled our minds with visionary herbs, experimental chemicals, and mandalas capable of interpreting the collective's messages . . . and for many years, our guidance was beyond reproach. We led the empire to heights that former scholars had considered impossible, even divine. Although we had already conquered war, famine, disease, and inequality, the Wellspring's prophecies ensured these issues would never again plague our people. Our truest aim was to ensure that all beings delighted in the fruits of this labor.

"Soon, however, the one formerly known as Narbu realized that our vision could not be achieved through passive means. Our brothers failed to understand the role of karma and intention in divining the future. Each time we see an outcome, it is colored by our mind. In that sense, the dreamer shapes its dream, and the oracle shapes its predictions . . .

all while thinking their vision is pure and unsullied. Our brothers' minds were powerful, but even they could not see this truth. Only *we* perceived reality to such a degree. With this sharpness of mind came the realization that my brothers could not accept my insights. They were too blinded by the dogma of the Wellspring. It fell to us to ensure the integrity of our empire's mission."

I listened with equal parts frustration and interest. After all this time, I was finally getting the inside scoop on Narbu's scheming. But even now, with all the facades stripped away, he maintained his air of superiority. The illusion that he, and he alone, was capable of seeing clearly. Just like every other dictator in history.

"On one occasion, we and our brothers performed a powerful ritual to divine the coming millennium. All saw what was to come: that the empress's son, heir to the throne, would someday become a Wayfarer. But our mind went deeper than that of the others. We saw the cycles between the boy's birth and his ultimate enlightenment. Buried in that interim were sins beyond all others, driven by a mind that was powerful yet darkened by defilements from past lives. In the heir's rise to power, he would claim the lives of five quintillion beings. He would destroy the sacred wisdom of half the universe."

Quintillions. Intellectually, I knew what it meant—a million million millions, a billion billions, a million trillions, or a thousand quadrillions— but my human meat-brain didn't have even an inkling of what that meant in real, solid terms. I'd balked when the ghost monk said *trillions*, and this was literally magnitudes beyond that. On top of that, the confidence with which Narbu said the figure suggested he wasn't exaggerating.

"Don't reveal the heir's identity just yet," the Unmade said. "I am quite enjoying the buildup."

Narbu tossed a look of what might have been annoyance (but was probably fear) at the Unmade, then moved along. "With our divine perception, we saw a horrible truth: even the Wellspring, our most unassailable source, condoned this barbarism. In their minds, such slaughter was inevitable, the best possible outcome, and subject to the immutable winds of this universe's karma. In brief, they believed this fate was as natural and inexorable as the death of a star. We did not agree. Instead of accepting their holy judgment, blindly playing the minor role they had given us, we turned our mind inward and sought an answer from the source: the Absolute. Our own nature. Our essence. It was the same substance that animated the Wellspring, only . . . we wished to access it directly. True wisdom could not be inherited, nor conveyed through the masses. It had to be seized from our own mind. After sixteen years of contemplation, just before the heir inherited his first taste of power, we broke through to the Absolute. In an instant, we saw our one path to survival. The sole remedy to such an apocalyptic course was to tame the boy's mind . . . and the only path to that end was a dangerous ritual."

"Destroying his Accretion," I guessed.

"This one is very sharp," the Unmade said. "Maybe you've trained him well, Scryer."

Taking advantage of the Unmade's focus on Narbu, I briefly activated Telekinesis and ran its mental wave around my environment to see what was within reach. Most of it was immovable stone or ice, both of which were impossible to wield. When my presence hit the Unmade, however, it was as though someone had dropped liquid nitrogen into my stomach. It was just . . . a void. A dark, frozen blot on reality where my mind could not go. Even the various weapons and other pokey tools driven into his flesh were beyond my perception. Dismayed, I shut off the ability and looked to Narbu.

His pulsing eyes suggested he wanted to retaliate against the Unmade's jabs, but he resisted that urge and pressed on with the sordid story. "The empress agreed to our path, though she was not informed of exactly what it might entail. She readily surrendered her son into our custody for training. When we became convinced he was ready, we performed the ritual on a barren planet."

The Unmade stopped circling my cage and faced Narbu. "Oh? And what happened next?" he asked with a steady yet taunting voice.

By now, I was beginning to form an idea of just what was happening. I didn't like it, but I sensed it all the same.

"He perished during combat with his Accretion," Narbu said in a tight voice. "It was the only possibility that had not emerged during our divination. The one course that would lead to an outcome even more dire than the boy's original path."

"What did you do with the body?" the Unmade asked all-too-knowingly.

"It was buried in isolation," Narbu replied, obviously for my benefit more than the Unmade's. "When we told the empress of what had happened, she was distraught."

The Unmade lifted a finger. "What *did* you tell her, Scryer?"

"She was told her son had fallen from a great height and died," he said quietly. "Overcome by her grief, she abandoned her advisors and uncovered books that had been sealed for a million years. She then performed ceremonies driven by dark magics and pain, all without the knowledge or counsel of the oracles. She believed she could undo death and return her son to his mortal body . . . a feat that surpasses even the highest of Wayfarers and gods."

"That sounds very promising," the Unmade said. "What came next?"

Narbu spent several seconds establishing eye contact with me and only me. Clearly, he was growing tired of the Unmade's drawn-out torment. "The rituals were conducted during the most sensitive part of rebirth: the transitory state. As such, the very winds of karma were infringed upon. The boy's mind was not reborn in a new body, but instead pulled to the void between life and death. He became stranded in his own universe. His own domain. There, he sank deeper and deeper into his defilements."

The Unmade nodded slowly. "Now we're coming to the finale. Do the honors for us."

"The empress refused to relent," Narbu said, his voice strangled to just above a whisper. "She continued with the rituals, unaware of what she had birthed. Eventually, the veil between worlds could no longer remain separate. Her longing, her desperation, called her son back into this world—and with him came his defiled creations."

"Chok'tals," I said, awestruck.

"Very, very good," the Unmade said. "Do you know why they rained down in that form, Dak? Why they were slugs?"

I shook my head, yet kept my gaze locked on Narbu.

"The 'boy' could only create using his broken memories," the Unmade explained. "And what did the boy remember? What images, sounds, and odors tortured him for innumerable eons in the void?" He gave a "laugh," but it was a purely mechanical sound. "Why, the slugs, of course. How they crawled all over his body when the holy sages placed him in the ground. How they dissolved and devoured his flesh. How they were his only comfort in the endless darkness."

"This is your doing," I said to Narbu, my voice calm despite the tremors in my body. "It's all . . . your . . . fault."

The Unmade ran a hand along my cage, slicing his flesh clean open and studying it as it healed in an instant. "Now, now, Dak. Scryer Narbu hasn't yet explained how we ended up *here*. You may not be as interested, but I believe you should hear it just the same. I have a last-minute addition that might cast things in a different light."

I gave Narbu a meaningful look. One that hopefully conveyed, *If you don't spill every last secret from your nonexistent guts, I'll change teams on the spot.*

It seemed to work, because the Scryer proceeded without missing a beat.

"The devastation swept across our empire, claiming cities and whole planets within weeks. The threads of karma became unreadable and dense. Once more overwhelmed by her decision, the empress retreated to a remote world with her advisors and oracles, then instructed us to take any necessary steps to undo the collapse."

Narbu halted, trying and backing away from various sentence openers. Eventually, under the Unmade's sightless yet withering gaze, he found his footing. "As before, our brothers' minds could not pierce the barricade of fate. Even we found ourselves at a loss, for the Unmade had tainted the well of universal karma. Still, the solution was obvious: more wisdom. We ventured deeper and deeper into arcane studies. We consumed overpowering doses of the visionary substances. We did anything we could to chart a path through this darkness.

"While praying in a palatial grove, the answer once again came to us in the form of total certainty. When we explained this newfound revelation to the oracles, they were distraught. Our vision involved abandoning our empire, our people, our empress . . . even our memories. In order to succeed, we could not be weighed down by the defilements of the past, nor could we withstand the toll of emotional attachments to the dead, both past and future."

"Except your memories," I spat. "You kept them, didn't you? That's how you remember all this, and the others can't."

"It was *necessary*," Narbu said, his voice rising to a booming shout. "We had seen the sacred way, and we'd also seen the numberless ways in which it could fail. We had *lived* them. Every breath, every pain. We risked our very mind for the wellness of this universe and beyond!" After a few unconscious bouts of tendril whipping, Narbu calmed himself. "We were the one who vanquished the memories of our brothers. It was not a painless process by any means. Because they still required some recollections—the teachings of the Wellspring, for instance, and the course of my prophecy, naturally—it would not suffice to merely wipe their mind of all contents. Instead, we dissected and removed each memory . . . one at a time. We experienced their pains, sorrows, attachments, fears—no matter how much we loved them."

At this, his gaze strayed to Tekshim's corpse. It lingered there for a long while.

"We then journeyed across the cosmos . . . to this world," Narbu continued. "Along the way, we did not sleep as the others had. We knew we could continue to refine our prophecy. We could drink from the whispers of the deep, dark void and divine a new course . . . a better course."

Inwardly, I gasped at that. I knew the monks had been alive for a long, long time, but only Narbu had kept every last memory—including high-resolution scenarios of the universe's inevitable collapses. He'd erased countless years of history with those closest to him, including his own flesh and blood. In essence, he'd held the weight of eternity (and its consequences) on his shoulders. And on top of that, he'd chosen to *remain conscious* during an interstellar flight that surely took hundreds, if not thousands of years. While his brothers had enjoyed the dreamless sleep of hibernation, he'd lain there motionless and alone, his only comforts being the cosmic radiation that drifted through his logic nets.

No wonder he'd gone batshit insane.

"Despite our best efforts, we only had inklings of a superior course by the time the ships landed on this world," he said at length. "To our brothers, it was a paradise. A place to hone the mind, train passersby, and actualize a sacred course with repercussions they had all forgotten. To us, however, it was a race against time. With every prophecy we left uncovered, every mote of wisdom we denied, we were sentencing beings to death and eons-long damnation. Still, we knew this world was our intended home. It was saturated in the quantum blessings of the Absolute. Even now, its energy moves through us, speaking, guiding . . .

"Through their benevolence, we came across the caves of the indigenous species. They were barely sentient, primitive, but we immediately sensed their connection to the prophecy. Their sacred Throne of Radiance—the very organism that now forms our body—was a living storehouse of wisdom. Since time immemorial, it had been consuming the minds and guiding visions of this system."

"So, you killed them and took it," I said bluntly.

Narbu's eyes flared, then dimmed as though in reflection on my statement. "The deaths of a few thousand beasts mean nothing when compared to failure. Besides, it was only the death of the body. They live within us now, the same as our cherished brothers."

"Let's return to the *meat* of the issue," the Unmade said, with a bored sigh.

"Your defiled tongue cannot dictate anything," Narbu bit back. After a moment of silent staring with the Unmade, however, he moved on. "Our brothers did not understand the Throne of Radiance. They feared its whispers, its hunger for flesh. But we continued to rely on its sap all the same. We partook in rituals and contemplations until we saw the path we had always sought: the Path of Paradox. Blood to prevent blood. Untruth to guard truth." He glanced downward with discomfort—just for a moment, but long enough to catch my eye. "You have seen the outcome, Dak. Even so, it was still done with love. We knew they could not accept our radical new course. They were too attached to the old prophecy, or perhaps to the mural they had built in its commemoration. They would never have consented to another erasure of their memories.

"Not all of them were killed, of course. Part of our perfect prophecy involved sparing the worthy. Tekshim, for example. Those we deemed useful were sent on an errand while the fungus did its work. Upon return, the survivors were quite upset . . . yet they did as our prophecy had foreseen. They gave up their memories and abandoned the old monastery because they believed in our hidden vision."

"What was their reward for loyalty?" I asked, my voice cold and low.

Again, Narbu looked away. "You do not understand. The Throne of Radiance is no ordinary beast—it is a manifestation of the Absolute, the mind's truest and deeper nature. It may kill the body, but it holds and purifies the mind in its embrace. It prevents the karmic defilements of the slain from leeching into reality."

"Listen to yourself," I barked. "You think it's alright to kill innocent people because their 'karma' gets trapped in the fungus' mind. I've seen the inside of those colonies, you son of a bitch. The only person being spared from their defilements is *you*."

"It is easy to judge without the burden of reality's fate upon your head," Narbu said coolly.

"We're almost to the finish line," the Unmade said, as he made another dawdling pass on the cage. "Tell him how you enacted this genius plan, Narbu. Tell him how you planned to use a Purifier—*any* Purifier, by the way—to defeat the evil Unmade." He paused before me. "That's right, Dak. Narbu didn't even need you. Just someone with a chok'tal."

Narbu seemed to bristle at this, if his bulging spores were any indication, but he kept it under control long enough to speak with an even tone. "His lying tongue does not err, in this instance. We will no longer lie to you, Purifier—our new prophecy did not require *you*. All it needed was a Purifier who had been touched by the Unmade. Preferably one who had touched his dimension in turn. With their Accretion destroyed, their mind attuned to the Absolute, any Purifier could've followed our course."

I didn't know whether to be relieved or more pissed off about this. Narbu's "old" prophecy, the one I'd seen in the ghost monk's mural, clearly featured *me* in the starring role. It seemed Narbu had been keen to nix that part. Maybe he'd foreseen my issues with authority and blind trust, all the way back then.

"According to our sacred vision, Akasha was meant to perish at the hands of the corrupted colony," Narbu said weakly. "Not knowing of her death, your mind—and those of her people—would have remained pure when you ventured to this place. Here, you would have consumed the sacrament and eagerly joined with the collective. You would have willingly contributed your knowledge of the Unmade and its weaknesses to the Throne."

"And what, pray tell, did you plan to do with this Purifier-infused colony?" the Unmade prodded. "It was quite ambitious, if I recall."

Here, Narbu's eyes dimmed to a new low. It was obvious the Unmade was enjoying the Scryer's slow, slow roasting over the coals of helplessness. I'm sad to report that I sort of did, too.

"Had you joined with the Throne at a moment of clarity, our expansion would have been unstoppable," Narbu said. "You have seen the dream the fungus weaves for its inhabitants, but only in its tainted form. The Throne of Radiance would have served as a permanent dwelling of enlightenment . . . a pure space untouched by the Unmade and its corruption. Every sentient being in this universe would have enjoyed its comforts, hearing and practicing the sacred teachings until they became a collective even stronger than the Wellspring."

"Wait," I said, squinting. "Your 'grand plan' was to assimilate every being in existence into the Throne, including the people in Akasha's cube . . . so they would be *safe*?"

"Your mind and chok'tal would have immunized the collective against defilement," Narbu explained. "The Unmade nourishes itself through the suffering of sentient beings. Deprived of sustenance, it would have withered and died in a few centuries."

"Let's not pretend all . . . *this* was purely altruism on your part," the Unmade put in, flippantly gesturing to the Throne of Radiance. "It was also about your survival. About your fate when this wretched body finally gave out."

I narrowed my eyes. "Narbu?"

The Scryer met my stare with great difficulty. "They speak nothing but falsehoods."

"Is that so?" the Unmade taunted. "Is it false to say your goal was to bypass your precious karmic debt and become an 'enlightened' being?" Narbu didn't respond—a tacit admission. "You might be wondering, Dak, why Narbu would be so interested in this outcome. Is it because he's afraid to die? No. Is he resolved to end my reign as quickly as possible? It sounds plausible . . . but no. Everything he's done has been for him and him alone."

"Close the doors of perception," Narbu told me. "He's trying to poison your mind."

The Unmade scoffed. "Scryer, you must think I've never met one of these 'enlightened' beings . . . but I've met plenty. I've devoured their worlds. I've digested their minds, complete with every useless platitude."

Narbu's eyes flickered in a display of aggression. "You're lying. Those who have overcome defilements and seen their mind's true nature are freed from birth and death."

"Birth, maybe . . . but not death. Even your universe's beautiful Wellspring was unprepared for my arrival. The sinew of Radiant Wayfarers still lingers between my teeth. Even now, my claws reach toward the next Wellspring in the next universe . . . and the next . . . and the next . . ."

"Deceiver!"

"Oh, no, this is entirely the truth," the Unmade said. "It's what you've needed all along. Now, back to my original point . . . Why, oh, why were you so hasty about achieving enlightenment in this form?"

"To vanquish you."

"Incorrect." The Unmade turned to me. "You may or may not know this, Dak, but these so-called Wayfarers slip right out of the karmic web. Every drop of punishment headed their way is nullified. Not even prophecies can touch them. And best of all, they can take birth in any realm, as any form . . . supposedly to help their pitiful fellow beings. Now, make a guess . . . who would be interested in rushing to that finish line?"

"A fanatic?" I guessed.

The Unmade's head wobbled back and forth, indicating I'd partially gotten it right. "A fanatic, yes, but not just any fanatic. A fanatic afraid of their sins coming back to settle the score. The instant I decide to end his worthless life, he'll know *exactly* what I've experienced. His precious Wellspring won't be able to make his next life cozy."

As I looked at Narbu, my gaze turned venomous. "He makes a pretty good argument. Is that true? You wanted to achieve enlightenment, or embody the Absolute, or whatever the hell you call it . . . just so you'd have immunity from all the shit you've done?"

Narbu hesitated. "Purifier, you—"

"How does all that goddamn Sparkseed you made factor into this?" I pressed.

By this point, I was done with his prattling and excuses. I wanted answers.

"Sparkseed raised the sentience of beasts on this world," he explained after a long pause. "Had you ascended to the Throne, you would have consumed these beasts and purified their minds. The Sparkseed would have fed you, sharpened you. It would have constituted infinite power for the Throne . . . an infinite source of expansion across the stars. Alas . . . the winds of karma move too swiftly. Defilement has threatened the certainty of our vision."

For a few moments, all I could do was blink and try to wrap my head around it. Only a literally heartless brain-in-a-vat could've come up with such a ludicrous plan. Enlightened or not, he had clearly missed the most important aspect of sentient beings: they don't like being consumed by superorganisms with hive minds. It was hard to believe that, in his endless wisdom, he hadn't foreseen hordes of people screaming and crying at their fate.

"There we are," the Unmade said, offering a mock bow as though Narbu's theatre performance of a lifetime had just ended. "I believe it's time for *me* to reveal something, Narbu."

Considering Narbu's monolithic size—which very likely spanned the entire planet through a network of roots and filaments—it was strange to see raw fear emerge in his eyes.

"Now, then," the Unmade began, walking back and forth with mutilated hands behind his back, "if I recall, Scryer, you mentioned that this system was abundant in . . . what was it? Quantum blessings?" He shrugged. "I have eaten enough minds to know that most humanoids refer to it as cosmic radiation. Of course, some humanoids still believe there are messages contained in that static. Usually the mad ones. So, if I've understood your plan correctly, you were guided in large part by that radiation. Including the radiation that had built up over a long, boring time in this . . . Throne of yours. It must have sounded quite convincing to make you murder your brothers—one *actual* brother, no less—and throw away your empire's ideals of nonviolence."

Narbu said nothing, which may as well have been an outright *yes*.

"What if I told you, Narbu, that the voice you heard wasn't the Absolute? What if it wasn't the Wellspring? What if it wasn't even the feedback from a distant neutron star?" The Unmade stopped moving, then turned directly toward Narbu. "What if, instead, this voice belonged to someone standing right in front of you?"

The spores all across Narbu's mound-like body—his equivalent of goosebumps—quivered.

"It . . . is not possible," Narbu whispered.

"It's more than possible," the Unmade countered, still in that droll and maddening tone. "In fact, it's *true*. Did you really think I would spend eternity playing in my own shit, simply *wishing* for retribution, for pleasure?" He shook his head, releasing a torrent of yellowish grubs from the eye sockets. "Even with your visions and schemes, you can't understand the sheer monotony, the ennui, of a single nanosecond in my dimension. No light, no sound, no feelings. Not even space. By the time you buried my bones and walked away from your crime, I had lived the equivalent of ten universal cycles. Can you even fathom that? No, of course not. You certainly can't grasp what it was like to endure so many cycles you begin torturing yourself to death just to experience something novel. Given such bondage, it was only natural to repay you for your benevolence when the veil began to fade. When my own mother called out to me, and the minds of countless beings begged for my miracles."

By this point, Narbu was squirming on an impressive level. Individual colony nodes lifted through the mountaintop and flailed in midair.

"I didn't smile, let alone laugh, for ninety septillion years. What a strange and delightful figure . . . *septillion*." He paused, seemingly relishing that tidbit. "But when my creations finally crossed the veil, and I could feel even the faintest sense of the pain they inflicted . . . why, I'd never guffawed so hard in all my existence. Even now, the memory of it warms me. The way they screamed and prayed . . . how they took solace in their rituals and prayers . . . how your own brothers turned them away from shelter to spare themselves." The Unmade let out a wistful sigh and glanced at me. "Still, I knew what my ultimate goal was. That's for me to know, and you to find out . . . when the stage is set."

"You can settle for taking this goddamn chok'tal out of me," I said casually.

The Unmade shook his head and wagged a finger. "Not so fast. I've learned better than most that the sweetness comes from *time*. You'll understand everything when you must. For now, let's stick to the subject of our conversation." Once more, he looked at Narbu's pitiful bulk. "You and your brothers may have feared my order, but the chok'tal didn't desire your minds anyway. Why do you think it was designed for humanoid *nervous systems*? Do you really think I wanted to kill you? No. I wanted to see you exposed as the useless tyrant you are. I wanted you to feel the hope of being saved, the hope of the prophecy redeeming itself . . . only to see it all collapse before your very eyes. And more than that, I wanted to see the look of anguish when you realized you had always been playing someone else's game.

"It took a few eons, but eventually I learned how to feel the threads of this universe. How to feel *your* presence, no less. When you called to the void, I called back. When you drank the sap, you drank *me*. When you listened to the stars, you listened to my counsel. You listened so well, in fact, that you willingly killed your own brothers and sent the blue witch to die without remorse. And as for the second leading role in this performance?" The Unmade gestured to Tekshim's frost-covered corpse. "How do you think Dak knew about your crimes, and your prophecies, and your hidden secret in the ruins? Why, your brother, of course. He didn't trust the sacrament, but he trusted the intuition he'd gained in his own rituals. *My* intuition. If you were the cogs in this machine, Tekshim was the wrench. And he played his role to perfection . . . all without suspecting a thing. How's *that* for a dramatic reveal?"

At this point, my head was almost ready to explode. I'd already known I was being manipulated by Narbu, but now the Unmade was pulling strings, too? The more I heard, the more convinced I became that this entire mess was a struggle between two mentally unstable beings. In fact, I was nothing but a pawn being shuffled about. This probably should have given me an existential panic attack, but in truth, it did the opposite.

For what seemed like the first time since my chok'tal merging, I viewed everything with a sense of gallows humor. It was just too absurd to make me angry. Too convoluted to make me hopeless. All I really cared about, at that moment, was ensuring that when Akasha returned to her body it was in the same condition as when she'd left it.

"Your defilement knows no bounds," Narbu said quietly, eyes locked on Tekshim's body.

"It's not about *my* defilements," the Unmade said. "I was always destined to make roaches like you squirm. No, this is all about you. It's about your pride and arrogance. Do you feel proud now, Scryer? Are you being carried through the skies on the wings of celestial creatures for your brilliance?"

"We can still offer you release. Purification. It is the only way out of your state of existence."

"It's far too late for that. You see, I've grown to enjoy my place in the cosmos. I savor the aromas of anguish."

Narbu's attention flicked to me, then back to the Unmade. "Then it seems we must engage in combat. Our sacred vision did not foresee this, but—"

"Even now, you cling to your prophecies. After all this time, you still give me the occasional surprise, Narbu. You would really be willing to sacrifice your champion for this? Not to mention the blue witch's form?"

The *champion* part didn't bother me much, but mention of a blue witch certainly did. Akasha's only sin had been following Narbu down his path of madness. She didn't deserve a grisly death just because she'd been transformed into the Unmade's temporary housing.

"Everybody, shut up and listen," I barked. To my surprise, they did. I fixed the Unmade with a serious look. "What exactly do you want? If it was to embarrass Narbu, you've done it. If it was to kill him, well, go right ahead. But Akasha and I have *nothing* to do with this."

The Unmade cocked his head. "Nothing? You're the centerpiece of this entire story."

Before I could probe deeper into what he meant, Narbu growled so fiercely it resonated in my sternum. "Do not listen to his words, Purifier. He has been stripped of any traces of logic or compassion. It is a fool's game to ask what he desires."

"That tends to happen to kids when you kill them, bury them in an unmarked grave, and trap them in eternity," I said bitterly.

"We have made mistakes," Narbu admitted, "but it was done for this universe and its inhabitants. If you forsake this task in favor of his machinations, you will never survive the guilt. Trust this well."

The Unmade lingered in the silence for a while, then put in, "Unlike you, Scryer, I've never asked anything of Dak. Nor will I. You see, he's not property to me. Partially my creation, yes . . . but not property. Whatever he does with his mind will delight me." He glanced in my direction. "It's an important skill, being able to amuse yourself."

"Then what do you want?" I asked in Narbu's stead.

"Well, we've left one key figure out of the story," the Unmade said, as he walked back to Akasha's upright meatsuit. He traced a black, jagged fingernail across her cheek. "Although I don't know why, Narbu, I do know that this woman is very special to you. Like a daughter, some might say. Given your treatment of youths, I find this rather ironic, but the point remains . . . You are fond of her. You always have been."

This was the point where alarm bells went off at full volume. The Unmade hadn't come here to kill me, or Narbu, or even the monks themselves—he'd come to this universe with the aim of tormenting the Scryer in every conceivable way. First with the loss of his empire, then his brothers, then his prophecies. This was revenge eons in the making. He'd had plenty of time (and obviously isolation) to find out *exactly* what was capable of hurting Narbu. That included Akasha.

To the Unmade, she was just another piece on the gameboard. A bargaining chip that he had no intention of using for anything beyond suffering.

My body tensed as though preparing to spring into action, but the metal rod still hovering in front of my eye put the kibosh on any movement whatsoever. All that nervousness, that horrible intuition that verged on prescience, built up in my muscles like battery acid.

"You deprived my mother of a child," the Unmade said to Narbu, as he reached toward the exposed halves of Akasha's brain. "Now I'll deprive you of something even more beloved."

27

Without so much as a quarter-second's thought, I activated Telekinesis, latched onto one of Tekshim's broken-off panel fragments, and threw it with the force of a crashing warship—right at the Unmade's head.

The icy, dented shard of steel whistled as it shot through the air. The Unmade seemed to detect the threat, based on the slight shiver in his hand, but it was too late. The fragment sliced into his cheek like a saw-blade. He staggered back a few paces from the impact, then lifted a hand and touched my projectile. The fragment was nearly the same size as his neck, and had evidently cut deep due to its velocity. No blood, though.

He can be wounded, I realized. The rage that had initially powered my strike simmered down to a cool, determined state of mind. Enough chatting. Enough concessions. I was going to kill the Unmade, then Narbu, then anybody else who dared to fuck with me on this terrible day. I was done being screwed with.

To my discomfort, though, the chok'tal didn't seem to recognize the Unmade as an enemy. There was no HUD, no Kill Point info. To make matters worse, the Unmade didn't seem bothered by the attack. Only while watching him tenderly stroke the fragment did I understand why. His *entire* body was a pincushion. Between the knives, skewers, nails, and other killing instruments driven into him, it was harder to find actual flesh than rusty metal.

"Impressive," the Unmade said, with genuine approval. "You must've done an excellent job with him, Narbu. That one was . . . almost a surprise. Almost."

I swallowed hard, but at the same time noticed something creeping out of the corner of my eye. Angling my head ever so slightly, I saw a throng of tendrils and spore nodes creeping along the cliff and approaching the

Unmade. It hadn't worked before, and the fact that Narbu was willing to risk Akasha like this brought up a flash of anger, but I also realized I'd been just as reckless—much more so, in fact.

Much as I resented it, I found myself holding onto the thinnest hope that Narbu was still in control of things. Maybe, just maybe, he'd already foreseen this moment, and was now playing it up so the Unmade felt the balance had shifted. If *that* was true, I could understand why Narbu wasn't cluing me in. The more people who knew a prophecy's course, the less likely it was to occur.

With that in mind, I decided to work with him—at least until Akasha was safe, anyway. That meant causing a distraction.

"Leave her alone," I said, causing the Unmade to look even further my way. The tendrils resumed their silent march. "Narbu doesn't give a damn about her. He sent her to die."

The Unmade nonchalantly ripped the metal fragment from their face and dropped it. "That's Narbu's way of showing he cares, it would seem."

"Then keep her out of it and deal with *him*."

"Ah, I see," the Unmade said, tapping his burlap-covered chin. "You've deepened your bond with the witch, haven't you? You've . . . felt things for her." Caught off guard by the truth of his statements, I found myself at a loss for words. "There's no need to be shy, Dak. She's a remarkable woman . . . inside and out, as you can see."

"Go to hell."

"I've been living there longer than most realities have existed, Dak. But don't worry—I'll *show* you hell in due time. Perhaps you can even visit Akasha there."

"You won't hurt her. I know you won't."

"Do you?" the Unmade asked. "I must admit, I'm beginning to believe this little charade has been more successful than I first envisioned. In each glimpse of this world, it was Narbu whose heart ached for her. Platonically, I grant you, but it ached nonetheless. Now I see it's *your* heart that desires her flesh and fluids."

"Yeah, maybe it does. So what? Why punish *me*?"

"I'm not punishing you. I'm making you into what you were always meant to be. If that requires the slow, excruciating death of your witch—"

"Coward," I snapped. "Let me out, and I'll show you slow and excruciating."

"I decline."

"Why? Because I'm the first Purifier to pose a threat to you?"

"A threat? Oh, Dak, let's be reasonable. You're nowhere near where you ought to be. That will take time."

"Ought to be?" I asked, frowning.

The tendrils were about twenty meters away now. Just a bit longer . . .

"It's improper to harvest fruit before it ripens," the Unmade explained. "You have potential, and I am eagerly awaiting its demonstration. But here, now . . . your only role is to witness. To understand the nature of your maker."

The tendrils continued to slither. Ten meters, nine, eight . . .

"God, you people sure do like to speak in riddles. Too afraid to be honest?"

"Fear means nothing to me," the Unmade said, in a cold tone that lent credence to his words. "Nor does pain, or guilt, or even the void. You see, Dak, I am not afflicted by these things . . ." Five meters from their target, Narbu's tendrils darted forth like a lethal forest. ". . . I *am* these things."

Still facing me, overshadowed by the literal tons of fungal matter preparing to rain down on him in an avalanche, the Unmade lifted his hand and snapped a finger.

The tendrils halted just before they struck. Then they began quaking, blackening from their tips all the way back toward their source. I watched in horror as large, fleshy chunks rotted and sloughed off the appendages, which were still locked in place and jittering as though being torn apart from within.

With relaxed, world-weary movements, the Unmade turned around and studied the dying mass suspended above his head. "Really, Narbu? I didn't expect much, but you've still managed to let me down. Even in your final moments, you remain a disappointment. Hopefully you're still aware enough to—"

By now, the dark rot had spread around the mountain, presumably carving its way to whatever served as this monstrosity's core. Even Narbu's eyes and mouth had already slipped into random, toxin-stricken spasms, indicating consciousness had left the building for the time being. But it got worse. In a few minutes, if that, the rot would overtake and infect the entire mass. From there, it was anybody's guess what might happen next.

All I knew was that *I* needed to act, because nobody was coming to help. Until I got out of this cage, though, I would be no use to anybody— least of all Akasha.

Which meant it was time for a drastic (and in hindsight, downright idiotic) course of action.

After taking a deep, shuddering breath, I closed my eyes and entered the misty void of Mind Cascade.

The moment I fully slipped into that mind-made realm, I realized my experience in the monastic ruins had spoiled me. I'd truly come to believe that, through Mind Cascade's recent neural bridge and personal experience, each foray into the immaterial world would be easier. The environment would be sharper, my power greater, my foe weaker. Here, though, it was just the opposite.

Unlike the relatively well-defined arena in which I'd fought the junnara-gol, this battlefield was a grove more obscured than ever before—even worse than the sloth's domain, in fact. And yes, it was a literal grove. As far as I could tell, anyhow.

I stood in a small, fog-carpeted circle, surrounded on all sides by trees that extended into the haze overhead. Glancing upward, I found that the "trees" also doubled as torture poles. The bodies of weeping, moaning humanoids had been *nailed* to the wood at strange angles, forming a canopy of writhing limbs. This was my first indication that I may have made a mistake in taking the fight to the mental realm. After all, the Unmade had just spent several eternities stranded in places that were probably made of the same "stuff." This was akin to challenging a sea monster in an underwater duel.

I'm no idiot, though, despite what you might be thinking as you read my story. The moment I understood I was outmatched, I tabbed out of Mind Cascade—or should I say, *tried* to tab out. No matter how many times I passed the mental command back to my body, nothing happened. It felt like I was flipping a switch with no wires connected to it. That, or someone was jamming the signal. I didn't know which was more unsettling.

Either way, I was trapped in here until I found a way out, and that meant fighting the Unmade on his terms . . . in his territory. I adopted the same tactic I'd used with the junnara-gol, relaxing my visual focus and trying to discern movement within the fog. It only took a few seconds to realize this wouldn't work. There was some kind of static in the air—a low, flickering background hum that threw off my focus. Everywhere and nowhere felt threatening.

"You've spoiled me with this twist," the Unmade whispered, his voice threading through the forest like wind. "Such a remarkable power for one so small."

My mental body circled rapidly, every sensory field strained to detect his presence. Second by second, the world grew denser, more "real," in some sense. It was as though gravity was slowly settling over the entire area. Before long, my previously airy form had condensed into a bulky mass that felt ill-equipped to navigate its surroundings.

"You can thank Chanzig for this one," I said.

"Do not make excuses for your own abilities. I've seen many, *many* Purifiers produce interesting mutations, but not like this. It's so robust. So beautiful. It's exactly what I envisioned for the chok'tal—not a source of power, but of infinite creativity."

I chewed on the Unmade's words, extracting their unspoken meaning. Part of the chok'tal "DNA" was the element of randomness, or at least the possibility to cobble together new abilities on the fly through determination. Repeated use, after all, was what had taken Mind Cascade from a weird blip in my Status Display to a full-fledged (and system-supported) power. By the same token, that also meant the Unmade didn't fully grasp what I was doing here. Morphic Imprints were akin to mutations beyond his control. That was something I could exploit.

"It's reassuring to see how . . . spirited you are," the Unmade continued. "I don't say this often, but you truly are my favorite. Even in my dimension, I could sense your potential."

"Means a lot, coming from someone like you."

"Myopic words. You might think I only crave suffering, but that's just another lie told by the Scryer. You'll know what I want in time, Dak. And deep down, it's what you want, too. You just don't know it yet."

"I doubt that, but hard to say without the full story," I replied. "Listen, how about a compromise? You kill Narbu, leave Akasha and I out of this, and spend the rest of your existence torturing your old friend."

"I considered that course several trillion times, Dak. I did. But you see, there's something you mortals can't grasp about reality. It's not about the ending of the tale . . . it's about the journey to reach it. Without some pain, some death, what good is the story?"

"We didn't ask to be characters in your little performance."

"Nobody does. Yet reality plays these games every moment of endless time. It births, kills, and recycles mortals in new bodies all the time. Why is that, do you think?"

I sighed. "Nothing good on the network to watch, I guess."

The Unmade gave a huff that might've been his take on laughter. "You're more correct than you realize, Dak. Don't you see? Beneath your world, beneath all worlds, there's . . . nothing. It's a void. Narbu, for all his stupidity, was clear-sighted enough to understand that the true nature of that void is the Absolute. Wouldn't you know it? It's also the material that makes up every single being . . . both mind and body. The material that makes up existence, even." He paused, growling as though disgusted by the very notion. "Do you grasp what that means?"

"Not at all," I said honestly, still spinning and trying to locate the Unmade through the mental fuzz.

"If the Absolute is *everything* that is, was, or ever will exist: the void, the worlds within the void, the beings that inhabit those worlds within the void . . ." He trailed off as though expecting me to put the dots together.

I didn't. "Get on with it."

"Nothing is *real*, Dak," the Unmade said calmly. "The Absolute—existence itself—is just masturbating . . . incarnating itself as universes, people, trees, neutrinos. All of it remains engaged in a war without beginning or end . . . against itself. Cycle after cycle, eternity after eternity, the Absolute devours itself." He hummed in pseudo-contemplation. "Do you see now? The Absolute is a dead god. It has no logic, no *purpose*. There's nobody at the wheel of this universal genocide. From now until . . . well, now—it's always *now* if there's no time, after all—the Absolute will carry on in its blind dance. Even if you destroy every universe in existence, more will be born."

"What the hell is your point?"

"*Nothing* matters. *Nothing* is permanent. Narbu launched his failed crusade because he's just like me . . . even if he doesn't know it. He, too, saw the horror of eternity. The terror of being forced to exist *forever*, simply because it's the law of reality. That which exists can never *not* exist. It's simply . . . how it works."

Suddenly, I latched onto *something* near me. Something tangible. Once again, it was distraction time. The longer he talked, the more accurately I could zero in on his presence. Once I had him in my sights, I'd unleash my plan.

"At least Narbu tried to do something for other people."

"That's just it, Dak. He can claim his heart bleeds for the masses, but I have seen its rotten veins . . . Him and I are nearly the same. Every action he took was a stand against the indifference of the Absolute. An attempt to carve a permanent marking into the sands . . . only to watch the tide rip it away and erase any sign it had ever existed."

"So, that's what you're after, then? Some kind of grand war to kill the Absolute?"

The Unmade actually chuckled at that one. "My, my. I've forgotten how titillating it is to interact with mortals. So, ignorant of reality . . . so . . .

spontaneous. You should cherish your oblivious mind while you still can. To be a mortal is meaningless, but to be a god is madness."

"Then *what's* your goddamn objective?"

"Now, now. I've said numerous times that comes later. For now, let me say this: I do not aim to kill the Absolute, because I can't. Nothing can. Gods, machines, the enlightened . . . all of them are forced to play this pointless game until they go so mad they forget they're playing . . . and then they keep playing in ignorance. Is it any wonder why mortals enjoy killing so much?"

"I think you're projecting," I said. "You're the one who's obsessed with pain and whatever kinky stuff you're into. Not to mention sending murder-slugs into our universe."

"Perhaps it's just my age, Dak, but I've learned a thing or two about humanoids. They don't fear violence—they crave it. It's their only reprieve from the eternal wheel of futility."

The signal was stronger now. So strong I'd narrowed it down to a patch several meters across in the deep woods. Still, I didn't turn or show any indication I'd found him. I needed to be precise for this to work.

"Again, that's what *you* think," I countered. "Most humans I know just want to avoid bullets in their body. So don't start selling yourself as some savior of reality because you forced people to murder each other for survival."

"And yet, you all consume vids of warzones . . . you're addicted to the networks and their gruesome tales . . . you fetishize your warriors . . . you bury your noses in thriller texts just to experience the rush of danger. Face your nature, Dak. You *love* being a Purifier."

"Wrong again. If you're really committed to this hero-of-the-people schtick, you can start by safely removing my chok'tal. Then, I'll tell every-one what a great guy you are."

"Oh, I couldn't *deprive* you of such a gift. Not until we reach the end of things."

While the Unmade spoke, I hurried to enact the next stage of attack planning. Thus far, I'd been relatively passive, only relying on my chest and its infinite source of light in moments of crisis. Now it was time to see what I could *really* do in the world of Mind Cascade. If this entire battlefield really was the product of our joined minds, it meant I theoreti-cally had just as much control as the Unmade. Maybe not when it came to shaping the environment—his power would always outmatch mine in that domain—but with regard to drawing on my own wellspring of energy? That might work.

Slowly, steadily, I pushed my mind-made fingers into my sternum until I sensed the burn of my inner light. Then I pinched off a glob of that radiant essence and cradled it in my palm, rolling it into a thin, pointed projectile without consciously knowing how.

Progress was glacial, however. I'd need at least a minute of real-world time to form the weapon in my mind. That meant keeping up my reliable strategy of talking bullshit.

"Lay it out for me," I said, glancing about for any overt sign of the Unmade. "Narbu's always going on about Wayfarers and their freedom from karma or whatever, but you don't seem to be getting smacked by karma. Does that make you enlightened?"

The Unmade hummed in ponderance of the question. "I don't care much for the monks and their archaic terms. What I do know, dearest Dak, is that I've gone beyond the boundaries of karma. Beyond *all* boundaries."

"Yeah, or maybe reality is winding up to give you the biggest sucker punch in history."

"I think not."

Suddenly, the mist that obscured the sky dispersed. Overhead, in the place of treetops or stars or space, was an insanely dense lattice formed by millions of interwoven threads. These threads wriggled at random, almost like nerve fibers trying to spread electrical impulses. The arrangement was so dense I couldn't see through it.

"This, Dak, is the web of karma," the Unmade explained. "Not in its 'real' form, I grant you, but in one that your mind can grasp."

Still kneading my radiant javelin, I studied the web in awe. Sure, it was *possible* the Unmade had summoned the entire illusion just to impress me, but I had a feeling this was the real deal. A feeling I wanted to resist, mind you, given my hatred of karma as a concept. It was just too intricate, too powerful to be anything but the living expression of universal causality. Even as I stood there, hundreds of meters below it, its energy crackled over me in waves.

"Each time an intention arises in a being's mind, a thread vibrates," the Unmade went on. "Each time they speak, eat, walk, or shit . . . a vibration. With each vibration, there's a vibration along every intersecting thread. Old Narbu thought he'd mastered these vibrations. He thought he could trace his way from a beginningless origin to a perfect end. It's a shame these monks never learned about chaos theory." The trees shuddered with a great wind, which I soon realized was none other than the Unmade's exhale. His breath caused an entire region of the karmic web to stir, sending out ripples in all directions from the impact point. "One breath, one word out of place, and the entire course of things is altered. Which is where the amusement begins."

My javelin was nearly ready. Only thing left was to sharpen the tip, which I did with great excitement.

"What's the point of showing me this?" I asked.

"Dak, Dak, Dak . . . you're more clever than that," the Unmade whispered. "You remember what that pitiful old Scryer said. What his entire order preached. By learning the mechanics of a system, you change its outcome."

"Like a prophecy."

"Yes. Very good. If one knows every step, they awaken the sleeping urge to step off their destined path. The highest hope of all mortals is to break out of this web. To be freed of the shackles placed on them by fate and predictive calculations."

"So, you're showing me the web . . . to free me from it."

"Voila."

When my fingers passed over the tip of the javelin, I felt a jolt of pain. It was sharp enough. It had to be.

"Well, thanks for the gift," I said, simultaneously gathering force in my chest and locking onto the Unmade's physical location at my back. "You must be pretty good at figuring out what's coming."

"Oh, I'm beyond—"

Whipping around, I dialed in on my enemy's signature, cocked my arm back, and loosed the javelin with a borderline nuclear level of power. It streaked forth like a bullet of liquid energy. No more than a half-second after the throw, it slammed straight into the Unmade's presence. There was a spray of dark blood and a scream, then silence. Even his ever-present aura seemed to fade.

Holy shit, I thought. *I just killed a god.*

I hadn't been ready for that throw, and evidently, neither had my body. Physical or not, my entire form was wracked with a surge of weakness. My chest, formerly a cauldron of light, was now a collection of sputtering embers.

It didn't matter, though. The son of a bitch was dead. Time to hop back into the real world, check on Akasha and Narbu, and then move the hell along before anybody caught wind of what had happened here. When I went to toggle off Mind Cascade, however, nothing changed.

My immaterial heart dropped into my intestines.

"That attempt was lackluster," the Unmade whispered, seemingly right over my shoulder.

I spun in a panic, but there was nothing in sight.

"You're supposed to surprise and delight me, Dak," he continued. "Do you really think your mind is so shielded from my teeth? Your intentions are known to me long before they're even seeds of possibility for you. I expect better from my children."

I didn't see what was coming so much as I felt it. There was a shift in the air pressure, a cold front that swept across my back for the briefest moment. That was all I needed. Twisting around once more, I leapt back, ducked, and dove as a barrage of heavy-duty strikes flashed out of the trees, their source moving too quickly for a good look. When the metaphorical dust had settled, my arms burned where the enemy's strikes had landed. There was no blood—not even any flesh to cut—but my mind-made form stung nevertheless.

Biting down on the pain, I glanced up to see what fresh hell the Unmade had cooked up. He didn't disappoint.

His formerly humanoid shell was gone, replaced by a deformed tangle of parts I could hardly term a body. The base resembled a mutant pastiche of a spider and a crab, with squat, mottled legs covered in patches of mold and keratin. Loops of tangled guts hung beneath it and scraped through the mist. Higher up were uneven and bulging sacs of fluid, some filled with half-digested corpses and others with knots of cancerous muscle.

It gets worse. Atop that beautiful mound was something that might've once been the head of a young child. *Might've* been, because it bore almost no similarity to an actual child's head. This version was easily twice the size of the legs and growths beneath it—which, by the way, were already twice *my* size. If anything, this damn head looked like it had been severed from a living statue. It was bloated in spots, bulging with pustules that leaked streams of tiny insects, and its eyes had the slimy, pale coating one tends to find on decayed fish. The hair sprouted in oily, haphazard clumps through desert-like cracks on the scalp. Then there was the mouth: bloody lips peeling off in chunks, rotten and twisting teeth, and a tongue that forked into five long, swaying tentacles.

"Alright, that's enough of . . . whatever *this* is," I growled, gradually backing away from the advancing abomination. "I'm done with your games."

A sound I can only describe as a chorus of screeching infants materialized from the back of the Unmade's throat. When the cries reached a deafening crescendo, they formed into a single voice.

"You don't fear me," the Unmade said, "but you will. I'll make sure of that."

"I'm still standing here, asshole."

"Have you ever seen an animal locked in a fight for survival? You'd swear a demon had entered their body. The way they howl, cry, bite, slash . . . it's a beautiful thing. An unpredictable, chaotic dance born of desperation." The Unmade lumbered farther out of the dark woods, revealing this spider-child hybrid also had a goddamn scorpion's tail. "That desperation is life itself. And that's what I'll rip forth from you, Dak."

Snarling, I propelled my mind-made body straight at the Unmade's milky eyes. Light ignited and burned on the tips of my knuckles mid-flight. Despite the speed and ferocity of my attack, however, the Unmade didn't flinch.

Just before I made impact, his tentacles snapped toward me and wrapped around me: four for my limbs, one for my neck. When I was firmly locked up and deprived of any hope of escape, the Unmade grinned.

"It doesn't matter what you do, Dak," he purred. "The immaterial dimensions belong to *me*. Before my presence, the gods and Wayfarers are nothing. Even Narbu now understands that my mind is the creator and destroyer of all reality."

While he spoke, I squirmed and strained against the tentacles' decaying flesh, but that was only another show. One more distraction to keep the mad god occupied. My real intention, and also my last-ditch effort, had to do with precisely what the Unmade had just said. *My mind is the creator and destroyer . . .* Assuming he was right, it hinted at something that should've seemed obvious from the start.

Narbu was a fanatic, but he'd taken a very specific course with one outcome in mind: stopping the Unmade. Each step of that course had prepared me for the next—the tortoise allowed me to harvest Sparkseed, which in turn allowed me to form the mandala, which in turn allowed me to master Telekinesis, which in turn . . . Well, I didn't quite know what his endgame had been, but I understood everything up until that point. It hadn't been explained in such a direct manner, but here, now, I understood the genius behind the progression. Nothing had been done without reason. I was equipped with everything required to win.

The Unmade kept jabbering on about something or other, but I was only half-listening. My external focus was invested in pretending to struggle against the tentacles, while my internal focus was reserved solely for scanning the soil around me.

Time to do something ballsy.

This wasn't a real, physical location, so the odds of finding inert matter I could handle with Telekinesis were next to nil, but maybe I didn't need that. I'd sharpened my Telekinesis skills on Sparkseed, after all, which Narbu had implied was somewhere between animate and inanimate material. A "training material," if you will. Yet another stroke of genius. He hadn't just been preparing me to defeat my Accretion; he'd been training my mind to command substances that went far beyond what the chok'tal had been designed to handle. Specifically, he'd been training my mind to work with the fabric of "mind" itself. That is to say, with the exact stuff that comprised this world.

The realization thrilled me, but it didn't mean I was automatically able to rip up the ground and start throwing telekinetic missiles. What it did do, however, was allow me to get my foot in the proverbial door. Everything around me, from the trees to the soil to the mist, all seemed slightly more porous on a quantum level, as though I could sink my awareness into anything I desired. It was the same sense I had in the physical world while establishing command over inanimate objects, albeit far weaker and less stable. It would have to do.

Still maintaining the illusion of resistance against the tentacles, I steadily directed my awareness out of my body and into the dirt beneath me. The first thing I noticed was how unwieldy it felt. Compared to the solidity of physical matter, this mind-stuff felt closer to foam in a sink basin. Each time I attempted to grasp it, it crumbled in my mental grip. This being the case, I switched tactics on the fly and tried out something I'd only explored in theory.

Instead of targeting any specific particles, I let my awareness relax until it was a broad, diffuse wave of presence. Then I latched onto the space *between* the particles. The instant I did this, it was like someone hooked my mind up to a hydrogen reactor. I intuitively understood the "secret sauce" of Telekinesis—including the very nature of the particles affected by it.

You see, taking control of a single nearby object was the first tier of control. A warmup, if you like. The second tier came in the form of manipulating numerous objects at once. The third tier, the one I'd just broken through, went far beyond the scope of the prior two. At this tier, I could sense the way each morsel of matter flickered in and out of the quantum field, simultaneously alive and dead. I could even sense the void that housed, produced, and consumed every particle.

Distantly, I heard the Unmade's continued monologue. The pressure of the tentacle choking my neck. The life flowing out of me, one mote at a time.

I didn't care. My newfound insight into Telekinesis and the matter it controlled had thrown me into a euphoric, infinitely vast space. This entire dimension danced with the energy of the void. The energy of the Absolute. Translation? Fuel to fuck the Unmade up.

Pushing aside final doubts, I poured my awareness into the space permeating the ground. A bubble of conscious control pooled soon after. Everything within that bubble—air, condensation, minerals, dirt—was mine, or at least intimately connected to me. Most pertinently, it responded to my will. Even as the Unmade ratcheted up the pressure on my body, I tore free a clod of earth and lifted it to the heel of my boot.

You enjoy eating people's minds, I thought, hoping the Unmade could hear me. *Try to chew on this one.*

In one chaotic instant, I steered my awareness back into my strangled, borderline dying body, slapped a grin on my numb face, and formed the universe's most defiant one-finger salute with both hands, all the while maintaining control over the dirt bubble below me.

The Unmade, who'd been in the middle of yet another wordy speech, suddenly shut up for once. A shadow of unease quirked the massive head's lips. Just what I wanted.

This was the make-or-break moment, and every part of my mind seemed to collectively understand that. For just a fraction of a second, everything else went quiet. No thoughts, no feelings, no intentions. The only thing occupying my focus was the bright, burning memory of the mandala I'd formed in the meditation hall. This version had to be perfect. Better than perfect.

When I shot my wad of willpower to form the symbol, there was little, if any, conscious involvement. My cocktail of panic, focus, and determination handled the heavy lifting . . . but there was something else, too. An unseen hand, a phantom presence. Through instinct alone, I *knew* it was the very force that had led me out of the junnara-gol's nightmare.

One moment, I was suffocating in front of the Unmade's ugly mug . . . and the next, my mandala erupted between us in a flash of blinding light. A shockwave of the same brilliance came a second later, burning away the forest's mist and turning night to day.

The Unmade's tentacles instantly went slack, dropping me to the soil below. Oxygen rushed, almost of its own accord, down my aching throat as I fell. I landed hard, sputtering and probably with a face that bordered on purple, but still grinning like a madman.

It had *worked.* But more than that, it had caused actual harm to the Unmade. The bastard was currently backpedaling through the woods, knocking down trees and screeching like a banshee all the while. Even from where I lay, desperately trying to stand up and prepare for the next round, it was easy to spot the sizzling flaps of tissue that had been scorched clean off by the mandala.

It was a damn good start, but I needed to press my advantage while I could. That meant taking the fight to the one place I truly understood: the physical realm. Time for another shot at toggling off Mind Cascade.

This idea didn't come a moment too soon, either, because I then realized that the Unmade had stopped retreating. In fact, it was *advancing* . . . this time in a fit of what seemed like fury. Guess that's what happens when you bruise an eternal being's pride. I watched in horror as the Unmade came closer and closer, their every step somehow causing the mandala to dim further. By the time they'd made it halfway back to the clearing, the symbol was little more than a hovering arrangement of dirt with a dull spark in the center. Then, piece by piece, the mandala began to dissolve.

Now or never. I shut my eyes, sent Halcius a truncated prayer, and tried to switch off Mind Cascade as though my life depended on it. Which it did.

Suddenly, I was back on the freezing mountaintop. Back in the real world. Never before had I been so grateful for the feeling of imminent frostbite. I was so excited to be out of that hellhole, in fact, that it took me a moment to notice the Unmade's cage was gone. The bars, the metal rod, everything. The same couldn't be said for the Unmade, however. They stood near Akasha's body, arms held casually at their sides and head tilted.

Beating their ass to a pulp would be my first activity as a free man.

"That was so . . . unexpected," the Unmade said with a note of awe. "You continue to surprise and amaze, Dak. I can only imagine what you'll do when you grow into your other abilities."

I moved toward them with brutish, amped-up hops, trying my best to look intimidating despite the fact that I was one walking stick away from being immobile.

The Unmade watched me with what seemed to be amusement, if his invisible yet highly tangible aura was any indication. "Time for round two already? Or is it three? No matter. I'm enjoying this more than you can possibly imagine."

Mere seconds ago, I'd been filled with pride over the notion of getting the upper hand in this fight. The same pride, I imagine, the Unmade had felt while holding me in its grasp. And just as I'd sullied the Unmade's pride through my mandala plot twist, my foe was now throwing dirt all over mine with his apparent lack of a shit to give. That was dangerous—not for me, but for him. He didn't seem to realize the direct correlation between how pissed off I became and the strength of my Telekinesis. Mental energy was mental energy, no matter the source.

Still advancing on him, I put my newly sharpened skills to the test. With one flick of awareness, I seized control of Akasha's empty rifle and launched it at the back of the Unmade's skull. The weapon impacted with a solid *thok* sound, not to mention the speed and velocity of a runaway tram. Unfortunately, the Unmade was sturdy enough to shrug the blow off as though he'd been slapped upside the head. Which was fine, since I'd already cued up my next projectile.

A meter-wide chunk of solid ice ripped from the mountaintop crashed into the Unmade's left shoulder with considerably more force. Enough to stagger him, at least. He shoved back against the ice, visibly straining, but I pushed harder . . . and harder . . . and harder. Eventually, his strength broke. My mind-controlled battering ram forced him to the ground, where I then diverted the bulk of my power to crushing him into paste. The stone beneath his flattening body began to groan and crack. At the same time, I felt the familiar trickle of blood working past my lips and down my chin. This level of exertion wasn't sustainable, but it didn't need to be. He was nearly gone.

Just before the Unmade became a two-dimensional spray of tissue, however, he delivered a strange, seismic blast straight up into the ice chunk. The entire thing crumbled around him. I did my best to rejoin the broken bits, but it was no use. Blood was already streaming past my collarbone, and I could feel the dense, tingling waves of unconsciousness coming fast.

Realizing the nature of this losing battle, I redirected my awareness from the ice chunk to the next "projectile": a shotgun-like blast of loose stone, mica, and calcium powder left behind by Narbu's rampage. The mere act of lifting the nearby pile using my "bubble technique" sent jolts of pain and vertigo streaking through my mind. It wasn't enough to stop me, though. Seeing the Unmade casually dust himself off and begin standing gave me an amphetamine-like rush—one so potent I almost feared it, given what I knew about Purifiers succumbing to bloodlust. That was a fear for later, though. Right now was murder time.

I fired the powder blast straight into the Unmade's eye sockets, obliterating patches of burlap and necrotic flesh. Yet even that damage wasn't enough to see the face beneath. Just like his body, his mask repaired itself almost instantly. Even his crumpled chest cavity, which I'd tenderized like a piece of beef using the ice chunk, showed no signs of damage. The last of his ribs slid back into place with a sickening *pop*.

Once he'd shaken off the blow, he finished getting to his feet . . . and hardly looked worse for the wear. In fact, I wasn't sure I'd done anything at all to him.

"Such good fun," the Unmade said, nodding in approval. "Alas, I think it's time for me to finish my business with the Scryer and his little witch. We can resume our playtime later."

I spat a mouthful of blood onto the snow. "I'm not finished . . . with *you*."

"Such is the nature of the spirited. Even so, I think you'd do well to pause and calm yourself. After all, you've already spilled half your own vital fluids from those parlor tricks. Since you're about to watch your former mentor and lover die in the worst possible ways . . . why, you may not survive the stress alone in your current state."

I stared him down, knowing full well he was right. I *was* on my last legs. One more reckless use of Telekinesis, and I might take myself out for good. Even as I stood there, weighing my options, I felt my body crying out for rest. For calories. Especially calories. Although it had only been a few hours since I left the junnara-gol's lair, my limbs, stomach, and chest were visibly smaller. Bordering on skeletal, if the feeling of my bones preparing to pop through my skin were any indication.

In summary, things were not great.

Then, like a siren song drifting over the mountains, a familiar voice cut through our silence.

"It . . . is time," Narbu announced. "You will know what to do, Purifier. The Absolute guides your hands in this sacred hour."

The Unmade and I looked at Narbu with equal confusion. The Scryer was still dying, his body now almost wholly hijacked by the toxin, but he'd spoken with remarkable clarity. I squinted at him for several seconds, wondering if his words meant anything or were simply the last gasps of a failing brain.

My answer came in the form of a massive rift in the fungus. The biofilm just above Narbu's face peeled itself apart, exposing layer upon layer of spores, vines, and bone-like calcium growths. At the very heart of the mass was . . . Akasha's cube. It levitated in a haze of green mist.

"Oh, *another* twist?" the Unmade asked, plainly unimpressed.

I, meanwhile, stayed silent. Something was different about the cube. It was as "alive" as it had ever been, but now I sensed a kind of telepathic call radiating from its core. A call that, without any language whatsoever, spoke directly to me. In fact, the cube felt as intimately connected to me as the Sparkseed that had comprised my first mandala.

Oh, shit, I thought as the realization dawned on me. *It's a weapon.*

To this day, I don't know how or why that conclusion arose. All I know is that I felt it with absolute certainty. That certainty, in truth, was the only reason I felt confident enough to do what follows.

With a silent mind and the burning confidence of *something*—the Absolute, if you want to get all metaphysical about it—I extended a shaking hand and transplanted my awareness into the cube. Instantly, my presence was hit by alternating blasts of light and pure energy. My body was a distant memory. The only thing that remained was a thoughtless (and frankly overwhelming) experience of concepts I'd only understood through metaphors or hyperbole: creation, destruction, birth, death. All of it occurred in a single moment that I can only describe as falling into the center of a black hole.

Then I was back in my body, blinking and gasping, hand still outstretched. Only . . . I wasn't reaching toward the cube any longer. There wasn't even a cube to speak of. In its place was a pulsing hammer with the exact shape and size as the one I'd used to murder the turtle. This variant, however, had one key difference: it was made of pure, completely solid Sparkseed.

My jaw dropped, only to drop even more when the hammer went flying out of Narbu's body . . . and straight into my waiting hand.

The hammer felt just right. Not in terms of weight, or balance, or anything in particular, but as a whole. It was as though it had been crafted for me, and me alone. And although it could've been my imagination, I swore I could sense the energy of Akasha's people humming through the grip.

"Well . . . it seems I've failed to appreciate Narbu's penchant for surprises," the Unmade said, huffing out a laugh. "Let's add another layer of spontaneity."

No sooner had he spoken than my stump of a leg began twitching. I looked down at the limb with unease, only to find it mutating like some out-of-control science experiment. Muscles and tendons rippled beneath the flesh. It reminded me of a pot about to boil over.

Before I could even figure out what was happening, a blinding jolt of pain raced from the bottom of the appendage up my spine. I sagged and cried out, but the pain only worsened. Just as I bit down on the torment and straightened, however, it multiplied by magnitudes. The flesh on the bottom of the stump split open like a bloody flower in bloom. Fresh, pinkish muscle fibers oozed out and dangled, followed by bones and tendons that literally grew from the air itself.

All I could do was shut my eyes and try to channel that pain into anger. Into rage, even. By the time the body horror ceased, I was ready to skin the Unmade with his own fingers. But that wasn't the only change. Hesitantly looking down once more, I found that I'd grown . . . a new foot. Almost a new leg. The only signs I'd even been injured were the faint stretch marks running up and down my bare ankle, but even these were fading rapidly. It was strange to be so grateful for the feeling of imminent frostbite.

"There," the Unmade said, giving a little clap to celebrate his magic trick. Then he lifted his hand and curled two fingers toward himself in the classic "come and get it" gesture. "Don't limit yourself on my account, Dak. I came here for blood, and I'd hate to be disappointed."

28

I charged the Unmade like a starving animal let out of its cage—which, in hindsight, I suppose I was. With a grimace on my face and hammer in hand, I sprinted faster than I had in my entire life. The five-meter window between me and my foe vanished in seconds.

The Unmade didn't seem to have anticipated this. He took a small but noticeable step back as I fell upon him, barely managing to twist out of the way of my hammer strike. I doubled back for a reverse swing, only for my weapon to clang against something that hadn't been there a second prior.

Held in the Unmade's hands was a long, wide blade that seemed to be made of obsidian. The way its material crackled against the hammer's Sparkseed, however, indicated it wasn't obsidian at all. Hell, I doubted it was even a product of this universe. As he pressed back against the hammer, his black eyeholes regarding me with unspoken curiosity, I sensed the blade's defiled energy seeping into the air.

Summoning feral strength, I simultaneously triggered Overclock and Indomitable. When my muscles began to tense and ache, I knew the effects had kicked in. That gave me the force needed to shove off my back foot and deliver a punishing ram to the Unmade's weapon. Or, at least, I'd imagined it would be punishing.

The Unmade took the full brunt of my charge without ceding an inch of ground. I kept pushing, exhausted and leaking nose blood by the second, but it was no use. After letting me tire myself out for a while longer, the Unmade easily stepped back . . . and caused me to stagger forward.

I had just a second's warning about the defiled blade sweeping toward my face. Thinking fast, I dropped to my stomach and felt the swing *whoosh* over the back of my neck. The Unmade hadn't expected that, it seemed, because the blade's momentum carried him slightly off balance. That was my opportunity. Just after hitting the ground, I rolled over, lined up my attack, and delivered a brutal swing to the outside of the Unmade's left knee.

Bone and cartilage popped with a wet, jarring sound, and the Unmade faltered on that side of his body. Still, he didn't cry out. The most I got from that savagery was a muffled grunt—and even that wasn't clear enough to indicate whether it was from pain or just amusement.

No time to dwell, though. The Unmade's dark sword came plunging down toward my stomach. I rolled, but I wasn't fast enough. The blade's tip still managed to catch me on the hip and spear all the way to my pelvic bone.

Swallowing a scream I knew would only satisfy him, I kept rolling until I'd cleared his follow-up strikes and gained the room to get to my feet. Left in my wake was a bright red smear.

"I expected you to dodge that one," the Unmade said, flicking the last of my blood from his blade. Even as I studied him, his *injured* left knee healed without a dent. "Getting slow, are we?"

I opened my mouth to reply, a fittingly spiteful remark on my tongue, only to notice something that worried me even more than the Unmade. High above the mountaintop, partially obscured by the planet's cloud cover and atmospheric haze, were throngs of starships in orbit. And not just any starships—*Hegemony* starships. There was no mistaking their dark green hulls or rows upon rows of gun batteries. From this brief glance alone, I estimated there were a handful of frigates, a few capital ships, and . . .

Oh, shit.

The big daddy drifted into view behind the frigate chain, its docking bays open for deployment and panels emblazoned with an elite battalion's black sigil. They'd really done it. They'd sent a goddamn flagship of the Hegemony fleet after me. In just a few brief minutes, this entire world would be crawling with gunships, ground troops, and containment drones.

This fight had suddenly gained a time limit. Just what I needed.

In truth, I didn't know if I could beat this asshole with all the time in the world. He regenerated at a rate even quantum medicine couldn't match, he could summon overpowered weapons on a whim, and he evidently didn't have any such thing as pesky "survival instincts" that might cause him to slip up. Add to that my starvation situation and increasingly thinning options for new tactics, and the outcome was dismally clear.

Get your head together, I told myself in the world's weakest pep talk. *What would Smart Dak do in this fight?*

Depressing as it was, nothing came to mind. Smart Dak had plenty of interesting ideas, but how many of those had actually worked? Most of them had only gotten me into deeper trouble. No, this wasn't the time to be Smart Dak.

This was time for Stupid Dak to shine.

Aided by a deep breath, I cocked my arm back and threw the hammer with everything I had—including a primal scream. The weapon flipped end over end toward the Unmade's head like a golden rocket, unstoppable, unavoidable.

Then it missed.

It sailed right past him and toward the mountaintop's edge. Just as it neared the drop point, I primed my frontal lobe for something ridiculous and straight out of an action vid. My awareness skimmed over the snow in pursuit of the hammer.

"Really, Dak?" the Unmade asked, letting out a disappointed sigh. "I was expecting something better."

I shrugged, moving toward him with the ease of a competitor who'd just decided to drop out of the match. This seemed to perplex him, if not outright *annoy* him, more than anything else I'd done. He let his sword's tip drop to the ice with a hollow ring.

"I've always liked traveling to new places," I said with a smile. "But the best part is the trip back. It always feels shorter, huh?"

The Unmade didn't get what I meant until it was much too late.

My hammer came screaming back toward me with unholy fury, its speed so amplified by Telekinesis that it literally cracked the sound barrier. A thunderclap split the silence an instant before the hammer smashed into the back of the Unmade's head.

He staggered forward, genuinely rattled, but I didn't give him the chance to recover. I dashed forward, hand outstretched and visually guiding the hammer as I swung it into his skull and jaw repeatedly. At two meters away, I leapt toward him, recalled my weapon into my palm, and delivered a rage-fueled downward swing . . . right into his forehead.

The Unmade dropped like a sack of bricks. He rolled over, trying in vain to readjust his blade and counter me, but I was on him in a heartbeat. I straddled his chest and delivered a few more whacks to his temples, then went full ape mode on his face. I swung with one hand, two hands, Telekinesis . . . anything possible to deliver as much damage as I could.

I drew sharp, bestial gasps as I wailed on him, punctuating each swing with a breathless shout.

"Fuck! You! You're! A! Massive! Prick!"

Before long, black sludge soaked the burlap mask and drained out onto the snow. The Unmade's only movements were those directly caused by my hammer knocking his face around. Each time I drew back for another swing, viscous trails of Unmade-fluid spattered all over me. I didn't care, and hardly noticed. At that moment, there was no humanity in me. I was an animal. A demon.

Eventually—after a minute, or maybe five—I gave my final *thwack* to his nose and stopped. My entire body heaved in a fight to secure oxygen. Every muscle burned as though I'd injected hydrochloric acid in my limbs.

Despite that, I was happy. The Unmade lay still beneath me, his mask concealing the fact that I'd managed to flatten his face to half its prior width. That wasn't an exaggeration, by the way. Toward the end, I'd felt entire pieces of his head floating around in a jelly-like pool.

Only when I glanced at Akasha and her split-open body did I return to remotely "human" consciousness. I shook my head and struggled to my feet, nearly passing out as I did so.

"Good . . . work," the Unmade croaked, causing me to reflexively tense up for another swing. I held off, seeing as I could barely stay upright and his regeneration didn't appear active. "This has been . . . most enjoyable. Keep . . . training for me. Keep slaying. Our next . . . reunion . . . will move entire universes."

I lifted my hammer for a desperate, halfhearted strike, but there was no point. The moment the Unmade fell silent, his body began contracting, rolling into itself in a manner that defied the logic of anatomy. In a handful of seconds, he went from a humanoid shape to a small, dense ball of burlap and gnarled metal. Even his dark blade was sucked into the singularity of flesh.

Not knowing what this was leading up to, I stepped back and lifted my weapon in defense. It wasn't needed. The ball rose from the ice and hovered in midair for a moment, then rushed back along its umbilical cord and into Akasha's central cavity. With the same impossible, dimension-warping power as he'd used to enter this world, the Unmade vanished.

A half-second later, Akasha's halves were yanked back together and stitched up with an invisible seam. She collapsed to the ice and lay still.

"Leave her," Narbu rasped from behind me. "It will take some time for her mind and body to heal. Meanwhile, we must speak. It is our last chance."

I turned to find the scryer-turned-fungal colony in even worse shape than before. Despite defeating the Unmade, his toxins were evidently not going anywhere. They lingered in Narbu's tentacles, spores, and biofilm, running through the healthy tissue like infected veins. Most of the appendages and nodes had already slipped out of his control or outright withered. The only bastions of Narbu's control were his own face and torso, and even then, I could see the stirrings of early-stage corruption.

Despite everything that had happened, the sight twisted something deep in my chest. In some ways, Narbu was the closest thing I'd had to a father. A stern, wise, commanding presence with a vision for my life that far exceeded my own. Even if that illusion had been irreparably damaged, I still owed him the dignity of a farewell. And *he* still owed me answers to questions I'd only formed during that last fight.

This being the case, I bit the bullet of leaving Akasha behind for a moment and approached Narbu's monolithic face. Up close, amid the slurp of interweaving tentacles and the glow of the scryer's eyes, I felt as though I'd entered an industrial plant. That, or a long-lost site of alien worship.

"The Hegemony's in orbit," I said. "I despise you, and I only came here to ask you one question: How the hell did you drop Akasha with one word?"

"We will explain everything, even if you do not trust us," Narbu said, his mouth overflowing with strings of mycelium and spores. "We ask that you listen with great caution. What we must say concerns not only you, or this universe . . . but Akasha as well."

I slid the hammer into my belt and cocked a brow. "Usually, you put the most important thing at the end of a list, not in the middle."

"We have felt your affection for her. We know her survival and contentment are vital to you."

Geez, did *everyone* but me know I was in love with Akasha? "Say what you have to say, Narbu, because we're not sticking around. You made this bed . . . and you have to lay in it."

"Akasha is not what you think she is."

I glanced back at the blue-skinned woman, frowning. "Huh?"

"There are things we could not disclose in the presence of the Unmade. Now that we are alone, they must be said." His eyes flared to their former blue, indicating a surge of cognition. "Think upon our homeworld, and upon the empress and her heir."

"The heir *you* killed," I said bitterly.

Narbu let the dig slide, instead continuing with rapidity that only an imminent Hegemony invasion could create. "Before we left the homeworld, we told the empress of our plans in this system. We told her every step of the prophecy."

"Why? You said it would throw things off if people learned them."

"It was necessary for one reason. In our prophecy, the empress played a role as vital as your own. Her karmic bond to that fallen child was powerful. Unbreakable."

Midway through Narbu's sentences, a cold, empty pit gathered in my chest. I wasn't skilled enough with karmic webs or divination or whatever to know *exactly* what was going on, but I had a pretty damn solid idea. In hindsight, it was ridiculous that I'd overlooked the most telling sign of all: an umbilical cord connecting the Unmade to Akasha. That hadn't been caused by whatever she ingested, I now realized. Something far darker was behind it.

"She's the empress," I whispered, once again looking back at her twitching form—this time with terrible concern. "She is, isn't she?"

"She is, and she is not," Narbu said unhelpfully. "The empress, having understood her place in the fabric of destiny, agreed to our course without hesitation. That is to say . . . she agreed to perform a ritual that would create an exact future birth."

"*What?*"

"We understand you are skeptical of rebirth, Purifier, but you must heed our words." Hard as it was to do, I set aside my doubts and listened as Narbu went on. "Our ritual divined a moment in time and space that would be optimal for her next life. A place in which she could fulfill the sacred role required of her."

"You're saying that you . . . *engineered* Akasha?"

"We guided the empress' mind through the void," Narbu explained. "We created the conditions that would allow her to actualize her full potential. The very same conditions that would lead her to this world, in this moment, with the cube you now hold."

I don't know why, but that response pulled the covers off a realization I should've seen coming ten miles away. "Holy *shit*. If she's the Unmade's mother . . . does that mean the Unmade used to look like *her*?"

"No. The prophecy stated that the empress's descendants would change their flesh. They would become unrecognizable, so as to hide themselves from the gaze of the Purifiers."

I began pacing back and forth, trying to control my breathing despite everything melting down in every area of my existence.

"You asked us about the command word," Narbu continued. "What we utilized was one of many commands implanted in her mind. Commands that have slept there since she existed as the empress."

"What the hell for?"

"Her mind is unstable, Purifier. It is still tainted by her Accretion. By all the guilt, fear, and pain of her past life . . . and the many lives before that. Thus, it had to be controlled using external logic."

"But she did the second trial!"

Narbu went silent for several excruciating seconds. "Akasha never destroyed her Accretion. It was too dangerous. Instead, she destroyed the image I had placed within her mind."

My mouth opened and closed several times, completely devoid of thoughts to translate into words. Finally, I managed to put something together. "Does she know?"

"Of course not. She cannot know. Not until the time is right."

"Are you fucking kidding me?"

"Her Accretion is what allowed the Unmade to cross into our world," Narbu said fiercely. "If she uncovers her past life too soon, it will emerge and consume her mind. She must be trained, Purifier, if she is to become what destiny requires. Our time is dwindling . . . so this task falls to you."

"No, no, no. She's been the one training *me*." By now, I was on the verge of hyperventilating. "You need to tell her. She deserves to know."

"The empress went forth with her decision out of unconditional love. If you reveal her nature now, it will destroy that love. She will become something as depraved as her son."

"You can't seriously expect me to hide this from her."

"It is now our only solution," Narbu said. "If this course had succeeded . . . if you had joined with the Throne and ascended to glory . . . she would have been purified in death."

"You made the empress take birth as Akasha, then decided your new prophecy was good enough to justify tossing her aside, huh?"

"There is no sense in discussing dead prophecies. The Throne has revealed all to us, Purifier. We have seen the end of every timeline, every world. There is only one remaining course that will prevent annihilation."

"No. No, no, no. No more prophecies. No more bullshit."

Narbu's eyes fizzled as he competed against the toxins for bodily control. "We cannot guide you from this moment onward, even if we desired such a thing. You must uncover and follow this course using your own wisdom. Each step must be spontaneous . . . yet precise."

"Enough with the wisdom talk," I snapped. "Just tell me how to help Akasha. What can I do to stop that son of a bitch from ripping her open again?"

Narbu studied me. "We cannot help you. The path is now yours and yours alone."

"What path!?"

"We shall offer just one instruction, Purifier. One you are not ready to hear, and one you may never be able to perfect. You must learn the art of pure killing. Merciful killing. Without this, there is no hope for you . . . or this reality."

"That's all you've got? All *this*, and that's what you give me?"

"Your path awaits."

I *wanted* to stand there, defiant and pissed off, ready to lecture the fading scryer until the Hegemony dragged me away—but I couldn't. After what I'd just witnessed with the Unmade, I wasn't afraid of the approaching soldiers blowing my head off and throwing the chok'tal into a black hole. Hell, that might've been the best (or at least most merciful) outcome I could ask for.

By the same token, I was deathly afraid for Akasha. Even if I couldn't get fully on board with the idea that she was a reincarnated empress that had given birth to the Unmade, I needed no convincing to understand how much of a threat he posed to her . . . and *through* her, no less. On top of that, I knew that if the Hegemony somehow realized her potential to serve as the Unmade's reluctant host, there was no telling what kind of brutal tests or trials she might undergo—nor how effective they might be in creating a new breed of soldier.

Anyhow, this is all a way of expressing why I couldn't afford to linger and vent my frustrations to Narbu. He probably deserved a death as cold and heartless as he'd been to his brothers, but it wouldn't be delivered by my hands.

Shaking my head, I turned away to retrieve Akasha.

"Stop, Purifier," Narbu said. He succeeded in making me do just that. As I turned back, he said, "We must ask you for a final kindness."

"What?" I got my answer a moment later—not in words, but in the way his gaze drifted to my hammer. "You want me to kill you?"

"If we perish at the hands of the Unmade, we will forever abide in his dimension. Our torture will be ceaseless. If slain by your sacred hand, however, we will be incarnated in the deep hells. In time, we might atone for our actions and become something praised by sentient beings."

Hell of a choice, I thought. Assuming rebirth was true, Narbu could either go gently into the toxic night and become the Unmade's torture toy, or he could let me kill him and wind up in some truly miserable births for untold numbers of lifetimes. The descriptions I'd read about the hells were enough to make me cringe, even if I still couldn't confirm their existence. You know, stuff like dipping people's genitalia into magma, having the goods regrow, and then repeating it . . . endlessly.

So sure, the hells were bad, but I knew they were nothing compared to what the Unmade would do to him. That dick had just spent the last googa-jillion years (or whatever it was) creating the longest, most elaborate "prank" in the history of reality. One could only imagine how he'd amuse himself with direct access to Narbu's mind and body.

Some small, angry part of me wanted to subject Narbu to the latter fate. He'd killed a child, wiped out his order, tried to sacrifice Akasha. If anyone on this world had earned their torment, it was him. And yet . . . I couldn't.

For better or worse, my "moral compass" was a lot stronger than I might've liked for dealing with these kinds of situations. Letting him succumb to the toxins, whether or not I believed in rebirth as a real thing, constituted cruel and unusual punishment. That was the Hegemony's style—not to mention the Unmade's—but not mine.

Nodding once, I moved back to his trembling chest panels and hefted my hammer. "How's this going to work?"

"Our death should not be wasted," Narbu said, his voice fraying worse than ever. "It is only good and proper that our final act in this world benefits you, Purifier. May you be nourished through our blood."

"You want me to . . . drink something? From inside you?"

Narbu rumbled with dissatisfaction. "We will do what we must, and so shall you. We hope you will bask in the Absolute's unending radiance, Purifier. It is the only thing that will spare this dimension." Suddenly, Narbu loosened the biofilm over his torso and began unfurling the chest panels to expose their contents. "Thank you for this mercy. Now, let us meet destiny in silence. Words are naught but the songs of lost birds."

Whether through extreme cognitive power or truly otherworldly prescience, Narbu seemed to know his time was up. Even during that last sentence, his voice had started to splinter and devolve with exponential speed. These were the final gasps of a superintelligence . . . and that realization hit harder than I'd expected. No matter how powerful or wise one grew to be, they would never outrun death in all its pitiless forms.

Narbu's chest panels fully swung out, revealing honeycombs of spore colonies and sludge. Cradled among that appetizing mass was the wide, transparent vat housing his brain in clear fluid. His real brain . . . from his real body. Nests made of intermingling wires and fungal roots descended from the top of the vat to interface with that lump of ancient, ambitious gray matter. It was hard to believe that all of *this*—the betrayals, the confrontations, the secrets—had been birthed by such a relatively small (and surprisingly humanoid) organ, which had no doubt evolved for tasks more suited to gathering berries and finding mates than uncovering universal destiny.

I lifted my hammer in preparation to smash the vat, all the while wondering what Narbu had meant when referring to his blood and trying to "benefit" me. There was no benefit here; just a casual mercy killing.

At least, that was what I thought. Right before I swung the hammer, the tendrils draped around Narbu's face—that is, those that were still close enough to the core to resist the toxin's spread—began to twitch and stiffen. I hesitated at the sight, though I didn't quite know why. Then the tendrils dashed toward me, their sharpened points more than ready to kill.

My HUD appeared in an instant.

[NEMESIS EVENT]
Narbu / Radiant Throne (UNKNOWN)
CALCULATING . . .
Estimated Kill Points: 3,407,800

In the handful of microseconds I had before being skewered, I met Narbu's eyes with utter serenity. He looked at me in the same manner. A tacit understanding passed between us—one that was far too complicated and emotionally nuanced to make sense to anybody who hasn't experienced what I did on that planet.

Then, just before impact, I switched on Telekinesis and pushed my awareness into the very glass that comprised Narbu's brain-vat.

With one swift, thoughtless impulse, I crushed the glass inward.

Narbu's tendrils instantly froze up and sagged as his cerebral juices drained out onto the snow. Shards of glass stuck protruded from his brain at every possible angle, with a few even penetrating one lobe and jutting out another. A thin cocktail of blood, vat fluid, and greenish dye bled from the many wounds. After a few final, rather depressing thumps, the brain went still.

NEMESIS ENCOUNTER SUCCESSFUL
Kills: 1

Kill Points Awarded: 3,407,800
Storehouse Time Awarded: 15 Hours

RANK-UP AVAILABLE: Rank 13

I stepped back from the dead titan, equal parts relieved and remorseful. That "fight" had just netted me a metric shitload of Kill Points (and enough Storehouse Time to stave off death), but it had also ensured death for an organism that had surely lived longer than most sentient beings. The Throne's assemblage of toxic fungus, bursting mushrooms, and haphazardly flailing tendrils put a knot in my throat. It was clearly in its final hour, acting out the random impulses of dying neurons and groping at anything that might keep it alive. Without Narbu, though, there was no hope of survival. It had been reduced to a mindless heap of fertilizer.

This bout of depressing contemplation was interrupted by a sound I'd hoped to never experience: the subsonic thrum of Hegemony gunship engines breaking atmosphere. Glancing skyward, I saw at least three dozen of them in ground-attack formations. The sleek, cannon-fitted ships were heading directly for the mountaintop.

Three dozen goddamn gunships, I thought with disgust as I ran the math. *That's well over a thousand soldiers . . . all for me?*

For some brief context, one of the few firsthand memories I had related to media coverage of a Hegemony counterterrorism operation on a small hub world. They'd only needed two platoons of infantry, a hundred recruits, to seize the capital city in a day.

Whatever way I sliced it, I wasn't fighting my way out of here. My body was a gust of wind away from dissolving, my mind was frazzled, and my guns were empty. So, instead of hurrying to take up a defensive position, I hurried over to Akasha, knelt down, and worked to settle her across my shoulders.

This proved almost as hard as taking on the entire Hegemony fleet, even with the aid of Overclock. Akasha was a head taller than me, and despite her thin figure, she had long, *long* limbs corded with muscle. Worst of all, when I finally managed to heave and heft her onto my back, her skin's quilted pattern of black studs bit into my flesh.

Struggling to my feet, I had just one thought in my mind. *I can't believe I'm about to snap my spine for the Unmade's mom.*

Now that I had Akasha on my back, there was just the teensy-tiny issue of getting down from the tallest mountain on the planet . . . which was also being destroyed by the second. By the time I'd lumbered over to the cliff's edge to look down, there wasn't much of a mountain to see. Where there had once been colossal sheets of stone and ice, there were now fungal nodes that had breached the surface. Massive fissures lined the entire mountainside.

This was already bad, but it got even worse when I felt (and heard) a fresh round of tremors beneath my feet. These weren't the light, tinny sounds of a mild earthquake's aftershocks, but the full-body groaning of a planet's crust undergoing some *serious* movement. Maybe I hadn't been far off in assuming Narbu's underground "body" spanned the entire world.

Then came another round of quakes, this one plainly originating behind me. I spun to find Narbu and the remains of the Throne sinking into the mountain itself, much like a naval vessel lost at sea. Plumes of pollen-like dust and pulverized stone clouded the air.

Although daunting to witness, it gave me an idea. I resettled Akasha and ran toward the dying creature. Sure enough, the fungal mass was descending into what essentially resembled an organic sinkhole. The reason for this was obvious: the Throne was dying, and dying plants tended to shed water and other vital substances. The pool of dark, greenish slime descending alongside the central chunk of the Throne backed up this theory . . . and further cemented my idea.

As this plant matter withered, it left behind the enormous channels it had carved through bedrock. If this pattern continued, the Throne would eventually shrivel enough to create a set of usable escape passages that connected to caves across the planet's surface.

Well, that or collapse due to a lack of structural integrity, thus ensuring the death of whoever was stupid enough to use these "tunnels" as escape passages.

It just so happened I *was* stupid enough to try my luck. The Throne had now sunken about two meters underground, and that depth was rapidly increasing. It was now or never. Clenching my jaw against the pain I knew was about to follow, I squatted down and jumped into the hole.

It was a quick drop, but hurt just as bad as I'd predicted. Between my own weight and Akasha's, not even the Throne's spongy, fibrous surface was enough to fully cushion the blow . . . which resulted in something popping out of my right ankle's socket. I stifled a few curses and bit into my lip, using the pain as energy in my war to stay upright.

Once on my feet—a tough task, since the fungal mass was constantly shifting and imploding in random spots—I looked around for our way out.

Even now, mere seconds after the start of the collapse, the sinkhole was already massive. There were no traces of the mountaintop's winds, nor its subzero conditions. Instead, I found myself in a dark, humid pit that only grew hotter by the minute. Probably caused by the Throne venting some kind of noxious gas from its core.

The mass beneath me shifted again with a groan, this time releasing a very visible gout of spores that confirmed my theory. Luckily, this shift also revealed the first of many passages leading into the deeper bedrock. The most promising option was a fairly narrow, biofilm-coated tunnel to my left. Promising due to its smaller size and lack of any major "roots" growing through it, which posed a serious cave-in risk once they'd shriveled enough to lose their load-bearing capability.

I hesitated, wondering if I should continue to ride the fungal elevator down in search of better options or bail out now. There wasn't long to decide, though—the sinkhole was deepening at an alarming rate, and soon that narrow passage would be high above me and out of reach.

I had to pull the trigger.

Dashing over to the passage's crooked mouth, I ducked and twisted inside to ensure Akasha's body (and especially head) didn't slam into any rock protrusions. Mere seconds after I'd squeezed into the passage's hot and earthy darkness, an ear-destroying growl echoed from behind me, followed by a long, violent rumble. I didn't need to turn back—not that I could, given the tunnel's diameter—to know the Throne had just plummeted like a stone in water. My best guess, as an uneducated would-be archaeologist, was that it had breached some kind of massive cavern or air pocket underground . . . and thus become a *real* sinkhole.

Ahead of me was a tight, putrid space with dubious air quality, its only promise of an exit provided by the gentle breeze on my face. Behind me was, well, a giant hole . . . and an overwhelming unit from the Hegemony fleet. Good options all around.

I worked my way deeper into the passage with Nocturnal activated, cringing every time I felt something small and slimy tickling my skin. My only touch of comfort was Akasha's measured breathing. In my position, some people might've been concerned about the fact that she was still unconscious, but it was nothing but positive for me. What would I even say when she woke up? How would I tiptoe around the fact that she was the Unmade's mother in a former life?

This opened another can of mental worms. Akasha had always been able to peer into my mind with varying degrees of success. Small, easy things—my mood, for example—seemed ripe for the picking. The larger things, especially ones I worked to keep suppressed, tended to give her more trouble. It didn't feel possible for me to fully obscure this revelation, though.

Narbu wasn't a good guy, but I still felt it was prudent to take his words *very* seriously when it came to Akasha and learning her past. If she managed to pierce my mind, to drag out the secrets Narbu had shared with me . . . it wouldn't be good. That much was certain.

On the other hand, however, how well could it possibly go if I hid those same secrets from her for days or weeks on end, then explained them when I felt she was "ready"? Even setting aside the issue of trying to determine how she was ready, I had a strong hunch she wouldn't be pleased to learn I'd kept something so important from her. It didn't take much of an imagination to consider how I'd have felt if she had done the same to me.

I could think of that later, though. I could think of it *all* later. Too much had happened in too short a time, and each attempt to put the pieces together ended in a migraine. For now, it was best to keep my head down (literally) and keep trucking through the passage. Our immediate concern, beyond simply surviving the Hegemony's landing and our time underground, was to find some way off this planet.

The Hegemony's trio of "scouts" had mentioned the cities scattered across the surface, as well as their ferry services. This suggested they probably also had ports for private ships. Not that I had the funds to buy them or the power to steal them, of course. Even if we *did* secure ourselves a vessel, we couldn't leave anytime soon. The Hegemony's tracking devices were top of the line, able to triangulate a ship's pinch pattern in seconds. No, we'd probably have to hunker down and wait for the Hegemony to finish scraping the surface. But where? Who would have any incentive to decline turning us in for a fat reward?

While considering these impossible dilemmas, I heard a new sound—one that rattled me even more than the sinkhole's collapse. The harsh, crackling hiss of gunship engines swept through the passage like a chill wind.

In hindsight, I should've seen that coming. Modri hadn't been kidding about the Hegemony's surveillance equipment. They really *could* spot a moving body from the high atmosphere, right down to the pores on their nose. This meant the Hegemony not only knew where we'd gone, but also how we looked. There was a good chance our beautiful mugs had already been plastered across hub stations and restaurants throughout the Hegemony's territory.

Don't think about the big picture, I told myself, trying to stay calm as gunships audibly descended into the sinkhole. *One step at a time . . .*

This logical approach to panic was quite effective . . . until I noted the whine of rappelling lines unspooling and the crunch of heavy boots landing on the stone far behind me. Much like when I'd been pursued by Kardinal Killa in the caves, I heard *everything*, and they surely heard me. The auditory-enhancement modules in Hegemony helmets were no joke.

My fear didn't improve much when the sound of boots kept coming . . . and coming . . . and coming. They had to be flooding the passage with several squads. Between the cumbersome weight on my back and my fatigue—the use of Overclock had already turned my thighs into quivering sticks of jerky without a spot of fat—there was no hope of outrunning them. The elite soldiers on my tail were itching for a fight . . . and probably loaded up on amphetamines.

This day just got better and better.

29

Our fate came down to one decision. One agonizing, reckless decision. Did I keep going and pray for the best, or use the last of my energy to collapse the tunnel—trapping us in an underground maze that potentially ran for dozens of kilometers?

I wasn't sure what to do until I saw the glow of reflected flashlight beams painting the walls around me. In my best estimates, I'd had several minutes of fleeing time before they caught up. I now realized it was closer to several seconds.

Leaning against the sticky wall to my right, I closed my eyes, left my body on autopilot, and began driving my awareness into the stone a few meters behind me. As expected, it was nearly impenetrable, both due to the rock's naturally dense composition and the fact that it was part of an entire goddamn mountain. The most I managed was tugging a few flecks of mica off the ceiling.

Now in a touch of panic, I abandoned that plan and moved my awareness back down the passage. It wasn't a perfect image, but I was able to cobble together a roughly accurate layout of the soldiers and their movement. The analysis didn't reveal anything comforting. Just thirty meters away, boots sent vibrations through the floor and filtration masks clouded the air with warm plumes.

Get your head in the game, I scolded myself. *This is for all the marbles, Dak. You either bring this shitty ceiling down, or you wind up in a Hegemony torture cell.*

With that inspiring thought, I returned my awareness to the nearby stone and tried again. Just like the first time, it felt as though the rock itself was shoving back against me, actively shielding itself from my influence. Still, it's like I've always said . . . pain and fear are energy. Tapping into that primal vein of terror, I managed to dig the first of my "hooks" into the wall.

Little by little, my awareness threaded through the rock's quantum structure, probing deeper to find purchase.

But little wasn't enough. The soldiers were already twenty meters out, then fifteen . . . If I kept working at a telekinetic snail's pace, I'd only succeed in showering our pursuers with stone confetti.

Suddenly, my awareness retracted against my will. A sense of hopelessness set in. I'd come all this way, killed all these people, and it was for nothing. Worst of all, I'd failed the woman draped across my back. Akasha had spared me out of a genuine desire to see what I might accomplish, and what suffering I might heal in this world. All she'd gotten from that decision was an impromptu dissection, Narbu's coma command, and, by the looks of it, a long, painful stint in captivity.

Dark thoughts swirled in my mind. I ran the unthinkable math of whether it was best to let her be taken, or to kill her now and spare her from that torment. Much as I hate to admit it, the latter option seemed preferable . . . until I remembered her past life. Again, I wasn't some die-hard believer in rebirth, but I also wasn't about to throw caution to the wind and turn her into a depraved goddess because I'd been arrogant enough to disregard what didn't mesh with my logical mind.

That meant I *had* to bring down this damn tunnel. Impossible or not, it was our—and specifically, *her*—only chance at survival. Even if it caused a brain hemorrhage, followed by a slow and excruciating death, I would do it.

Drawing a deep breath, I took a third whack at the walls using Telekinesis. This time, I saved no energy for monitoring the soldiers' approach. Every drop of my focus and power was reserved for shattering stone. I didn't play nice with the rock by trying to gradually slip between its particles or attune to the empty space beneath and between them; instead, I attacked my target with fury. I punched my awareness through the quantum flux and seized control of the particles without mercy.

Then I strained, pulling inward with everything I had in an attempt to implode the ring of rock and seal the passage. Despite my aching jaw and the fresh blood running down my face, my only accomplishment was widening a crack in the ceiling. I needed more power. More energy. And since there was none left to pull from, I'd have to create it.

Tugging even harder, I called Akasha's face to mind. I pretended I was gazing into it, cherishing her, enduring this vast pain for the sake of her well-being. The strain didn't lessen, but I felt my awareness brightening and expanding. Before long, the crack in the ceiling was spewing dust. *That's it*... I exerted more and more force, ignoring the throb of my eyes rolling back into my skull.

Akasha's face came closer in my mind's eye. I saw her smiling, at peace ... I sensed her well of compassion for me and all other beings throughout the cosmos. Placebo or not, it kindled the fire in my mind.

"Stay right there," a heavily scrambled voice ordered. That of a Hegemony soldier, I dimly acknowledged. "Lower the woman and raise your hands."

The words didn't jar me; in fact, they only heightened my grip on the rocks. I was ready. I had to be. Driven by a cold, emotionless swell of energy, I triggered my pent-up focus. The ceiling, floor, and walls just behind me exploded with a deafening roar. This was followed by the longer yet equally deafening clatter of debris sifting down amid the implosion. And then, finally ... there was silence.

When I opened my eyes, dust was wafting past my ankles like a thick, slow-moving carpet. The biofilm all around me was coated in a thin veneer of the same powder.

That was all I had time to see before the severe energy cost registered in my body. I slumped to the side, nearly dropping Akasha. The wall was my only savior. Given my wobbly legs and blurred vision, I had a good hunch that I was currently slipping toward fatally low levels of glucose and overall calories in the body. I'd had low blood sugar before, but this was its steroid-boosted cousin. Even my thoughts, which came in zany, looping snippets, were too affected to be considered trustworthy.

Still . . . it was done. For now, anyway. The fact that I couldn't hear anything on the other side of the cave-in, including the shuffle of boots, gave me hope that I'd either killed or thoroughly blocked off the passage. A good sign, but not a guarantee of our safety. For all I knew, the Hegemony could still map these caverns using echolocation and cut me off at the exit. That meant I had to keep moving, no matter how wrecked I was.

I pressed on in a daze, excluding everything from my mind except breathing and walking. The minutes turned to hours—something I only confirmed when I finally paused to pull up my Status Display and get myself to Rank 13. At a bare minimum, I figured the rank-up's boost to Anima would help delay my death. After I triggered the rank-up, my info looked like this.

STATUS DISPLAY
PURIFIER RANK: 13
RANK-UP NOT AVAILABLE (1,638,400 KP required)

Kill Points: 0
Genofacturing Points: 3,334,240

Rank Points: 1

Rank Time: 21 Hours, 59 Minutes, 56 Seconds
Storehouse Time: 25 Hours, 18 Minutes, 41 Seconds

Anima: 360%
Dominion: 0/5

First, the good news. I was topped up on Rank Time, and my Storehouse Time had finally been replenished to a level that didn't trigger a heart attack. I wasn't too keen about seeing the ugly minutes and seconds on the latter number—I'd grown used to having nice, even hours—but I couldn't complain about more wiggle room. I also now had a Rank Point capable of purchasing my long-sought love: the flying upgrade.

Next, the bad news. Even with my increased Anima, I was screwed when it came to healing and overall energy levels. As I've mentioned, I was probably hanging out around 4 percent body fat. In case you're not a nutritionist or biologist, a little primer: below 3 percent body fat, males are at death's door. Females kick the bucket below 12 percent. Turns out fat isn't just a way to stay warm; it's also what keeps your organs pumping and brain-juices flowing.

This was bad enough, but made worse by the fact that Akasha and I were stranded on a planet that would soon be under the Hegemony's complete control. Depending on how things went, there was a real risk we'd have to spend literal years underground waiting for the occupation to get bored and move along—which I didn't see happening, given the Hegemony's fanatical interest in the chok'tal. Hell, my eternal thirst for Kill Points probably meant I'd end up having to fight them in the near future . . . and for years beyond that.

It was enough to drive a man mad. Instead of heading down the rabbit hole, I tabbed over to the upgrade paths and checked out my options. Yes, yes, I know, flying had been my dream for a long while . . . but it wouldn't be worth much if I got lasered out of the sky the moment I went airborne. My meager supply of calories probably wouldn't even get me off the ground, let alone me *and* Akasha.

Therefore, it was time to weigh options.

MUTATION [Tier IV] (*2 Rank Points required for Tier V access*)

Genofacturing III (REQ Rank 15): Enables creation of all Stage-III products. *Does not require a Dominion slot.*

Soaring Death (REQ Rank 13): Sprouts a pair of wings made from cartilage and stem cells, suitable for low-altitude travel. (0/3)

Photosynthesis (REQ Rank 11): Converts starlight into energy, enabling accelerated healing and decreased nutritional requirements. (0/3)

Mind Cascade (REQ Rank 10): Triggers a sudden release of repressed mental impressions, often causing disorientation or madness. (1/3)

Telekinesis (REQ Rank 8): Forms a strong quantum link between your mind and any inanimate object within 10 meters. (3/3)

Blindsight (REQ Rank 6): Projects a sonar signal up to 20 meters from your nervous system, rendering a three-dimensional readout of any environment. (0/5)

Polyps II (REQ Rank 3): Enables bonding with a second Polyp. *Does not require a Dominion slot.*

Omniphile (REQ Rank 3): Increases homeostatic efficiency in harsh environments. (0/3)

Nocturnal (REQ Rank 1): Further enhances night vision when active. (2/5)

Internally, I felt like screaming. I finally had the Rank Point and proper requirements met for Soaring Death, but it would have to wait. There were far better options for navigating subterranean tunnels than a pair of wings.

Blindsight was particularly appealing, given its ability to "map" environments, but I'd already developed a weak version of that power through Telekinesis and its projected awareness. A mild pass, then. Next was my old nemesis, Omniphile. It had always felt like a strange, underwhelming choice, given its vague description, but I now wondered if it could help me down here. Maybe it could help me better utilize calories, or give me the ability to draw water out of the air, or even grow spores all over my skin to make use of the ambient gases . . .

With *that* nasty bit of imagination, I put Omniphile back on its shelf.

That left Photosynthesis. You might find it odd that I was even considering the choice, given my present situation deep underground, but hear me out. If and when I found an exit to these passages, the one resource I could *guarantee* access to was sunlight. The lack of any hard numbers was concerning—did it reduce caloric needs by 10 percent, or 50?—but its general concept was promising. As far as I knew, it was the only available upgrade that would *give* energy instead of requiring it.

With great regret in my heart (not to mention a mournful glance at Soaring Death), I spent my Rank Point on Photosynthesis. Then I trudged onward, trying not to imagine what could've been in a world with aerial travel.

Around two hours later, I snapped out of a fog I hadn't even realized I'd slipped into. The reason for my sudden alertness was . . . noise. Some distant signs of life. Unlike last time, though, these sounds didn't put me on edge. They were too dim and irregular to belong to sentient creatures.

Filled with a blend of hope and wariness, I approached the origin site with careful steps. The nearer I got, the louder it all became. It was almost . . . a roar. Not of a beast, but of something larger, less defined. *A waterfall*, I realized with a start. *There's water down here.*

I didn't *need* water yet—not as bad as food, anyway—but I soon would. When you're stranded in an underground labyrinth, you'd do well to capitalize on any source of water you come across. In my personal situation, however, there were other, equally significant reasons to get excited about water. Especially water in the form of waterfalls.

For one thing, a waterfall was a stream descending from a higher altitude. If there was a waterfall down here, it meant the flow was pouring in from a reservoir or river on the surface. The very same surface where I'd be able to soak up starlight and work on securing a way off this world.

This probably explains why I began hurrying toward the noise, tongue lolling out in anticipation of that sweet, hydrating goodness and the freedom it implied. Before long, the cool smooch of mist filled the air and prickled my face. It was so close I could literally taste it.

By the time I arrived at the final bend in the passage, the floor was covered in glistening, muddy pools of water, and the waterfall was startlingly loud. It was a wonder it didn't wake Akasha up.

I leaned against the wall for a moment, half-laughing and half-groaning, overjoyed to have reached something as small and simple as water. Then I rounded the corner to soak in the miracle.

The cavern before me didn't disappoint. Well, I'm calling it a cavern, but that doesn't quite do the scene any justice. It was a bright, lush sprawl of moss and neon flowers and twittering birds, all arranged around a central pool that appeared too cerulean to be real. Shafts of sunlight and white, thrashing water spilled down through the massive hole in the ceiling.

"Oh, shit," I whispered, clutching Akasha even tighter to ensure she didn't fall off during my oohing-and-ahhing session.

Then the full exhaustion of my journey hit me. After limping over to a particularly soft-looking patch of moss, I knelt down and shifted Akasha onto her makeshift bed. I plopped down beside her and sat there for a few minutes, my eyes closed, chest aching, mind filled with nothing but the chirps of birds and the waterfall's static.

Weird as it is to say, I *felt* Narbu's presence here. This calm, serene slice of nature was exactly what he'd desired, even if he hadn't known it. All that bloodshed, all that betrayal . . . it had all been in service of a quiet world without cruelty. As I lay back and stared up at fungus-dotted stalactites, I wondered if that aspiration could ever be made real. Personal experience told me it couldn't. So long as sentient beings existed, they would always be cruel to one another. They would always lie, steal, rape, and destroy to satisfy their urges. The Unmade wasn't the cause of that; he was the result. A malignant tumor on the face of reality.

And yet . . . I couldn't afford to think that way. The minute I wrote humanity (and in fact, all sentient beings) off as broken, sadistic things, I would become just as wicked as Narbu. He, too, had seen humans and other organic creatures as droplets of defilement. He'd blinded himself to all the goodness and compassion of which they were capable. Worst of all, he'd lost hope in their intuition about what was right and wrong—and instead substituted his own moral code to disastrous effect.

I let out a deep breath, wishing I could just forget everything Narbu had ever taught me. But I couldn't. I wouldn't. Insane or not, he'd shown me something real about my own nature. He'd pointed out that, deep down, my "essence" was identical to that of reality itself. The Absolute.

Now my task was to remember this about everyone and everything I encountered. Each being was nothing but an expression of the Absolute, a microcosm of the macrocosm, a pixel among the fractal of existence. They were like me, and I was like them. So, if the Unmade wanted to devour all life, he would have to start with his number-one foe.

And I *would* be ready for him.

While contemplating this refreshingly optimistic idea, something bizarre happened. My Sparkseed hammer, which had been tucked in my belt since Narbu's death, began thrumming against my hip. That thrumming rapidly turned to burning. I hissed a curse, plucked the hammer free, and tossed it to the nearby moss . . . only to realize it was also glowing.

Waves of light bubbled up from its core and spread across its surface in a pattern too orderly for my liking. It was almost as though the weapon was trying to communicate through the flashes. To tell me *what*, though?

I wracked my brain, desperate to understand what the hell was turning my new weapon into a glowstick. Then it hit me: *the cube.* This thing had been crafted directly from Akasha's heirloom, meaning it probably contained some traces of its original abilities—not to mention the minds of her people.

What did she use it for, again? I asked myself, annoyed with how little I actually remembered about the thing in my brain-fried state. *Weapon? No. Prophecies? Nope. Cooking? Absolutely not.*

Suddenly, I remembered.

"Chok'tal!" I shouted to my nonexistent audience. "It tracks chok'tal activity!"

I inwardly applauded myself for recalling that detail, but that celebration was short-lived. Even with my crippling exhaustion, I was lucid enough to realize the hammer hadn't been glowing all this time. Put another way, this change hadn't been triggered by *my* chok'tal. That meant there had to be another one in close proximity, or—

That thought stopped dead in its tracks when I noticed ripples on the water. They weren't the normal type kicked up by the waterfall, but deeper, more vibratory crests, almost like they were being artificially driven by subsonic pressure.

Then, lifting my eyes with dread, I detected the faint outline of something *massive* hovering over the surface. Water vapor began beading up all over its outer panels, gradually revealing the form of a sleek, yet undeniably frightening, ship.

The damn thing was using active camouflage—highly illegal, highly prone to meltdowns. Highly despised by the Hegemony. And if *that* wasn't enough to mark it as a vessel that didn't fuck around, there was the fact that I still couldn't hear it. Active camouflage was almost exclusively used by the worst criminals in the 'verse, but auditory dampening that completely silenced everything from the reactors to the exhaust ports? I couldn't even think of a profession cruel enough to need that (or afford it).

Casting Akasha a nervous glance, I stood on jelly-like legs and retrieved the hammer. If a Purifier had somehow found me here, I'd give them the fight they'd come seeking.

"Too afraid to duke it out on your feet?" I shouted at the looming behemoth. "Come on, coward! I'm right here! After the shit I've just been through today, you're just the dessert course."

In spite of my bold words, it took a lot of guts to stand there and look menacing as the ship's rear panel dropped out of active camouflage. The metallic crimson square hung in place, almost like it had popped into existence of its own accord.

I tightened my grip on the hammer, ready to engage in a fight I had no business fighting, as the floating panel slid upward. Inch by torturous inch, the ship's interior was revealed: dark bundles of wires, grimy weapons racks, and a pair of heavy-duty boots.

A Purifier's boots.

Everything in my bones said I should skip the niceties and take the fight to them right now, bashing their skull in before I even saw their face. Still, I resisted. Something was weird here—weirder than usual, that is.

The panel continued rising, revealing long, muscular legs . . . a utility belt crammed with grenades and other devices . . . a hulking, pressurized breastplate . . . arms coated in thick bands of nano-weave mesh . . . and finally, their face. Their horrible, monstrous face, with all its—

Wait.

Their face wasn't horrible at all. It was that of a young woman, no older than thirty. She had long, silky black hair, freckles, crimson eyes, and lips covered in reddish glitter.

"Howdy, fellow Purifier," she said, smirking. "You look like you could use a ride."

ABOUT THE AUTHOR

Curator Omega is an interdimensional traveler, archivist, and occasional author from the deep reaches of the void. He is best known for curating tales from the Cutthroat Cosmos, including the Purifier series. In his free time, he enjoys sailing in the hearts of dead stars and studying cookie recipes from extinct empires. He resides in the quantum flux right behind you.